D0191161

My Life
for Yours

BOOKS BY VANESSA CARNEVALE

The Florentine Bridge
The Memories of Us

My Life for Yours

VANESSA CARNEVALE

Bookouture

Published by Bookouture in 2020

An imprint of Storyfire Ltd.
Carmelite House
50 Victoria Embankment
London EC4Y 0DZ

www.bookouture.com

Copyright © Vanessa Carnevale, 2020

Vanessa Carnevale has asserted her right to be identified
as the author of this work.

All rights reserved. No part of this publication may be reproduced,
stored in any retrieval system, or transmitted, in any form or by
any means, electronic, mechanical, photocopying, recording or
otherwise, without the prior written permission of the publishers.

ISBN: 978-1-83888-653-0
eBook ISBN: 978-1-83888-652-3

This book is a work of fiction. Names, characters, businesses,
organizations, places and events other than those clearly in the
public domain, are either the product of the author's imagination
or are used fictitiously. Any resemblance to actual persons, living or
dead, events or locales is entirely coincidental.

For Mum

PROLOGUE

Paige

Sometimes I spend a lot more time than I should on Pinterest. It's usually when I'm putting off things like paying bills or making mundane appointments or cooking dinner. Sometimes I use it to imagine how things could be. Like your first birthday party. I chose a cake for you. It's a Peter Rabbit one – pastels, styled on a table with fairy lights – and I'd spell your name out with gold foil balloons across the wall. I'd also have fresh flowers and handwritten place cards. And I'd order one of those fancy art easels, and in gorgeous typography I'd have your name on it. Oh, and let's not forget, I'm a sucker for bunting (fabric, not the plastic kind).

My password is your name in lowercase. (I changed it an hour ago, right after I finished brushing my teeth because that's what I was doing when we decided on it!)

Anyway, enough about Pinterest and first birthdays. I'm sure you'd be just as happy with a ten-dollar ice-cream cake and a packet of streamers and whistles, and those cheap cone hats from the supermarket – the ones with the elastic that always slips out of the staples.

I have a present for you. It's a picture book. The Little Engine That Could has always been my favourite. I recorded myself reading it for you. My voice is a little shaky and you can hear Piper barking in the background, and Nanny Evelyn opening the front door when she popped in to visit, but I hope you don't mind.

By now you might be walking, or close to. Sometimes when I look at baby photos of Daddy and me, I go cross-eyed until the images go blurry, trying to imagine what beautiful shape your face might have.

I love you. I hope you never forget that. I hope you have a very happy first birthday, whether it's with a Peter Rabbit cake or a ten-dollar ice-cream cake from the supermarket.

Love,

Mummy

P.S. Do you like the outfit I bought you? I chose it because not only did I think you'd look cute in it but the colour reminds me of Daddy's eyes. I wonder if yours will be the same.

PART ONE

CHAPTER ONE

Paige

'I cannot for the life of me find the fig paste anywhere,' says Mum, poking around the fridge. It's one of those refrigerators where you can tap on the glass and see what's inside so you don't have to open the door. According to the manufacturer, this handy feature keeps food fresher for longer. But Mum has been searching for the fig paste long enough to almost guarantee the early demise of her groceries. She finally registers me and Nick, and blows the stray hairs away from her face with a single breath.

'What are you looking for?' asks Dad, piping in.

'The fig paste,' we all say in unison – me, Nick and Mum.

'Oh. Finished it yesterday.' Dad almost looks proud of himself, and I marvel at how after spending more than three decades of his life alongside my mother, he's practically oblivious to the level of despair this will cause her. My mother, like my sister, is a perfectionist, though my mum has nothing on Caitlin. And even though it might not seem like it at first, the fig paste's absence from this evening's platter will be forgotten by the time she's ready to serve it.

'You didn't,' she says incredulously. 'It was gourmet from Leo's! I needed it for…' She lifts her hands in despair. 'Never mind. Let's forget the antipasto altogether.'

Dad flings me and Nick a sheepish look. Ever since he retired from his thirty-plus-year career as a commercial airline pilot, he's been driving Mum loopy. Incidentally, as Dad spends more time *at* home, Mum has started to spend more time *outside* the home. Every month she seems to tack on yet another activity to her rotating roster: mosaic classes, reformer Pilates, tai chi, macramé. 'It preserves my mental wellbeing and my relationship with your father,' she recently told me as she lifted an empty carton of milk from the fridge. 'I love your father but I like my space and my coffee white,' she added, her face turning a little sour.

Nick and I have been married for seven years, and ever since then, our Sunday nights have been reserved for dinner at Mum and Dad's. The only exception is when Nick is on call at the hospital, though I'm still required to attend, mostly on Mum's insistence. I'm the one with normal work hours – a regular job in a regular aged-care home, which I've been working at forever. My brother Ryan moved to Canada five years ago after meeting his wife, Susannah, on the first flight he took from Melbourne to Vancouver, so that rules out their attendance, and Caitlin and her family occasionally miss Sunday night dinners due to various excuses pertaining to their kids' health and sleeping habits.

'I need help in the kitchen,' feigns Mum, knowing full well I am never any help in anyone's kitchen, much less hers.

'We brought wine,' I say cheerfully, holding up the bottle. I uncork it and take some glasses down from the cupboard. 'It's a Derwent Estate Calcaire Pinot Noir.'

'I don't care what it is. Pour,' commands Mum, her eyes trained on Dad.

'I've got to finish clearing those gutters,' he says, making his way outside. 'C'mon, Nick.' Nick, ever the obedient son-in-law, follows Dad outside.

Shortly afterwards, the doorbell rings, signalling Caitlin's arrival with Mark and the kids.

'I'll go,' I say, setting my wine glass down.

'Anyone home?!' yells Caitlin.

'I'm coming!' I call, speeding up.

Ella peers through the window, her nose pressed against the frosted glass panel. She's dressed as a ladybird, in a red-and-black leotard with a matching tutu. I unlock the front door and step aside as Caitlin, carrying two-year-old Ethan on one hip, comes inside. She nods at me with his dummy in her mouth, a nappy bag slung over one shoulder and a plastic container in one hand, which no doubt contains dessert. I extend two arms out to peel Ethan from her. 'Hey, Ethan, Aunty Paige has missed you!' I nuzzle my face against the soft skin of his neck, inhaling the fragrance of vanilla soap and laundry detergent.

Ella squeezes through the door and grips my leg. 'Aunty Paige! I haven't seen you in years!'

'I know!' I crouch down to her level. She is all freckles and wide eyes. 'It's been so long I don't think I can remember your name.'

She bursts into a fit of giggles and whispers into my ear, 'Ella. But you can call me Ellabella.'

I wink at her. 'Okay,' I whisper, feeling my heart expand.

We trail into the kitchen and Mum squeezes Ella, delivering a loud kiss on her cheek before prying Ethan from my arms, but not before I blow a raspberry on his neck and wait for the delightful laughter to ensue.

'Hey, Mum,' says Caitlin, pecking her cheek. Mum tries to slap her hand away when she goes to pinch a freshly baked cookie from the tray, but Caitlin is too quick.

'Are these white choc and macadamia?' she asks, snapping it in half and handing a piece to Ethan.

'Yes. And we're about to have dinner soon,' says Mum, sliding the tray away from the bench.

I snatch a cookie for Ella, handing it to her as I hold a finger to my mouth. 'Do ladybirds know how to keep secrets?' She cups her mouth with her hand, stifling a laugh as she accepts it.

I scoop some of Mum's home-made olive tapenade onto a cracker. 'Unusual for you to be this late,' I say to Caitlin.

'Mark got caught up talking to some people at the country house. We need to finish the renovation by the end of next summer. I've had to cancel the interior designer and now I'm on another waiting list. So… well, it needs to be ready, and that's that.' She rubs her temples. Four months ago, she and Mark bought a fixer-upper – a moderate-sized weatherboard on acreage in Castlemaine, under two hours away from Melbourne. They plan on transforming it into a B & B as well as a home to retreat to over the kids' school holidays. The renovation process is turning out to be an arduous one riddled with ongoing dramas that Mark, who works in the corporate office of a bank, deals with only on weekends when time actually permits, which of course isn't as often as Caitlin would like. Foundation issues, leaking pipes and council hurdles. They haven't even begun physical work on it yet. And judging by Caitlin's wrinkled forehead, it's taking its toll. Not that she isn't trying to hide it. Caitlin normally has the poise and grace of Kate Middleton, but not when it comes to discussions about the country house.

'What a nightmare.'

'No, not a nightmare. All part of the renovation process,' she says, trying a bit too hard to appear all Zen-like in her response. She prises my wine glass from me and drains the contents. 'Nothing we can't handle. Any more wine?' She holds up the bottle to check it.

Mum gives me a questioning look.

I shrug.

'Ooh, what's in here?' asks Mum, lifting the lid of the cake container to inspect the double-layered heart-shaped pastry slathered in piped white chocolate drops and a perfectly arranged mismatch of pink macaroons, fresh roses, strawberries, raspberries and sprinkles. 'Oh, it's divine.' She puts Ethan down and carefully lifts the Instagrammable dessert out of the carrier. 'Don't tell me you made this.' It is no secret that Caitlin has inherited all of Mum's baking and organisational genes – genes that have completely skipped me.

'Cream tarts, Mum. Everyone's making them now. I'll give you the recipe.'

How Caitlin manages to find the time and patience to present a dessert like that at a regular Sunday night dinner at Mum and Dad's is beyond me. I imagine her days are filled with the constant pinging of notifications alerting her to all the various commitments in her life: meal planning, doctor's appointments, Pilates sessions, PFA meetings, ballet and swimming lessons, coffee and play dates. She's the kind of mum who turns up at a school fete fundraiser with two cakes if she's been asked to bring one – usually decorated with perfectly piped buttercream or edible flowers – while the other mums scramble to present their Donna Hay packet brownies. Me, I'd be the kind of mum who would stop by the supermarket with an empty Tupperware container after an attempt at making a simple vanilla sponge failed.

Once Mum finishes cooing at the cream tart, I have my quick turn, which is interrupted by Mark's grand entrance. He releases the numerous things he's carrying onto the floor: a pink backpack, another nappy bag, a ball, a hula hoop and a small ride-on tractor.

'Hi, ladies,' he says. He kisses Mum on the cheek before turning to me.

'Hey, Mark.' I point to the back door. 'Dad's got the beer outside.'

He nods gratefully, excuses himself and makes his way outside, completely ignoring Caitlin.

'Everything okay with you two?'

'Everything's fine,' Caitlin snaps.

'Where's Granddad?' asks Ella.

'He's outside with Uncle Nick. Let's go say hello,' I say, leaving Mum and Caitlin to chat. If there is any tension between Caitlin and Mark, it's unlikely Caitlin would discuss it with me anyway. She usually keeps those kinds of things to herself.

'Uncle Nick!' says Ella when she spots him.

Nick grins. 'Uh, you don't look like Ella. You look like a pixie to me.'

'No, I'm Ella dressed up.' She bends over in a fit of laughter.

'Uh, no, I'm *pretty* sure Ella doesn't wear green shoes with bells.' He makes a face.

She takes her felt hat off, revealing her unruly blonde curls. She really is a miniature version of Caitlin.

'It's *me*!'

'Oh my God, it really is you!'

Ella grins a toothy smile. 'Told you!'

Meanwhile, Dad's dragging a ladder out from the shed. He calls out to Ella.

'Granddad!' Ella skirts around in his direction and jumps up to give him a high five.

Dad reaches into his pocket and produces his wallet, fishing out two twenty-dollar notes. 'One for you and one for your brother,' he says, winking. Ella thanks him, and in unison the two of them point fingers at each other and declare in a sing-song voice, 'Make sure you spend it wisely!' By now Ella is used to Dad's usual routine of providing cash on greeting. She skips to the deck, diligently hands the notes to Mark for safekeeping and makes her way to the trampoline.

Dad joins me on the veranda and greets Ethan by giving him a kiss on the head. 'Hey, little fella,' he says, ruffling his hair. 'About time you and Nick made yourselves one of these little guys.'

'Daaaad.'

'Just stirring, love. We all know you'll make a great mum someday.'

I kiss Ethan on the cheek and nestle my face against his. 'I know,' I murmur, my lips against his delicate skin. 'One day.'

It's no surprise that at each family gathering, someone is ready to ask questions about the state of my uterus. Mum often jokes, saying things like, 'You're over thirty years old, Paige. Your uterus is getting as impatient as I am. I know it wants to make me a grandmother.' Once when I questioned why she never asks the same of my older brother Ryan, she replied, deadpan, 'Ryan doesn't have a uterus,' and that was that.

Mum pokes her head out onto the veranda. 'Nick, darling, would you mind picking some basil for me? It's in one of the pots in the corner.'

'Sure thing,' replies Nick.

Dad's now standing on a ladder, clearing the gutters. No matter how hard Mum tries to keep him from overdoing it since his recent hip operation, he always manages to find one odd job or another to keep him occupied outside.

'Oh, and do me a favour and ask David to get down and have a shower.'

I follow Mum back into the kitchen, where she opens the oven to check on the roast, a flurry of steam escaping as she does so, fogging up her glasses. 'Honestly, he's like a fourth child,' she mutters. 'Never listens to me or his doctor for that matter. Maybe Nick could have a word with him.'

'Or you could leave him to his own devices, Mum. Besides, Nick is a kids' doctor.'

'Speaking of kids.' She pauses, maintaining eye contact with me.

I roll my eyes.

'Any changes? I haven't asked in a few months.'

'You asked me two days ago,' I say, correcting her.

'No, I didn't. I just asked whether you thought you and Nick would be in a position to join us on a cruise next Christmas,' she says as the sliding door screeches open.

Nick re-enters the kitchen with a handful of basil. 'He needs a few more minutes,' he says, referring to Dad.

'I really wish you'd drop it,' I say as I slosh a rather large amount of wine into my glass. I tilt my head back, taking a long sip.

'I suppose there's no change then,' retorts Mum under her breath as she takes the basil from Nick, winking at him as she does this.

I exchange a glance with Nick, who reaches for an empty glass and starts pouring wine into it.

The usual, I mouth.

'Mrs Hutton?' he says, extending a hand with a full glass of wine.

Mum accepts the glass from him and he pours another for himself. 'Cheers,' he says, raising his glass. 'To future Hutton–Bellbrae babies.'

This is so out of character for Nick that Mum almost chokes on her wine, spluttering discreetly into her hand, while I simply smile into my glass and pretend not to giggle. *Nice*, I mouth as soon as she turns her back to finish setting the table.

Nick winks at me and I feel a surge of love move through me.

'And hopefully they come sooner rather than later,' she says, waving a hand in the air. 'Don't think I don't notice all those cute little gestures between the two of you,' she says with her back still turned to us.

Nick snakes his arm around me and squeezes. 'One day,' he whispers, only there is something different in his voice. Something that makes it sound like he knows something I don't.

A pang of mixed emotion whirls through me. One day how far away? One day soon? Nick squeezes me harder as if he understands my thoughts. Yes, I've been waiting a while. Being a paediatric surgeon is more than a job to Nick – it's a vocation. And to get there, study and work have had to come before family. But the honest truth is that I hope that *one day* comes sooner rather than later.

CHAPTER TWO

Nick

'I've been thinking about what your mum said,' I say to Paige one day, which is exactly three days after Evelyn's Sunday roast. We're in the light-filled kitchen of our Bayside Melbourne home, an area we settled on because we love the beach. My commute to work takes an hour in peak traffic even though we live less than twenty kilometres from the children's hospital. Then again, I rarely travel to and from work during peak traffic anyway.

'Yeah, which part exactly?' Paige asks, snapping the snow peas in half. She adds a handful of grated carrot to the salad and moves on to chopping the cucumber.

I slide the tray of salmon into the oven and check on the potatoes. 'Well, we've been married a long time now.' I suppress a smile. Paige has no idea what's coming, and I can't wait to see her reaction when I tell her. There is nothing, absolutely nothing, that she wants more than what I'm going to surprise her with tonight.

'I know. *Seven* years. We're on the road to becoming old together. I don't even complain about the fact you leave your T-shirts and socks inside out when you put them in the washing basket. I've reached a place of acceptance when it comes to your faults.'

I chuckle and open the fridge. 'Why is this in here?' I ask, pulling out a box of cereal.

'Huh?' she says, glancing over her shoulder.

I lift up the cold box of Weet-Bix.

'Oh, I must have had a moment.'

This doesn't surprise me at all. Paige has been having these kinds of 'moments' since the day I met her, and it's one of the many reasons I fell in love with her.

'I love your faults, Paige Hutton. You are the quirkiest woman I know.' I dig my hand into the box and shove a dry Weet-Bix in my mouth, and she reacts exactly as expected, with a giggle and a small shake of her head.

'You're worse than a child, you know that?' She eyes the floor. 'And you're making crumbs.'

I slip away into the laundry room and return with the stick vacuum, gliding it over the floor and down the gap between the fridge and the cupboard. Paige loves it when I vacuum without her having to ask me to.

'Who eats Weet-Bix like that anyway?' she asks.

'Your faulty husband,' I joke, washing the last of my Weet-Bix down with a glass of water.

She smiles into the salad bowl.

'So, don't you want to know what I was thinking about?'

'Let me guess. Mum needs her windows washed and you know someone who can do it,' she says, resting her hand on her hip. 'At a good price,' she adds, waggling a finger at me.

Paige and I have an ongoing joke that if we are ever in need of any kind of service, advice or assistance, I can find a contact able to help. I keep telling her that one of the most interesting parts of my job as a paediatric surgeon is getting to understand the dynamic of a family better. I think I can do a better job if I feel like I know my patients and their parents. Paige, however, is convinced it's so I can come home and declare things like: 'I met a guy who travels to seventeen countries a year and is a fountain pen doctor who fixes nibs for a living. He has a four-year-old son who he hardly ever sees.'

'No, actually,' I say.

'Well, don't keep me in suspense here,' she says as she drizzles balsamic vinegar over the salad.

I raise a finger in the air. 'Can you hear that?'

'Hear what?'

'That,' I say, tilting my head.

She tilts her head in response, and it's nothing short of adorable. 'Nick, I can't hear anything.'

'Exactly.'

'Okay, what has gotten into you tonight?' she says, shaking her head.

'Well, I was thinking that this house is pretty quiet with the two of us, would you agree?'

'Nick…'

I can tell she's holding her breath in anticipation of what I'm about to tell her.

'And I'd really like to share my love of Weet-Bix with a little person. Who knows if genetics will come into play as far as preferences for dry or wet ones go.'

Paige doesn't move. 'Hold on a second. What did you say?'

I move closer and envelop her from behind, resting my chin on her shoulder. 'I can feel that you know – going all thoughtful on me.'

'Um, I don't know what to say.' She flips around to face me. 'Are you sure? I mean, is this really something you want – as in *now*?'

She surveys me, trying to work out whether I'm actually serious. I am, and I couldn't be more ready for it. *We* couldn't be more ready for it. Paige has been more than patient with me about this next step in our life. When we met at Windsor Lakes, the aged-care home she works at, after my grandmother moved in there ten years ago, I was studying. It's been a long road of hard work and study, and having a baby is something we decided to wait for until I was more established in my career. We are now finally ready.

'You don't need to say anything. But there *is* something we could do.' I lean forward, pulling her body close to mine, and run my hand behind her neck and kiss her.

'Paige, would you do me the honour of becoming the most perfect, loving, heart-stoppingly beautiful mother of my children?'

I can tell she's trying not to laugh. 'Nick, would you do me the honour of becoming the faulty, ever so smart and often hilarious father of mine?'

I smile against her lips. 'Baby – it's a deal.'

CHAPTER THREE

Paige

I take a pregnancy test while Nick is in the shower. I'm bloated and my boobs are sore and my period is three days late, which is no real surprise since it's never usually on time, but I've convinced myself that this month's test will be no different to all the others – it will be nothing but another disappointment. Over the past seven months I've done everything right – all the prenatal check-ups and vitamins, diet and exercise – but despite all this there's no denying that *nothing has been happening*. Nick's tried reassuring me that we have nothing to be concerned about, and we should wait at least another five months before we entertain the idea of going to see a fertility specialist. I know I shouldn't, but I'm quietly clinging to the misguided assumption that every other woman in the world is blessed with a functioning body and mine isn't. It isn't healthy, but I'm tired of having my hopes crushed. So, this morning, I decide I will have no more of it. I leave the test on the bathroom sink while I go and hang out a load of washing.

'Hey,' says Nick, joining me outside, his hair still wet from the shower. He picks a towel from the basket and hoists it over the line as if he's playing with a basketball.

'Hey,' I reply, handing him two pegs.

He helps me hang the rest of the washing and steps back as if he's assessing what a great job we've done, not dissimilar to how a painter might admire a work of art. 'We're going to need a bigger line,' he surmises.

'Uh, what?'

'Do you have *any* idea how much washing we're going to need to do for an infant?'

I take the empty laundry basket and start to make my way inside. 'Yes, I do. But that's the least of my problems right now. I know you said there's no cause for alarm yet, but I really think we need to start seeing someone now.'

Nick tilts his head. 'Aww, you look so sad.'

'Don't,' I say, trying to be serious despite Nick's endearing expression. 'I took another test, which is pointless since my period's going to arrive any minute now. Look at me,' I say, pointing to the red spot on my chin. 'It's like my period is teasing me. The minute I decide to take a test, it shows up. Cruel, right?'

'You mean this test?' says Nick, pulling the plastic stick from the pocket of his jeans. He pats it against his palm, an expressionless look on his face.

'What? Yes?'

He shrugs. 'Is it meant to have one or two lines to make you smile?'

'No way,' I whisper. 'Show me.'

Nick turns the stick around so I can see. Two pink lines.

'Oh my God! We're having a baby?!' I throw myself into Nick's arms. He hugs me back, nestling his face against my shoulder.

'Can't wait to become three,' he murmurs into my ear.

I laugh and frame his still-wet face with my hands. 'Well, he or she is the size of a poppy seed. Did you know that, Dr Bellbrae?'

He shakes his head, still smiling at me. 'Well, yeah. It's made of two layers: the epiblast and hypoblast.'

'I love our poppy-seed-sized epiblast and hypoblast already. Oh my God, Nick. We're having a baby. I wonder if he or she will like yellow jelly beans like me. Do genetics play a role in taste preferences?' Nick and I have had a thing for jelly beans since our first date, when he surprised me with a jar after I'd joked that gold stickers for his patients were boring.

Nick chuckles and taps his front tooth with his finger. 'No jelly beans. Bad for teeth.'

'Oh. Yeah. Course.' I grin at him and start counting on my fingers. 'Summer baby.'

Nick raises his eyebrows. 'Summer baby,' he repeats.

'This is the best moment of my life. Aside from meeting you.'

'Our biggest moment,' he says, admiring the test.

'We made a baby, Nick.'

'Epiblast and hypoblast,' he says, correcting me.

'Yeah, whatever.' I close my eyes and kiss him.

Nick's phone rings.

'Can you leave it?'

Nick slowly prises himself away from me. 'Sorry, I'm on call.'

I stand there, watching him as he nods into the phone and gives whoever he's talking to some instructions. He glances at his watch. 'I'll be there in twenty minutes.' He turns to face me. 'Paige, I'm sorry. We'll celebrate tomorrow. I'll organise something special – I promise.'

'It's fine,' I reply. 'Everything is fine.'

'You sure?' He takes a moment to survey me.

In response, I hold up the pregnancy test and try to hide my disappointment at our interrupted big moment. Someone's child needs him more than I do right now.

'Of course. Go,' I say, nodding in encouragement.

Nick hugs me. 'Sorry,' he whispers into my ear.

This is our life and will be our life as long as Nick stays in this career. It's who we are. We want this baby and will make sure we give it the best possible life. Everything will be fine. All families strive to find perfect balance – even Caitlin's.

Nick and I are going to become parents.

We are starting a family.

Somehow, we will make it work. Because that's what other families do, and ours will be no different, I tell myself. But I can't help wondering whether I really believe it.

CHAPTER FOUR

Nick

I can't recall whether the woman behind the Level One gift shop counter is Cindy or Meg. I *should* know – over the years, both Cindy and Meg have delivered countless orders of teddy bears, balloons and bouquets to the wards upstairs.

'Dr Bellbrae! Fancy seeing you here!'

Cindy-Meg obviously knows me, and seems thrilled I've come to visit. I can't recall the last time I set foot in here even though I pass this place every day.

'Night, Nick,' says Leo, one of the pharmacists who works from the dispensary at the back.

'Night,' I reply as he squeezes past me and ducks under the half-closed roller shutter.

Despite the fact I'm bone-tired having spent the better part of my shift operating on patients, I feel like I owe it to Cindy-Meg to wander around and pick up a few errant items along the way. A scented candle for Paige, a bunny with lopsided ears in a fabric that I'm pretty sure is velour for the baby, even though I should probably know better. It's a bit soon for a gift like this, so I put it back and opt for a safer option. Flowers. At this hour, there are only two bunches to choose from. The one with proteas, eucalyptus and a mishmash of red berries appears to be the most alive, so that's what I go for.

'Are these for a patient?' asks Cindy-Meg, when I deposit the items on the counter. It's at this point I remember. This is

Cindy. Winner of last year's Christmas raffle. Grandmother of three. Enjoys sailing and wants to retire on a sailboat. With her short, jet-black, curly hair, Marilyn Monroe beauty spot and fire-engine-red lipstick, she looks more like she belongs on Broadway.

'They're for my wife, actually. Paige. She's, uh… she's pregnant.' We found out three days ago and this is the first time I've said the words out loud to anyone. I'm not even sure *why* I'm telling Cindy in the first place. Paige and I haven't even told our family members or our close friends yet. It feels odd – like it's not quite true yet. I'm going to be a *father*. When I think about it like that, it's impossible not to feel excited by everything this means, but I can't ignore the statistics: around one in four pregnancies end up in miscarriage – one in three for women over thirty-five. One in two for women over forty. There's promise in the fact that age is on Paige's side. But still, I should probably maintain a level of cautious optimism at least until the first scan. When it comes to the human body, you never really can predict for certain how things are going to go.

Cindy takes off her bluish-grey tortoise shell glasses and lets out a congratulatory, 'Wow! That's wonderful news! Is this your first?' We're in friendship territory now, Cindy and me.

'Yeah, it is.'

'Ooh, how lovely. How far along is she?'

'We only just found out. We're assuming probably around five weeks.'

Cindy looks positively delighted. 'So, it's *very* early.'

'Yes,' I agree, 'it is.' And this is why I probably should have kept my mouth shut. There's no telling whether Cindy has a big mouth. For all I know she might share the news with Leo first thing tomorrow morning, or anyone on Level Two for that matter, by the time I return to work for my next shift.

Cindy starts tying a huge pink ribbon around the bouquet. 'I'm sure she'll love the flowers. Hopefully she won't get morning sickness. I was sick for six long months with my Alfie. And don't get me started on what a rough pregnancy I had with Faith. Jane was my easiest. Didn't even find out I was pregnant until fourteen weeks with her!'

'That's… amazing.' I tap my credit card against the machine.

'Ginger,' she says as we wait for the receipt to roll out.

'Excuse me?'

'Ginger. For the nausea. Don't bother with those acupuncture wristbands or any of those gimmicks. Good old fresh ginger.'

I click my tongue. 'Got it.'

Cindy waves a dismissive hand in the air. 'You're a doctor. Who am I to be telling you what works for morning sickness?'

'I'd never heard about the ginger,' I say, mostly to appease her. She winks theatrically.

My phone starts vibrating in my pocket.

'Excuse me.' I fish the phone out, expecting it to be Paige. We have a dinner reservation at Zero Fifty-Five tonight – the third one, since we had to cancel the last two due to some surgical emergencies. Luckily, we're on good terms with the owners, Francesca and Luca, who understand our need for last-minute cancellations. There's no way I can't get home on time tonight, yet it's upstairs calling and I know this does not bode well for mine and Paige's celebratory dinner.

'Lorraine, what's up?'

'By any chance have you left yet?'

'No, not yet.'

'Five-year-old. Peritonitis. Can you take this one?'

Paige or the kid with the burst appendix? It's a no-brainer. Even if it does push me into shitty husband territory.

'Nick? I can get Ben to take this one if you prefer – he's on call tonight.' Ben is another paediatric surgeon I work with, and I know for a fact he's planning on proposing to Pamela tonight on her birthday unless he gets a call.

'No need. I'll be upstairs in a minute.'

'Great.'

'Lorraine?'

'Yes.'

'What's the patient's name?'

'William Summers.'

Paige will understand, I tell myself, but as I ride the lift up, it dawns on me that I walked out of the gift shop without the flowers, without the candle and without saying goodbye to Cindy.

Will's mother, a tall woman with blondish, short, curly hair and glasses, grips her son's hand as they wheel him in. She looks familiar, though I can't pinpoint why. Without the smudged mascara and blotchy skin, and the bright lights of the operating theatre, I might have some context to place her.

'Hey, buddy, would you like to give the car to Mum for safekeeping?' asks Briony, one of the nurses. His mother gently prises the car from his fingers. She's taking in the sights and sounds of the operating theatre, and I can tell she's petrified. To most people, the operating theatre is a scary place. My work environment is one of those places no parent wants to be in, and I understand it can be quite confronting: the sterility of the equipment, face masks, blue scrubs, nurses chatting about the weather or the morning traffic, or even joking while their most precious person is about to be operated on.

Alicia, the anaesthesiologist, strokes Will's forehead. 'It's okay, sweetheart, we're going to give you something to fall asleep. Right where we put the special cream. Can you count down from ten?'

'Ten… nine…'

'Okay, Mum, you can give him a kiss now,' instructs Briony.

Will's mum bends down, presses her lips against Will's cheek and watches as his eyes close by the time he gets to five. This is the moment most mothers start crying. She stands back, cupping her mouth. A stream of tears already runs down her cheeks.

'He's not going to… *die* is he? Please don't let my baby die. There's no way I can lose him.' She directs this to me.

This isn't the first time I've heard this and it will not be the last. She can't possibly know that I've already told *myself* I can't lose him – once when I was riding the lift up here, and also around thirty seconds ago.

'Not if Dr Bellbrae can help it,' interjects Briony, in her usual upbeat tone, when I don't answer straight away.

I give Will's mum a nod of reassurance, the only thing I *can* give her, aside from a living, breathing child on his way to restored health after the surgery. Without this operation, Will could face life-threatening complications like septicaemia, potentially leading to death.

Eddie, one of the other nurses, steps in and gently guides Will's mother by the elbow, escorting her out, and then it's time to get started.

I never allow myself to think too deeply about what happens to the parents who walk back through the theatre doors, but this is exactly what I'm thinking about as I watch Eddie guide this mother away. She'll fall into a family member's arms, Eddie will give them instructions on where the best coffee vending machine is located. If he's feeling particularly helpful, he'll suggest the best sandwiches from the self-service booth. Whether they're chatters, weepers or silent worriers, there is no doubt they'll be out of their minds until someone in this room walks out to give them the news that their child has made it through the operation. It's up to me and my team to make sure that can happen.

Briony starts chattering away. She's now the proud owner of a rescue dog, she's booked in holiday leave to the Whitsundays for April. She thinks that this is the year she's going to meet her long-time partner in life, only she's got no idea how she'll achieve this, but she's definitely steering clear of online dating.

'You know, his mother – she took him to the GP three times before they ended up in the ED. She said their doctor ruled out appendicitis and told her he had gastro,' says Eddie.

'Did he take his vital signs? Order any pathology tests?' I ask.

'Nope.'

My hand hovers in mid-air, forceps in hand. A tremble. Just a slight one. And just for a moment. Nobody notices. Not even Briony, who never skips a beat. This is not the time to think about Zac. I count to three and then return to the task at hand. There is no way we are losing William Summers on my watch.

No child should die from something like this. The sad fact of life is that sometimes, they do.

CHAPTER FIVE

Paige

It's Saturday morning, and rubbing eyes that are still puffy from sleep, I follow the smell of melted butter and pad into the kitchen, where Nick is in his boxer shorts and a T-shirt, whistling as he stands in front of the hob, flipping pancakes. I yawn, stretching my arms in the air. Nick's gym T-shirt, the one I claimed when I grew out of my normal pyjama top, rises up, exposing the bulge of my belly.

'I made you a smoothie,' he says, pointing to a tall glass on the island bench. He switches the gas off and carries the stack of pancakes over, setting them down between us.

'Thanks,' I say, reaching for the glass. 'I waited up for you again last night.' I don't mean to sound harsh but that's how it comes out. I pick up a card from the stack of pregnancy milestone cards we keep on the bench. *Today I am 32 weeks. My baby is the size of a head of lettuce.* I raise my eyebrows and turn the card around to show Nick. 'Our baby boy is about the size of an iceberg lettuce.'

He smirks. 'You were in bed when I got home,' he says as he pours himself a coffee. 'I got home around two.'

'We had a reservation for Mr and Mrs Brigg's at seven thirty.'

He watches me as I sip on the smoothie. Blueberry and apple with a hint of cinnamon and honey, exactly how I like it.

'Mr and Mrs Brigg's,' he repeats, furrowing his brow, his eyes darting right and left. 'I thought the reservation was for this Fri—' He stops himself. 'Paige, I'm sorry. We had a surgical emergency – gastroschisis needing immediate closure.'

And the day before that it was a small bowel obstruction. There is always something or someone needing Nick's time and attention. He rarely goes into detail about his patients, but I always want to know whether they are at least okay. On occasions where things aren't, he normally replies, 'Scrabble,' to which I nod and pull out the board game, and over a nice wine and a few slices of pizza, Nick opens up to me. He keeps the details fairly vague, maintaining balance between sadness and complete detachment. The scales have never tipped – in the ten years I've known him, I can tell when he's been on the verge of tears, never quite getting to the point where he's actually cried, and I've never seen him demonstrate total indifference.

'The mother went into premature labour at thirty-six weeks,' continues Nick, leaving it at that. He *tsks*, annoyed with himself. 'I totally forgot about dinner.'

He waits for me to answer him, and when I don't, he adds, 'It was major abdominal surgery. I need to head in soon to check on the little guy.'

Biting down on my straw, I mindlessly pick up a pancake and tear a piece off. Unable to stomach another bite, I drop the rest of my pancake onto my plate and push my glass away. 'This is only going to get harder, isn't it?'

'Is this about the Singapore trip? I told you months ago I didn't have to go unless you were comfortable with it.' Months ago, before we knew we were expecting, Nick was invited to a work conference to present a keynote on paediatric surgery advancements. It's important, and it would be unfair for him not to go.

'No, it's not about the conference. You should go to the conference.'

'You and this baby are top priority for me.'

'I know that,' I say finally.

'It really couldn't wait, Paige.'

I nod silently, offering a weak smile as I approach the kitchen sink. I rinse out my glass, look up at him and sigh. 'But I did.'

After his shower, Nick pops his head into the laundry room. 'Hey, I was thinking that tomorrow we could go to that winery in the Yarra Valley you love.'

'It closed down six months ago.'

'It did? Wow, doesn't seem like long ago we were last there.'

'Eight months,' I say, pulling the clothing out of the dryer. I fill the basket and lift it onto my hip. 'Also, I can't drink wine.'

Nick extends his arms to take the basket from me, but I forge ahead, deposit it on the sofa and start haphazardly folding the towels at the top of the pile.

Nick isn't having it. 'What did those poor towels do to deserve that?' he asks as he reaches for a T-shirt from the basket, which he folds with irritating precision. Normally I'd appreciate Nick's ability to defuse a potential argument with a bad joke. It is, after all, a trick I often use myself.

When I don't answer him, Nick prises one of the towels away from my fingers and gives me a knowing look. 'This isn't just about me forgetting about last night's dinner reservation, is it?'

'No, it's not,' I admit. 'What if it happens when our child has a school concert? Or a parent–teacher interview?'

'Hold on a second,' says Nick, giving a quick shake of his head. 'Aren't we getting a bit ahead of ourselves here? Shouldn't we be concerned with sleepless nights and breastfeeding and nappy changes right now?'

'Of course. But babies grow, Nick. They grow into little people like Ella and Ethan. They go to piano lessons and swimming lessons, and they have birthday parties and play dates and sports presentations. Where is that going to leave us? Or me? Have you even given any of this any thought? What's going to happen when I go back to work after my maternity leave?'

'You said you didn't really want to go back to work.'

'Yeah. For a *year*. And then? What if I want to go back?'

I love my job at Windsor Lakes but I'm not wedded to it in the same way Nick is to his. In truth, I haven't really decided whether I want to go back at all. I like the idea of not working outside the home, but what if staying home with a baby bores me to tears? Or worse still, what if I'm not any good at it?

'You go back. We get a nanny, or sitters, or politely ask your parents to help us. We work it out, like everybody else does.'

'You make it sound so easy.'

'Well, I'm not expecting it to be a walk in the park, in case that's what you're thinking.'

'That's not what I mean.'

'Well, what do you mean?' His eyes fill with genuine intrigue rather than frustration. This is one of the qualities about Nick I love the most: his ability to stay calm, listen and play down any kind of situation. Even in life-and-death situations, he is able to maintain level-headedness. After all, that's what he's been trained to do.

I think about how to frame my words so I don't sound completely selfish. 'You're going to miss out on parts of our child's life.' I hesitate. 'Your work... the long hours, being on call and needing to leave at a moment's notice whether we're in the middle of a birthday party or at a sports game. You're going to miss out on things. And I know it sounds selfish, but I really want you to be around. When I was growing up and Dad worked for the airline, he was always away. And you know yourself how hard it was for your mum to raise you on her own. Up until now I've been the one missing out on you – waking up in an empty bed, attending weddings and functions on my own, eating meals by myself when you're home late or on call – and

I've been okay with it because it only concerned me. But soon it'll affect our baby too.'

Nick sucks in a breath. 'I'm hearing you. I guess I didn't think it was going to be too much of an issue.'

'My dad used to be away for twenty-one days out of a month when he worked for the airline. I missed him, Nick,' I say, handing him a stack of folded towels. 'I know he loved us but he missed out on all the things – birthdays, his twenty-fifth wedding anniversary with Mum, Ryan's graduation, Caitlin's "epic piano recital of 1999", my stage debut in the high school musical.'

A brief smile crosses Nick's face. 'Thought you said you hated performing in that musical.'

'I did. But that's beside the point. Tell me something. In all seriousness, have you thought about what our life is going to look like once we have a baby?'

Nick picks a towel up from the basket and folds it. 'I think about it all the time. Sure, there will be some things that I'm going to miss out on, and I understand that it won't always be easy for you. But you know what? No family is perfect. I never had a dad around, and my mum worked two jobs most of my childhood. She was hardly ever around and I turned out fine.'

'What, so because I'm a woman, I can automatically do this?'

Nick tries to reach for my hand, but I scoop up the pile of folded towels and walk towards the linen closet.

'That's not what I mean. But it would be helpful if you could suggest how you'd like me to fix this,' says Nick, trailing behind me down the hallway.

I squeeze the towels onto one of the shelves and turn around. 'So, you're saying it's up to me to come up with a solution?'

Nick takes his time in responding. 'Well, what do you want me to say? I could look at reducing my hours and taking on a teaching load. Is that what you want?'

Nick sounds sincere, but I know this isn't what he seriously wants. He hasn't worked this hard to move away from surgery and into teaching. Our marriage has to work around it, and soon, like it or not, so will our family.

'No. Because I know *you* don't want it. But I don't know what we can do to fix this.' I lean my back against the linen closet door to shut it and meet Nick's gaze. 'What I do know is that babies don't like it when their fathers work seventy-hour weeks.' Neither do their wives, is what I want to add, but I hold my tongue.

Nick steps forward and takes my hand in his. He kisses it and pulls me closer to him. 'I might work crazy hours and occasionally forget dinner reservations, but I'm committed to our family. When I'm with you, I'm with you 100 per cent. I promise you I'm going to be the best dad I can be, Paige.' He holds my eyes with his and lifts my T-shirt. He bends forward, pressing his lips against the bulge. 'Did you hear that, baby?'

I run my hands through his hair. 'Yes, we heard you. And you need to go check on that little guy at the hospital.' I let out a small sigh. As clear as Nick's words are, they aren't exactly ones I want to hear.

CHAPTER SIX

Nick

She looks different today, Will's mum. For starters, her hair is styled, and she's wearing make-up – lipstick, a pinkish-red shade similar to what Paige wears. She seems taller, not only because of the heels but the navy pantsuit.

We're both standing in the hospital cafeteria queue. At this time of morning, staff flow in and out for their takeaway breakfast bowls, coffees and teas. I'm on rounds today, and then officially free until I fly to Singapore on Sunday.

A young guy wearing AirPods, even though he's standing behind a coffee counter, calls out, 'Next!'

Will's mother seems unsure whether she should step forward first.

I take a step back. 'Go ahead.'

'Oh, no, it's fine, I can wait.' A pause while she maintains eye contact and recognition dawns. 'Oh, you're the doctor – Will's *surgeon*.'

'Yes. Nick, Nick Bellbrae.'

'What can I get you?' asks the barista.

Will's mum steps forward, orders a coffee and then turns to me. 'Let me shout you.'

'Oh, not necessary, but thank you.'

'Please, it's the least I can do.'

'Sure. Well, a flat white. No sugar. Thanks.'

We step aside to allow other customers to step forward, and she introduces herself as Miranda.

'Miranda Addison?'

'It's Summers now.'

Of course. Miranda Addison. Minus the braces. And the weird bob.

'My God, I think I know – knew – you,' I say. 'University – you went to Melbourne Uni.'

'Yes! We took a couple of classes together. I think we had some mutual friends at the time – Lisa and Derek. I didn't think you'd remember so I didn't mention anything during Will's hospital stay.'

'I remember now. So, you're a doctor? Do you work here?'

'I transferred to psychology, actually. I think I'm better for it. I'm here for a job interview in the psychology clinic. I think it went well.' She crosses her fingers.

'Well, good for you. Hopefully you get some good news soon.'

'Thanks. I've been a single, stay-at-home mum for the past year, but now that Will's at school, it's time to get back into the workforce.'

'So how *is* Will?'

'He's great. Really great. I still can't believe he got so sick that he ended up in your operating room though.' Her voice goes quiet, like someone's turned down the volume. 'I should have listened to my instincts earlier. I felt so guilty about it having progressed so far, like I failed as a parent. Like I failed *him*.'

Unlike me, Miranda has nothing to feel guilty about. I wonder if I should tell her about Zac but then I think better of it. Some things are better left unsaid. Especially this.

'You didn't fail him.'

'The main thing is he's okay, I suppose.'

'Well, let him know I said hello.'

The barista calls out our coffees and Miranda hands me my cup. 'I don't know what I would have done if I'd lost him. We came so close to losing him, didn't we? I owe you so much more than a flat white.'

'Not necessary, really. It's my job.'

What she doesn't know is that patients like her son are the reason I'm here.

'So, are you ready to name our baby?' asks Paige as we plate up Sunday morning breakfast. Poached eggs, spinach and mushrooms. We need to leave home in a little over an hour. She's still wearing her pyjamas, or rather an old T-shirt of mine, that stretches around her belly, making her look all the thirty-three weeks pregnant that she is. Sometimes she complains about her changing figure, the stretch marks, the fact her hair needs a good tint, but to me it's the most magical thing, watching her grow our baby, and she couldn't be more beautiful.

I take two forks from a drawer and hand her one. 'Yep, let's do it.'

'Okay,' she says, moving a glass jar to the centre of the island bench. Earlier, we filled the jar with names that had made it onto our shortlist. All twenty-seven of them. 'You go first,' she says, unscrewing the lid and holding the jar for me.

I swallow a mouthful of spinach and pick a name out, making an effort to give nothing away. 'Okay, your turn.'

She puts the jar down and spins it around three times. 'For good luck,' she says, no doubt sensing my eye roll.

This is typical Paige, drawing out the moment, making it one to remember. Part of me wishes I could skip boarding the plane and just stay here at home with her, doing goofy things like this all day.

She places her hand into the jar and closes her eyes. 'Okay, here goes.' She picks a folded piece of paper and peeks at it.

'Ohhhh,' she coos.

She holds it up to show me.

MAX

This is Paige's top choice. She holds the paper against her chest. 'Show me yours. Go on… Oh my God, I hope it's not Brodie.'

As far as I'm concerned, there's nothing wrong with the name Brodie, but Paige doesn't think it's the kind of name that would suit our little guy.

'Come on, show me. What did you get?' She leans across and tries to pry open my hand. 'Liam? William? Dante?'

I laugh, keeping a tight fist. 'Do you know how much I love you?'

'Of course I do.'

'I don't think you do,' I tease.

'I do. I promise you, I do.'

'You don't,' I reply, and her eyes light up. She laughs and it makes me feel like I'm falling in love with her all over again. I open my palm, take the square of paper and hold it in front of her so she can see.

MAX

She draws in a breath. 'But *I* got…'

I nod, take another piece of paper from the jar and reveal the name on it:

MAX

I repeat this another time

'They all say Max?'

'Aha.'

'No, I did not realise you loved me this much.' She slides off the bar stool and hugs me, her belly pressing against me.

'You're welcome.' And then I bend down, lift her T-shirt, graze my lips across her belly and say, 'Love you too, Max.'

We pull up to the international short-term car park line an hour later.

'See you in a week.' She leans across, a little clumsily given the belly, and kisses me – one of those kisses that under normal circumstances would lead to something more. If I could, I'd tell her to turn the car around and forget about the trip altogether.

'A whole week. How am I going to live without you for a *whole* week?' she says.

I'm on call at the hospital one night per week and one weekend per month. The overseas and interstate conferences aren't all that frequent though, and neither of us is used to being apart for seven days at a time.

'What's a week when we have the rest of our lives to spend together?'

She frowns at me and giggles. 'Gee, who knew you could be so deep and romantic?'

'I'm kissing my sexy, thirty-three-week-pregnant, hormonal wife goodbye at an airport – it seemed appropriate.'

'Get out of here. The taxi driver behind us is having connip-tions.' Another toot erupts from the car behind us.

'I love you,' I tell her. 'Be careful, eat as much ice cream as a pregnant human can and don't forget to take your vitamins.'

She gives me another kiss, which tastes like the cinnamon gum she always keeps in her car console.

More honking ensues from the vehicle behind us.

'Go!' she says, waving me away. 'See you Sunday night at ten!'

Exiting the car, I haul my duffel bag over my shoulder, and for some inexplicable reason, I turn back.

Paige winds the window down. 'Forget something?'

'No. I just… I wanted to tell you that I wish I didn't have to go.'

'I know. But this isn't the time to talk about it if you don't want to miss your flight.' She taps her wristwatch, closes the window and blows me a kiss.

For the first time ever, I'm questioning whether I've made the right decision to put work in front of family.

CHAPTER SEVEN

Paige

Of all the places we could have decided to meet up, Hope has chosen a packed city bar. I waddle in and manage to perch myself onto one of the stools with as much elegance as a woman in her third trimester can muster.

Hope slides a vibrant, peach-coloured drink in front of me. 'Paige Hutton is *finally* about to become a mother, and something appears to be off here.' A decades-long friendship with Hope means she knows when something is up with me before *I* know something's up with me.

'Does this have mango in it?' I lift my glass and inspect it for a trace of the offending fruit.

'It's a mango and berry mocktail, Paige, not lighter fluid.'

'Meh,' I say, making a face.

'Talk to me. What's troubling you?' She wraps a length of brown hair around her finger, letting go again as it springs to life. Hope's hair is hopelessly curly, something she sees as a flaw and I see as exotic and beautiful. Everything about Hope is exotic and beautiful. She has olive skin and dark chocolate eyes which appear larger than they are thanks to a double application of mascara.

'I'm having a hard time picturing how it's going to work.'

'You balloon to a size you never thought imaginable, and eventually you get these cramps that feel like period pain and they get worse and worse until—'

'Not what I mean,' I say, quick to shut her down. Never has Hope pandered to any of my irrational anxieties, nor would I ever want her to. This is what makes Hope my perfect best friend, so her response is somewhat expected.

'Sorry, go on.'

'First it was his hours, all the study. Do you remember when I was talking to you in this very bar when Nick and I started dating? And I was worrying about all the times he stood me up for work?'

'Okay, so now you're having a baby with Nick, also known as the love of your life, and the problem is?'

How can I explain it to Hope without sounding completely precious? Nick's a good man trying to do a good job, and I came into this relationship knowing full well that it meant I'd be on my own a lot of the time. Which isn't too much of a problem when it's only me it affects. But soon, we'll have Max.

'I want him to be around more, but I don't know how we can actually make that happen. In all these years, nothing's changed. I'm still the girl who waits at home in her pyjamas with a plate of cold spaghetti on the table waiting for the sound of a key turning in the lock. He's going to miss out on so much. And what if I can't handle it? When he's not around to help me?'

Hope puts her drink down. 'Hey. It's normal to freak out before you have a baby.'

'That's not what I'm...' I bury my head in my hands and groan. 'Is that what I'm doing?'

'Yes. Believe me, I googled it about three hours into labour with Ollie.'

Hope waits a beat for the laugh she knows is coming and then gives me one of her signature grins – a satisfied smile that stretches across her face and makes her eyes look bigger.

'Is this what hormones do? I've turned into Needy Wife, haven't I?'

'A bit. As usual, you're worrying about the way life will be before you're even there.'

I hold my finger up. 'Hormones aside for a second. How's it going to affect Max though?' I know I'm prodding but I can't help myself.

Hope stops sipping through her straw. 'Let me tell you something, Paige. No family is perfect. You're never going to get it perfect. Now I know you have a hard time believing that since you are Caitlin's sister, but for a moment let's pretend you're not. Max is going to be fine, believe me. And so are you.'

'Okay,' I concede, straightening myself in my chair. 'I'm going to calm down about it all and see how things turn out. Got it.'

'Good,' says Hope, clapping her hands together. 'Because you and Nick love each other and you will find a way to make this family stuff work. It will likely involve sleep-deprivation and fumbling around while convincing yourself every other mother around you knows what they're doing, but that's simply not the case. My theory is nobody knows what they're doing – of this I am unequivocally convinced.' Hope finishes off the last of my mocktail. 'Tread carefully with Mother's Group. That's where you're likely to find the worst offenders,' she says, finishing with a wink. 'Wait until I tell you what the Perfect Hipster Mothers of Melbourne have to say about baby sunglasses. And did I tell you they banned plastic toys at midweek catch-ups?' She rolls her eyes. 'It's all Nina's doing. She thinks the reason we all don't have calm babies like hers is because we didn't birth ours in a blow-up pool in the middle of our living rooms.'

'Bet she live-tweeted it too,' I chortle.

'Uh-uh,' says Hope. 'Instagram.' She pulls out her phone to show me.

'Oh my God, who is this woman?' I say, pushing the phone away.

Hope shrugs in defeat.

'Well, you know I don't need to look very far for the world's most perfect mother, remember? Did I tell you Caitlin recently announced she wants another baby?' I ask, moving the conversation along. I curl my upper lip. 'She wants another one before it's too late. She'll probably be pregnant by next week.' It's so typical of Caitlin to have every element of her life go to plan exactly the way she wants it to.

As expected, Hope bounces right over my comment and goes back to the heart of things. 'You're going to be a great mother, Paige. You've waited a long time for this, so try to enjoy it.'

Hope catches the barman's attention and orders another mocktail for herself and a sparkling water for me. 'So, I'm going back to work in six weeks.' Hope is a human rights lawyer, and an excellent one at that. She'd had her eye on Melbourne Law School since she was in high school, and that's exactly where she went. She let nothing stand in her way.

'Yeah? That's great. Is Paul on board?'

'Yes, thank God. Though there is one problem,' she says. 'Aside from the inevitable judgement that will be bestowed upon me by the Perfect Hipster Mums.'

'Tell me.'

'What do I do with the baby?' she asks, deadpan. 'And these?' she says, pointing to her breasts.

'We find you a terrific day care centre. Or a nanny. And a quality pump. We work it out.' Just like Nick and I will work things out, I think to myself. If Hope and Paul can go with the flow and tackle things as they come their way, then so can we.

Seven days later I'm putting the finishing touches on the freshly painted nursery with Mum and Caitlin. Weeks earlier I'd come home from the paint shop with ten swatch cards, in varying shades of blue. Nick was adamant there was no difference between

Windmill Blue, Milan Blue and Cool Lilac, which didn't matter since we ended up going with Dew Kiss.

On the floor lie disassembled pieces of what will eventually become Max's cot.

'You need to talk to her,' I whisper to Mum the moment Caitlin leaves the room.

'Let it go, honey,' says Mum as she removes a screw from the frame.

'She won't let up.' Earlier, Caitlin had been educating me on the importance of pelvic floor exercises. 'It's never too early to start,' she'd warned, and followed this by reeling off no fewer than five reasons why I should take this advice seriously.

Mum sighs. 'She wants to help. You know how enthusiastic she is.'

'I don't have the energy for her today.' I fold the instruction booklet and let it fall to the ground.

'Why don't you have a nap, sweetheart? You look tired. You've been tired all week. I told you you've been overdoing it.'

I lift a framed picture and position it on one of the hooks on the wall. The frame isn't particularly heavy but I still have to pause to catch my breath from bending down to lift it.

'I might have a nap actually. Once we manage to get this cot assembled.'

Caitlin returns a few minutes later, brandishing a drill bit. 'I think this is the size we need.'

'Hand it over,' says Mum. She points to two pieces of wood that make up the base of the cot. 'Let's get these off and start again.'

'Paige, I can check the instructions if you like,' says Caitlin, in a tone that suggests I'm incapable of the job.

'Well, what am I supposed to do in the meantime? Just watch?'

'Try out the rocking chair and practise your pelvic floor exercises,' she says, chuckling.

I manoeuvre myself into the seat and let my eyes drift shut.

'She's right, you know,' agrees Mum. 'A few sets of power squeezes a day never hurt anybody. You don't want to live your life feeling too scared to sneeze, honey. The reality is that—'

I stick my fingers in my ears.

Squeeze and release. Squeeze and release.

'Paige, do you want to answer that?' says Mum.

'Huh? What?'

'Oh, sorry, didn't realise you'd dozed off. Someone's at the door.'

'It must be the delivery from the baby shop. I'll go.'

I make my way downstairs and sign for a large box from the courier that contains almost everything I imagine I need to welcome a baby into the home: a baby monitor, a breast pump, breast pads and probably more knick-knacks than I know what to do with. I barely make it halfway back up the stairs when I stop to catch my breath.

'Everything okay out there?' calls Mum, hearing the thump as I drop the box at the top of the stairs.

I bend over and draw a long, laboured breath. My heart is hammering in my chest like a woodpecker. Lowering myself on the top step, I sit down and wait for my heart rate to normalise.

Eventually Mum comes out of the nursery to check on me. 'Paige!'

'Just resting,' I say breathlessly. 'Didn't realise I was so unfit.'

Mum helps me up. 'What do you expect? You've been painting and redecorating, and you're still working full-time. I've been telling you to take it easy.'

'I'll have an early night tonight and I'll take Monday off.' If this is what late pregnancy is like, I'm not sure I'll be able to keep working to thirty-six weeks. I flick off my ballet flats and examine the red marks on my swollen skin from the elastic. My ankles resemble two thick stalks. 'You know, I'm not enjoying these third trimester symptoms at all. I can't even wear my wedding ring any more. What am I going to be like in six weeks' time?'

Caitlin removes a screw from between her lips. 'I was full term with Ella during summer. Puffed up like a blowfish. Make sure you drink lots of water.'

'Have been,' I say in a sing-song voice. I start coughing.

'That's it, girls, we're taking a break,' commands Mum.

'Have you decided on a car seat yet? And the pram?' asks Caitlin when we reach the kitchen.

'Not yet but it's under control, thanks,' I say, staring into the fridge. 'I'm staaaarving.'

'Good, because there are so many other things to prepare. Things you haven't even thought of yet. Trust me.'

I roll my eyes and pull out a bowl of hummus and a bag of carrots.

'Oh, dips are a no-no,' warns Caitlin.

'It's home-made,' barks Mum.

Caitlin continues prattling on. Something about getting a Thermomix to make the baby food. It would save me so much time and then I could freeze the food in those ice cube trays and blah, blah, blah.

Mum passes me a large glass of water, and as I go to drink, my heart starts thrumming away in my chest again.

Caitlin continues serving her sales pitch for the Thermomix.

'Order me one,' I say, munching on a mouthful of carrot.

Caitlin's eyes widen. 'What? Really? You want one?'

'Yep,' I say, reaching for another stick. At this point I'm happy to agree to anything in order to have Caitlin give me a break. I drain my glass of water and set it down on the bench, but I start to lose my balance, and it tumbles over.

'Paige!' says Caitlin, rushing over to me. She snakes her arm around my waist to steady me.

'Dizzy,' I say, still wobbling. It's as if the room is floating.

Mum rushes over and loops an arm through mine. 'Sofa,' she says firmly, grabbing me by the elbow.

'Put your head between your knees,' instructs Caitlin. 'I used to get like this when…' She stops herself. 'Never mind. It might be low blood pressure. You're hungry and you probably haven't had enough to eat today.'

I do as she tells me, lifting my head after a few seconds to cough.

'Maybe you should call your obstetrician,' she adds.

'No, I'll be fine. I'll be okay in the morning.'

'Get that cough checked out,' says Mum. 'You've been coughing all day.'

I nod and close my eyes. I can barely keep them open.

'I'll get dinner on and then you're getting straight into bed,' warns Mum.

'Okay,' I whisper, leaning back into the cushions. I don't have the energy to argue with her.

'Paige, honey,' whispers Mum, her palm pressing against my forehead. The living room is now dark, the blinds drawn shut. I sit up and cough into my blanket.

'You don't have a temperature, but maybe you're coming down with something.'

'What time is it?' I ask groggily.

'It's after eight. The nursery's all finished. We unpacked the box too.'

'Oh, Mum. Thank you.'

'Did you really need to buy ten boxes of breast pads?'

'I don't really know what I'm in for, do I?'

She titters and moves my hair behind my ears. 'No, but that's the magic of becoming a mother for the first time. So much to learn and lots to look forward to. Listen, there's some soup in the fridge – want me to heat it up for you?'

'Sure. Where's Caitlin?'

'She went home half an hour ago, she didn't want to wake you.'

'She missed bath and bedtime with Ella and Ethan?'

'Mmhmm,' Mum says, smiling warmly.

She heats up some soup for me and carries it over. 'It's your favourite. Chicken and corn. Remember when I used to make this for you when you were little?'

When I was younger, Mum would always joke that her soup had special healing ingredients in it – according to her, the ingredients knew exactly how to get to the heart of any ailment or problem. 'Thanks for taking such good care of me,' I say, accepting the bowl from her.

'That's what mothers do, sweetheart.' She pats my thigh. 'Rest up, and take it easy tomorrow, okay? What time does Nick get home tonight?'

'Around ten.'

'Okay, good.' She kisses me goodbye. 'You'll feel better tomorrow. I used magic parsley.' She winks at me and scribbles the recipe on a Post-it note lying on the kitchen counter. She hands it to me before grabbing her keys and making her way down the hallway. 'See you next Sunday,' she calls before she clicks the door shut behind her.

I stare into my soup bowl. Magic soup. I scan the note Mum left behind.

> *Chicken, corn, garlic, salt, pepper, chopped parsley. Sauté the garlic, brown the chicken, throw in some water and the other ingredients, and voila!*

'We've got this, Max,' I murmur, rubbing my belly. I'm just not sure I believe it. I have no idea about what it takes to be a mother. What if I'm not going to be as good at this as Mum or Caitlin? I don't know how often or how many times a day I'll need to feed a baby; ditto for nappy changes. All I know is that it's a lot. Crying sounds like, well, *crying*. What if I turn out to be incapable of identifying Max's different cries? According to Caitlin and a book she's read – back to back, twice – there are several types.

Before today, I was largely oblivious to the perils of leaking and sneezing. There is so much to think about. Maybe Caitlin is right. I should have ordered the car seat and pram weeks ago. I should have read the stack of books she gave me the day after I told her I was pregnant. Who am I kidding? The nursery is ready, but I've ordered a boxful of stuff I don't know what to do with.

After showering, I start changing into my pyjamas. Even dressing leaves me struggling for air. It's like a rope has tightened around my chest. I wriggle under the bed covers and text Nick.

Our baby is making Mummy feel really tired, but the nursery's done! I had a big nap this afternoon and I think Max has been sleeping all day. Okay if you take a cab home? Wake me when you get here. Love you. xo

Leaning back into the pillows, I rest my hands against the smooth skin under my pyjama top. Max is generally quiet during the day and more active at night. I love poking and prodding my tummy when I lie down at night, feeling him respond as if we're speaking our own secret language. I cast my mind back to this morning, trying to remember the last time I felt him move. After breakfast? Or was it lunch? Last night even? I've been so busy with the redecorating and deliveries, I've lost track. As I press down on the side of my belly, anticipating a gentle kick in response, I replay the day's nesting events through my mind: washing baby clothes, vacuuming, folding baby clothes, setting up nursery furniture. Not once can I remember feeling Max move. I prod my bump again and wait.

Nothing.

CHAPTER EIGHT

Nick

Thankfully, the flight home isn't delayed. Truth be told, it's a relief the conference is over. I miss the routine of the operating theatre, my rounds and my private consults. And, of course, I can't wait to get home to Paige.

After the meal service, I check next week's roster and the unread emails sitting in my phone. Sarah, my receptionist, has flagged a few important ones for me and forwarded along another with the subject line: *This is too sweet!*

> *Nick,*
>
> *Miranda Summers popped by today with a note she dictated on behalf of her little guy, Will. She told him she bumped into you at the hospital last week and he decided to write you a letter. See attached!*
>
> *Hope you're not working too hard. Ha! (As if you're not.)*
> *Sarah*
>
> *P.S. Have you given any more thought to how much time you'll take off once Junior arrives?*

I open the attachment, and a note penned in elegant cursive appears on my phone screen.

Dear Dr Bellbrae,

My name is Will Summers and you did my operation after my appendix broke. My friends thought it was cool, but it hurt a lot and I got very scared. My mum said there was an infection in my body and we were lucky to go to the hospital when we did so you and your doctor friends could fix me. When I grow up, I want to be a doctor like you. But if I don't become a doctor, then I will be a soccer player instead. I would rather be a doctor because you get to make people better when they don't feel good and I think that would be a really good job to have. I would also invent time-travel so I could go back and save my dad with an operation after his car accident so he wouldn't die and have to go to heaven.

Thank you,

Will

By the time I finish reading Will's note, my knee is jerking up and down in an anxious twitch.

'Fear of flying?' asks the guy beside me. 'Or was that some bad news?' He points to the phone in my seat pocket.

'Nothing the drinks trolley won't be able to fix,' I reply.

He snort-laughs. 'I know what you mean. A few years back I was on an aircraft that had an emergency landing in India. Utter nightmare. Pilot did a great job though.'

'Wow,' I tell him.

'They say if you breathe through one nostril and then the other, it helps.' He closes his eyes and demonstrates.

I'm almost tempted to try the technique myself, but I leave him to it. When I close my eyes again, a memory comes back like a flash – so clear and real, it steals my breath. It was two days after Zac's eighth birthday. We were in our small, three-bedroom house in one of Williamstown's quietest streets. We loved it there because there was a path that led to the bike track just two doors down from us. The trick was you had to know how to get to it via a well-hidden gate that the council left unlocked.

Like most Sunday afternoons, Mum was supposed to be working a shift at her retail job in a homewares shop. They paid better rates on Sundays. And since my Dad left when Zac was too young to remember him and never paid a cent of child support, she was the first to put up her hand for the weekend roster.

Zac had vomited again, the second time that morning, right before Mum made her second attempt to get into the car.

'There's no way I can work today,' she said, retreating to the kitchen to call her boss. She made that call, and then another, to the doctor's clinic, which was closed, but they gave her the number for a locum, which could be a six-hour wait, maybe more. 'If he vomits again, I'm taking him to the ED. This is ridiculous, he's been sick for days. He should be getting *better*, not worse.' She poured a glass of water. 'Here, sweetheart, take this to him.'

Dutifully, I took the glass of water to the bedroom Zac and I shared. His half was plastered with space paraphernalia, whereas mine had everything to do with car racing.

'Have some,' I said to Zac, holding the glass for him to take. He simply shook his head and groaned. 'My tummy hurts.'

'Do you want to play Nintendo?'

'Uh-uh.'

I sat on my bed, legs crossed, and tipped a box of Lego Technic onto my bed, a Christmas present from Grandma Elsie, who was away in Queensland with Grandpa Rob.

Mum was in the bathroom, and by the sound of it she was rifling through the medicine cabinet. She returned to the bedroom with a thermometer and a wet face towel for a crying Zac. She pressed her hand to his cheek and stroked his face while she waited for the reading. 'I'm just going to pop round to the chemist to get you some medicine, sport. You know what the doctor said, it's just a tummy bug so in a day or two you'll feel lots better and we'll go down to the beach.'

He smiled then. Zac loved the beach. We all did. Mum had enrolled us in Nippers at our local life-saving club as soon as we each turned five. Zac was a better swimmer than I was. A natural. He wanted to learn to surf.

'Knew that would make you smile.' She ruffled his hair and stood up, moving quickly to the door.

'Nick, grab some crackers from the pantry. See if he'll eat some. I'll be back soon, okay?'

'Okay.'

'There's a bucket next to his bed in case he needs it.'

I wrinkled my nose.

'*Nick.*'

'Yeah, okay. Zac, if you need to throw up, wait until Mum's back.'

Minutes after Mum left, Zac started groaning. Really groaning. There was no mistaking he was in pain. A *lot* of pain. He rolled onto his side and clutched his stomach.

'Nick, I don't feel good.'

'Use the bucket,' I told him.

But he didn't. He got up from the bed, his face pale with a greenish tinge. 'Toilet.'

He hobbled to the bathroom, leaning against my frame for support. Thirty seconds or so later, he called out for Mum, which meant I had to go in and attend to him, and I didn't like the sound of what I was hearing. I pushed the bathroom door open, and there was Zac, on his knees, a pool of murky, syrupy liquid on the cream tiles.

'Mum?' he called out, breathless, the kind of panic in his voice that made my heart gallop. He must have sensed me standing there behind him.

'No, it's me.' I tore my eyes away from the mess and put my hands under his armpits, helping him to stand. 'She'll be back soon. Go back to bed and lie down. Mum won't be long.'

Crackers. Mum said he needed crackers. And towels. Towels could also be useful, I thought. As I took the crackers from the kitchen pantry, I heard a thud, like someone had run into a wall.

'Zac?'

In the bedroom, Zac's body was sprawled on the floor. He'd vomited again, this time on the carpet.

The crackers slid out of my hands as I dropped to my knees. 'Hey. Get up.' I shook him a little, but he didn't move.

'I said get up.' I shook him some more, the way he'd come and shake me on a Christmas or birthday morning. 'Zac!'

His eyes rolled back and his teeth clenched. Sometimes we played games like this and Zac was the worst offender of all. But I knew this wasn't a game – not when he was lying in a pool of that strange-looking liquid.

'Not funny, Zac! You need to get up, *now*!' I screamed. My eyes searched the room for Mum, which was futile because she was at least another ten minutes away. 'Mum! *Mum*!'

I shook him more vigorously. Slapped his face with my hands. Still nothing.

'Zac, please! Wake up! You can even have my whole Star Wars collection – whatever you want. Just open your eyes! I won't even tell Mum it was you who broke her watch!' I begged for him to come back to me. My best friend, my sidekick, my little brother who slept with the night light on because the ghost stories I told after Mum left the room scared him to bits. Sometimes he crawled into my bed with me, and I pretended I hated it but I was just as scared as he was.

I wasn't trained in CPR. I didn't yet have my Surf Rescue Certificate, but I'd watched some of the kids in other groups practising. I knew you had to lay the unresponsive person on their back. And you needed to start compressions. I didn't know how many or how frequent they needed to be, or how many rescue breaths you needed to do in between, but I did the best I could until Mum came home and took over.

It was futile. Zac never opened his eyes again. He was already gone. Right there, in front of me, Zac's heart had stopped, and despite what the paramedics said, I did absolutely nothing useful to help revive him.

Later, the doctors that worked on him told my mother that Zac had died from peritonitis. His appendicitis had been misdiagnosed by his GP, who'd said he had gastroenteritis after he threw up his breakfast and presented at the clinic with a tummy ache. After two visits, they hadn't ordered any pathology tests. No blood test. Not even a blood pressure check. Mum had another appointment for the Monday, one they never made it to. The locum knocked on our door nine hours after Mum had called him.

Things were never the same after we lost Zac. But that's the moment I knew I wanted to become a doctor. I didn't want to be responsible for anyone else around me dying. I'd become someone who saved lives instead.

CHAPTER NINE

Paige

There are no more ice cubes in the freezer.

In the last hour I've drunk two glasses of iced water, which has done nothing to evoke even the slightest kick, punch or hint of a somersault. I resorted to crunching on the ice cubes one by one, and now my fingers are numb and stiff from scooping them out of the plastic tumbler, which is now empty. I've tried everything, and that includes eating a handful of jelly beans, turning onto one side and then the other, and then onto all fours on the ground. Now I'm rummaging through one of the tool drawers in the garage, desperately trying to find a torch to flick on and off against my belly. I open every drawer to no avail. I check the time. Nick's flight will be landing any minute. He'll know what to do. I repeat the mantra in my mind as I shuffle back to bed.

'Come on, Max, one little punch... Let me know you're okay,' I whisper, clambering back into bed, out of breath. My heart flutters again, and I raise a hand to still it.

My phone beeps.

Landed. See you soon, babe.

I grip the phone tightly, and between moments of wakefulness and dozing, I watch the minutes tick by until Nick finally walks through the door.

'Nick,' I call with relief upon hearing the front door open. I listen for his footsteps as he makes his way down the hallway. I call out again, this time more loudly. 'Nick!'

I hear him set his keys down, and with each step he takes up the stairs, I start to unravel. He drops his bag on the floor and sits down beside me. Nick's home and now he can help me *fix* this. He has to help me fix this. The cool air from outside radiates from him. 'Hey beautiful,' he whispers. 'What's wrong?' He moves the loose strands of hair away from my face and tries to meet my gaze with his.

'Something's not right. The baby. I can't feel... I can't remember the last time he moved.'

Nick nods, showing he understands. He rubs his hands together to give them some warmth and places one on my belly. 'Do you remember any movements today?' His voice is calm, smooth, void of even a hint of panic, and for one brief moment I let myself relax.

I don't want to admit it. 'No,' I whisper.

'You said the nursery's finished. You've been busy, you might not have noticed the movements.'

'I think something might be wrong.' I take a staccato breath. 'God, I'm so tired.' I rest my head back against the pillow.

'Why are you breathing like that?'

'I told you – I'm tired.'

'Are you struggling for breath?' he asks, narrowing his eyes.

'I don't know. My chest feels tight when I'm lying on my back.'

'And what about when you're not? What about when you're moving around?'

'Well, yeah, but especially when I'm climbing the stairs or taking a long walk. But Caitlin and Hope, they said this is all normal...' The creases on Nick's forehead indicate otherwise. I swallow hard. Maybe I'm imagining the flicker of concern on his face.

'Since when?'

'I don't know. A week or so? I only really noticed it getting worse in the last few days. Maybe I took on too much. Work plus the nursery stuff. So, it's probably that, right? I overdid it?'

Nick doesn't answer.

As much as I want to convince myself that there isn't anything wrong, I know I have to tell Nick about all the things I've been experiencing. 'Um, I've been noticing this weird kind of hammering in my chest. Like flutters, but they kind of last a little while. Is that... is that normal?' I wait for his response. It never comes. 'Could it be I'm low in iron?'

'Palpitations? When are you getting them?'

'What do you mean?'

'Lying down, sitting up? Throughout the day?'

I cough before answering him. 'All of the above.'

'And how long have you had the cough?'

'Umm, a few days?'

He lifts the sheets, exposing my swollen legs and feet.

'Caitlin and Mum said the swelling is normal. It's normal, right?'

Nick doesn't answer me, just mumbles an inaudible sound that resembles, 'Hmm.'

'What is it...?' I cough again. 'What are you looking for, Nick?! What's wrong?'

'Hold on.' Nick leaves the room, returning with his medical bag and a stethoscope in hand. He helps me sit up while he listens to my heart. I go to speak but he raises a finger to his mouth. Instinctively, I touch my belly. Nick's expression sharpens, the way it sometimes does when he is on the phone with colleagues asking for advice or if patients need to report specific symptoms to him.

'Are you feeling any pain?'

I shake my head.

'I'm taking you to the ED,' he says finally, pulling my pyjama top down.

'What? Wait. What's wrong? Do you think—'

'I'm just being cautious.' Nick pulls his phone out of his pocket and begins searching for a number. He keeps his eyes trained on his phone as he scrolls through his contact list.

I turn my body so I'm sitting on the edge of the bed. 'I need to get dressed.'

'No, Paige. Car. Now.'

'What?' My hand flies to my mouth, tears forming in my eyes. Nick's jaw is tightly clenched, his eyes dark with concentration.

'You're worried! You're worrying me. So, if there's something to worry about, *tell me*. And if there isn't anything to worry about—'

He kneels down in front of me and takes my hands in his. 'I need to rule out a few things. Okay?'

I can see he is trying to be calm and professional with me, but Nick's quick to get up. His body turns away from me briefly as he runs a hand over his face.

'Nick…'

'Everything's under control.' He takes a deep breath and reaches out to help me up. 'Come on, let's go.'

Nick secures my seat belt for me, slams the passenger door closed and races to the driver's seat. He dials Dr Sanders as we turn the corner from our safe and quiet cul-de-sac. One of the street lights needs a globe replacing. The car is emitting a desperate beep, urging Nick to put his seat belt on. He fastens it as we pull out into the main road.

'James, sorry to bother you at this hour. I've got Paige in the car with me and I'm taking her to the hospital. Would you mind meeting us there?'

'Uh, yeah, sure. What are we dealing with?'

Nick glances at me briefly and squeezes my hand before answering him. 'Orthopnea, dyspnoea, tachycardia, unexplained cough, pitting oedema…' He hesitates, drawing a breath. 'And reduced foetal movement.'

'Remind me, how many weeks is she?'

'Thirty-four.'

'I'll see you soon,' says Dr Sanders.

His voice cuts off and I sink deeper into my seat, gripping the edges of it, practically gasping for air.

Nick has already run two red lights and is about to run another.

Dr Sanders, my obstetrician and a good friend of Nick's from university, is already waiting for us in emergency. He shakes hands with Nick, who asks whether Victoria has been paged.

'She's on her way,' responds Dr Sanders.

I have no idea who Victoria is, and before I can ask, a nurse is standing beside me with a wheelchair. My body sinks into the seat, slumping against the backrest, my eyes closing without me willing them to. Hours ago I was putting finishing touches on a baby nursery, and now I'm a patient about to be evaluated in a hospital emergency room. I want to turn back the clock, go home, bypass this blip in time. Come back tomorrow.

'Hey, Paige, how are you feeling?' asks Dr Sanders, turning his attention to me. He smiles the way he does during our normal appointments together, which isn't at all necessary now, but I know it's out of politeness, to help me stay calm.

'Not great.' My hands hug my belly tighter. 'I'm worried about…' I'm struggling to speak in full sentences. I close my eyes and gulp for air and try again. 'The baby.'

'We're going to check you both out now.'

A nurse wheels me through a corridor while Nick and Dr Sanders forge ahead, discussing my symptoms. Everything becomes a blur once we reach the cubicle in emergency. Nurses and midwives come in and out, hooking me up to oxygen and a pulse oximeter. Someone takes my blood pressure while one of the midwives, who introduces herself as Jo, straps a foetal heart rate monitor to me and sets up an IV.

'Nick?'

When he doesn't answer, I tug the bottom of his jacket.

'Where's Victoria? She needs an echo and a plasma BNP test,' Nick says impatiently, directing his question to Dr Sanders, who is performing a pelvic exam to make sure I'm not dilated. In this moment, Nick isn't the guy who's my husband, the one who holds me when I need him. No, as midwives and nurses come in and out of the room, Nick is the guy who's the doctor – the guy who's away eighty per cent of the time dealing with patients.

'Let's sit you up a bit higher,' says Jo once Dr Sanders confirms my cervix is long and closed. She guides me up. 'Is that better? Easier to breathe that way?'

There's a marked difference in how much easier it is to breathe in this position. I nod.

'Here I am,' says a female doctor, poking her head through the gap in the curtain. She smiles at me. 'You must be Paige. I'm Dr Bridgeman – you can call me Victoria. I hear you've been feeling a little short of breath lately?'

'Yes,' I reply.

In language that sounds almost foreign, Nick updates her on his assessment of me, to which she nods and responds with things like, 'Right,' 'I see,' and finally, 'Okay.'

'How far away is the echo tech?' asks Dr Sanders.

'Too far,' says Nick. 'We need Luke in here right now for a bedside echo.'

Within moments, another doctor – Luke, who introduces himself as an anaesthesiologist – squeezes lubricant on my chest and starts sliding a Doppler around until he finds the correct placement for it. And then it dawns on me. *Echo.* The Doppler isn't on my belly. I glance over at the screen, trying to get a better look, but Victoria distracts me by asking me a series of questions about my symptoms – when they started, what brought them on, when they got worse. Every now and then Nick's eyes dart to the monitor.

'How long have you got to go, Luke?' Victoria says, her eyes glued to the monitor, a stony look on her face. She turns to one of the nurses. 'BNP as soon as you can.'

I question Nick with my eyes.

He wraps his hand around mine. 'We need to check your heart.' He tries to reassure me with his eyes, but they dart back to Luke's screen.

'But the baby. Why are you… why are they checking my *heart?*'

Victoria explains this is for a brain natriuretic peptide test to check the amount of BNP hormone in my blood. In other words, to show her how well my heart is working.

'What about Max? Is Max okay?' I ask Nick.

'Luke,' prompts Nick, with a tone of urgency in his voice.

'Almost done,' he replies without lifting his gaze from the screen.

Nick is grinding his teeth, something I've never seen him do, and at this point I don't know where to look.

'We need to deliver this baby,' says Dr Sanders, finally breaking the silence. He mentions something about there being significant heartbeat deceleration to sixty bpm. Sixty beats. What is it supposed to be? Eighty? Ninety? One hundred and twenty? I can't remember.

'Shit,' mutters Nick, running his hand through his hair. He turns to Dr Sanders. 'How long do we have?'

'Nobody's doing anything until we stabilise the mother,' says Victoria.

Dr Sanders chews his lip, appearing to think.

'James! Can the baby tolerate waiting ten minutes? What's the deal?'

No response.

'James!' repeats Nick.

Dr Sanders shakes his head. 'No, I don't think so.'

Seconds later, the room fills with nurses and midwives pumping me with drugs, calling out figures, while a nurse hooks me up to more monitors. I can hear Nick and Dr Sanders in the background discussing things with Victoria and Luke. I try to stop myself from calling out to Nick, which lasts all of three seconds, even if I can barely keep my eyes open.

'I know it's hard, Paige, but please, try to stay calm,' says Victoria, but her eyes don't meet mine.

'I'm here. Right here,' says Nick, reaching for my hand.

Victoria nods to the nurse standing beside me, who I haven't noticed before. 'We need the defibrillator in here, just in case.'

'Vic, Luke, if there's a chance of saving this baby, we really need her in the operating room,' says Dr Sanders. 'If we're going to initiate a crash section, we need to do it now.'

Nick turns to face Luke. 'What's her left ventricular ejection fraction?'

'It's only twenty per cent.'

'There's no way you're giving her a general, it's too dangerous,' says Nick. 'Luke?'

'Yes, I agree.'

'In my opinion, even a C-section right now poses too high a risk for the mother,' says Victoria.

'You sure?' Nick asks.

Victoria looks at him sternly.

'Dr Bridgeman, are you sure?' he repeats.

'Surgery is going to place additional stress on the heart, and I'm not confident enough with the outcome.'

I muster as much energy as I can to tug on Nick's jeans. 'Please, Nick. Let them do the C-section.'

'It's way too risky,' he replies, blinking at me, his eyes turning glassy.

I manage to raise my hands to cup his face. 'Please. I want them to save our baby.'

Nick pinches his nostrils and gives a small nod. Straightening up, he locks his gaze with Victoria's. 'With proper monitoring – Luke's the best anaesthesiologist we have. Are you willing to—'

Victoria's response is blunt. 'I need time to talk with Paige – she needs to understand the risks before she makes a firm decision.' The hospital room starts moving in slow motion as each of the doctors explains the extremity of the situation and the risks to my life and the baby's life if surgery is to go ahead.

'We don't have a lot of time to decide on this one,' says Nick. 'We – you – need to make a call.'

'Do it,' I say.

'Paige,' says Nick, his face close to mine. 'Are you sure you want to do this?' He's gripping my hand with both of his.

'We have to – it's our baby. Dr Sanders, please get me a consent form. I understand the risks and I want you to do whatever you have to do to deliver this baby.'

By the time I finish my sentence, Luke is already on the phone to theatre, briefing staff. 'We have a critically ill woman coming around to theatre for an immediate C-section. Please set up an arterial line and get out a combined spinal epidural set ready for me.' He briefly turns to Nick. 'You stay here.'

Nick goes to protest but Victoria grabs his arm. 'Too close, let us handle it.'

Dr Sanders is already out the door. 'Someone get a consent form!'

Before they whisk me away, Nick bends down and presses his lips against mine, where they linger for a beat. 'It's going to be fine – they're going to take care of you.'

CHAPTER TEN

Nick

Evelyn is walking towards me, an oversized cream leather handbag bobbing against her thigh. It's more of a power walk really, and it doesn't give me much of a chance to think about how I'm going to tell her what's happened in the hours since I got home. I'd spoken to Paige before I left for the airport – a brief three-minute chat. Did I ask her how she was? Did she sound any different? It was hard to hear her in the hotel lobby with so many people around. I should have called her again from my room, or the taxi to the airport. If only George, the conference delegate I shared my ride with, hadn't been so damn chatty.

Evelyn grabs my hand and squeezes it. 'Nick, we came as soon as we could. David couldn't find the keys to the car. He left them on top of the fridge. The *fridge*. Of all places! He's parking now. Tell me about Paige. Is she… Where is she? Where's the baby? Has she had him already? When can we see them?'

When I called Evelyn and David, I kept the details to a minimum: Paige was very unwell and had been admitted to the hospital. Doctors were going to be delivering the baby early due to distress, and I thought it was a good idea for them to be here. Caitlin too. I knew how harrowing the drive over would be if I told them exactly what was transpiring, and I wanted to save them from undue stress until I could explain things calmly and clearly. Now that Evelyn's here, I'm practically lost for words.

'No, she—'

'Have you called Bette? She didn't want to miss the birth. She'll need to get a last-minute flight.' My mum, Bette, lives on Tasmania's East Coast, where she operates a B & B, about an hour's flight from Melbourne. And no, I haven't called her yet.

'Why aren't you with Paige?' asks Evelyn suddenly. 'Shouldn't you be in there with her?'

'The doctors feel it's better I wait out here since she presented...' I correct myself. This is Evelyn, not a colleague. 'She isn't well.'

'She said she was coming down with something. She napped on and off all day. I didn't think she'd be giving birth this early though. The baby will just need a bit of extra monitoring, true?'

'Evelyn, it's a bit more complicated—'

'It must be pre-eclampsia. She was so swollen. You should have seen her legs. I mean, she was a bit puffy in the face and hands but her ankles—'

'*Evelyn*...'

'It's a late pre-term though so I think it'll be fine. The lungs are fully formed at this stage so—'

I cut through her blather. 'Evelyn, I need you to listen to me. There's a chance that Paige might die.'

Evelyn goes quiet. Her creamy complexion loses colour almost instantaneously. 'From pre-eclampsia? That doesn't sound right.'

No, this is much, much worse.

'I don't understand, Nick. Pre-eclampsia is common. It's not something I hear soon-to-be-mothers dying from.'

'We aren't dealing with pre-eclampsia.'

Evelyn straightens her shoulders as if to regain composure. She glances around, eyes pinned on the door, obviously searching for David. She probably doesn't want to hear me deliver this news without him by her side.

'Then what are we dealing with?' she asks finally.

'Heart failure.'

*

In the time I've been a part of this family, I've never seen the Huttons like this. Nobody is talking. Not even Caitlin. Evelyn is sitting on one of the waiting room chairs beside a passive David, who looks completely dishevelled. She takes a small amber spray bottle with a yellow label from one of the pockets of her handbag. She spritzes the Rescue Remedy onto her tongue and stares into her lap.

'This is insane,' says Caitlin eventually, standing up. 'She was working on the nursery, climbing stairs – she seemed fine.' Her frantic expression mirrors Evelyn's, only she's way more intense.

'She didn't seem fine, Caitlin. She seemed exhausted,' says Evelyn.

'We thought… I told her…' She pauses. 'Nick! I told her it was normal! I told her to put her feet up and rest, and now you're saying—'

'Shhh, darling, you're making a scene,' says Evelyn.

'This is my fault,' she says, bewildered.

'No,' I tell her. 'It's not your fault.'

It's hardly fair to let any of the blame fall on Caitlin when I am the one who should have been around for my wife and unborn son. Instead, I was having drinks in a hotel in Singapore while my wife's health was deteriorating so badly she could die. I eye the wall clock again. That stupid, boring, old black-and-white clock, typical of the ones you see in any hospital or school setting. Any place you want the minutes to tick by more quickly so you can go home and get on with your life.

'She's going to be okay though, isn't she? I mean, there's so much they can do for weak hearts.' This from Evelyn.

This isn't the time for me to comment. I don't know enough about Paige's condition, though I have my suspicions around what's happened. I just don't know *why*. What I do know is this is more than just a 'weak heart'. Late trimester pregnancies aren't meant to end like this.

'Nick?' says David, looking up at me. 'Please give us your opinion. Is she... Are they going to be all right?'

It dawns on me how patients must feel when they ask me to try to answer questions about their children's recovery and prognosis. I'm a man who can never seem to give anyone an absolute. My expression must tell them what I'm thinking, and what I'm thinking is, *I don't know*. I'm on the outside here, and I hate it. I want to be in the room with Paige. And Max. Out here there isn't a single thing I can do except wait.

Evelyn lets out a small moan and leans into David's shoulder, her words something along the lines of, 'We can't lose our daughter,' coming out in a muffled sob.

Caitlin scoots to her side and puts a hand on her back. 'Mum... how about we grab a coffee? Or tea? I've got some chamomile in my bag.' She digs through her handbag and produces a handful of lemon-coloured sachets.

'Any idea if there's a kitchenette nearby where I can boil some water?' she asks me.

That's when I notice the doctor in his scrubs. It's James. I have known James for over ten years, and this is not how he walks when he delivers good news to people. He's slightly hunched over and his pace is slower than usual. Of course, none of this is intentional – he's probably thinking about what he's going to say and how he's going to say it.

As he approaches, I breathe the words, 'This is us,' and Evelyn and David sit bolt upright. James stops a safe distance from us, slides his cap off and holds it with one hand, as if he's at a church service. He turns to Evelyn and David. 'Mr and Mrs Hutton?'

'Yes, I'm Paige's mother, Evelyn, and this is my husband, David. Our daughter, Caitlin.'

'I'm Dr Sanders, Paige's obstetrician.'

'Yes, we met at one of her appointments,' says Evelyn.

'Oh, yes, of course.'

'What's the latest?' I can't help myself from interjecting.

'Is she okay? Is my grandson okay?' asks David.

My body stiffens and I break out in a cold sweat. Maybe I'm not ready for this news after all.

James stands there, impossibly composed. 'Well, I have some news,' he starts. 'As you know, Paige came in…'

His eyes dart to his hands and then back up to me. That's when I know. One of them is gone. The strange thing is, I don't know which is worse: my wife or my baby.

CHAPTER ELEVEN

Paige

Three days after my C-section, I'm still in ICU. It's cruel the way my body is not able to behave the way it should after I delivered a baby. The midwives told me that suppressing my milk with drugs was going to be easier on me than the alternative, since I have no baby to feed.

I'm finally being moved to a private ward. Judy, one of the midwives, pushes me down the corridor. My breath catches as we pass a new mother in her pyjamas, trying to soothe her crying baby. Further ahead, a group of visitors is waiting at the unmanned reception desk with an enormous helium balloon sporting the words *It's a boy!*. A small moan unintentionally escapes my lips, and I hope Judy hasn't noticed.

'Almost there,' she says, which gives me reason to believe she *has* heard me. My body stiffens as I try to keep it together. In ten seconds, nine, eight, seven… I'll be in my private room and all the reminders in the outside world can disappear.

'Here we are, love,' says Judy as we approach the last room – the one that is conveniently located farthest from the nursery. 'It's actually our best room.'

I don't know Judy, but I can tell she's lying. She goes over to the window and opens the curtains, allowing the natural light to filter through the room. I take a few deep breaths and go to stand up.

'How about we get you settled back into bed?' She helps me into bed, and once she completes all her checks, she takes something that is hanging off the back of the wheelchair. I try to get a better look at it as she fastens it to the outer side of the door with some Blu Tack.

'A butterfly? But I… I don't have a baby.'

'I know, dear. That's why we give you the butterfly. It's so all us nurses on the ward know that whoever's in this room is going to need some extra-special TLC.'

A few hours later, Nick and I are waiting for Victoria to come by to give us an update on my most recent echo. Nick has been spending as much time as possible here with me and he hasn't shaved in days. Even though Mum brought him a change of clothes, he's wearing the same T-shirt and trousers as yesterday. He's been peeking at my chart, and quickly puts it back when he hears the two gentle knocks on the door.

'How are you feeling, Paige?' asks Victoria. She sits down at the end of the bed near my feet and crosses her legs, balancing her clipboard against her knee. Nick pulls up a chair beside me. She's dressed in a pale-lemon-coloured shirt with a Peter Pan collar and tight-fitting jeans, and a stethoscope wreathes its way around her neck alongside a chunky necklace. She's wearing thick-rimmed plastic glasses, with her long brown hair swept to the side.

'A little better,' I admit. Although that isn't taking into account the fact that I'm still in pain from the C-section or that my body feels as if it's been hollowed out like a pumpkin.

'I know Nick has probably explained to you what's been going on, but now that you're on the mend, I wanted to give you a proper explanation of what we were dealing with when you came in as well as give you a chance to ask any questions and discuss your most recent test results.'

'Okay,' I reply, not exactly sure that I'm ready for the details. I'd asked Nick to keep the information vague for now. My voice is small. I can't bear to think about that night. All I want is to be able to forget.

'As you know, when you came into the ED our tests showed that you were experiencing heart failure, and in your case, more specifically, PPCM or peripartum cardiomyopathy, which we were able to conclude after running tests in ICU and ruling out all the other possible causes for your heart failure.'

'What caused it?'

'We don't know why some women develop this. It's not like other forms of heart failure, where we know the cause and can treat that. And that's why we call it PPCM. This can usually manifest in the last month of pregnancy or in the first five months or so post-partum. Or it can occur sooner, as in your case.' She pauses to open the folder in her hands. 'Paige, when we did the first echo, we found that your heart was abnormally enlarged.' She points to a laminated A4 poster she's brought with her. 'Like this,' she says, holding it up. 'As you know, the heart is a muscle, and what happens in cardiomyopathy is that the heart is unable to pump blood as effectively as it should. Now, when you came in, your left ventricular ejection fraction, or your EF, was twenty per cent. That is to say the amount of blood pumped out of the ventricles with each contraction was extremely low.' She points out the ventricles on the diagram to show me. 'You still with me?'

I nod. It's raining outside and it has been all morning.

'Okay, so to give you an idea, the normal EF range is around fifty-five per cent or above. That's why I was so concerned with you having a C-section. Due to the weakness of your heart, emergency surgery with a general anaesthesia was very risky to perform, and even the epidural posed a lot of risks for you.'

A bird – one I can't name, with a lapis-blue forehead and brown wings – perches on the windowsill before taking flight into the unrelenting drizzle. It's early summer. It shouldn't be raining. Cars are banked up in bumper to bumper traffic, their red brake lights flicking on and off as they inch forward slowly. Victoria is still talking, her voice like white noise.

'Paige, did you hear that?' asks Nick softly.

The bird returns to the sill, carrying a tuft of dry grass in its beak. 'Yes, I understand.'

Victoria takes her glasses off and folds them. She drops them into a case and clamps it shut. 'I want to let you know, as I'm sure Nick has already told you, that PPCM symptoms, especially given the fact they often appear in late pregnancy, can often be confused with late trimester symptoms…' Victoria is prettier without the glasses, I decide. Her eyes are large and deep-set. Her eyelashes most certainly false. Her brows – they are perfectly shaped. I have an appointment booked for mine for this afternoon.

'… from what you described, it seems your condition deteriorated fairly rapidly after the onset of those early warning signs. The promising news is that your echo showed a very slight improvement in your EF.'

I need to call Marcia, my beauty therapist. She hates last-minute cancellations, and if I miss this one, I won't be able to get in for another week at the very least. I'm not supposed to be here. I'm supposed to be getting my eyebrows done today.

'Paige?' says Victoria finally.

'Yes.'

'I'm recommending a few more days in hospital to make sure we properly establish the correct amount of medication your body can tolerate.'

'Sure thing,' replies Nick, when I don't.

'Do you have any questions at this point, Paige?'

What kind of bird is that?

'Um, no, I don't think so.'

Nick interjects with questions about the anticoagulants, diuretics and beta blockers she's prescribed, along with things like the size of my left ventricle, and my BNP levels. And is there a need for an implantable defibrillator? She patiently answers all of his questions and then redirects her attention back to me.

'Now, there's one more thing I'd like to discuss with you both. I mentioned before that PPCM is usually reversible with the right treatment, although I want to stress that there's never a 100 per cent guarantee of full recovery. There is a chance your condition may worsen, remain stable or, as we all hope, improve. Generally, you can expect to be on the medication I've prescribed you for at least twelve months.'

Nick reaches for my hand then, signalling that he knows what's coming next.

'I know things are very raw for you both right now, but since you were about to become parents, we should talk about the fact that a future pregnancy would be contraindicated as long as your EF levels are under fifty-five per cent. Currently, your heart simply isn't strong enough to supply blood to you and a baby. Research tells us that a pregnancy with an EF under fifty-five per cent would pose significant threat to your life, so I'd recommend thinking about what method of contraception would suit you – an IUD could be a good option, or I can have Dr Sanders prescribe a low-dosage progesterone pill if you'd prefer that.'

'The pill will be fine,' I manage, nauseated by the very thought. *Pregnancy is contraindicated.*

Victoria pats my leg. 'I know this must be tough to hear, but you're an otherwise healthy woman – you exercise regularly and have a good diet. I'm optimistic about your recovery.'

I muster a quiet, 'Thank you,' and Nick does the same, closing the door behind her.

'I need to call Marcia, from Lush, the beauty therapist. I have an appointment at five thirty. Eyebrows.'

Nick sits back down beside me and pulls me into his arms. 'Oh, Paige.'

'It's not fair,' I say, my words muffled against his chest.

He holds me tighter. 'I know, baby. I know.'

'I want to hold Max,' I manage, pulling away gently. 'Could you bring him to me?'

'Knock, knock.' Caitlin is standing at the door of my hospital room with a bright Cath Kidston tote hanging off one arm and a small brown paper carry bag in her free hand. Nick has gone home to shower and get some rest, and Mum's at home preparing some cooked meals we'll be able to freeze. 'Up for a visitor?' she asks quietly. She's wearing a long yellow dress with cream polka dots and a scarf belt cinched at the waist, and it radiates sunshine.

'Sure. What's in the bag?'

She hands it to me and I tip it upside down. A few bottles of essential oils, a vial of Rescue Remedy and a crossword puzzle fall out onto the bed.

'The crossword is from Frank. Nick was in touch with Bette, she told Elsie, she told Frank and he wanted to send these along.' She shows me a small stack of newspaper cuttings from the *Herald Sun* crosswords section. Frank is a resident at Windsor Lakes, and he and Elsie, Nick's grandmother, are inseparable. When he was sick in hospital last year, it was my job to make sure he had an endless supply of crosswords, and now he's doing the same for me.

Windsor Lakes. Meeting Nick. One tiny moment that changed my life forever. That's the thing about tiny moments. They seem tiny until you look back on them, registering how big they were. Me, Nick, a chance meeting at an aged-care home, a wedding, two pink lines, two red lights and a street lamp that died and needed its globe replacing.

Caitlin pauses and takes in a deep sigh when she registers my expression. 'God, I didn't want to upset you. Paige… say something. Please.'

I try to blink away the tears but it's impossible. I'm like a leaky tap. There are simply no words to convey how much I don't want to be here.

'If you want, I'll take it all back. I can go if you don't want me around, or—'

'Stay,' I blurt. 'I want you to stay.'

She flings her arms around me and I welcome the soft curves of her body against mine. I hold the fabric of her bright yellow happy dress tightly in my fist. I can't let go. Don't want to let go. I need something – someone – to hold onto.

'I love you. And I'm so, so sorry,' she whispers into my hair.

My body shudders against hers as she holds me tightly. She combs her fingers through my hair, and when I release the fabric of her dress from my grip, I look into her eyes. 'I was wondering if you... if you wanted to hold him?'

Caitlin pulls away and holds me by the elbows. 'Yes,' she whispers. 'Of course. I would love to hold your son.'

Ten days after being admitted, Nick and I leave the maternity ward and all the flowers in it, without our baby. It's Christmas Eve. The street lamp globe has been replaced, the black pillars now adorned in glittering silver and red tinsel.

As we pull into the driveway, the wooden candy canes and joyful bright lights draped along the front façade of our house tease me.

'Could we shut the lights down, please?' I say to Nick as he helps me out of the car.

'Course. Yes. I'll do it ASAP.'

Inside, he helps me up the stairs and towards our bedroom. Nick has closed the nursery door. Wooden polka dot letters spell out Max's name at eye level. I stop outside the door, taking in the letters: M A X. All the slips of paper had spelled out Max.

I'm clutching the blue paper butterfly that Judy had fixed to the door of my hospital room. I hold my thumb in place and press the butterfly against the door, sticking it firmly.

In my bedroom, I pull a set of clean pyjamas from my dresser drawer and sit them on the edge of the bed. I simply stare at them, knowing I need to shower, to wash my hair, to find some way to function, to grasp life again, to accept that I'm a mother – albeit a mother without her baby. I enter the bathroom, feeling Nick's eyes on me as he leans against the doorframe, watching me as I lift my top to examine the scar on my belly where they made the incision for the C-section. I blink at Nick, meeting his eyes in the mirror.

'Hey,' he says softly. 'I know it hurts.' From behind, he envelops me in his arms, resting his head against my shoulder. My breath hitches in my chest, and while I don't necessarily want it to, my body stays rigid despite his embrace. 'You don't have to believe me yet, but I promise you, we're going to get through this.'

My eyes scrunch closed at the impossibility of it. 'I don't know…' I whimper, feeling my knees buckle. 'I don't know how to be a mother without her baby. How do we be parents without Max here with us? We left him there.'

Nick's arms tighten around me.

I continue, 'He's still there. All alone in the hospital and he should be here, now, with us.' I turn around to face him and hug him as tightly as I can, moving my hands underneath his shirt so I can feel his warm, soft skin against my hands. I want to feel as close to him as I possibly can. His body shudders as I attempt to hold him in my arms. Here we are, holding each other in the dim light of the bathroom, and it's the first time I've ever heard him cry.

My gaze falls on our toothbrushes: one pink, one green. His and hers. Husband and wife. A couple. We are supposed to be a family. I will never ever get to recognise Max's cries. Why couldn't I have recognised the signs?

CHAPTER TWELVE

Nick

We chose a tiny white casket with flowers that Evelyn selected. Cream ones, small and strong-scented, like vanilla and honey. I didn't ask the name of them.

'Nick, darling, how are you holding up?' Evelyn is standing beside me with a full plate of sandwiches.

I run a hand over the stubble on my face. I can't remember the last time I shaved. 'Uh, it's going to take some time.' What else is there to say? Somehow these words, along with ones like, 'I'm fine,' and, 'Could be better,' have become my go-to phrases whenever someone asks me how I'm doing. Frankly, I'm more concerned about Paige. She's barely eating, barely sleeping and has not stopped crying.

My mum keeps her hand on my arm. She travelled to Melbourne from Launceston the day after Paige was discharged from the hospital. She wanted to stay in a hotel but Paige insisted on opening up the guest room. Mum and Paige have always got on well, and I think having her here has helped a bit.

'Yes. You're right. Course it will.' Evelyn says this in a way that sounds like she's trying to reassure herself. Which she probably is. 'Have you eaten anything at all? You should eat... if you haven't.' She thrusts the plate in my direction, inviting me to take a sandwich. 'Nobody's touched them.'

'I'm good. Not all that hungry. But thank you.' All I've eaten this morning is a bite of cold toast and a sip of coffee. I can't remember the last time I ate a full meal.

'Um, David said to tell you that he and the others are ready when you two are. He was also wondering if you'd chosen a song to play?'

'Uh, no, we never got around to choosing one so I think we'll skip the music. Paige and Hope have gone for a walk. I'll let them know when they come back.'

'Okay, well, I'll put the sandwiches in the fridge, and if you want some later, you can help yourselves.'

Her words fade. Like most of the conversations we've been having over the past few days, all the words come out stilted, forced, unnatural, as if they don't belong to us at all. Being at home is becoming almost unbearable. There's no escaping the reality of losing a child who did not get the chance to live. I'm hankering to get back to the hospital, away from it all.

'Excuse me, I need to make a call. I'll be back in five minutes.'

Evelyn feigns a smile that evaporates quickly. It's an expression I recognise. It's the expression of someone trying to be strong for someone else when they're hurting just as much themselves. I quickly leave the room and go upstairs to the study, closing the door behind me.

I slouch into the chair and plant a fist on the desk.

Goddammit, why did I have to go to Singapore at all?

With a brush of my arm, the papers on the desk fly across the room – outstanding bills, a quote for a new washing machine, a note from Paige reminding me to change the smoke alarm batteries.

I fish my phone from my pocket and dial my colleague Ben at the hospital to let him know I'm ready to come back to work. The smoke alarm batteries can wait. The washing machine can wait. And those stupid bills can wait, too.

Ben answers the phone as if he's expecting a call from me. 'Hey, Nick. How's it all going?'

The words don't come. Why won't they come? I pinch the bridge of my nose, a stinging sensation building up.

'Nick? Hello? Can you hear me? Are you there?' There's a pause. And then, 'Is everything all right, mate?'

In one swift motion, I hurl my phone across the room, where it hits the glass door of a cabinet, shattering the glass like a thousand stars falling from the sky.

I drop my head into my hands and sit there, elbows on the desk, trying to fight the urge to cry. I'm struggling to hold back all these feelings – *emotions* – that are inside me, I don't know where they come from.

When I look up, Paige is standing there with Mum's arm around her shoulder, one hand cupped over her mouth, tears streaming down her cheeks, holding onto a small bottle of bubbles in the other.

'I'm sorry. I shouldn't have – I just… I don't know what came over me.' I stand up and run a hand through my hair. The last thing I want is for Paige or Mum to see me upset. I need to be strong for them – especially for Paige.

Mum moves quickly across the room towards me. 'You know, you two should come down for a break when you're ready. Can you take some time off, Nick?'

'Thanks, Bette,' says Paige. 'I think that would be a good idea. Maybe once the weather improves,' she says, her eyes focused on me.

Mum tries to hug me. I raise a hand to stop her and soften my voice. 'I'm fine, Mum, thanks,' I say, giving her shoulder a squeeze.

Paige is still standing there, something I have never seen before shadowing her face, dimming the brightness in her usually bright green eyes. Sunlight is streaming through the window and the glass shards shimmer in the light. 'Dad said they're waiting downstairs for us. Are you ready to…? I mean, do you still want to …?'

'Why don't I duck out and get a dustpan and brush,' Mum says, taking the opportunity to exit the room.

I reach for Paige's hand. 'We don't have to say goodbye today… or like this… if we don't want to.'

We both came up with the idea to have a bubble-blowing ceremony in the back garden in Max's memory after the service. We thought that spending time with family afterwards would be a good idea, and together we'd be able to let go. But now, I get the sense we're both regretting those decisions. The truth is, we have no idea how to navigate this road we don't want to be on at all.

'What do you want to do?' she asks earnestly.

'It's up to you.'

'No,' she says, moving towards the broken glass. She bends down and picks up a photo frame that has fallen to the ground. It's a photo of the two of us on a holiday in New York. We are standing under a tree in Central Park, clutching paper cups of coffee, watching the snow fall. Paige is holding her free hand out, trying to catch a snowflake. It is a photo of a girl filled with wonder and innocence. 'I think this is one of those magical moments we won't ever forget,' Paige had said, smiling up at me, her teeth chattering. I'd proposed then and there, knee in the snow, with the ring I'd held onto for eight months prior to our trip.

She runs a finger over the cracked glass. 'It's up to us.'

I hold my palm out for her to hand me the frame. 'Maybe if they want to, they can do the bubbles thing and we…'

'Could just be together?' she says, leaning into my embrace.

Half an hour later, the people we love the most – our parents, Caitlin and Mark, Hope and Paul – gather in a circle on the lawn in our back garden beside the freshly planted lemon tree. Paige and I stand together in Max's nursery, watching our hopes and dreams and expectations float away; a stream of bubbles against a periwinkle sky that disappear moments after they appear.

*

Three days after the funeral, I drop Mum off at the airport and come home to Paige opening and closing cupboard doors in the kitchen. A saucepan clangs to the floor. 'Hey, what's going on?'

'I can't find the measuring cup. I think Mum put it away somewhere.'

'You're planning on cooking – baking – at seven thirty in the morning?'

She sticks her arm into the back crevice of the pantry and fumbles around. 'Got it.' She holds up the plastic measuring jug, takes it over to the tap and fills it up, noting down the volume in a notebook before pouring it into a glass.

Paige has been given strict instructions to follow a low-sodium diet while continuing to take the diuretics. It means she needs to limit her fluid intake to one and a half litres per day to ensure minimal strain on her heart. Once she finishes the diuretics, she'll be able to up it to two litres. It's hard to believe that not so long ago she was healthy and fit, and now she's following instructions that are handed out to *sick* people. Paige shouldn't be one of them.

She drains her meagre glass of water before lining up her pill bottles in a row. She pops the lid off a container and starts counting them out like little beads, ready to divide into a day-of-the-week pillbox.

'I can do it for you,' I offer.

'Nope, no need, I'm perfectly capable of doing it.' She continues sorting the pills.

Everyone keeps telling me I need to *be there* for Paige, but no matter how I try to be there for her, it doesn't seem to be working. I make a mental note not to offer to sort out the meds again. Or the washing. I can also make myself scarce of an evening as apparently Paige doesn't need me to babysit her on the sofa while she's watching Netflix either.

'What's this?' I muse, picking up a gift box.

She shrugs. 'Not sure. Hope brought it round yesterday.'

'You're not going to open it?'

'It can wait,' she murmurs, not taking her eyes off the task at hand. 'You can open it if you want.'

I tear open the package and hold it up to show her. She barely registers the 5,000-piece puzzle of a spring butterfly garden. I think it's a great idea on Hope's part. But I can just imagine what Paige is thinking: *A puzzle is a thoughtful gift but it's hardly going to make this better, Nick.*

'You should probably open the card yourself.'

She doesn't respond so I change tack. We both look like hell and could benefit from a shot of caffeine. I inch towards the coffee machine. 'Have you had breakfast?'

'Not hungry.'

'You need to eat though.'

'Not hungry,' she repeats, and I know this isn't going to end well. Paige isn't in the mood for talking and it's clear she doesn't want me around.

I put my mug away, closing the cupboard door a little more forcefully than usual. I don't *mean* to do this but she flicks her eyes up momentarily, her expression indifferent.

'You know what? I'm going to go for a run.' I hesitate for a beat because I don't know how she'll take what I'm about to say. 'Drop past the hospital after that.'

'I think that's a good idea,' she says. This time she doesn't look at me. 'Sorry, I'm counting.'

I'm halfway down the hallway when I tell her, 'I shouldn't be longer than a few hours. I'll aim to be back by early afternoon.'

I don't know why I even bothered. She doesn't answer me at all. Instead, she continues dropping pills into the box.

Ping, ping, ping.

CHAPTER THIRTEEN

Paige

The early days are hard.

I forgot to cancel a major delivery from the baby shop. The bakery called on the day of my baby shower asking why nobody had been in to pick up the cake. An early baby present arrived in the mail from Ryan and Susannah in Canada. I've gone up one shoe size and two bra sizes. The skin on my lower belly is scored with purple lines where it's stretched to accommodate a baby.

I've taken leave from my job at Windsor Lakes. Brian, my boss, is for the most part very understanding. He and his partner Chase lost a baby via a surrogate about eight months ago. While it was an early miscarriage, it was still devastating for them. It had taken them years to find an altruistic surrogate.

'Wait, you resigned from work?' asks Hope when I fill her in on the details. We're sitting at the dining table, puzzle pieces sprawled out around us, Ollie sleeping in the pram beside us. It looms there with its four wheels and pale blue muslin blanket draped over it, like another cruel reminder of what I've lost. Ollie is two months old and I've gone from doting, step-in aunt to someone who is trying to pretend he doesn't exist, another thing to feel guilty about. If Hope has noticed, which she most certainly has, she doesn't make a big deal about it, and that's something I'm thankful for. She hands me a mug of tea.

'Thanks, but I need to check how much I've had to drink today.'

'Don't worry, I already did. You're within your limits, and I recorded it in your notebook.'

'Of course you did. I didn't resign. I just don't know if I want to go back.'

'What about Elsie and Frank? It might do you good to get out and be with people, even if you just go for a visit.'

I do miss them, but there is a problem. A big one. Getting out and *being* with people means having to *talk* to people. And there's nothing worse than talking to people about anything except the actual thing everyone is too scared to talk about. Going back to Windsor Lakes, even for a visit, feels too hard.

'I just need some time to—' I motion to the puzzle '—finish this.' Somehow, the puzzle I'd initially resisted starting has become part of my routine. I wake up, say goodbye to Nick, bypass the shower and head straight for the dining table. Nick and I have resorted to eating meals on the bar stools at the kitchen counter. Every morning, I sit in my pyjamas, trying to force pieces that don't belong together until I finally find the ones that do. In the past week, I've declined a lunch invitation with Kate and Lori from work and ignored the phone unless it's Nick, Mum, Caitlin, Hope or Ryan calling. And sometimes I find myself making excuses not to answer their calls too. The truth is, when I'm working on the puzzle, it's like I'm somehow closer to Max. It's the two of us and my thoughts in a corner of the world I can inhabit without thinking about the fact he's gone.

I've dreamed up Max's entire life while fitting together the forty pieces that have begun to shape the left-hand corner of the butterfly garden. Once the January mornings became warmer, I'd nurse him on the wicker chair on the back deck before taking him for a walk in the pram I never got around to ordering. We'd go to the park two blocks away, the one with the massive willow tree and flying fox. When Nick would leave for work, I'd hoist him onto one hip, and we'd wave goodbye, counting the hours together until he got home. We'd bake failed cakes that collapsed onto themselves, dip buttered soldiers into runny eggs, paint huge sheets of paper with our hands and eat ice cream for fun. At night I'd lie down in bed with him – me on one side, Nick on the other. We'd marvel at the way his hand fit perfectly into ours – soft, spongy fingers lengthening and growing into strong hands that belonged to a pre-schooler, then a teenager, a young man we could be proud of. A happy, respectable, capable, funny, loving, wonderful person we were proud to call our son, and lucky enough to love, protect and care for.

'This all fucking sucks,' declares Hope, jolting me from my thoughts.

'You're not meant to finish it in a day,' I say. We've been working on the puzzle for an hour and have managed to fit no more than six pieces together.

'No, I mean you losing the baby… Max.'

Until this moment, nobody aside from Nick has referred to Max by his name.

I run my finger over the edges of the puzzle piece, turning it around, thinking about what I want to say. 'He was so beautiful. He looked like Nick. Same eyes.' I smile to myself, remembering his tiny features. 'He had the most gorgeous little chin. And the midwives, they told me they were the cutest toes they'd ever seen. They were so tiny and perfect. They took photos and I can't stop looking at them whenever Nick's not home.'

Hope reaches out and holds my hand in hers, keeping her eyes trained on mine as I speak.

'Does he look at them?'

'I don't think he wants to.'

She nods thoughtfully. 'Tell me more about him – about Max.'

I welcome Hope's invitation to talk about him. Dad finds it too hard, Mum seems to be more comfortable making sure we're fed and taking care of ourselves, and Caitlin skirts around the fact we've lost a baby. She's more preoccupied with making sure I'm keeping in good spirits, all things considered. She's already brought me three care packs I haven't managed to bring myself to open yet, plus a stack of novels I know she's thoroughly vetted for happy endings. Aside from Bette, who's had to navigate life after the loss of a child herself, and now Hope, nobody seems to feel comfortable talking about Max with me.

'They cut a tiny handful of hair from his head. It was light brown. Not much of it, but enough. The midwives took his tiny prints on a piece of cardboard.'

'Will you show them to me? When you're ready?'

I nod, pleased she's asked. 'I still feel like I'm a mum. Max's mum. Even though he's not here – with us – right now.'

'God, Paige, I'm so sorry,' says Hope, shaking her head.

I chew the inside of my lip and ask the question I've been asking myself for three weeks. 'How can I feel like a mother if I don't have a baby?'

'It's a boy!'

'Sure is, kiddo,' says Nick, watching Ella tear away the last shreds of hot-pink wrapping paper from the box.

She races over to me and hugs me. 'Thank you, Aunty Paige.'

I ruffle her hair, sending bits of sparkling glitter into the air. 'Is that the doll you were wishing for?'

'Aha,' she says, all eyes and gappy smile. She lost her front tooth last week and another the week prior to that. She takes me and Nick by the hand and leads us inside. 'Mum and I made fairy bread. Look!' She points to a platter of sandwiches covered in rainbow sprinkles.

Caitlin is behind the kitchen counter wearing an apron over a pair of jeans and a loose-fitting sleeveless cotton top. 'She has been hounding me for one of those dolls for weeks,' she says, pulling a tray of mini pizzas from the oven. She sets them on the bench and I help her deposit them onto the plates she's lined up.

'How many kids do you have here?' I ask, looking out the window. Mark is blowing bubbles, entertaining a gaggle of younger kids around Ethan's age, while Mum and Dad are helping kids on and off the enormous jumping castle that occupies part of the back garden. The sound of kids' music filters into the house.

'The whole class and then some,' says Caitlin, wiping the back of her hand across her forehead. She looks a little weary, as if she's overworked and hasn't had much sleep. Understandable, I suppose, since she's probably been planning this party for weeks. She'd called Dad over early to help with the paper lanterns and helium balloons, and Mum helped by sticking Freddo frogs into jelly cups, setting up the long table outside and making the 'entertainers' – a face-painter, a fairy named Betsy and her Shetland pony Trixie – feel welcome. 'So around twenty-two, plus siblings.' She reaches for a platter and nods to me and Nick to help her. 'Let's pop them on the table out the back.'

I follow behind the two of them and deposit the pizzas on the table.

'Do you need a hand, babe?' asks Mark, directing his question to Caitlin. 'Hey, Paige,' he says with a wink. I step forward and give him a quick hug and kiss. Mark is wearing a pale pink gingham shirt, a pair of old jeans and a worn baseball cap that looks as if it's been through the wash too many times.

I've always liked the way Mark manages to appease Caitlin while maintaining his own sense of self. They met in her last year of high school when Mark moved into a house on our street and started at the same school as us, in the same year level as Ryan. His parents and siblings have long since moved from the house across the street. It all fell apart when the Callaways divorced eighteen months after they first moved in. After that, Mark no longer lived across the road but spent more time than ever before at our place. He got a job in finance after finishing university, just like he said he would. And Caitlin, who dreamed of becoming a pastry chef who would travel to France for a gap year in the hope she might find a way to an apprenticeship in Europe, parked her carefully plotted ideas for her life after high school shortly after the Callaways moved in. She ended up graduating from university with a public relations degree.

Mark pinches a mini pizza from the platter Caitlin has set down. She doesn't accept his offer of help but responds with a brief cold stare that she holds long enough for me to notice.

'Hey, is everything okay?' I say, under my breath.

Caitlin turns to face me and gives me a look that says, *I don't know what you're talking about.*

I shrug and turn my attention to the garden. Caitlin has really gone all out for this party. There's a small marquee in the far corner of the garden near the apple tree, set up for the adults. A few women are sitting together. One of them has a baby on her lap – a girl, dressed in a white cotton jumpsuit with tiny elephants embroidered on it. The woman is gently bouncing the baby on her lap as she squeezes her chubby legs and laughs at something one of the other mothers is saying.

'Should we sit over there?' asks Nick, pointing to the empty chairs in the marquee.

'Um, I think I might see if Caitlin needs some help inside.'

'Oh no, I'm fine, Paige, it's all under control. You relax.' She then raises a hand to her mouth and calls out, 'Kids! Time to eat!'

Within moments, they start emerging from the jumping castle, like ants leaving a nest. They swarm towards the long table set up with plastic plates and cups and party hats.

'These are for the adults,' says Caitlin, making her way towards the marquee with a platter of food. Reluctantly, I trail alongside her and Nick across the garden.

'Laura, Joy, this is my sister, Paige, and her husband Nick.'

'Hi, nice to meet you.' I give a little wave. Nick does the same and pulls up a chair, leaving the one beside Laura free for me to sit on.

'Oh, nice to meet you both – we've heard a lot about you,' says Laura. Joy nods as if to echo what Laura is saying.

I smile uncomfortably, hoping no one will notice. There is no doubt in my mind they *know*. Joy drops her gaze to her lap as soon as I reciprocate my own forced smile.

'So, your kids go to school with Ella?' says Nick, diving into the conversation. Yep, he's definitely noticed my discomfort.

The three of them make small talk while I try my hardest to keep my eyes away from the baby on Laura's lap when, suddenly, Laura jolts forward and says, 'Uh oh!'

A young girl has tripped over and is crying on the lawn, clutching her ankle. Laura stands up and turns to the closest adult, which happens to be me, and thrusts her baby towards me. 'Would you mind holding her for me?'

Without a chance to think about it, I am now holding a newborn baby girl in my arms. A warm baby, a baby that blinks and moves and smells like warm milk and honey. She stretches her arms out, makes two tight little fists, and I watch her face contort into a grimace as she takes a long deep breath in. In slow motion, her face becomes the colour of a turnip before she opens her mouth and lets out a long wail. I bounce her in my arms for a few seconds, the crying getting louder and louder and louder until it rings in my ears and I can barely hear my thoughts. Eventually, Nick stands up and extends his hands to relieve me. I relinquish the baby to him and watch as he deftly places her against his chest, patting her bottom. My heart is racing.

'Paige,' he whispers, reaching for my hand. 'It's okay.'

No, it's not.

Nick turns to Joy. 'Joy, would you mind taking her for me?'

'Oh, sure,' she replies, extending her arms. 'Come here, you gorgeous little thing,' she coos.

By now I'm already making my way inside. I turn to face Nick. 'My God, what's the matter with me? I can't even make it through our niece's birthday party without falling apart.'

'We knew it was going to be—' Nick settles on a word '—testing. It's only been six weeks.'

Yes, this first major outing since the hospital has been testing all right, but it also feels like torture, as if life is purposely poking fun at us. 'Can we go home? Do you think they'll understand if we miss the cake?'

'Yeah. Course. Apparently it's a caramel mudcake so everyone should understand.' Nick hates the taste of caramel. I want to smile the way I usually do when Nick makes one of his bad jokes that I love so much. It's like the tiny ball of happiness inside me wants to puff up into a balloon but loses all its air before I can grasp it. Happiness seems so far out of reach I can barely remember what it feels like.

Nick pats his jeans. 'Sorry. That isn't funny. Where'd I leave my keys?'

CHAPTER FOURTEEN

Nick

'Hey, Nick, before you go home could I have a word?' asks Ben. He slaps his hand on my shoulder as he squeezes past me in the corridor.

'Give me five minutes.' I slip my phone into my pocket. 'I just need to check on a patient. I'll let you know when I'm done.'

I enter Rory's room – six years old, tonsils and adenoids, funny little laugh, freckles, pet monkey called Fred. According to one of the nurses, Rory's been a bit sulky this morning and it's imperative I address Fred in my best monkey voice. By now I have monkeys, donkeys, giraffes and elephants nailed. 'Afternoon, Fred!'

Rory giggles. His mother smiles to herself.

'How's your friend Rory feeling today?'

'Okay,' replies Rory, sitting up straighter.

'Mind if I check him out?'

Rory nods.

'Okay, this won't take a second.' I assess Rory to make sure he's ready to be discharged today, and when I see he is, I turn to his mother and brief her on all the usual things to avoid and be mindful of.

'Fred, I hereby declare Rory ready to go home. But before you go, you need to decide: gold star or—' I pull a small jar from my pocket '—magic jelly beans?'

Rory laughs. 'Jelly beans.'

'Please,' interjects his mum.

'They're magic. And the magic only works if you eat one at a time and brush your teeth every day. Make sure you let Rory know.' I ruffle Rory's hair and hand him the jar. 'Good job, sport. You were brave. Make sure you share the jelly beans with Fred.'

After I finish my rounds, I dash downstairs to pick up two take-away coffees. As I'm ordering, someone taps me on the shoulder.

'Fancy seeing you here,' says Miranda. She's dyed her hair lighter, and she's wearing another pantsuit, this time in a shade of dusty blue.

'Let me guess, you got the job?' I ask, clocking her official lanyard.

'I sure did,' she says, with a smile that reaches her eyes.

'And it's going well?'

'It's going great, actually. I love it.' She takes a sip of the coffee the barista has just handed over and eyes me over the rim of her cup. 'So, uh... I heard about your baby, Nick. I'm really sorry.'

It shouldn't, but this throws me. Miranda is a psychologist and, yes, we work in the same hospital, and it isn't exactly a secret, but this is a big hospital. How on earth does she know about Max?

She touches my arm softly. 'I found out purely by accident. The lady in the gift shop... Cindy? I go in every week to pick up little presents for my patients. Erasers – giraffes, elephants, ice creams... cute shapes. They smell like bubblegum and the kids love them. Anyway, she was telling me about what had happened while she was putting some flowers together, and I noticed your name on the card. I'm sorry to spring that on you.'

I'm pretty sure at this point I look like a fish that's been hauled out of water and can't wait to jump back into the ocean. This is the thing about losing someone – you want people to talk about it, yet when they do, you don't know what to say.

'It's hard isn't it – to find a way to talk about it?'

Somehow, I manage to find my voice. 'Yes, but it's fine. Thank you for asking about Max. Paige and I are doing okay. Nice seeing you again.'

I couldn't sound more awkward if I tried. What's worse, Miranda follows me out, the sound of her heels click-clacking behind me.

'Nick?'

I spin around.

'You forgot your coffees.' She thrusts the tray in my direction. 'My husband, Jake. He died last year. I know what it's like to lose someone precious. So, if you want to talk… I'm here. I volunteered as a counsellor for a pregnancy and newborn bereavement organisation for six years, but I can also lend an ear, as a friend… if you need one. Give me a call. We can do coffee or beer, or we can just stand around in the foyer chatting.'

I give her a half-hearted smile. It's a nice offer, but I hardly know her. 'Sorry about your husband.'

'I know it's only been a couple of months but it does get easier, I promise.' She says this with conviction, like it's almost guaranteed.

Strangely, she sounds convincing enough that I actually believe her.

'Okay, two coffees, one with a double shot,' I say to Ben as I enter the tea room. 'What's up?'

Ben slides a muesli bar out of a wrapper and bites into it. The guy lives on muesli bars and Granny Smith apples. 'Just wanted to see how things were going for you. Is there anything I can do? What I mean is… do you need anything?'

Ben and I met in our first year at medical school and he was my best man. Later this year I'll be his when he finally ties the knot with Pamela, his on-and-off girlfriend for the past six years. And in all the years I've known him, I've never seen him stumble over his words the way he is now.

'Thanks, but I'm okay. To be honest, it's Paige I'm worried about. She's still not herself.'

'Understandable. Pamela said she would try to pop past your place to see her this week. She wasn't sure if it would be too soon? Do you think she'd be okay with her visiting?'

'Yeah, course. I'm sure she'd like that.' In reality, as much as Paige adores Pamela – they bonded over their love for the royals – I suspect she won't. It might be easier to arrange a dinner out for the four of us together, but then again, trying to get Paige to socialise with anyone at the moment seems impossible.

My stomach rumbles, loud enough that Ben can probably hear it. I help myself to an apple from the fruit bowl. I haven't had a thing to eat all day. 'You want to go for a beer sometime next week?' I rub the apple against my shirt and bite into it.

Ben's shoulders relax. 'Yeah.' He nods. 'Let me know when it suits.' He finishes the rest of his muesli bar and tosses the wrapper in the bin. 'And Nick – if there's anything at all. Just—'

'I'll let you know,' I say, pasting on my most reassuring smile.

'If you need time off, we can work it out. I can cover… we'll make it work.'

'No need.'

'You've been spending a lot of time here, that's all. So I thought…'

'I'm good, Ben,' I say, chewing on my apple. I'm not going to explain to Ben that being at work helps me to forget. And going home, *being* at home, is when I remember.

I readjust the satchel on my shoulder and head for the door. 'After-work drinks next week. Just let me know where.'

*

In a way, you could say that our life started spiralling out of control the moment we got home from hospital. I'm trying. Really trying. But nothing seems to be working. With each passing day, Paige seems more distant than ever.

Paris for Two is our favourite restaurant. It's French-inspired and it reminds us of our trip there four years ago. Paige is sitting at a table in the far-right corner of the restaurant, the same one we sat at the first time we discovered this place. Her hair is down, gentle curls resting on her shoulders. It's pinned back at the front, giving it a softer look, making her look younger. She hasn't styled her hair like this in ages. She's wearing a floral blouse with a pair of jeans, and to look at her you'd never know that not all that long ago she had to say the hardest goodbye of her life. The woman in front of me looks like my wife, but there's a vacancy in her eyes, an emptiness that makes me want to reach out and pull her into my arms. Will I ever get her back? Will Paige – the fun-loving girl I met all those years ago – ever be the same?

'Hey, there.' I lean forward and kiss her. She leaves a berry kind of taste on my mouth from the lipstick she's wearing. 'What did you do today?'

Her voice is small. Flat. 'Same as every other day. The puzzle. Mum called in the morning. Tess, the dry-cleaning lady, called before I left home. We need to pick up three of your shirts, two pairs of trousers and a tie. Caitlin called in the afternoon. And Hope called me when I was on my way here. I swear they've got a roster going on behind the scenes.'

'They care about you.' Even though I know the menu off by heart, I pick it up and cast an eye over it anyway. 'I think I'll go for the cassoulet.' This dish always over-delivers, but I don't have much of an appetite, since it's almost too early to be eating dinner. Paige has rescheduled her first two appointments with Imogen Banks, a counsellor Dr Sanders recommended. She missed the first appointment when she feigned a headache; the second time she didn't bother feigning anything. Now Imogen has squeezed her in for an after-hours appointment and I hope Paige is going to keep it.

'So, you ready for your appointment?'

As soon as I ask this question, I want to take it back, afraid she'll back out forty-five minutes before she's due in Imogen's practice. And if I'm totally honest, I want to talk to Paige about other things – *normal* things. Like when the cars are due for their next service, or about plans to visit my mum in Tassie. At this point, I'd even be happy to talk about her favourite Netflix series, *The Crown*. Heck, I'd even be happy to sit through every single episode of every *season* of *The Crown* with her.

Paige lifts the menu up so it partially hides her face. 'I know you think she can help, but there's nothing that's going to change what happened, and dredging it all up again with Imogen, no matter how good she is, is only making this nightmare more painful than it already is.'

After giving it only a cursory glance, she sets the menu down. 'I'll have whatever you're having.'

'The cassoulet.'

'Is that what you're having?'

'Yes, I just told you that's what I'm having.' I stretch out my legs. 'Never mind. Just tell me what you need from me, Paige.'

She stares into her lap, and her shoulders sag, making her look smaller. 'I don't know. I don't know what I need from you. I don't even know what I need for myself.' She gives a small shake of her head, like she's totally confused. But I get it. I feel the same way. 'I can't talk about it without crying.' She's blinking away tears now and I'm sitting here like an idiot, not sure what I can say to make it better, as if that's even possible. She rummages through her handbag for something to dry her eyes with. 'No tissues,' she says desperately.

'Here,' I say, handing her my cloth napkin.

She wipes her eyes with the stiff corners and then starts rubbing the fabric against her lips, removing all traces of her pink lipstick. 'Jesus, I feel like such a clown,' she mutters. She folds the napkin and moves onto her cheeks. I stare at her as she takes an elastic band from the zipper pocket of her handbag and ties her hair back.

'I don't know how to make this easier for you,' I say once she finishes.

'You could just *be* there for me.'

'But I am.' I pause. 'Aren't I?'

She waves a hand in the air. 'You're right. Forget it. Sorry.'

'I'm not going to forget it – we need to talk about it.' I'm trying to be patient, gentle, a listener. All the things everyone tells you to be when someone is grieving. This is the only way I know how to be. But, of course, it isn't enough. Because nothing can bring Max back.

'I don't *know* how to talk about it! Just *thinking* about it makes me cry, so how are you expecting me to find a way to talk to you about it? We lost a baby, Nick! A beautiful little baby. We walked out of that hospital *alone!*'

She bunches up the napkin and puts it on the table.

'And dressing up for a nice dinner in these… these clothes that belong to someone who hasn't just lost a baby is…' She shakes her head and stands up. 'It's wrong. And I can't do dinner at Paris for Two. Because all I can think about is the fact I really, really, really wish we were three.'

I leave some cash on the table for the waiter and follow Paige outside.

'Paige!' I call, jogging to catch up to her. 'Talk to me. Please just talk to me.' As I speak the words, it occurs to me that I'm asking of Paige something I haven't been especially good at recently.

She turns around in the middle of the street to face me and yells, arms up in the air. 'I can't!'

I know, I want to call back. *It hurts too much to talk about it.* But it's too late. By the time I manage to say anything, my wife is sliding into a cab without me.

CHAPTER FIFTEEN

Paige

Windsor Lakes is a sandy-brick building that sits happily in the middle of an expansive boulevard thronged with Californian bungalows and well-maintained buffalo grass nature strips. Inside, it smells of old furniture and citrus air freshener, and I don't realise how much I've missed working here until this moment. The main reason I'm here is because of Imogen. We've had eight sessions together, set two weeks apart from each other, and this is my big step towards getting some semblance of normality and routine back in my life since I haven't been working for almost six months.

'Morning, Mr Healy.'

Frank jerks his head up. 'Call me Frank,' he croaks, his sultana eyes coming to life.

'Okay, Frank.' I smile to myself.

'Ah, Paige. You're back.' I turn around to face Elsie. 'When's that grandson of mine going to visit?' she says, pointing a knobbly finger at me.

'Well, he's been pretty busy at the hospital lately,' I say, placing her blanket over her lap.

I give her a smile with no heart to it. 'I'll come back a little later. Let me go say hi to Viv.'

Viv, one of the Windsor Lakes cooks, is in the kitchen, peeling potatoes, swaying her hips to an Ella Fitzgerald tune. A rotund woman in her late fifties, Viv believes that love is cultivated in the kitchen, which is why she never turns down an opportunity to reach for her baking tins. Cupcakes when Beryl informed her she had glaucoma, hummingbird cake when Giuliano was discharged from hospital after his hip replacement, lemon meringue pie when Claudine became a great-grandmother for the fourteenth time. Oh, and petit fours when Bill proposed to Bernadette. She was four days shy of her seventy-ninth birthday and wore that ring of hers with as much pride and excitement as a twenty-five-year-old.

'Well, hello there!' She holds her arms wide open and locks me in an embrace. She smells of lemon rind and cake batter. She turns the music down. 'Phone not working?' she says knowingly.

'Bad service at my place.'

'Mmm, so I noticed. For what it's worth, we didn't miss you a bit. Except for maybe Frank.'

'I'm sick of Frank's crossword puzzles.'

'He insisted.' She gives a small chuckle.

'I read eighteen books. Eighteen! And I've seen everything there is to see on Netflix, Stan and Amazon Prime.'

Viv laughs. 'But how *are* you?'

'Well, there have been times when I need every ounce of willpower to wash my hair.'

'And your heart?'

'Is improving. Well… *slowly* improving.'

She hesitates. 'You want to help me peel some potatoes?'

In all these years, Viv has made it quite clear that she needs no help in the kitchen. Ever. 'Potatoes. *Really?*'

She shrugs. 'Well, are you going to have a heart attack if they ask you to replace the water jug on the cooler?'

I laugh. 'With any luck, no.'

It's good to be back. It almost feels like I can start to believe that life will get back to normal someday.

*

'I feel like I haven't seen Nick in ages,' Mum says from behind the screen of her computer a few weeks later. She recently remodelled her study on Caitlin's advice, replacing the old brown leather armchairs with grey wingbacks, and putting up baby-blue floral wallpaper that had left Dad shaking his head.

'How's he going?' she continues. The casual tone of her voice makes it obvious that the question she's really asking is how things actually are between us. Nick has missed the last few Sunday night dinners due to work but of course Mum thinks there's more to it.

I slump into a chair and curl my legs up. 'He's fine. We're fine. I'm fine.'

'Just fine?'

'Fine means things are fine. We've reinstated date night.' I take a sip of coffee. Somehow it always tastes better when Mum makes it for me. 'Imogen says it should help,' I add.

'Well, date night sounds great.' She takes her glasses off and I know I need to change direction or else be subjected to Mum's questions.

'So, tell me why you wanted us here?'

Mum called me and Caitlin a couple of days ago asking us to come over. She's been a little obsessed lately with tracing the family tree since she discovered that she can access billions of historical records with the simple click of a mouse. What that has to do with Caitlin and me is still a mystery.

'I wanted to show you some stuff,' she says, waving to a wooden trunk beside the fireplace. I vaguely recognise it as one of the many items Mum has stored in the attic, along with all the other belongings she and Dad have collected over the years they've been together. 'You know, my father always said we had a little Scandinavian in the mix.' She pushes up her glasses and surfs a series of web pages before she pauses and reaches for the wallet in her handbag. She pulls out her credit card.

'They can test my DNA and find out my heritage – did you know that, girls?'

Caitlin looks at me and frowns.

'Oh no, Mum, you're not...'

'What's the point?' says Caitlin. 'What difference is it going to make to your life knowing this?'

Mum sighs. 'Oh, I don't know. I've been thinking a lot about legacy. The things we keep, the things we let go of, the things we remember about those who've left us. Like, who is going to remember, 200 years from now, that I lived in this lovely clinker-brick house on this leafy street, drove a car to the supermarket every Friday morning to buy my groceries, had a husband always up a ladder if he wasn't up in the air, three beautiful children...' Her voice tapers off. 'Well, you get the point,' she says. She finishes tapping her credit card details into the computer and stands up. 'What I mean is that I have been thinking about my contribution to the world and how I'd like to be remembered one day.'

Caitlin and I exchange glances. This does not sound like Mum at all.

'Mu-um, you're not sick, are you?' I can always rely on Caitlin to get to the point.

'Oh, God no,' she says, waving that idea away. 'Never felt better. I'm the fittest of all the women in my walking group. And did I tell you I've started water aerobics? You should see the instructor. His name is Jose. From Chile.' She's smiling like a giddy teenager.

Caitlin shakes her head in amusement and reaches into the trunk. 'Oh, look, Paige. Remember these?' she says, picking up two journals, one belonging to each of us.

'Have you read them, Mum?' asks Caitlin, smirking as she flicks through the pages of mine. She holds up a page decorated with glitter around thick letters that spell out *PH Loves RB*. 'Who was RB?'

I groan. 'God only knows.'

'Ah, Paige, listen up…' She starts reading. '"My name is Paige Hutton. My best friend is Hope Edwards. She is the funniest! My sister Caitlin is the best at lots of things but she is annoying sometimes and won't let me use her perfumed notepaper. Who cares anyway? It kind of stinks. I like Ryan better because he lets me play in his room and he let me name his turtle. When I grow up I want to be a circus performer…"'

Caitlin's voice trails off but I continue reading over her shoulder. 'I will have a horse, plus two dogs, one cat and a rabbit called Humphrey.'

We all laugh and Caitlin hands me my journal. 'You'd make a terrible circus performer.'

'Just as well life doesn't always turn out how we'd like it to,' I say. I turn to face Mum. 'It's because I nearly died, isn't it? This is why you're thinking about all this stuff?'

Mum bites her bottom lip. 'Oh, I don't know,' she says, letting out a sigh. 'Yes… no… maybe…'

'Well, luckily enough, Paige is still with us and doesn't need to go thinking about who remembers what about her,' says Caitlin, standing up, brushing her hands on her trousers. 'We have plenty of family photos, and a mother who held onto most of the junk from our childhood, so we're good.'

'She's right. Let's get some more coffee.'

I feel the weight of the journal in my hands, the weight of unrealised dreams and innocent memories. And once Caitlin and Mum leave the room to prepare another pot of coffee, I walk outside to the garbage bin and push my journal of unrealised, ridiculous dreams to the bottom, as far as it will go.

When I return inside, Mum and Caitlin are locked in an embrace. As soon as they notice me, they separate awkwardly, and their smiles disappear.

My brow furrows. 'What's going on?'

Caitlin looks at Mum for encouragement.

'Sweetheart, Caitlin has some news…' Mum's voice fades, like the way the automatic sound leveller in my car reduces the volume when I press on the brakes. Caitlin starts to speak as my eyes travel down her body, resting on her midsection.

I shake my head. *No*, I mouth. I repeat the words in my head. *I'm pregnant. It's early. I just found out.*

'Paige, honey…' Mum takes my hands in hers and squeezes. My face tightens and every other muscle in my body follows.

'I wanted to tell you, but with everything going on, I couldn't find the right time and I didn't know how to let you know, and I know how you must be feeling.'

'Congratulations,' I manage, resting my body against the bench, my lungs searching for air. I need space to breathe, to not think about babies. 'I know you wanted another baby. You've always said you wanted three.' I choke on the word *three*, the unfairness of it leaving a burning taste in the back of my throat.

Caitlin's shoulders sag. 'Paige… I'm sorry.' Her voice is small and I feel sick thinking about the fact that she's apologising for something so special.

'I'm happy for you. I really am.' I throw my hands in the air. 'It's not like you can put your life on hold because of what happened to me.'

'It isn't fair, though,' she says. 'I know that.'

No matter how hard I try, I can't keep the sadness bubbling away inside of me from surfacing up, up, up. Caitlin's eyes glisten with wetness, meet mine, and I start sobbing. Her arms wrap themselves around me and I nuzzle my face into her chest while she holds me. It reminds me of when we were small, of the time we got lost at Wilson's Prom on a camping trip. We'd been foraging for fairy house items: bits of paperbark and gumnuts, moss and the odd twig. We'd ventured too far into the national park and had no idea how to get back to where we were. I started crying and Caitlin held me, telling me we needed to wait it out. We did, and Dad and Ryan showed up thirty minutes later.

'I wish this never happened to you. I wish you didn't have to go through this. And I wish the timing could be better.'

So do I.

In a little over seven months, when Caitlin's perfect body gives birth to a healthy baby, knowing my luck I'll still be here, with my broken, defective heart, still on meds, waiting for my turn to *possibly* come around again.

CHAPTER SIXTEEN

Nick

Date night is not going well. Paige hates the supposedly 'safe' flick I chose as evidenced by the fact she's gotten up twice – first for popcorn she hasn't touched, and now for the bathroom.

When she doesn't return after fifteen minutes, I get up to look for her. She's standing beside the snack bar, on her phone, talking to someone. Though it looks more like she's having a heated discussion with someone, and it doesn't take much for me to guess who it is she's talking to. By the time I reach her, she hangs up and slips the phone into her bag. 'Sorry, I'm coming back in.'

I nod, my impatience turning to slight annoyance. 'Really? Cause it looks like you hate the movie.' Never mind that I'm not loving the movie either, but I'm not the one getting up out of my seat in the middle of what's supposed to be date night.

'You're mad at me. Sorry.'

'I'm not mad,' I tell her. But I sort of am. It's clear Paige doesn't even want to be here. For one night it would have been nice to just enjoy each other's company.

'So, who were you talking to?'

'Caitlin. She wants me to babysit for her on Saturday night.'

'Okay, well, I'm home this weekend – I'll come too. I'll make tacos. The kids love them.'

'I told her I can't do it.'

'Why would you do that?'

'Because I can't.'

'You have plans?'

She wanders towards the snack bar, unfazed by the fact the movie is playing inside Cinema 2. She pulls her wallet out of her handbag and joins the long queue. 'Choc Top?' she asks.

I give her a look that says, *Are you kidding me?* 'We're almost halfway through the movie.' I can't help it. Something's off with Paige, and I wish she'd just let it out instead of making me guess what's wrong. 'Why can't you babysit for Caitlin?'

She groans. 'Do we have to talk about Caitlin? Can we just get through one night without bringing up my sister?'

'Hey, you're the one who walked out of the movie to take a call from her.'

'I didn't walk out to take a call from her. I walked out to go to the bathroom and *then* she called.'

'And you answered.'

'And now she's ruining date night.'

'No,' I tell her. 'I think you're the one doing that.' We stare at each other. 'You don't even like Choc Tops, so why are we even standing here?'

'I'm allowed to change my mind.' She crosses her arms around her chest, and just when I think this is going to escalate into a petty tiff, I notice her eyes – still fixed on the board advertising the current popcorn combo – are watering.

'It's okay,' I say, immediately regretting my harshness. 'You're allowed to change your mind about Choc Tops.'

She breaks into silent laughter, but the smile disappears as quickly as it appeared, and now she looks so sad I can barely stand it. I want to pull her into my arms and transport her back to a time and place where she knew nothing of heartache and loss. Sometimes I don't know what's worse – losing Max or not being able to make things better for Paige.

'Caitlin's having another baby.'

For a second I think I haven't heard her properly. Caitlin *wants to have* another baby. We know this. This isn't something we haven't heard before. Caitlin wants four kids. A girl, a boy, a girl, a boy. In that order. She even has their names picked.

'You mean now?'

'Jesus, Nick, no, in about six months.' She rubs her forehead. 'Excuse me,' she says to the people in the queue as we squeeze past them to the foyer. 'Everywhere I look. Pregnant women. Prams. Crying babies. They're everywhere.'

Caitlin's *pregnant*. I know what this means. Paige is going to have to endure her sister's third pregnancy. As much as I love Caitlin and want to be happy for her, I know that in Paige's eyes her timing for this could not be worse.

'I'm happy, but I'm not, you know?' she continues. We are now walking out of the foyer and through the cinema doors onto the street. So much for the movie. I'm still clutching a half-eaten box of popcorn.

'It's not that bad,' I offer, mostly because I don't know what else to say, and also because I don't have a consolation prize. The fact is we don't know if Paige is going to be healthy enough to ever carry another baby.

'Really? Why?'

'Because eventually, we're going to get our turn again.' I don't know why I say this to her when it's a matter of *if* not when.

'We don't know that.'

'True.'

Paige stops in front of a bookshop on a corner. 'I used to be able to read books without worrying about whether or not they had a happy ending,' she muses before pushing the door open.

I follow her past the fiction new releases and towards the cookbook section, which is her favourite even if she never can follow a recipe. 'There are alternatives, Paige. We can look at different ways to become a family.' Truthfully, this is the first time I have ever thought about this.

She picks a book up – some guide to a healthy gut – and mindlessly flicks through it.

'We'll find a way to become parents, I promise you.'

'But are you even prepared to wait two, three, five more years for me to get better? At what point do we call it a day and stop waiting?' She tucks the book under her arm and picks up another.

'We decide together.'

She starts walking to the counter.

'You're actually buying that?' I ask.

'Yes, haven't you always wondered how to make sauerkraut?'

She pays for the book, and when we reach the next street corner she comes to a stop. We stand there, under the street light, while a small group of people wait for the lights to turn green, the cadence of laughter streaming behind them as they cross the road.

'Would we want the same things if I can't do it, Nick? I mean, what are the options? Adoption takes forever so we can pretty much rule that out. How would you feel about something like… surrogacy? Are you even going to want this? What if we can't find a surrogate? What happens then?'

I squeeze her hand. 'Shhh…' I whisper. 'Let me answer you. When I held Max in my arms, I realised that I wanted nothing more than to become a father. So, as far as options go…' I pause, choosing my words carefully. 'I'm definitely open to surrogacy. However…' How to tell Paige something she doesn't want to hear? I can't bear to deliver another blow but I need to be honest with her. She deserves this.

'What?' she asks, searching my eyes.

'There's some information out there that indicates that the precipitating factor for PPCM can be transferred from the biological mother to the surrogate, so—'

'So I wouldn't be able to use an egg?' Her eyes widen. She shakes her head in disbelief. 'Oh my God,' she whispers.

'I'm not saying that,' I say, quick to stop her jumping on the worst-case-scenario train. 'I'm trying to explain—'

'Oh God, this wasn't a good idea.' She wriggles her hand away from mine and slams her palm against the pedestrian crossing button.

'It's not an absolute,' I point out. My words come out strained. I'm doing a terrible job of reassuring her.

'Right, but I wasn't expecting to learn that the next best thing might not even be a possibility for us!' She starts crossing the road, despite the little red man, and stops on the island.

'We'll find a way to become parents. Why don't we give this another six months and see how things turn out, okay? You never know what your next echo will show.' I make it sound so easy, so hopeful, when I know that all she can think of right now is the fact she might not ever be able to have a baby, and Caitlin – with timing that could not be worse – is pregnant. It's just one more blow.

Paige forges ahead, crossing the street at a much faster pace than usual. I dump the popcorn I've been carrying all this time into the closest street bin and take her by the hand.

'She always gets what she wants,' she murmurs. 'Always.'

'She didn't do this to spite you.'

'Either way, I can't be around her right now, Nick. It's too awkward and I don't like the way it makes me feel. Trust me, it's better for everyone if I keep my distance.'

'She's your sister, you can hardly avoid her.'

'Actually,' she says, 'I can.'

And that's when I start to worry. The last thing Paige needs right now is for her family to fall apart too.

CHAPTER SEVENTEEN

Paige

Despite the fact I said I wouldn't do it, I am here on Caitlin's doorstep to babysit her kids. Both Ella and Ethan rush towards me like a tsunami to say hello, all flailing legs and happy grins.

'Uncle Nick will be here soon. He's at the supermarket picking up the ingredients for your favourite dinner.' I pinch Ella's nose and tickle Ethan under the chin.

'Tacos!' they say in unison before retreating back to the living room.

As soon as Caitlin and I step into the kitchen, I can immediately tell something is off. Her enormous stone sink is filled with unwashed dishes, and the kids are sitting in front of the television watching cartoons at six o'clock. The strict cut-off is usually five thirty.

'Thanks so much for coming. I was going to call a sitter if you couldn't make it.' She starts rummaging through her handbag. This is a lie. Caitlin never employs sitters. Not since the Norwegian au pair she hired when Ella was three. Astrid, the petite young blonde who smuggled her American backpacker boyfriend into her bedroom one night and forgot to turn the gas burner off when Ella jammed her pinkie in the kitchen cupboard door, had been the first and the last. 'Where'd I put my phone?'

I spot a phone near the fish bowl on the counter. 'This it?' I say, holding it up.

Caitlin snatches it from me. 'Oh, thank you.'

'What's wrong?'

She straightens up and tilts her head. 'Nothing.'

I roll my eyes. 'Puh-lease.' I motion to the sink and then turn around and point to the cartoons.

'I've been busy, okay? Mark's been working long hours fixing up the cottage since it was supposed to be finished months ago, and I've been feeling tired and I didn't get a chance to do the dishes.' If this is an attempt to make me feel sorry for her, it isn't working. Nope, not a bit.

'Or the vacuuming,' I say, as I hear the crunch of cracker biscuits on the glazed ceramic tile floor. 'Which would be normal for someone like me. But since it's you and you live a much more orderly and perfect life than me, I call a problem.'

Caitlin holds up a hand for me to stop. 'Paige, there is no problem. But is everything okay with you?'

I won't let her turn it around and make it about me. Caitlin's always been good at that.

'Never been better.'

'Good because I was worried this might—' she pauses before settling on a word '—change things between us.'

'No, I can handle it.'

Of course, this is not how I feel at all. I can barely stand to be around my sister right now, but I can't exactly say that. What kind of person would that make me? Sorry, but you're pregnant and I'm not, so we can't be sisters any more?

'Okay, good. Because if you don't want me to talk about the pregnancy, I can keep the updates and news to myself.' She says this as she takes an ultrasound image off her fridge door and shoves it in her pocket. I save her the effort and pass her the bottle of pregnancy vitamins from the bench. 'Here. These belong in your pristine bathroom.'

'Paige.' Her voice leaks disappointment.

'Just helping you tidy up.'

Thankfully, she lets it go. I'm pretty sure neither of us is in the mood for this. 'So where are you going?' I ask coolly as I search the kitchen cupboard for a dish sponge.

'Jesus, look who inherited all Mum's sleuthing genes.' She checks her watch. 'I really need to go. I'll be back before midnight. Sponges are on the left in the labelled container. Blue Chux for dishes, green for surfaces.'

Caitlin is always in bed before ten thirty, and since she's wearing no make-up, I know she isn't heading out with her girlfriends. 'Midnight?' I repeat.

'Eleven thirty at the latest.' Caitlin makes to leave but then turns back. 'Oh, Mum mentioned you had another echo appointment coming up…'

'Yeah.'

'I was thinking, I could come with you.'

'Thanks, but Nick said he'd manage to get the morning off.'

'Do you think it'll be good news?'

Do I? Honestly, I have no idea. I feel better than I did right after my diagnosis, but have I improved enough to be able to try to conceive another baby?

'I hope it'll be good news. I mean, wouldn't it totally suck if Victoria tells me my heart isn't improving and I should give up on this whole idea entirely?'

'Of course it would.'

'Nick and I spoke about surrogacy.'

Caitlin's cheeks instantly turn pink. 'Surrogacy,' she repeats, like she's never heard of it.

'Yes. When some altruistic human being carries your baby to term, births it and then gives it to you.'

'Is that… the next step for you two? Is that what you're saying?'

I shrug. 'There might be some issues with it so we're not really sure yet.' Maybe that's the part that bothers me the most – the not knowing. The waiting.

Caitlin, who never seems to be lost for words, goes unusually quiet. I know what she's thinking. And it's not what I'm thinking, not at all.

'I wasn't asking you to do this for me. If I was going to ask, I would just ask. But just to make it clear, I'm not asking.' There is no way I am ready to have this conversation, and now I'm annoyed with myself for even bringing it up in the first place.

'It would make sense that you would ask me though, right? I'm your sister.'

It would make sense. But the last thing I want to think about right now is Caitlin having *my* baby. 'I wouldn't want you to anyway,' I blurt. This is a lie. A total lie. If anyone was going to be a surrogate for us, I would want it to be Caitlin, but I can't bring myself to admit it.

Caitlin literally backs away from me. 'Gee, Paige. You really know how to deliver a punch where it hurts.'

'Sorry, but I don't want this.'

'You know what, Paige? Nobody *wants* this. And blaming me for the challenges you're facing right now feels a little unfair. Who knows, maybe I wouldn't want to do it anyway.'

Of course. She'll be busy with her own baby for at least the next eighteen months or more anyway. Clothes shopping, feeding, burping, changing, with all milestones documented on Facebook along with the perfect photo taken in the perfect light. Well, maybe not the oversharing on Facebook. She once waxed lyrical about a child's right to privacy in the online space, but certainly she would bombard Mum, Ryan and me with photos via text message just like she did with Ella and Ethan. The thing is, before all of this, I loved getting those text messages. I love being an aunty to Ella and Ethan. And I want to love being an aunty for this new baby, too.

'Do what?' asks Nick, appearing with an armload of groceries that he dumps on the bench. He's obviously let himself in.

'Have your baby,' says Caitlin, deadpan.

Nick shakes his head, obviously trying to catch up on what he's missed.

'Don't worry, she's not having our baby. She doesn't *want* to have our baby. She's too busy having her *own* baby.'

Nick fires me a look that says, *Shut up*. He's right, I should shut up before I say something else I'll regret.

'Good, so it's settled,' says Caitlin, but I can tell she's offended. She turns on her heels and pops her head into the living room, sending Ella and Ethan an air kiss goodbye.

'I really need to go,' she says. 'For what it's worth, thanks for helping me out tonight.'

'No problem,' I reply sheepishly. I walk her to the door and wave from the doorstep as her pristine, cherry-red Mazda backs out of the driveway, and I think about how I'm going to explain this to Nick.

After we finish putting Ella and Ethan to bed, Nick turns the TV on in the living room and surfs a few channels. 'Netflix?'

I carry the tower of board games over to the entertainment unit and start putting them away, 'It's that or Hungry Hungry Hippos.'

'Ella's got Uno all worked out,' he says. 'She's doesn't miss a beat.'

'Nope. She's all Caitlin.' I feel a surge of guilt pulse through me. 'It was bad, wasn't it?' I frown at him. 'I don't know what got into me.'

'She'll come around. So will you.' Nick helps himself to a cracker and a wedge of cheese from the coffee table. 'All I'll say is that pushing her away isn't the answer. It's never the answer. It just makes things harder.'

'Well, maybe that's why I needed some space. I knew I shouldn't have agreed to babysit but I let you push me into it. I knew I shouldn't have let you do that.'

'What happened tonight isn't my fault, Paige.' He flicks his shoes off and angles his body towards mine.

'Well, maybe you can just trust that I'm handling this in a way that works for me. And if that means keeping my distance from Caitlin for the time being, then so be it.'

'How's that working for you lately? The whole keeping the people you love at a distance thing?'

'I'm sorry?'

'I've been trying my hardest to support you but you're making it really hard to help you. This jealous weirdo stuff with Caitlin? This isn't you. And you don't need another major stress like this in your life.'

'I'm upset about it, Nick. It hurts.'

'Of course it does. Over the coming months, you're going to have a constant reminder of what you lost. But you're going to have to accept it otherwise you'll live to regret it. Because tonight you told your sister something that you can't take back. And if you don't get a hold of yourself, you're going to say something else, and then things might really break and you'll be worse for it. You might lose her entirely, and you've already lost so much.'

He has a point. A valid point. You're always bound to lose when you push away the people who love you. Then again, how do you keep close the reminders of what hurts you the most?

CHAPTER EIGHTEEN

Nick

The next time I talk to Miranda Summers is when I call her on the way home from a particularly hectic day at work. Only I don't let the call connect but hang up just before she answers. It's crazy, calling someone like this – a woman I barely know and who isn't my wife.

I'm stuck in traffic when she returns the call no more than a minute later. I'm sorely tempted to block it but decide that would be weird, so I answer.

'This is Nick.'

'Oh, Nick, hello. How are you?' She sounds caught off guard. 'Sorry I missed your call. I was cooking. I didn't make it to the phone in time.'

I turn the radio down and wind my window up. 'Oh, that's okay. Sorry if I've interrupted dinner.'

'It's fine,' she says, almost cutting me off. 'It's just me tonight. Will's at basketball with his granddad.' The line goes quiet for a beat. 'I'm glad you called. Were you calling to take me up on that offer of a chat?' she asks, and I admire her directness. Actually, I'm thankful that she said it so I don't have to. Admitting I need help isn't one of my strong suits by any means.

I must take too long to answer because she lets out a melodic little laugh. 'It's okay, you don't need to confess to that. So, tell me… how are you?'

'Are you going to regret that you asked?'

She laughs again. 'God no. I'm about to pour some wine. My brother's a sommelier and brought back a case of something or other from Bordeaux. All I know is it's red and good.' It's refreshing to hear someone laugh so easily. I wind the window back down and it occurs to me suddenly that I'm not bothered by the bumper to bumper traffic any more. Before I know it, I'm pouring everything out on the phone to Miranda, and by the time I pull into my driveway, not only does she know all about my favourite wine but I feel like a different man. A weightless man. A man who isn't heading home to problems.

That of course changes the moment I get home. Whatever I was feeling in the car is gone by the time I put my bag down. There are dirty dishes in the sink, a pile of unfolded washing on the sofa. I haven't seen the house like this since those early days after Max. To be clear, I don't expect my wife to keep the house looking pristine – we have always shared the load when it comes to domestic chores, even though I'll admit that Paige does more than I do, but that's mostly due to the fact she's home more than I am. We love this house, and while we're not tidy according to Caitlin's standards, breakfast dishes in the sink at nine thirty at night can only mean one thing: Paige has other things on her mind.

I find her in the bathroom, in the tub, surrounded by a mountain of bubbles, green face mask on, a stack of paper on the small table beside the tub next to a glass of champagne and what's left of a block of chocolate. 'What are you doing?' I ask, trying to get a better glimpse of the printouts. They look like academic research papers I would read, not something Paige would opt for. She's more like a Kristin Hannah groupie ever since she read that book of hers that was set during the Second World War. So, of course, my mind wanders to why the house is in disarray, and how these papers have something to do with it.

I bend down and kiss her.

'You taste like alcohol – were they serving late-night cocktails at the hospital?' she asks. Surprisingly, her mood is lighter than I thought it would be. Lighter than it was last week at Caitlin's place. Caitlin, who she hasn't spoken to all week. I have no idea if Evelyn knows about this but she won't be happy when she finds out.

Paige tilts her head, waiting for an answer.

'Um, no actually, I stopped somewhere for drinks with a friend.' This isn't exactly a lie of course, but it also isn't exactly the truth of my detour off the freeway to Miranda's. That wine from Bordeaux turned out to be a 2015 Château Vignol Clairet and it was every bit worth the glass. I eye the paper she's been reading, which looks like it's been dunked in bathwater. 'So... the papers?'

'Oh,' she says, taking her reading glasses off. 'I'm trying to find that information you were talking about. About the surrogacy and my egg...' She waves a hand in the air, splashing some bubbles around. 'Problems. Problematic eggs.'

'You know what they say about looking for problems,' I say, perching myself on the side of the tub.

'I printed out all this stuff but I couldn't find the information, Nick. I want to know exactly what the issue is.'

I should have known mentioning things would lead to this, which is why I never should have said anything in the first place.

'What the issue *could* be,' I point out. 'We don't actually know for sure. There isn't conclusive evidence around this side of things because there aren't any formal reports on this. There was just one case I read about that talked about PPCM transferring to a surrogate, so it doesn't mean we need to be alarmed – we just need to be aware.' It's not clear if this reassures Paige or not because she rolls her eyes and starts wiping the face mask off with a face washer.

'You're always so careful about what you say,' she says shortly. 'Can't you just come out and tell me exactly what the issue is? I'm not a patient, you know.'

'Well, there could be a genetic factor playing a role.'

'Oh, great.' She reaches for her champagne glass and finishes off what's left in it.

'But we don't know for sure,' I quickly add. 'Honestly, I don't think we need to be concerned about this right now. I also don't think it's a huge risk. Like I said, it's simply worth noting.'

'How do you know that?'

'Because I searched the literature already.'

'You could have told me that and saved me all this trouble.' She steps out of the bath. I hold out a giant fluffy towel for her and she wraps herself in it.

'I didn't know you were going to go looking for it.'

She shakes her head. 'Why wouldn't I? This is the most important thing to me. I wish you'd told me earlier.'

I frame her face with my hands and meet her eyes. 'So you could start thinking about surrogacy prematurely? I wasn't going to do that to you, Paige.'

She bites her lip. 'I think I'm just nervous about tomorrow.' Tomorrow Paige is having another echo with Victoria.

'It's not a race. Just because Caitlin—'

'This isn't about Caitlin.' She shuffles closer and hugs me, her wet skin still warm from the bathwater. 'I just feel like I need to prepare myself for the worst, even if I don't want to.'

We've been through the worst already, I think to myself. There's nothing that could beat what we've just been through with losing Max. Nothing.

'Course,' I say, kissing the top of her head, wondering what happened to my once relatively optimistic wife. 'My calendar's free until midday tomorrow, so why don't we go for an early lunch after the appointment?'

It's an offer that brings a smile to her face, but to me, it's an insurance policy. There's no way of knowing how she'll take the news tomorrow if Victoria doesn't tell her what she wants to hear.

CHAPTER NINETEEN

Paige

On Tuesday morning, the day of our appointment with Victoria, I choose three outfits from my closet and lay them on the bed. A floral skater dress (too pretty), a grey pencil dress (too formal), a pair of white capris and a poplin shirt (just no). Finally, I settle on a navy-and-white spotted shirt dress with a pair of white tennis shoes.

Nick and I return to Victoria's consulting rooms for my latest echo results. It's eight months to the day since my diagnosis. My insides are sloshing around like milk in a butter churn.

'Don't look so worried,' whispers Nick. We are in the waiting room, the same magazines on the coffee table, the same posters on the wall.

'I want the news to be positive.' Nick's hand lands gently on my knee and he gives a small squeeze. I deposit a 2015 copy of *Women's Health* magazine back on the coffee table and clamp my fingers together to stop fidgeting.

'There's every chance it will be.'

Eventually, Victoria calls my name. Her face brightens when she sees me and Nick. I wave back and follow her into the room, Nick trailing behind me.

'Good to see you both again. How are things?'

'Things are good,' I say, taking a seat. Well, not great if we count the fact I haven't spoken to my sister in nine days. Or the fact there is a chance my eggs may be *problematic* though nobody can tell me why. Glancing up at the split system in the corner of the room, I notice the heating is on. I eye the paperwork on her desk. 'Um, would you mind if we turned the heating off?' I fan my face and loosen my scarf.

'Oh, yes, sure,' she says, getting up to find the remote. 'Let me put you out of your misery. We have an improvement,' she says as she sits back down. Victoria looks as proud as Mrs Fletcher, my sixth-grade piano teacher, when I went back to class after practising all summer holidays. 'Your EF levels are up to forty per cent, so things seem to be heading in the right direction.'

I blink, wondering if I've heard her correctly. I frown at Nick. 'Only forty per cent? I was hoping it would be a bit closer to—' I shrug '—fifty-five per cent, so we could think about another baby soon.'

'Your current EF level isn't high enough to safely attempt another pregnancy, but the main thing is there's an improvement here, Paige. Sometimes all we can do is wait and see how your body recovers over time. I know it's hard.'

Well, *that* is an understatement if ever I heard one.

Nick clears his throat. 'Uh, could I ask a couple of questions?'

'Sure,' replies Victoria.

'Size of left ventricle?'

Victoria and Nick spend the next few minutes discussing the more intricate medical details of my condition. All I can think of is that I've been on medication for over six months and my heart still isn't completely back to normal, and it's not going to be my turn any time soon by the sound of it.

Eventually, Victoria's attention swings back to me. 'So, Paige, tell me, what are your energy levels like?'

I explain that I'm feeling better overall, but there are days when I fatigue on exertion and I need to rest, sometimes nap, and in general take it a lot easier than I did before as far as exercise is involved. She takes notes and surmises that it's all normal and part of the recovery process.

'At this point, I think we'll follow up with an echo in another six months and hopefully by then we'll be able to wave the green flag for you.'

Nick looks at me, smiling, seemingly pleased with today's results.

Somehow I manage a small, 'Sounds good,' followed by the biggest smile I can summon. As I follow them both out of the room, I swallow back the lump that has formed in my throat, and wish I could tell them both how I'm really feeling. I'm happy about my health improving but I also really want my green flag *now*.

'Paige, this isn't the end of the world,' Nick says as we walk through the park towards the car.

'Then why does it feel like it is? I hate this, Nick! I hate that my body isn't working the way it should be. I hate not knowing whether we are going to get a second chance at becoming parents. All I ever wanted was to have a family and now I might have to imagine a different life for myself – for *us*.' I stop walking and sit down on a park bench. 'What if we can't have what we want? What if one day you wake up and decide you do want kids and… you don't want… *me*?'

Nick takes a seat next to me and grabs my hand. 'That is not a deal-breaker for me. That is not going to happen, I promise you.' He guides my face towards his. 'You cannot let this news or the news about your sister be the things that cause you to spiral. You are doing great, Paige. We just need to be patient.'

'And not angry,' I add.

'Exactly.'

Be patient. This is what you say when there is nothing else to say. 'So that's our strategy? Be patient?'

He shrugs. 'That's all I've got. I think it beats "be hopeful".'

I cringe. 'Fine. Just don't go printing it on my coffee mug.'

He laughs. 'Hey, I was thinking of taking a couple of weeks off soon. Maybe we can go visit my mum and forget about everything except being patient.'

After Nick goes to work, I head home and find Mum there. She's in the back garden, standing in the raised vegetable bed with her gumboots on, bent over, planting out the globe artichokes we talked about last week.

'Mum?' I call out.

'Oh hey! Paige! I let myself in. Did you forget it was planting out day?' She rubs a gloved hand caked with dirt over her apron. 'This was in bad shape, honey.'

This yearly tradition of ours has completely slipped my mind. My mother helps me plant out my garden at the tail end of every winter.

'Totally forgot you were coming. I had an echo this morning.'

She springs to attention. As in, she literally goes from kneeling to standing as if she's a puppet on a string and someone is controlling her moves. 'And?' she presses.

'And all things considered it's good news.'

She beams at me and I don't have the heart to tell her why good isn't great.

'Great,' she says. 'We should celebrate.' She lifts an eyebrow. 'I brought a bottle of pink champagne with me. And your sister gave me the recipe for some amazing fillings for ribbon sandwiches. She found it in a vintage cookbook from the 1930s!'

'Sorry, Mum, I've already eaten.'

'It's barely even twelve o'clock,' says Mum, stepping out of the raised bed. She tosses her gloves onto the wheelbarrow and takes her hat off.

'Early lunch. Nick had to go to work.'

'I'll have to give you the recipe. I got up at seven this morning and started mashing and pounding and grating. Cayenne, watercress, cream, mushrooms... all these different combinations.'

'They're sandwiches, Mum. Fancy sandwiches.'

'It's all about reverence in the kitchen, Paige.'

We trail back into the house and Mum follows me into the kitchen, where she washes her hands in the sink. I open the fridge and search for the champagne. 'Now you sound like Caitlin.'

'Maybe we should call her. She said she was free today. Ella's home. She has a Curriculum Day.'

'No,' I say. 'Let her enjoy the day with Ella.'

Mum squints at me. 'Pa-aige,' she says with a sternness that demands answers.

'Pretty sure the fillings aren't going to be great for her morning sickness.'

'But she's feeling fine.'

'I need to go out.'

'But it's planting out day. We still have all the salad greens to plant out.'

'We might need to reschedule it.'

'But the garden's half done! Besides, my new mah-jong group is now meeting on Wednesdays. And my Fridays are filling too. Flower Club. We deliver posies to nursing homes. Starting next week.' She looks so pleased about it, I am almost tempted to ask if I can join her. 'Ella can come and help. You can drink champagne, and Caitlin can help me plant out. She's always had a good eye for garden design.'

I roll my eyes.

'I saw that.'

I pour us both a glass of champagne and sit down on one of the kitchen stools. 'I need some space from Caitlin right now, Mum.'

Mum stares into her glass, watching the bubbles fizz against the surface. 'That's interesting because she told me the exact same thing when I spoke to her this morning.'

'It's too hard.'

'Of course it's hard. But let me remind you that in this family, this isn't how we do things. And I won't have my daughters having "space" from each other when the only thing distance does is drive a wedge into a family.'

'That's not true. It won't be forever.'

'Oh, it'll be just while she's pregnant? Or just while she's got a newborn? Or just while she's raising a toddler? Before you know it the two of you will be estranged and I'll be hosting our Sunday night dinners on different nights of the week just like Margie from macramé. Her daughters stopped talking to each other when they were in their twenties. Over a boy who never even stuck around!'

'I promise you, that won't happen,' I say flatly, suddenly feeling like all the energy has drained from my body.

'I know the timing of this is not ideal, but like you said, you got good news today.' She slides her glass across the stone bench top until it clinks against mine. 'To your good news, darling.'

CHAPTER TWENTY

Nick

Ben and Pamela's wedding is the biggest social event Paige and I have attended in months. They're holding their wedding at a flashy reception centre on the banks of the Yarra River.

For the most part, everyone who knows us politely skirts around the topic of Max, asking how we are with sympathetic smiles. There's no denying the fact that talking about losing a baby – an almost full-term baby – makes people uncomfortable. Nobody ever knows what the right thing to say is, and nobody ever seems to ask the questions Paige wishes they would, such as: *How old would he have been today? Do you have a picture of him? What was his nursery like?*

As soon as the canapés start making their way into the dimly lit ballroom and the drinks start flowing, I lose track of Paige. It's not until I search outside that I see her, sitting on the jetty alone, head stretched up towards the sky.

I take a couple of glasses of champagne and some hors d'oeuvres in a napkin out to her. Plonking down beside her, I open my palm for her to take one.

'They're just trying to be nice,' I offer.

'I know.' She stares into her lap. 'It would be nice to be able to forget. Just for one night.'

Yes, it would. I would love nothing more than that. Paige bites into her hors d'oeuvres while I try and think of something to say that might be remotely helpful.

'Where'd you get the bracelet from? Do you like Pamela's dress?' I'm firing too many questions at once, and I know she knows I don't give a fig about where she got the bracelet or Pamela's dress. At every wedding we go to, Paige usually gives me an in-depth rundown of the bride's dress on the way from the church to the reception, only this time we didn't travel together, and I would be surprised if she even gave it much thought today. 'You look beautiful tonight,' I add. I inwardly cringe at how I'm making *small talk* with my wife. She's wearing a pale blue dress with a plunging neckline, with her hair falling in soft curls around her shoulders, and she looks more than beautiful, actually. She's exquisite.

'Thomas Sabo. Love it. Thanks.' She twirls the bracelet around her wrist and sighs. And then, 'Honestly, it's the best dress I've seen a bride in since my cousin Katrina's wedding in 2016.' She manages a smile. 'Pamela has amazing taste.'

'Well, rumour has it that the antipasto platters are nothing to rave about, and there's no way their pan-fried gnocchi can compare to yours,' I continue, changing tack as I swallow my food.

It's a joke – the home-made pan-fried gnocchi she attempted to make three years ago for my birthday dinner had been a disaster, leaving us with one big clump of sticky gnocchi and a burnt pan. We'd opted for cheese toasties and a good red wine instead while we watched my favourite movie of all time, *Top Gun*.

'Could we go home and eat cheese toasties?' she says, and I can tell she's only half-joking. Something jolts inside of me. I miss – *really* miss – the usual banter between us.

I stare out to the water. A houseboat is passing by with party music blaring from the distance and people dressed in eighties-style clothing dancing on the deck to Madonna.

'Think we could wave them down and hop on board? Looks kind of fun and I haven't struck a pose in a while.' I demonstrate for fun, and it's enough to see a smile break over her face.

I reach across and wipe a crumb from her mouth, our eyes locking. *Safe*, I want to tell her. This is safe. This is *us*. Suddenly, I don't even care whether I'm best man and we leave early. Nothing is more important to me than Paige tonight.

She shuffles closer and rests her head against mine.

'If you really want to, we can leave early.'

'Mmm, I do really want to. But we won't.' She takes a long sip of champagne and holds up her glass. 'Think there's more of this inside?'

'I think we can probably arrange it.'

'Tonight went pretty well, don't you think?' I say on the way home, reaching across the car for Paige's hand. She gives it a squeeze and it fills me with hope that this is the beginning of getting our lives back on track.

'I lost my appetite after Annoying Emily congratulated me. She assumed our baby was at home with a sitter.' She looks over at me and smirks.

'Shit,' I say, shaking my head.

'Yep.' She rummages through her bag and produces a Chupa Chups. 'These things are impossible to open without chipping a tooth or ruining a nail,' she says, trying to unwrap the lollipop.

'Give it here.' I unwrap it with my teeth. 'She recently got back from an eight-month trip to Europe. She had no idea.'

'I know.' She sighs deeply. 'Did you know she came back pregnant?' She reclaims the Chupa Chups from my mouth and pops it into her own.

'She has a partner?'

'Well, yeah, apparently somewhere between Mykonos and Barcelona.'

I start laughing. 'Oh, what?! Are you serious?'

A ripple of laughter escapes her. It's like music. The most beautiful music I've heard in ages. 'Yeah. She has no idea how she's going to find him. Which is very sad if you think about it.'

'We really shouldn't be laughing at someone else's expense,' I say, turning the indicator on. We are around the corner from home. 'Especially since it involves a baby.'

'Think she wants to give it up for adoption?'

We're still laughing at Paige's terrible joke when we pull into the driveway.

'You know, I don't really feel like going home right now.' I angle my body towards hers. 'Want to head to the beach? We could exchange theories on how Annoying Emily might be able to track down Pedro.'

'How'd you know his name?'

'I don't – call it a wild guess.' I lean back, loosen off my tie and toss it on the back seat. 'So, is that a yes?'

'You asking me out on a late-night date?'

'Do you want it to be a date, Hutton?'

'Um… well… usually I only date guys who bring jelly beans.'

'Is that right?' I reach over to the glovebox and produce a jar of jelly beans. They say that life is full of defining moments, if only you know how to look for them. Ours is a jar of jelly beans.

CHAPTER TWENTY-ONE

Paige

Two months later, Nick and I are in Tasmania, staying in one of Bette's five beachfront stone cottages. Here, on the edge of Great Oyster Bay, where the spring sky turns lavender and chalk-blue in the evenings, where the pebble-stone stretch of beach curves around the bay, we manage to settle into a new rhythm together.

Bette meets me in front of the cottage we'll call home for the next two weeks carrying two grey hand-knitted blankets to put around our shoulders. While the days are pleasantly warm, the nights here are still quite cool. Nick has gone out to pick up some fresh seafood for dinner. Bette hands me a blanket and we set off, following a narrow path to the sandy patch of beach and onwards to the pebbled part of the bay.

'Things getting easier?' she asks as we stop to sit on a couple of large rocks. The sun's setting, and the sky looks as if someone has brushed it with pastel watercolour.

'Things are much better,' I say. 'I mean, I still think of Max all the time. We both do. But the fog's lifted.' It's true. Once Nick and I started talking about things, it *did* become easier. I bend down and pick up a shell, smoothing off some of the sand. 'You don't think it's... too soon, do you?'

'No, darling. There are no "shoulds" with this kind of thing. Your time is the right time.'

I half-smile.

Bette tilts her head and gives a small nod. 'It's okay for you to feel happy, Paige, so please don't feel guilty over it.'

'That's what Nick says.'

'And how is Nick?' she asks.

'He's okay. He's not spending every waking hour at the hospital, and we found a way to talk to each other, so things are good.' I squint at the sky. 'We're in a good place now. We like it here.'

Bette smiles and pats my knee. 'Good work, kiddo.'

'I can't help wondering what it would have been like for Nick if the baby had survived and I hadn't,' I say as we make our way back to the cottage. Until now, I haven't admitted this to anyone, not even Imogen.

Bette wraps an arm around me and rests her head on my shoulder as we walk. Her flowery scent mixes with the gentle salty breeze. 'Thankfully, you don't need to think about that.'

'I couldn't imagine him as a single dad.'

'And I couldn't have imagined myself being a single mother. But I did it. You somehow find a way to work with the hand life deals you. It wasn't always easy. Let me tell you – behind that oh-so-handsome and serious demeanour, there was a kid that *loved* to get into trouble when I wasn't looking.'

'No way. You're lying.'

'Well, not the bad kind of trouble, but he used to sneak out at night. And to this day he still has no idea I knew.'

'Really? To do what? Meet girls?'

She grins. 'Nope.'

'Go drinking?'

'Nope. It was much more innocent than that.' She stares out along the coastline and adjusts the blanket around her shoulders. 'He would get up at three in the morning, ride his bike down to the fruit shop and go make deliveries. It took me an entire six months to figure it out.'

'What gave him away?'

'I eventually realised no bills had arrived. No phone bills, electricity, gas, water. He'd been keeping tabs on the mail and went and paid them all at the post office as they arrived. I tried to hide how hard it was to make ends meet but he was perceptive, like most kids are. I don't need to tell you what a good man he is. You already know.'

I smile, nodding in agreement, feeling a burn in my chest that makes me want to be with him right here and now. 'He is. He was raised by a beautiful woman.'

Bette smiles. 'It wasn't easy. Losing Zac, or raising Nick alone.' She pats my thigh. 'But you don't need to worry about that, and neither does he. He told me your last echo showed improvement?'

'*Some* improvement. Which means he is… we are hopeful. We'll see what the next one shows.'

We stand up and make our way to the white Adirondack chairs positioned in front of the cottage.

'I can't imagine my life without a son or daughter,' I admit after some minutes pass.

'Don't ever stop hoping,' says Bette as we watch the skyline morph into a shade of plum. 'You'll find a way, whatever it takes.'

Minutes later, Nick whistles at us from some distance away. His jeans are rolled up to his ankles, and he's wearing a wrinkled linen shirt with the cuffs rolled up to his elbows. Everything about him shows how relaxed he is here. The way he moves, the way he smiles, the way his hair, due for a cut, is unkempt and messy. He's holding a package containing fish and chips and waves to us with his free hand.

I get up from the chair and start running towards him. When I stop in front of him, completely out of breath – it's moments like these that my heart's weakness is most apparent – I fling myself towards him. He drops the package and lifts me up. He twirls me around in circles, and as I close my eyes, the wind sweeping up my hair, I'm thinking that if we've gotten through this, then together we'll be able to face anything at all.

By the time we turn around, Bette has started walking away.

'Hey, Mum, why don't you join us for dinner?' calls Nick. He holds up the package. 'I got scallops for you.'

She waves a hand and continues walking. 'Thanks, but I've got to sort out a late check-in,' she calls out.

'I thought you said you were booked out until next week,' calls back Nick. He creases his brow. 'Isn't that what she said this morning?'

I laugh. 'Yeah. She definitely did say that.'

Back at the cottage, Nick slides the key in the lock and holds the French door open for me, revealing a living space with a fireplace, a lounge and two sash windows that afford us clear views of the beach. There's a rectangular dining table to the right near the small kitchenette, and to the door on its right, an ample master bedroom with windows offering a view of the deck and the waters of Great Oyster Bay beyond it.

Nick opens one of the kitchen cupboards and produces two wine glasses. I open the fridge and take out a vintage local chardonnay. 'Does this go with fish and chips?'

Nick grins. 'Perfect. Let's go.'

We eat on the beach, our bare feet burrowed in the sand, the cool evening breeze burning our cheeks. Nick jogs back to the cottage for a jacket, which he drapes over my shoulders. He opens another bottle of wine and refills my glass. By now I'm starting to feel light-headed. 'That's my last one,' I say. Nick moves closer to me so his shoulder is touching mine. We sit for a bit, listening to the waves crashing gently and receding.

'I've been thinking we should get a dog,' says Nick, seemingly out of nowhere.

'A dog? Since when?' I ask, swallowing a mouthful of hot chips.

Nick shrugs. 'Since now. Maybe introducing a furry new member of the family could be a good thing for us both.'

A puppy, no matter how adorable, would never take the place of our lost baby.

'We'll get a good-natured one. One that'll be good with kids,' adds Nick, sensing my hesitation. 'A cavoodle.'

I've always wanted a cavoodle. I picture the two of us welcoming a dog into our home. The baths, the walks, the feeding, the snuggles. A distraction, a pet to love and care for. Something to bring us closer together. We both love animals. It makes sense. 'Okay,' I agree.

Nick's face brightens. 'New beginnings,' he says, thoughtfully.

I nod. There's something I need to tell him first – something that's been on my mind for a while now. 'I want to apologise for something. Something I should have said a while ago,' I confess.

'You don't need to apologise for anything. We're past that stage now.'

'I need to know something,' I explain. 'All those times I'd catch you standing in the doorway of the nursery with that pensive look on your face, I should have asked you how you were feeling – *what* you were feeling. I'm sorry that I never asked you. I think I was scared of your answer.'

He pulls me close to him.

'Let it go,' he says. 'It's all in the past.' He intertwines his fingers through mine and kisses my hand.

I hold up my glass. 'To the future. Oh, and to Dr Bridgeman giving us—' I make air quotes '—"permission".' I put on my best Dr Bridgeman voice. 'Your chances of a full recovery are solid, Paige.'

Nick laughs. 'I think you've had too much wine,' he says, tickling me.

I move over so I'm now straddling him. 'What should we do? With all this time we have here?'

'This,' he murmurs, right before his lips settle on mine.

The trip to Tasmania has worked a treat. We are finally back to being *us*.

PART TWO

CHAPTER TWENTY-TWO

Paige

On any other day, I would have been more sensible and not tried to make such a good impression, but while we were in Tasmania, I promised Nick I would make even more of an effort to get back to being my usual self. It's Mum's birthday, so I decide I can start by getting back into the kitchen. Today's *effort* takes the form of a cake, which emerges satisfyingly round and golden from the oven.

'How's the baking going?' comes Mum's voice down the line.

'It's fine,' I reply, cradling the phone in my neck.

Nick enters the kitchen with Piper, our two-month-old cavoodle, waddling behind him. Her fur is a milky-cream colour, with uneven patches of cappuccino around her face and ears, and she's every bit as attached to Nick as I hoped she would be. Nick admires the cake. I mirror his expression and hand him a coffee cup.

'What about yours?' he whispers.

'Don't feel like one,' I say, covering the mouthpiece. The toaster pops, and I snatch up a piece of bread, dropping it onto a plate before lathering it with butter.

'You've got so much going on right now, love. Why don't you let Caitlin make the cake?' suggests Mum.

'Because Caitlin has two kids, is pregnant and always gets to make the cake,' I say with a mouthful of toast.

Nick gulps down a mouthful of coffee and pecks me on the lips. *Love you*, I mouth.

He snatches an apple from the fruit bowl. *Love you more*, he mouths back. 'Be good to your mum, Piper,' he says, bending down to pat Piper goodbye before he bites into his apple. She pitter-patters behind him all the way to the front door.

I turn my attention back to Mum. 'I know you're saying that because you think baking isn't my forte.'

'It's not your forte,' she replies matter-of-factly.

'Thanks,' I say, rolling my eyes.

'You are good at many things, Paige, but the kitchen will never be your temple.'

'Way to crush a girl's dreams,' I say dryly.

She mutters something about there being more to life than a perfect cake.

I resettle the phone against my other ear and watch the cake slowly collapse into itself. My gaze shoots around the kitchen and lands on the empty egg carton. I scan the ingredients list. The recipe called for six eggs. I count the empty shells on the bench. Eight halves. I exchange a look with Piper, who's chewing on my shoelace. 'And we're out of packet mix, too, Pipes. Not even Donna Hay can get us out of this one.'

'What's that, honey?'

'Nothing, Mum. It's all under control. Happy birthday. I'll see you later.' I eye the deflated sponge once more and grimace.

After I set the phone down, I give up on preparing the coffee cream filling and ceremoniously pour the fresh brew of espresso down the sink. As it gushes down the plughole, the brown liquid splashes around the porcelain, sending up a strong, bitter odour. I step back and groan, a sudden wave of nausea catching me by surprise. Trying not to gag, I exhale slowly. Jug still in hand, I stare into it as if I'm expecting it to reveal an answer. Two things enter my mind: coffee and queasiness.

The jug slips from my hand and onto the floorboards with a loud clang. Piper skids out of the kitchen so quickly she bumps into the wall. My hands move to my chest, where I press down, trying to gauge whether there's any tenderness in my breasts.

Another wave of nausea surfaces. My foot hits the pedal of the bin, just in time for my sourdough to come up.

No.

Surely not.

There's just no way.

Nine hours later, I'm in the bathroom, peeing on a stick, when Nick pulls into the driveway. I purchased the test this morning but haven't been able to bring myself to take it. I finish up, shove the test into the empty box and speed into the walk-in wardrobe, where I thrust it under a pile of folded clothes.

Piper zooms to the front door and starts circling. 'Easy, girl,' I say, nudging her out of the way with my foot. I fling open the front door to greet Nick.

'Hey,' I say, breathless.

Nick lumbers up the two small steps leading to the porch. He's wearing the new Italian shirt we bought last week from 7camicie, the sage-and-white striped one that we weren't sure about. Would the mint do a better job of bringing out the blue in his eyes? Nick's gaze lands on me and his expression sharpens. No, it seems the shirt we've picked is doing a fine job.

'You seem puffed out.'

'Just raced Piper to the door.'

He bends down and plants a kiss on my lips before glancing back over his shoulder to the two teenage boys from across the street who are playing basketball. They stop when they notice me standing there. It occurs to me that I'm only wearing a bra and knickers. I burst out laughing.

Nick's satchel falls off his shoulder and onto the floor as he slides his arm around my waist. He nuzzles his face against

my neck, tickling me with his five o'clock shadow, and closes
the door behind him with his foot. 'Maybe you should put
some clothes on next time you race Piper to the door.' Piper
is still running around in circles, her tail thumping against the
whitewashed floorboards. 'Now we'll really give them something
to talk about,' he murmurs. He motions towards the bedroom.
Piper starts yapping.

I pry myself away from him. 'Raincheck? We're already
running late.'

He checks his watch. 'Yeah, about that. Sorry, I had an
emergency. Six-year-old. Ruptured appendix.' He bends down
and pats Piper. 'Good to see you too, Pipes.'

'All okay?' I ask, following him into the bedroom as he loosens
his tie and undoes the buttons on his shirt.

'All sorted. Ben took care of it. Let me take a quick shower
and we'll get going. Give me two minutes,' he says as he enters
the en-suite bathroom.

Two minutes.

I sneak into the walk-in wardrobe and pull the test from the
box. I hold my eyes shut, my heart pounding as I slowly open
one eye then the other.

Two lines.

I cup a hand to my mouth as I steady myself against the chest
of drawers, before plonking down on the tufted ottoman in the
middle of the wardrobe.

'Do we need to stop anywhere to buy a gift?' Nick calls as he
steps into the shower.

Images of pastel polka dot blankets, plush toys and limited-
edition melamine plates and cups briefly flash across my mind.

'Paige? Your mum's gift?'

No need – taken care of.

In my mind I've answered him, but he calls out again. 'Paige?
Did you hear me?'

Gift, right: the cake, flowers and a subscription to *Delicious* magazine.

'Uh, no, it's all under control.' Hopefully the running water hides the wobble in my voice. I force myself to take a deep breath.

It's all under control, Paige.

I hold my palm over my chest, adrenaline flooding my body. My heart is still pounding furiously against my chest.

As I stare back at those two lines and try to register everything this means, I tell myself many things.

It's simply a shock.

It will all be okay.

Babies are gifts. These two lines are a gift.

Good God, this is a gift I don't know what to do with. It's one that says: 'Here you go, Paige, here is everything you ever wanted. Enjoy this happy time in your life. But don't expect it to last long.'

With a trembling hand, I shove the test back in the box and drop my head to my knees.

I know what Imogen will say. Imogen will say that what I'm really dealing with is a choice.

And I'll tell her that this choice is one I'm not ready to handle.

'Are you nearly ready?' says Nick half an hour later, swiping the keys off the side table in the hallway.

'Did you feed Piper?' I call as I rummage through my dresser.

'Uh, yeah. You've asked me three times already.'

'Oh, did I? Sorry. So you put her outside?' I continue tearing my dresser apart. 'Does she have Potato?' Ever since we brought her home, Piper has had a tendency to fret if she's ever put outside without her soft toy, one I bought for her when I brought her home from the rescue centre. A fabric version of Mr Potato Head, he's lost one eye and his nose is barely hanging on by a thread, and I wonder how I'll go about finding her a new one once the stuffing inevitably starts to come out of him.

'You seem a bit on edge. I know Caitlin's coming but   '

'I'm not on edge,' I say, interjecting. 'I'm fine. Everything with Caitlin's fine.' I close the drawer and open the one below it. 'If only I could find what I'm looking for.' A waterfall of clothes spill from the edges of the drawer and onto the carpet.

'What exactly are you looking for?' says Nick, leaning against the doorway.

'My cape scarf. The Ted Baker one. It's black satin with pink flowers.'

From my peripheral vision I catch a glimpse of him checking his watch. 'I can see you. And I wish you wouldn't do that.'

'We're going to be late. You look fine like that.'

'Aha! Here it is.' I chew the plastic tie off with my teeth and hand him the label.

'Two hundred and twenty-nine dollars for a *scarf*?'

'It's Ted Baker,' I explain, slipping it on. 'Okay. We can go now.' I spray a little perfume into the air, taking a deep breath as I register the fragrance that curdles as it settles into the silk. Repulsed by the scent I normally love – I've been wearing the same Dior fragrance for years – I tug the scarf away, thrust it into the drawer and close it.

Nick's gaze lands on the drawer for a few seconds and then on me.

'It's a bit too warm for it. Changed my mind,' I say, waving my hand in a kind of dismissal. I scratch my head. 'Uh, yeah... so Piper's outside with Potato?'

Nick looks at me as if to say, *Are you for real?*

'Oh, yeah, you said she was. Sorry, I'm just... I don't know. A little distracted.'

'What's going on?'

'Nothing. Let's go,' I say, but it comes out in the wrong pitch. I go to make my way past Nick but he catches me by placing his hand on my waist. My breath hitches in my chest. Teasing me, he whispers into my ear, 'You haven't finished doing your make-up.'

Caught off guard for a second, I blink. I've never forgotten to do my make-up before leaving the house. 'We're already late. You know what Dad's like with firing up the barbecue nice and early. I'll finish doing it in the car.'

'Same with your hair?' he says, his forehead creasing as I wriggle my way out of his embrace.

I purse my lips, nod and then raise a hand to my head and release the jaw clip. With a shake of my head, a mass of loose curls falls around my shoulders, which I comb through with my hands. 'Better?' I pinch my cheeks until they flush pink.

'Aren't we bringing the cake?' he asks, nodding towards the kitchen.

I lift my empty Tupperware cake container in response. 'Change of plans. Let's go – we're stopping by the cake shop on the way. Chop-chop!' I take him by the hand. 'They better not be out of vanilla sponges,' I mutter.

'You know, I can tell when you're lying,' he says, holding the front door open for me.

'I'm not lying,' I reply as I turn to face him. I lower my voice and look him in the eyes. 'I promise.' I stand on my tiptoes, frame his face with my hands and peck him on the lips. 'I've had a lot on my mind lately.'

This is the truth.

Unless you count lying by omission.

'What kind of stuff?' asks Nick as we click our seat belts into place.

I flip my compact mirror open and take out my mascara. I try to keep the wand steady as he reverses out of the driveway.

'The usual,' I say, closing one eye. 'Tell me if you're going to go over a bump.'

'Baby stuff?' He surfs playlists before settling on the latest Coldplay album. 'Bump,' he says, raising the volume.

I hold the mascara wand away from my eye and glance down at my belly, trying to ignore the surge of emotions that have begun to surface. *Bump.* I blink away the tears that have started forming in my eyes, dip the wand into the bottle and remove it, scraping off the excess from the sides. 'Yes,' I admit, after a long silence, not wanting to lie to him. 'Baby stuff. But could we... could we talk about it another time?'

'Sure.' Nick pretends to sound unaffected by what I've told him.

I glance over at him before I attempt the other eye but he looks straight ahead, his jaw set firmly, the way it does whenever he's thinking things he isn't yet ready to share with the outside world. He turns the music up and slides his sunglasses on, and when we reach the next bump, he doesn't say a word. But I know what he's thinking. Nick, my husband of eight years, the man who knows all my secrets, and all my shortcomings, knows something is up and knows that I am lying.

CHAPTER TWENTY-THREE

Nick

Evelyn is melting chocolate over a bain-marie for the profiteroles she has lined up on a tray on the island bench.

'Happy birthday,' I say. She beams a smile of appreciation my way and pats my cheek.

'Happy birthday, Mum,' says Paige. She steps away and mindlessly plonks the flowers we've brought for Evelyn on the bench beside the Tupperware container that does not hold a vanilla sponge but a chocolate raspberry semifreddo that looks too perfect to have been created in Paige Hutton's suburban kitchen.

'Oh, you shouldn't have,' she says, admiring the blooms. 'I love freesias.'

Paige stares out the window to where Ella and Ethan are bouncing on the trampoline with Mark.

'Paige chose them,' I say, trying to make eye contact with Paige, but it's like she's in a different world. There's no mistaking it, something's on her mind, only I don't know what it is. Evelyn's too busy burying her nose in the bouquet to notice.

As if on cue, David opens the sliding door and crosses the open-plan living area to the kitchen. He's wearing his favourite red apron that says, *Stay Calm! The BBQ Master is Cooking*. 'Hey, kids!' He gives me a friendly thump on the back. 'What's happening?' He ruffles Paige's hair.

'Did Paige tell you yet? She's decided to officially go back to work,' I tell him. This evokes no more than a tight smile from her.

'That's great news,' he says, and out of the corner of my eye I notice Evelyn smiling at him, a relief in her eyes I haven't seen in a while. David starts lifting the apples from the fruit bowl on the kitchen counter. 'Have we got any lemons, Evelyn?'

Evelyn turns her head slightly and eyes them on the bench – they're sitting there ready for him, right under his nose. David clicks his tongue and scoops them up one by one. Evelyn stands there, shaking her head as she turns back to the bain-marie.

Paige and I follow David outside to the rear deck, where the long wooden table is already set, and David's getting ready to drop the meat on the barbecue. Ella's and Ethan's delightful squeals carry over the drone of the neighbour's lawn mower. The motor stops and gives way to the smack, smack, thwack of boxing gloves pounding a bag. The neighbour's son must have moved back home.

'Hey, what's up? Are you feeling okay?' I ask Paige in the small window of time we have alone on the deck before Caitlin reaches us.

'Please, Nick, not now.'

'So something *is* the matter.'

She closes her eyes and inhales before opening them again. 'Nick, please…'

'Loop me in, don't make me guess what's wrong. First you act all weird at home, now you look like you're close to tears.'

'Hello, hello!' says Caitlin, bounding up the merbau steps. 'Did you bring the cake?' she asks Paige.

'Yup. Choc raspberry semifreddo,' she declares, unchanging in pitch.

'A semifreddo?' She gives me a mild smirk. 'Weren't you making a vanilla sponge with coffee cream?'

'Didn't work out,' she says, deadpan, avoiding eye contact with her.

Ella races up the steps and hugs Paige, then me, with Ethan trailing behind her. I pretend not to notice her.

'Hey, Ethan! Have you seen Ella? She's six years old, about this high, blue eyes...'

'Uncle Nick! I'm here, hugging you!'

'Where? I can't see you anywhere.' I scan the lawn, pretending to look for her.

She bursts out laughing. 'Here, silly!' She jumps up and down in front of me, flapping her hands around.

'Oh my God, there you are!'

'You need glasses, Uncle Nick!'

'I think I better get my eyes checked, Ellabella.'

She turns to Paige and tugs her by the hand. 'Come on the trampoline with us, please!'

'Sure, let's go,' she replies.

'I'm trying, Nick,' says Caitlin, when Paige is out of earshot.

'I know you are. I think she's just having one of those days. Something's bothering her.'

Suddenly, it feels like all the progress we made in Tasmania has dropped away. So much for open and honest communication with each other.

Paige barely touches her food over dinner while we discuss the best and worst birthday gifts we've ever been given. So far, Evelyn's winning both categories: a ticket for a South Pacific cruise for her fiftieth birthday versus a bromeliad that never flowered and a lettuce spinner. David, of course, is arguing the value of a lettuce spinner. Oil and vinegar stick better to dry salad leaves. And who knew that bromeliads could take years to flower, only to ever bloom once?

By the time we sing 'Happy Birthday' and Caitlin and the kids bring Evelyn's cake out, there is no doubt in my mind that whatever is bothering Paige must be significant. She's sitting next to me, twirling her wedding band, her knee jerking up and down – something she never, ever does.

Caitlin thrusts a piece of cake in Paige's direction. 'Paige, cake?'

She shakes her head. 'No, thanks.'

'Are you still upset about the comment I made earlier?' asks Caitlin.

'Oh, Paige, I'm sure she didn't mean anything by it. Nobody cares that you bought the cake and put it in your cake carrier,' says Evelyn.

David chimes in, his mouth full of cake. 'I don't care where the cake came from, but it's a ripper. Great choice, Paige.'

'I couldn't care less about a stupid cake right now.'

Mark flicks his gaze away out of politeness and turns his attention to the bottle of champagne he's opening.

Caitlin inhales. 'I really didn't mean for you to get upset over it.'

'I don't want cake because I'm not feeling well, okay? We don't need to make a big deal about it.'

'Champagne?' asks Mark, waving a flute towards Paige, who hasn't touched a drop of alcohol.

She shakes her head. 'No, thanks.'

That's when I feel the goosebumps on my arms. 'I think Paige said she had a headache,' I say. Now I'm the one who wants everyone to drop it.

'Headache? What? No, not a headache.'

Evelyn chimes in again. 'You're feeling okay, though, right?'

'Yes. No. Could we drop it? Caitlin – cake, please. I've changed my mind.'

'Well, which one is it? Yes or no?' presses her mother. 'Is it your heart? What's going on?'

Paige scrunches her eyes closed. 'Actually, I'm pregnant.'

It's like the breath has been completely knocked out of me and someone needs to remind me to breathe. Paige cannot be pregnant.

If Paige is pregnant, this means…

Actually, I don't want to think about what this means.

CHAPTER TWENTY-FOUR

Paige

Caitlin releases her grip on the plate. It drops in front of me with a smack, sending loose berries across the table. Everyone is silent, even Ella and Ethan.

'You're *what?*' says Caitlin.

Mum pales and freezes with her spoon still lodged in her piece of cake. She resembles a street performer, locked in one moment in time. Aside from the kids, Caitlin is the only one animated – her eyes dart from Mum's to Nick's to mine and back again. Dad reaches for his beer and chugs down the rest of its contents before setting it down with a thud. 'Shit. I think I left the gas on,' he says, standing up.

'Guys, that's… uh… great… congratulations,' says Mark. I've never seen him look so awkward. He offers me a smile, but I sit there mutely, feeling the burn in my cheeks amplify. He extends a hand in Nick's direction, congratulating him with a handshake. Nick mutters a barely audible 'thank you' in response.

By now Nick's face is so flushed I think he might actually combust. He is staring at his plate, avoiding eye contact with anyone at the table. I cannot imagine what's going through his mind right now. We are not prepared for this situation. When a doctor sits you in a room after you almost died and warns you that another pregnancy could cost you your life, you are not meant to fall pregnant. And yet, here I am. I am thirty-four years old, and I am supposed to have many more years in front of me.

Mum reaches for a plastic cup belonging to Ella, fills it with water and drains it. 'Um… how far along are you?' she asks, finally breaking the silence, her words coming out in the wrong pitch.

'Who wants to watch some cartoons inside?' Mark stands, scoops Ethan into his arms and whistles for Ella to follow.

I sit up straighter. 'Um, around five or six weeks…' I grimace, feeling like an irresponsible teenager. 'I think?'

Nick coughs. He coughs so hard Mum reaches for the plastic cup and refills it for him. I can't help noticing the way her hand is shaking as she does this.

Instinctively, she places a hand on Nick's back. His Adam's apple bobs up and down.

'Nick? Let's go inside and talk,' I say. 'I—'

'Save it, Paige. I really don't want to hear it right now.'

With that, Nick slides his chair out from the table with a deafening screech and excuses himself.

I close my eyes, dip my head and groan. 'I think I'm going to be sick.'

The tiles in the bathroom are cold, but the body enveloping me from behind is warm. I can tell it's Mum, not only by the softness of her body but from the scent of her perfume, Youth Dew. No matter how many times Caitlin and I have tried to introduce her to something more contemporary, she always insists on wearing the same fragrance, asking for a bottle each year for Christmas.

'What am I going to do?' It's silly to even be asking Mum to answer this impossible question – it's not like the time I had a minor car accident and couldn't find the money for the excess payment when I was nineteen, nor is it like the time I decided to break up with my boyfriend at twenty-three, right before I met Nick. Mum had the answers then, but she certainly doesn't have the answer now.

Mum squeezes me tighter. 'It's going to be fine. We're going to work this out.' I know she means well, but this isn't exactly something that can be easily worked out. Not in this situation.

I throw myself back into her arms. 'I'm scared, Mum.'

'No need, honey. It's all going to be fine,' she repeats. She says this in a way that sounds like she's trying to convince herself. 'Nick didn't know, did he?'

My voice is muffled against her chest. 'I didn't have a chance to tell him. I wanted to but I… I wanted more time to get used to the idea – to figure things out. I couldn't have chosen a worse way to tell him.'

By now, Caitlin is standing in the bathroom doorway, her eyes glossy as she watches us both. Mum is gently rocking back and forth, presumably to calm herself as much as she is trying to soothe me. Caitlin joins us on the bathroom floor and hugs me from behind.

'Sorry about before,' she says, resting her face against my back. 'What are you going to do?'

'I don't know,' I whisper, trying to hold back the tears. 'I really don't know.'

CHAPTER TWENTY-FIVE

Nick

We were so close to putting it all behind us. And now *this*.

The air in the car is thick. We drive home from Evelyn's birthday barbecue in silence, aside from my rhythmic tapping on the steering wheel. The air is weighed down by my thoughts and Paige's probable thoughts and the reminder of the toll the last ten months have taken on us.

When we're a couple of blocks away from our house, Paige manages a weak, 'I'm sorry.'

But answering her doesn't come easily. I can't believe this has happened. Already I'm fast-forwarding to what this means for us.

'Your timing sucks,' I say eventually and I hate the way I sound – cold and prickly, nothing like my usual self.

'It just came out. I should have chosen a better time to tell you…' Her words, ones that don't stand an infinitesimal chance of making things better, fade.

We travel through the streets in our neighbourhood, past the local primary school and the strip shops positioned along the same road. As we take the corner, something in me snaps and I realise it's my voice rumbling through the air like thunder, disrupting the silence. 'I thought you were on the pill!'

'I *was* on the pill!' she spits out.

I flash a glance in her direction. 'Was?!'

Her arms flail about. 'I was on the pill! Well, obviously not any more, but yes, I was on the goddamn freaking PILL!'

Air. We need some air. I let the window down. 'I don't believe it,' I mutter, shaking my head. 'I honestly can't believe it.' And I can't. I mean, she almost *died*. I nearly lost her. And this? This could kill her.

I should have been more careful. *We* should have been more careful.

'So, tell me then – how does this happen?' I ask, this time trying to sound a bit calmer, though I am anything but.

'Gee, Nick, all those years of medical school never taught you anything, did they?'

One more block and we'll be ready to pull into our driveway. All I want is to get out of the car so we can give each other some space to calm down.

I sigh. 'Legit question.'

Paige crosses her arms and squirms in her seat. She squeezes her eyes closed and then opens them. 'It was our second-to-last night in Tasmania – the one where we opened up the hundred-and-twenty-five-dollar bottle of sparkling rosé.'

I know the one. She argued that it was ridiculous to spend that kind of money on a bottle, even if it was French and vintage and a rare treat. According to Hope, you could provide enough life-saving peanut paste to a child in East Africa for three months with that kind of money, and she made sure I knew it.

'Well?' I prompt.

'I must have made a mistake. When we were travelling I think I forgot to—'

'You *forgot*?'

'The oysters. The Bollinger. We'd been out all day and I had a glass more than I should have and I think I must have forgotten to take it…'

I inch slowly up the driveway, leaving the ignition on as we continue sparring in the dim light.

My chest flickers with anger, heat pricking my cheeks. 'You forgot that accidentally falling pregnant could threaten your *life*?'

'You know what? I'm not having this conversation with you right now! You know I hardly ever drink and I have spent months measuring out every ounce of liquid I consume! I take the pill every night at the same time. We were *busy* that night, Nick. *We* were busy doing *other* things. I had a *moment*. For the first time in months, I let myself forget about everything else, and I got the days and dates mixed up. We were on *holiday*!'

'Okay. *Okay*.' I turn the ignition off and sit idly in my seat.

'Please don't make me feel worse about it than I already do. Blaming me isn't—'

'I'm not. But I don't think you realise what kind of situation we're in now.' I blow out a measured breath.

'Of course I realise! What do you think I am?' She unbuckles her seat belt and pushes the car door open. 'I'm finding you a little condescending right now. Listen to yourself.' She shuffles out of her seat and snatches up her handbag.

'Sorry, I didn't mean it like that. I just—'

Paige slams the car door closed and storms inside.

And then I put the car into reverse and back out of the driveway without her.

How long does it take to cool down after your wife springs her life-threatening pregnancy on you at a family barbecue? Obviously a fourteen-hour shift plus a side trip to the local pub isn't enough. I head straight into the bedroom and into the en-suite, where I turn on the shower and start peeling off layers of clothes, tossing them onto the floor – Paige's pet hate. I haven't spoken to her at all today, despite a string of text messages from her I couldn't bring myself to respond to.

'Hey,' she says, stepping into the room. 'I left you some dinner. I made coq au vin – and for dessert, baked Alaska.'

No, she didn't.

'Okay, fine. Pre-prepared chicken skewers and frozen veggies. Coq au vin is overrated.' She waits to see where her joke lands but I don't take the line like I usually would. I can't even look her in the eyes.

'Nick,' she says, her shoulders sagging. 'Please say something. I feel really terrible about this.' She shifts her weight from one foot to the other, waiting for me to speak.

'Why didn't you let me know so we could take other precautions?'

'Oh, come on. What am I? On the stand now?'

The stand? She's pregnant and this is possibly *the* most terrible thing that could happen to us, not that I ever thought that would be possible after losing Max, but it is. Here we are.

'What? No, you're not on the stand,' I reply. 'I thought you wanted to talk about this.'

'But you're asking me why I didn't let you know we should have taken other precautions,' she says, her voice even.

'Well, why didn't you?' It's a fair question but I'll admit it comes out a bit accusatory and, judging from Paige's expression, she's noticed.

'Maybe I would have if I actually *remembered* that I forgot to take the pill.'

Jesus.

'My bad.'

'Your bad? That's all you have to say? *Your bad.* As if this is a carton of spilt milk or you forgot to pay a bill.'

'Well, I'm sorry if I'm not so perfect like you, Dr Bellbrae, who thinks everybody should be as perfect as he is! Let's not forget that I didn't do this alone and you could have checked or reminded me! Besides, the pill isn't 100 per cent effective and we both know that.'

'Especially if you forget to take it,' I mutter as I concentrate on unfastening my watch.

'Where'd you go, anyway? Your clothes smell like smoke so I'm guessing you didn't come home straight from work.' She picks up my jacket and brings it to her nose. Yep, it smells like a dirty ashtray.

'George and Johnny's. I was with Ben.' I grab my toothbrush. I haven't smoked a cigarette since my first year of university.

'Oka-ay,' she says.

I know why she sounds surprised. We haven't been there in years. In fact, nobody our age seems to go to George and Johnny's any more.

'How much have you had to drink?'

'I only had a couple of beers and I took an Uber home. Don't worry, I'm not that irresponsible.'

I know I've gone too far when Paige gathers up the pile of clothes and thrusts them in my direction. 'These go in the wash basket. It's disrespectful to leave them for me to tidy up! And once you're done with the shower, for the love of God and all things holy, hang up the bath mat to dry!'

She stomps out of the room and calls out, 'And speaking of irresponsible, the water storage levels in this city are only sixty-two per cent and the shower's running!'

I stand there wearing only my underwear, with a pile of dirty clothes in my arms and nothing left to say.

CHAPTER TWENTY-SIX

Paige

The next morning I wake up to Piper's doggy kisses in bed. Nick has left for work early without waking me, and I'm counting the hours until he'll be home again so we can talk about things. I take my meds, throw on a pair of grey yoga leggings and my favourite black T-shirt, and take Piper for a walk, stopping only when I reach Hope's doorstep, hoping she'll be home. Her house, four blocks away from mine, is a semi-detached Edwardian that she and Paul renovated four years earlier and only managed to finish six months ago. She still jokes that it almost ruined their marriage.

Paul opens the front door, his large frame towering over me. He's sporting a blue football jersey with a black nylon jacket and a pair of black shorts. Around his neck is a lanyard. Paul, an avid lover of football, studied sport science at university and now works for Football Victoria as a sport trainer.

'Hey, Paige.' He beams his wide smile at me and pulls me into his usual Paul-style hug.

My arms snake around him, possibly too tightly and for a moment too long. I pull away and take a step back. 'It's good to see you,' I say in a small voice.

A glimmer of curiosity flashes across Paul's face for a moment before Piper distracts him by tugging at his shoelaces. 'Come on in. You're just in time. Ollie's spilt his breakfast all over the kitchen floor.' He lifts Piper into his arms and calls out down the hallway, 'Ollie, look who's come to visit!'

Hope's kitchen looks as if it has been messed up by four wild animals, not one almost twelve-month-old baby. There's a sink full of dishes, dishcloths over the bench, coloured plastic blocks strewn across the floor and a trail of spilt cereal and milk leading all the way from Ollie's high chair to the fridge. Piper scampers across the floor and starts licking it up. Ollie, who is sitting in his high chair, squeals with delight and bangs his spoon on his tray at the sight of her.

Paul shakes his head and laughs with him. 'Hey, how's Nick?' he asks. 'I've been meaning to drag him out for a game of golf now the weather's better.' He opens up his wallet. 'I've got tickets for the next Victory game. You want them? We're playing Melbourne City.' He holds them up for me.

'I don't know if we'll get the chance to use them.' Not only is Nick on call this weekend, I'm not convinced that either of us will be in the mood for a soccer match.

'Here, take them anyway,' Paul says, pushing the tickets into my hand.

Hope enters the kitchen with a bottle of Spray 'n' Wipe and roll of paper towel. She has oats in her hair, which is sticking out haphazardly. 'Hey you! Aren't you meant to be at Windsor Lakes today? Why so early?' She brushes her hair away from her face as Paul leans over to kiss her goodbye. He ruffles Ollie's hair and pecks him on the cheek. 'See you later, Paige. Say hi to Nick for me.'

'Will do. Thanks for the tickets.'

Hope crouches on the floor and starts tearing off sheets of paper towel so she can mop up the mess Piper is helping her with. 'Aren't you gorgeous?' she says, rubbing her hands over her fur. She stands up, the paper towel dripping milk across the floor as she ventures towards the kitchen bin. Ollie bangs his spoon on the high chair, sending splatters of sloppy cereal across the kitchen. Hope looks at me, exasperation on her face.

'He does this every single morning,' she mutters. 'I can never keep the kitchen clean. Welcome to Monday in the Barrett household.' Hope works four days a week, often bringing home work to catch up on in the evenings. I know how hard the long days are on her and wish I'd been around more to help her out in the early days.

'Let me deal with it. Go take a shower,' I say, waving her away.

Ollie starts crying for his spilt breakfast. I scoop him into my arms and carry him across to the bench. Securing him with one arm, I reach for the cereal box, hand him a spoon and then fill his bowl, drowning the Weet-Bix with a splash of milk.

'Go on,' I say to Hope, nodding.

She smiles with relief before heading for the shower.

'Okay, little guy, let's eat,' I say, returning Ollie to his high chair.

I wipe down the walls and help Ollie finish his breakfast. Between spoonfuls, he claps his hands together and smiles, his little mouth opening in anticipation, his dark brown eyes so full of innocence, I feel an overwhelming surge of love for him. And then, my body floods with warmth, and my thoughts flash backwards to Max and forward to the baby in my belly. Max would have been one soon. If life had gone to plan, I'd be at home spooning cereal into my baby's mouth, most likely on the phone to Hope while we challenged each other as to who could get to have their own shower first. And I wouldn't be sitting here, pregnant, my heart threatening to rob me of ever getting to bear witness to my baby spraying mushy Weet-Bix all over my kitchen.

I don't realise I'm holding the spoon in mid-air, teasing Ollie with it, until I hear him squeal, jolting me from my thoughts.

'Oh, sorry, honey,' I say, guiding the spoon into his mouth.

Hope has re-entered the kitchen wearing a pair of jeans and a black T-shirt, her wet curly hair in a messy topknot. She smells of pomegranate and lime soap. 'Okay, so what's wrong?' she says, flicking the kettle on. 'I know it must be bad.'

I look up at the ceiling and cringe. 'It's up there. But how can you tell?'

'Because you were sitting there spaced out, in your own little world, while my son was opening and closing his mouth like a fish and you didn't even notice.'

I busy myself by scraping the sides of the bowl clean and give Ollie the last spoonful of cereal before wiping his mouth with his bib. I lift him up from his high chair and he crawls to the centre of the living room, where he starts playing with his toy blocks.

'Pa-aige?'

'No coffee for me,' I say. 'I'm pregnant.'

Hope tilts her head and mouths, *Pregnant?*

I nod.

Her eyes search mine. 'Oh, shit. So what did Nick say?'

'He's still coming to terms with the news.'

'And you? Have you come to terms with it?' Hope's eyes are filled with concern.

'I have an appointment with my cardiologist at ten to sort out my meds.'

'That's not what I asked.' Hope chews the inside of her lip and reaches for her phone.

'What are you doing?'

'I'm skipping Mother's Group. I'll go with you to your appointment and then we'll go to the boathouse after that.' The boathouse is our go-to place to visit whenever one of us is going through a particularly bad time. Its cherry sundaes have massaged us through exam failures, bad job interviews, family arguments, boyfriend break-ups, one engagement break-up, one baby loss and now a wanted but very badly timed pregnancy.

'No, I'll get out of your way,' I say, going to stand. 'You can't mess up your day because of this. I'll be fine on my own.'

'Uh-uh,' she says, pointing a finger at me. 'I've been meaning to quit Mother's Group for weeks. This'll be the third week I've missed in a row, and got-it-all-together Nina's already snitchy about the "level of effort" I put into the group, so it's probably time to do it.'

'You're *quitting* Mother's Group? I thought you loved your Mother's Group. Why?'

Hope puts her hands on her hips. 'Why? I'll tell you why. I'm sick of hearing about how Beau is most likely gifted, and vaccinations might cause this or that. I'm a little cheesed off with the way Georgie makes Tash feel inferior because she bottle-feeds and uses a dummy, and how Nina always has to compare Lila's sleeping habits with Ollie's. I mean, really, are there not bigger things in the world to worry about than how many hours' sleep someone else's kid is getting?'

'Yes, there are much bigger things to worry about.' I sigh.

Hope's shoulders drop. 'Sorry - didn't mean to make it about me.'

'You know I don't think that. Send the message and tell Nina it's none of her business,' I say.

Hope taps a message into her phone and hits the send button with gusto. 'Done,' she declares, with an air of satisfaction. 'And now?'

I reach for a cold piece of toast that Hope has most likely intended to be her breakfast and start buttering it. 'Tell me something...' I say, my eyes focused on Ollie. 'Back when you were studying and you...' I can't bring myself to say the word "abortion", but from the look on Hope's face, I know she's aware of what I'm referring to. 'Did you... or do you... ever regret it?'

Hope puts her phone down and looks me squarely in the eyes. 'I mostly felt a sense of relief. The decision itself was the hardest part. I didn't want to be a single mother struggling to make ends meet, which is how things would have been. Leon would never have been the kind of dad our child would have needed him to be. He was too young, and even I knew back then that it was never going to last.' Hope's boyfriend at the time, Leon, was an international student studying in Melbourne for six months, and as soon as she told him about her pregnancy, he pretty much ghosted her overnight.

'I put in all those years of study for a reason. I love my career as a human rights lawyer. I love that I can make a difference to other people's lives doing what I do,' she continues. In addition to her work as a lawyer, Hope runs a not-for-profit company called Poppy and Willow. She started it over ten years ago. Her company is involved in the manufacture of artisanal clothing, ethically produced by women in Peru who are paid a fair income, with the proceeds going towards feeding hungry children around the world. 'Do you remember what you said to me when I was trying to decide what to do?'

'No, I don't,' I reply, the details of that time a little hazy.

'Well, that very year, the abortion law in Victoria changed. And you told me that I was lucky enough to have the freedom to choose, and I needed to choose what was right for me. And the same thing goes for you today. But the difference is that you need to keep in mind that you *can't* choose the way your body is going to behave during this pregnancy. Your circumstances are completely different to what mine were. Your life's at stake here.'

'I know,' I whisper, the horrible realisation of what is at stake dawning on me. 'But it's so much more complicated than that. My health, the baby's health. My feelings about this baby. I think I feel love for this baby, Hope. It's not some clear-cut, black-and-white, easy thing to decide.'

Hope nods slowly in agreement. 'Exactly. These kinds of things never are.'

CHAPTER TWENTY-SEVEN

Nick

I haven't spoken to Paige all day, though she texted me to let me know how her appointment with Victoria went and what medication she was prescribed. The experience of finding out we are expecting our second child is nothing like I imagined it would be. The strangest part is, I'm not thinking about becoming a father at all. How can I, when Paige's life is at risk? How can I focus on anything but her right now?

As I push my key into the lock, I steel myself, reminding myself to stay calm, knowing Paige is going to be emotional and I need to cut her some slack even if I am still angry that we are in this situation in the first place.

'Hey,' I say, depositing my keys on the bench. I let my satchel slide off my shoulder.

She steps forward and hugs me. 'Hi,' she says, her arms enveloping me. She looks up into my eyes. 'I couldn't stop thinking about you today.'

'Me too,' I say, but it's hard to meet her gaze.

She peels herself away from my unusually stiff body. We need to figure this out, and until we do I won't be able to relax.

'So, I made eggplant lasagne for dinner. I've never paid so much close attention to a recipe in my life.'

I smirk, the natural response I usually have to Paige when it comes to her adventures in the kitchen, and then, without willing it to, my face goes serious. 'We really need to talk.' I'm already moving towards the sofa in the living room. I haven't been this jittery since taking my university exams.

We sit opposite each other, and she props a cushion in front of her and hugs it, waiting for me to speak first.

'Okay, so when was your LMP?' I say. I know I sound like a doctor but I'm too preoccupied to care.

'My what?' She frowns at me.

'Your last menstrual period.'

'You're speaking to me like you're a doctor.'

'I am a doctor.'

'You're my husband, not my doctor.'

My expression doesn't change. 'When was it, Paige?'

'I don't know exactly.'

'Well, can you check your diary?'

'My diary? I don't keep tabs on my period in my diary,' she says, and I can tell her irritation just spiked. 'I can barely keep tabs on my own birthday.'

'But you use a diary.'

She screws up her face. 'Not for that! What woman keeps tabs on their period in their diary? Diaries are for birthdays and holidays and appointments and—'

'Surely you have some idea,' I press, rubbing the back of my neck.

She stares at me blankly. 'I can't think straight. And you putting pressure on me isn't helping.'

I sigh and remind myself that she hasn't had a chance to sort through all this yet. 'When did you find out?'

'Mum's birthday. Right before you came home. And I didn't mean for you to find out the way you did. I was just... I was in shock and I couldn't hold it in.'

I replay the scene in my mind and quickly push it aside. 'When did you realise you'd forgotten the pill?'

'Around ten days ago.'

'So why didn't you tell me then?'

'Because I thought for sure I couldn't be pregnant. It took us a while to conceive Max and I thought the odds of falling pregnant after only missing one pill were going to be next to nothing. I mean, how unfair could life be to us? It was *one* slip-up. I'm not exactly a "young" woman any more—'

'What?!' I can't believe what I'm hearing.

'I think you need to calm down before you say something you're going to regret,' she warns, hugging the cushion tighter.

'For ten days you were in total denial of this, Paige! Ten days! And then when you finally realised, you dropped the news like a bomb in front of everyone!' I rake a hand through my hair. She had suspicions but didn't bother telling me? 'Jesus!'

Paige bites down on her lip. 'I was worried and scared and I didn't want to say anything until I had the chance to wrap my mind around it. You make it sound so nefarious.'

When I don't answer, she continues. 'Hurting you was never my intention. I admit I made a bad judgement call to not test sooner, but we are here now and I can't do anything to change the outcome, Nick.'

I ignore her, instead focusing on the dates. The next steps. We need to sort out these dates. 'Okay, now your meds are sorted, we need to have a scan to confirm how far along you are.'

I can't believe I am going to say this. I inhale and finally look up at her. She's so beautiful sitting there opposite me, and I hate myself for what I'm about to say, but it needs to be said. 'I don't think we can keep this baby.'

Paige stares at me, dumbfounded, as if she's waiting for the dots to connect. As if she didn't see this coming.

She backs away to the far side of the sofa. 'I can't believe you said that,' she says slowly. She sits there, shaking her head, and then all of a sudden, she throws the cushion to the floor. 'Nick, what the heck? You're talking to your wife. We are a couple. This is *our* baby you're talking about. You don't come out and say it like it's some business transaction we need to take care of! We are supposed to decide something like this *together*.'

'Surely you knew this was a possibility,' I say.

'Of course I know it's a possibility. But…'

My expression remains stoic. 'Paige,' I say softly, but there is still a firmness in my voice, a firmness that sends a wall up between us, one that becomes thicker and more blurred with each word that follows. 'I'm sorry… but we can't do this. It's too risky. Given your history, it's too much of a gamble.'

'No!' she says.

'You almost died! I almost lost you!'

Her hand moves under her top and rests against the space between her pelvis and belly button. She's thinking of Max.

'It's not your body! This isn't only your decision!'

I lean forward. I'm not angry any more, just sad – sad that we are having this conversation in the first place. 'Nor is it solely yours. You need to take the emotion out of this one and think about the risks.'

The oven timer gives a shrill beep, warning us that our dinner's ready. She stands up and shakes her finger at me. 'I can't believe, after everything we have been through, that you think not keeping this baby is the way to go without even considering the alternative.'

I follow her into the kitchen.

'Dammit, Paige. *Think* about what you're saying. Take a minute to really think about what you're deciding and how it affects not only you but me.'

Paige yanks open the kitchen drawers, trying to find an oven mitt. 'I don't want to think about that today,' she says, pulling the tray out of the oven. 'Dinner's ready. You can eat alone. With all this talk about getting rid of our *baby*, I've lost my appetite.' She slides off the oven mitt, storms down the hallway and yells, 'And don't you dare lecture me on the importance of nutrition and pregnancy!' She snatches her keys from the buffet and steps out the front door, but she doesn't drive away. She just sits in the driver's seat of her car, alone in the driveway, until the lights inside turn off for the night.

Ben's back from his honeymoon in Bora Bora. He's come back with a tan that would make anyone envious, and there's a three-centimetre gash above his eyebrow from an accident with a catamaran. Obviously Tahiti, or marriage, or both, agrees with him because he's perched on my desk with a beer as if he's still on holiday. The only thing missing is a wedge of lemon and some sunblock.

'I thought Sarah drew the line at stocking the fridge with Red Bull,' I say.

'Not if you know how to ask nicely.'

'I always ask nicely.'

'Oh, but do you score her tickets to *Billy Elliot*?'

'This is why you're much more brilliant than I am.'

'I told her they were from you.'

'Why would you do that?'

'Because she likes you better. And she was pretty firm about the no beer in the fridge rule. She thinks it would encourage us to stay back even later when we should be at home with our wives.'

'That's because we should be at home with our wives.'

'Agree.'

'We should get her tickets to that day spa she keeps talking about – I'll have to ask Paige the name of it.'

'She's a one-in-a-million receptionist.'

'She is.'

We run out of words and the room goes silent except for the hum of the printer in the corner. As much as I appreciate Sarah, this whole Ben and the beer thing is bordering on weird.

'There's something I want to tell you,' he says finally. 'I want you to be one of the first to know.'

This can only mean one thing: Pamela is pregnant.

'Congratulations. That's great news.'

'Jesus. Can *anything* get past you?'

'You're smiling like an idiot. Drinking beer in my office. What else could it be?'

He shrugs.

'Really, I'm happy for you.' Only I don't sound all that happy, which makes me sound like a complete asshole. Thankfully Ben doesn't seem to notice.

'I know it's probably a bit awkward.'

'It's not. This is a good thing. A really good thing.' This time I sound more sincere. And I *am* happy for Ben. He'll be a great dad. Hands-on. Definitely the good cop.

He chews his lip. 'Okay.'

There's a beat of silence, which only makes the printer sound louder than it is. It's churning out pages and pages of documents. It stops and beeps, protesting for more paper. I go to get up.

'I've got it,' he says, handing me a beer. 'Finish writing that email. Or whatever it is you're staring at there.'

I go to protest, but it's too late. Ben's at the printer, gathering up the documents and refilling the tray with paper. He walks back to my desk, stealing a glance at the papers, and I know what he's thinking. He will be asking himself why I've got a stack of research papers on the topic of pregnancy outcomes in peripartum cardiomyopathy.

'Thanks,' I say, taking them from him. I shove them into my briefcase and down half my beer in one go.

Ben stands there, expectantly.

I fire off the email I've been obsessing over for the past half hour – one to a doctor in the US specialising in PPCM to see if he can shed some light on his experiences with expectant mothers like Paige – and shut my laptop. Ben's still standing there, all the joy that was on his face moments ago gone, like it was never there to begin with.

'So, you heading home soon? To celebrate?' I ask.

'We already celebrated.' Next thing, he pulls out a chair. Right opposite my desk, as if he's setting up camp for the night and doesn't intend to go anywhere. And then he helps himself to the papers in my bag and talks to his watch. 'Hey Siri, send a message to Pamela. I'm going to be home late. A friend who would never in a million years admit it needs help with something.' He licks his fingers and starts reading, glancing up at me briefly. 'We should order a pizza. We'll be here for a while. Don't forget I hate anchovies.' And then, 'How many weeks is she?'

By the time I head to my car, it's eight thirty and my head feels woolly, like there's too much information stuffed in it with nowhere to go. I could go to the gym, the pub, the beach for a jog, but I need to talk to someone who isn't Ben, someone who doesn't know me or Paige or how messed up this whole situation is. Someone impartial.

And that's how I end up in the corner booth of a packed bar on a Tuesday night with Miranda Summers.

CHAPTER TWENTY-EIGHT

Paige

Mum is potting flowers on the back deck when I let myself in through the side gate the next day. There are packets of flower and herb seedlings sprawled on the steps beside a small speaker that's playing some easy-listening music she's quietly humming to.

'Hey, Mum.'

She pulls her hands out of the dirt and stands up. 'Honey,' she says, her voice thick with relief.

Honey.

One word is all it takes for a lump the size of a ping pong ball to lodge itself in my throat.

'Oh, Paige.' She flings her arms around me. 'I've been calling you. Why wouldn't you answer? I came by three times. Didn't you get my notes?'

I got her notes, but I haven't had the heart to read them. I know they'll be written in Mum's sentimental style and that isn't what I need right now.

Mum pulls off her gloves and leads me inside, where she sits me down at the kitchen table. She switches the coffee machine on and takes two wonky hand-thrown pottery mugs from the overhead cupboards. She made them last summer when she went through her ceramics phase and gifted us all entire dining sets for Christmas. 'I spoke to Ryan last night. He says he tried to call you, too.'

'I know. I saw.'

'He's going to try again later tonight,' she says, as if to say I better pick up.

'You told him.'

'Caitlin did. And then he called me.' This isn't a surprise. News travels fast in the Hutton family, and it's near impossible to keep a secret for long. 'It's hard for him, being so far away,' she adds, like an afterthought. 'In times like these I miss him so much more than usual.'

'Is he still planning on visiting for Christmas?'

'Well, that all depends on Susannah,' says Mum as she opens the milk carton. She stiffens momentarily, seemingly annoyed with herself when she realises what she's said.

It seems that no matter where I look lately, there is someone having a baby, trying to have a baby, trying to keep a baby…

'Shouldn't you be at Windsor Lakes?' Mum asks, quick to change the subject.

'Yes. And no coffee for me,' I say. I get up and open the pantry, helping myself to a peppermint teabag and her secret stash of Iced VoVo biscuits – the ones she keeps in the limited edition Twinings tin.

Mum narrows her gaze as I wrestle it open. 'You know about the tin?'

'We all know about the tin, Mum. We have known about the tin for years since Ryan found it stashed there circa 2001.'

'Oh,' she says, blinking slowly.

I hand her a biscuit and take one for myself.

'So, how are things with Nick?'

'He's pretty much made his opinion on things clear.' I start licking the icing off the biscuit. VoVo-therapy is the term Caitlin and I used for these biscuits when we used to live at home. I faintly smile at the recollection of the two of us sitting in the fork of the oak tree in the back garden, biscuit tin in hand, discussing boy problems and girl problems and world problems. How different our conversations would be if we climbed up that tree today.

Mum is gripping her mug. Her face has lost some of the colour it previously held.

'Oh, Mum, don't look at me like that. Please.'

She gives a small shake of her head. 'Sorry. What are the doctors saying?'

'Not much yet. We'll know more next week when I see my cardiologist again.' Victoria told me that's when we would talk about 'the situation' in depth. In the meantime she needs to consult with some of her colleagues. I set my biscuit down. Thinking about Victoria and our next appointment has a disarming effect on my appetite.

'Right, so let me understand. You need to find out what you're dealing with and what the risk is so you can decide whether to…' She waves her arm vaguely, encouraging me to finish the sentence for her.

'You're assuming there's a decision to make.'

'What does Nick think?' she asks in a tone that gives her away.

'You've spoken to him, haven't you?'

Mum dips her head and gazes into her lap before finally looking up at me. 'Yes, I called him,' she admits.

'Mum!'

She shrugs helplessly. 'I was worried about you, sweetheart. We all are. Your father just tore up the veggie patch and replanted it. He's gone to Bunnings again. Fourth trip in two days. Caitlin's been messaging me every day. Your brother keeps calling.' Wisps of hair have dislodged themselves from behind her ear. She looks completely frazzled.

'You all need to calm down! And you shouldn't have called him. Please don't take this the wrong way, Mum, but this isn't your business.'

She crosses her arms. 'You're my daughter. So, like it or not, this is, to a certain point, my business.'

'No, Mum. It's not. So do not call him about this again, okay? Please. Not until we've had a chance to...' *Sort it out.* Like laundry. Mismatched socks. A billing error. Taxes. A hole in the roof. A leaky tap. Those are the kinds of things you sort out. Not a baby. Not when you are what is supposed to be one half of a supposedly happily married couple who have quite frankly, in my opinion, suffered enough and worked really hard to get back to where things are good again. I remember the words Mum told me on the morning of my wedding: 'A long-lasting marriage takes hard work.' Dad echoed the same in his wedding speech. 'And a bit of distance,' he joked, referring to his career as a pilot.

Mum stares at me thoughtfully for a few seconds as if she's trying to decide on whether she can agree to my request. 'I'll try,' she says finally.

I nod, satisfied.

'Darling,' she says, after a beat. Yes, this is typical of Mum. She can never let things go.

'Mmm,' I say, waiting for her to continue.

'Have you thought that maybe Nick does have some valid feelings about this? That maybe he's feeling a little more emotional about something other than the... baby?'

'What do you mean?'

'He loves you very much, Paige.'

'I know that.'

'Well, he's probably feeling scared right now.'

Mum's words hang in the air. I haven't wanted to think about why Nick might be scared, because a decision needs to be made according to what is best, not what scares us. Best for whom, I wonder. I bat the question away.

'Fear isn't a reason to suggest terminating a pregnancy. And the doctors don't know for sure how my body is going to respond to the pregnancy.' I pause. 'You know, you were always the one who told me that your children came first – that mothers would starve rather than let their children go hungry. Grandma Catherine told you that and now…'

'Oh, honey, but this is different. This is so, so different.'

'How is it *different*, Mum? This is still my baby. Even though the baby's not born, aren't I still its mother? Isn't it my responsibility to protect it, to keep it safe, to give it the best possible chance at life? Especially after everything that happened with Max?'

Mum hesitates. 'Your life is at risk. That changes everything.'

'You're only saying that because it's me. If it were anybody else, I know you'd be thinking differently about this. I remember when there was that story on the news about that woman who had a car accident while she was pregnant and the doctors had to decide whether to save her or her unborn baby, and you said that—'

'I know what I said, Paige! But you are my daughter! I'm your mother and it's my job to keep you safe, to…'

I flinch as Mum's voice rises to a pitch I haven't heard it rise to in years. Before responding, I take my time to consider my words. 'I'm a grown woman. Your job is to support me. You already got the chance to keep me safe, and now it's my turn to do the same for my baby. *If* that's what I decide to do. I get to choose, Mum. Not you or anyone else. So please don't make this harder than it already is.'

She closes her eyes momentarily, and when she opens them she shakes her head. 'You almost have your health back. Please think about that.'

'You're a hypocrite,' I say, tears spilling from my eyes. 'You are supposed to make me feel better!'

'Hey,' says Dad, entering the kitchen with a box full of gardening supplies. He sets down his keys. 'I can hear you from outside. What's going on?'

Mum looks relieved to see him. 'Paige and I were discussing—'

'The fact that Mum's a hypocrite and is taking sides with my emotionally detached husband! I can't believe you can't see things the way I do after everything you've ever taught me about being a mother!'

'Paige, give it a rest,' says Dad, chiming in.

'You're on her side, too, I suppose?'

'It's not about sides,' he says evenly. 'It's about your life.'

I stand up from the stool and grab my handbag. I've heard enough.

'Exactly. My life. My body. My choice,' I say, making my way to the front door.

'Where are you going?'

'I have a doctor's appointment for a blood test. I was going to ask you if you wanted to come with me. But now I think I'd rather go on my own.'

'Don't be like that. Please...' says Mum. 'Let me get my bag.'

I fumble through my bag for my keys. 'I know it's not easy for anyone, but I really think I need some time alone right now.'

Dad trails behind me. 'Call us when you get home,' he says as I step through the doorway. 'To let us know you're all right.'

'I'm all right, Dad. And I'm going to be all right. This is going to be all right.' He's looking past me, not at me. '*Dad*, did you get that?'

'Yes. Yes, I got it.' He's nodding but I catch the flicker in his eyes. A flicker of something I haven't seen since Ryan was hit by a car when he was sixteen.

Fear.

CHAPTER TWENTY-NINE

Nick

I visit Evelyn and David after work instead of going straight home. It's been a while since I've seen them, since Sunday night dinners at their place have fizzled out for the time being with everything that's going on. I let myself in through the back gate. David's staking tomatoes out the back while Evelyn is shelling peas on the table outside.

David waves hello and tells me he'll be over in a minute. I pull up a stool opposite Evelyn and she pushes the bowl closer to me.

'Make yourself useful.' She smiles to herself. 'How are you feeling?'

'I think we need to concentrate on how Paige is feeling. I couldn't get through to her. It's like she doesn't want to hear the truth about the risks involved. She's made her decision,' I explain to her, snapping a pea pod in half.

'I gathered as much when she was here the other day.'

'She's not thinking clearly. She has an ultrasound tomorrow and that's only going to bring more emotion into all of this.'

'What she wants more than anything in the world is to have a baby, Nick. She wants to be a mother. At any cost.'

'And that's the issue.'

Evelyn reaches across the table and presses her hand into mine. 'Nick, honey. I love you like a son. So I'm going to tell you something right now and you're not going to like it. I don't like the fact I have to say it but here's the thing. I don't blame Paige for wanting to go through with this pregnancy. David can tell you – he and I have fought about it; he spent two nights on the living room sofa because of it. He thinks I should be doing everything to convince her to not go through with this. So does Caitlin, but I refuse to get involved any further. I told her how I feel and she has every right to make her decision now. If we lose her, I'm going to have to live with the consequences of not saying anything more. But here's the thing, love. I'm a *mother*. My children are my life. I don't want to lose my daughter – no parent should ever have to lose a child. No husband should ever have to lose a wife. But I *understand* why she's making this choice. I'm not saying it's right, but I understand where she's coming from. And if I were in her situation…' She shakes her head. 'Honestly? I'd probably make the same decision.'

'But the risks.'

Evelyn wipes her hands on a tea towel.

'I'd bet my award-winning secret pavlova recipe that she's done as much research as you on the entire matter. Granted, hers probably isn't as medical. She knows the risks. She just doesn't need all the facts and figures like you do. Paige is carefree and laid-back, and most of the time she can't keep up with what day it is. But she's not stupid.' She sighs.

'Gambling your life away is stupid, Evelyn!' booms David's voice, startling us both. 'And as her mother you should be convincing her of this. The way you're talking, it's like you're as crazy as Paige. What'll you do the day you have to bury her?'

'Oh, David, calm down.'

'I'm not going to calm down when this is our daughter we're talking about. We can calm down once she's out of danger. But *this*, this is not the time to bloody calm down!' He drops his gardening tools onto the deck, the sound of metal reverberating as they fall onto themselves.

'I spoke to her about it. You were there, remember! And as far as I recall, you just walked her to the door and let her leave without telling her the way you feel!'

'Well, I can tell you I'll be letting her know how I feel all right.' David turns towards me, his face red and sweaty. 'Nick, you have to find a way to save our daughter – even if she's too stubborn to see it for herself.'

'David! How dare you put this back on him? *Think* about what you're saying. This is not about stubbornness. She lost a baby – she's still grieving for goodness' sake.' She follows him through the glass sliding doors into the kitchen.

'And we'll all be grieving again if this madness continues!' David searches his pockets for his keys. 'Excuse me, but I need to get to Bunnings before it closes.'

Evelyn tosses him his keys from the fruit bowl. 'Bunnings closes at nine, and the last time I checked, you prefer to eat risotto warm, not cold.'

'I won't be home for dinner.'

'Honestly, after all these years of marriage, you'd think you'd learn how to argue like an adult.'

David doesn't hear any of this, of course, because he's already halfway down the hallway.

Evelyn returns outside, closing the sliding door behind her.

'I think I might need a chamomile tea. Or is it lemon balm that's better for this?' She holds her hands out and inspects her hands, which are trembling. 'Never mind,' she whispers. 'I'm sorry about that, Nick. Lucky you're family.'

But it's not Evelyn's words that weigh on me. It's David's. I can't let them down.

A few hours later I'm at Mark and Caitlin's country house. Mark greets me in the driveway with a wave. He's wearing work boots, a tool belt around his waist and a T-shirt with holes in it – a contrast from his usual suit and tie for his job at a bank.

'This look suits you,' I say, pulling my own pair of work boots out of the back seat of the car. I've had them for years and they've never been worn.

He laughs. 'If I could do this kind of work all day, every day, I'd be a happy man.'

I wonder if he realises this statement implies he's currently *not* a happy man, but I brush it aside. Mark and Caitlin have their lives together – he's got a great job, they have a beautiful house, two amazing kids with another on the way, and a supportive family if we don't count the current Paige–Caitlin drama that's been unfolding. They have everything going for them. This country house – and all the hiccups that have come with it – is seemingly the biggest problem in their life.

'Maybe it's time for a career change?' I offer as he leads me inside.

The house is nowhere near complete but I can tell already it's going to be an absolute stunner by the time it's finished. It was originally a miner's cottage, and Mark has retained much of the original character of the home: the floorboards, the marble fireplace, the crown moulding.

'Actually, I've been thinking maybe it is.'

'Yeah?' I'm impressed. Mark's always been focused on his corporate job, and it takes guts to pivot into another career.

'Yeah, I feel like I'm missing out on the kids. By the time I get home they're usually already in bed.'

'Everything looks great so far,' I say, changing the subject.

'I'd love to move out here. Caitlin won't have a bar of it though. She prefers the suburbs.'

He opens an esky and pulls out two cold beers. 'I've been meaning to ask you about Paige. Caitlin thinks it's too risky... for her to keep the baby. Is that true?'

I pop the cap off my beer and nod. 'It's definitely risky.' Of course, I was hoping we could avoid this conversation, but this is my brother-in-law and it's only natural he's asking the question.

Mark lifts his eyebrows. 'You don't deserve this, Nick. Neither does she.'

'It's not a question of deserving anything. We just need to figure out what to do from here. I don't think she should go ahead with things but she has other ideas.'

He nods, understanding. 'Wow, so where does that leave you?'

This is a question I am not ready to answer. I have no idea where this leaves me, but I know it means that maybe Mark won't be the only one making a career change. Only mine might be out of necessity. I never pictured myself as a single dad, though I'm sure nobody ever actually does, unless it's by choice.

That would never – could never – be my choice.

CHAPTER THIRTY

Pulge

The cotton from the hospital gown feels cool against my skin. I lie on my back, a sheet over my legs, as the ultrasound technician, Jack, tries to explain how a transvaginal ultrasound works. As he rolls the protective sheath over the probe and tells me where he's going to put it, I decide that he isn't doing a very good job. All I can think of is that I would give anything right now to duck out of the room and empty my already supposedly empty bladder. But seconds later, a fuzzy image appears on the monitor and I forget about the discomfort.

I turn my head sideways to get a better glimpse at the screen. Jack is silent, deep in concentration, his fingers typing and clicking and zooming.

When I can't bear the suspense any longer, I ask, 'Is that it? The baby? Does it have a heartbeat?'

Jack keeps his eyes focused on the image. He points to a grey mass. 'This is the gestation sac here,' he says finally. 'And this here is…'

'A heartbeat?'

'One hundred and sixteen beats per minute,' he says as the *whoosh-whoosh-whoosh* sound reverberates through my ears. My insides come alive as I crane my neck, unable to tear my eyes away from the tiny little flicker. Max's little brother or sister.

'Want a photo?' he asks as a roll of pictures spits out of the machine.

'Yes, please.'

Jack hands me a series of images – hazy pictures of my future son or daughter.

He exits the room and leaves me to dress. I take my time, legs dangling from the bed, one hand on my belly, holding the pictures close to my chest, keeping the moment all to myself before this becomes something I have to share. I don't want to think about anyone else's reactions to this. These images are proof that I have a baby growing inside of me and I cannot bear the thought of anyone spoiling my moment.

Six weeks, four days. EDD 14 July.

I text Nick and wait for his reply. It comes two hours and thirty-four minutes later, while I'm grocery shopping.

Sorry I couldn't be there today. I should be home around seven tonight if all goes well. Should we grab a bite to eat? Meet you at Provincial's?

My stomach drops. I don't know what reaction I was expecting, but this isn't it. I text back:

Yes to Provincial's. We have a heartbeat!

See you then. Gotta go.

I stand in the middle of the supermarket, feeling my cheeks burn as I slip my phone into my pocket. Years from now, how will I describe this moment to my son or daughter? When we found out we were expecting you it went like this...

I enter the fruit section and start loading my trolley. Week Eight: Your baby is the size of a raspberry. Week Nine: Your baby is the size of a grape. Week Thirteen: Your baby is the size of a kiwi.

The unbearable weight of doubt anchors itself in the pit of my stomach like an undigested meal. What if I won't be around to tell my son or daughter anything at all? Dad's face enters my mind. Ryan's voicemails. Caitlin's text messages. Mum's secret phone calls to Nick. They're all scared.

And then, right there in the grocery store, in front of the forty-week melons, I start sobbing.

I arrive at Provincial's early. I'm starving, not having been able to stomach breakfast or lunch. I help myself to a grissini and wait for Nick to turn up. While the minutes tick by I text Caitlin back. She messaged earlier asking how I was doing.

'Hey there,' says Nick as I slide my phone back into my bag. He pecks me on the cheek. 'Sorry I'm late. I got side-tracked with a colleague. Miranda. She invited us to her son's birthday actually. If you want, I can pick you up on the way home from work tomorrow and we can go together.'

'Yeah, sure,' I say, without really thinking. I just want to get down to business.

He slips his jacket off before sitting down. 'So, uh, how was your day?' he asks.

'The usual.'

Moments of silence pass, and when I can't think of anything else to say, I slide the ultrasound images across the table.

Nick sucks in a breath and flicks through them before finally looking up at me.

'Can I get you any wine?' asks the waiter.

'Uh, a glass of house red will be fine,' says Nick, shifting in his seat. 'How about you?'

'I'll stick with water, thanks,' I tell the waiter.

'So, your day…' says Nick, dismissing the photos completely. This is so unlike him and I hate the way it makes me feel.

He helps himself to a grissini, but he doesn't bite into it straight away.

'I… uh… I got to hear the heartbeat. One hundred and sixteen beats per minute,' I declare, as if I'm relaying news that our kid has won a sports game, or achieved something particularly noteworthy in life. 'The sonographer told me, "Baby has a nice strong heartbeat,"' I say, mimicking Jack's tone of voice.

Nick remains silent, his eyes flicking to the grissini between his fingers before snapping it in half.

'I wish you could have been there. Because maybe seeing it would help you bond or at least see that this is our child – a baby we made together.'

'Paige,' he says softly, his eyes closing briefly.

'What?'

'No,' he whispers.

'No means what?' I take a deep breath, bracing myself for his response.

'I… the photos… the fact that there's a heartbeat. It's not going to change my mind.'

'But—'

'Why don't you hear me out?' he suggests.

'Oh, I have to hear *you* out, but you're apparently unwilling to negotiate. How is that fair?'

Nick's eyes dart around the room. He lowers his voice. 'It's not. None of this is fair. This isn't about being fair. It's about looking at the facts and—'

'Making an informed decision.' My jaw tightens. God, how I hate that expression. 'What if I told you I definitely don't want to go ahead with a termination?'

'I'd tell you that the woman I love more than anything in the world would be making a mistake.'

My eyes sting with tears but I manage to hold them back as the words settle on us. Every muscle in my body tightens. A *mistake*. A risk. No matter how I look at it, all I can see is a miracle, just like Max was.

My gaze settles on the aquarium positioned in the far-right corner of the restaurant while I contemplate how I should explain it to him. 'I feel attached to the baby. I feel like a… like a mother.'

Nick leans back in his chair. 'We lost our son. Your maternal instincts, that attachment – these are all normal feelings. But this isn't Max.'

'This isn't about Max. It's about this baby,' I plead.

'You keep talking about the baby, but you're completely avoiding any kind of discussion around the fact that a decision like this could cost you your *life*. It's not a game. It's serious. And I don't know what easier way to say it, but it could also cost us the baby's life. Have you thought about that? Or have you considered, at all, the fact that *I* could lose you both?'

I swallow uncomfortably.

Nick nods. 'That's right. Who is going to be left to pick up the pieces?'

'I don't want to hurt you.'

'It's not only about hurting me. It's an unnecessary risk.'

'If I can get to term – or as close to it as possible – this child would have his or her whole life ahead. I've already lived mine.'

'You're thirty-four years old! Don't you think you're being selfish? Think about what you're asking of me. Think about what you'd do if you were in my shoes.'

I try not to take offence. 'I'm not trying to be selfish here. I'm not trying to hurt anyone. I am simply putting the life of our child ahead of my own.'

Nick shakes his head. 'Sometimes matters of the heart don't necessarily always lead to the best decisions. And I'm telling you now, this is not a good decision.'

'You don't get to take out the emotion on this one, Nick!' I say, raising my voice a notch. 'This is *your* baby this time. It's your life, not someone else's. You don't get to distance yourself from things.'

'No emotion? Really, Paige? No emotion?'

I rub my temples. Mum's right. Nick is emotional.

The waiter arrives at the table carrying our drinks. He slides a glass of wine in front of Nick.

'Ready to order or—'

'Another five minutes, please,' says Nick, keeping his eyes on mine. He takes a long sip of wine before he continues.

'When I married you – in fact, the moment we started dating – I knew that I would do everything in my power to be the best damn husband I could be. And that didn't only include loving you, it also meant protecting you. How do you expect me to agree to this when I know the risks? What kind of man would that make me, Paige? You tell me, because it seems you have this all figured out.' He lifts his hands in defeat.

'I don't have any of this figured out. All I know is that I don't think I can have an abortion. There's no guarantee that things are going to work out for the worst. There is a chance this is going to turn out fine. I'm feeling great so far.'

'You have another thirty-three weeks to go. Probably less since you most likely won't make it to term.'

'You don't understand.'

'I do understand. I can't meet you in the middle on this one if you don't make any space for me.'

This is the problem. How can I make room for Nick when there is no middle ground here?

'But there is no meeting in the middle, is there? We either keep the pregnancy or we don't. What other choice is there? It's black and white. What could we possibly do to meet in the middle? Toss a coin? Draw straws?'

'No,' says Nick, unflinching.

'Then there's nothing more to say for now, is there?'

'Unless you want to hear the stats, I guess not.'

I sigh. 'Okay, tell me the stats.'

Nick starts citing some research papers he's been reading over the past several days. '"... what they found with a group of women in Haiti was that ... and with an ejection fraction of less than fifty-five per cent ... maternal risk was too great..."'

I'm always so proud of Nick, so in awe of the way his work allows him to perform everyday miracles on human beings. How his hands, his commitment to healing others, can make the difference between someone living or dying. He doesn't often talk about the ones who slip away. I remember the time early in Nick's career when he couldn't find a way to express the pain involved in losing his first patient in a neurological emergency, a ten-year-old boy who'd suffered a haemorrhagic stroke. Nick lost him on the table. He came home that night, dishevelled, with the saddest look in his eyes. 'I didn't sign up for this,' he said as he dropped his keys on the kitchen table.

'You did,' I told him.

I took the box of Scrabble from the linen closet, wiped a layer of dust away, and as we sat on the floor around the coffee table in front of the open fire, empty wine bottles gathering around us, he spelled out the words: IT HURTS.

I responded, tile by tile: I KNOW.

'Then why do I do it?' he questioned.

'You do it because you can make a difference. Because you are hope when parents have lost all hope.'

But now, as I look at my husband, sitting across the table from me, I want to retract that statement entirely.

CHAPTER THIRTY-ONE

Nick

Even though I'm around children every single day, it takes me forever to decide on a gift. I've been wandering through this toy shop for almost forty-five minutes after Paige decided she didn't want to come with me after all.

'Is there anything I can help you with?' asks a shop assistant, a freckly young brunette with her hair swept into a messy bun. 'Not to rush you, but it's almost nine o'clock and we're about to close.'

'Um, yes, probably.' I hold up the box of Lego and a science kit. 'I can't decide between these.'

'Are you buying for a boy or a girl?'

'A boy.'

'Sure, and how old's your son?'

'My uh… no, this isn't for my son.' I practically croak the words out and she makes a face like, *Why does this guy sound so weird about buying a box of Lego?*

She waits for me to say more, and when I don't answer she prompts me. 'So how old is he?'

'Um, he's six.'

'Has he got much Lego already?'

'I'm not really sure.'

'Oh, then I'd go for the science kit. If he already has one, you can keep the receipt for a full refund or exchange within thirty days.' She smiles at me, revealing a mouth full of braces and pink elastics.

'Okay, that's settled then.' I put the Lego back and settle on the science kit.

'Oh, one more thing,' I ask her as we walk to the counter. 'Do you offer gift wrapping?'

By the time I make it to Miranda's place, all the party guests are gone. My shift went overtime and it's a miracle I've been able to show up at all.

'Nick! I'm so glad you could make it.'

'Looks like I'm a little late.'

Will enters the kitchen wearing his pyjamas. He steps over a pile of streamers, following a robot that walks and shoots laser beams out of its eyes.

'Wow,' I say.

'Hi, Nick! You missed the cake. It was a space cake. Did you know NASA is going to send the first woman to the moon by 2024?'

Of course I know this. I am a NASA groupie. The question reminds me of Zac in so many ways. He would have loved Will. 'I did not know that,' I say, trying to sound impressed.

'We saved you some cake anyway,' says Miranda. 'Did you come straight from work? Are you hungry? I could warm up some sausage rolls.' She smirks. 'Or some hot dogs. That's pretty much all I have left. Unless you want some fairy bread?'

'I'm fine. Really.'

'Well, in that case, how about some wine?'

'Sure,' I say. 'Hey, Will, I got you a gift.'

Will scoots over to me and looks up innocently. He extends his arms to accept the box. 'Thank you, Nick.'

'You're welcome.'

He tears the paper away.

'What did I say about cards first?' says Miranda, but Will's not listening.

He turns the box over to inspect it, his eyes brightening. He lets out a gasp. 'Mum! Look!'

'Looks like you just nailed Will's birthday,' she says to me. 'What do you say, Will?'

'Thank you so much. Mum, can I play with it now?'

'Have you brushed your teeth?'

He bares his teeth to show her.

'Good work. Fifteen minutes, and then it's bedtime, okay, sweetheart?'

With that, Will retreats into his bedroom with the science kit, leaving the robot behind.

'He's wanted one of them for ages.' She pulls the cork off a bottle of wine.

'I won't stay. It's Will's bedtime. I just wanted to bring him his gift. Sorry I couldn't make it earlier.'

'It's fine, Nick.' She picks up two glasses and hands me one. 'Now, I'm going to ignore the mess for the time it takes to get through one glass,' she says, motioning for me to follow her down the hallway. She retreats to the sitting room, the one she mentioned last time is out of bounds for Will. She flops onto the beige Chesterfield and tucks her legs underneath her, straightening her dress, a flowy navy material that falls around her ankles. I sit next to her, maintaining a safe distance, but I can still smell her perfume. Lemon and fresh flowers.

'So, how are things? Any news? What's been happening since I last saw you?'

I take a long sip of my wine while my brain tries to figure out where to start. I am sitting next to Miranda, at her son's birthday party without Paige, and suddenly this is all I seem to be able to focus on. Paige. Risk. An impossible decision. A problem I can't seem to fix.

'Nick? Anyone home?' Miranda waves a hand in front of my face to get my attention.

There's a brass clock in the wall unit, and in the silence I can hear it ticking. Tick, tick, tick.

Then I feel Miranda's warm, perfectly manicured hand on mine. She squeezes. 'What are you dealing with? Is it that bad?'

Yes, I want to tell her. It's that bad. But just then, Will appears in the doorway and yawns for so long it makes me yawn in response.

'I'm coming, sweetheart. Just give me five minutes.'

'Nick, could you read me a story tonight?'

'I, uh…' There's no doubt about it, he's caught me by surprise. I clear my throat.

'Please?'

Miranda puts her glass down. 'I'll come now, darling.' She mouths, *Sorry*, as she squeezes past me.

'Please can Nick read it? I want to show him the book about the boy who went to space.'

'Why don't you bring your book out here and I'll read it to you?' I offer.

'In the special living room?'

'You don't have to,' says Miranda quietly.

'It's fine. Really.'

A minute later, Miranda goes back to the kitchen to tidy up and Will returns with no fewer than eight books. He settles himself onto the sofa, crosses his legs and puts a cushion on his lap.

'Okay, so what are we reading?'

'This one,' he says, patting the cover. 'My dad gave me this one. He used to read it to me every night.' He hands it to me. 'Now you can read it to me.'

'You want me to read it?'

He nods expectantly. 'I already know all the words.'

I start reading and he stops me after the first page. 'You're supposed to make the rocket sounds.'

'Oh, okay.'

'Just letting you know.'

'Sure.' I read on, making the rocket sounds wherever I think they're appropriate. At the end, I close the book and ask, 'So, how did I do?'

He's quiet, like he's weighing things up. This small kid, taking this – a story – so seriously.

'You didn't do it as good as Dad.'

I turn my body so I'm facing him. 'You want to know why?'

'Why?' he whispers.

'Because I'm not your dad. No one can replace him.'

He nods thoughtfully.

'Was it the rocket sounds? Were they not all that good?'

He screws up his face. 'Yeah, they weren't that good. You need some practice. Mum says with practice you get better at things. You need to be louder. Like this.' He demonstrates.

'You must miss him a lot.'

'I wish he was still here. Mum gets sad sometimes. I heard her tell my Aunt Zoe she's lonely.'

'I'm sure she's not lonely when she's with you.' I hand the book back to him. 'You're going to be okay, Will. So is your mum. You just have to keep remembering him. And remembering he loved you both, and you both loved him.'

He doesn't answer, just starts making another rocket sound. I join in, louder than before.

He smiles. 'That was a bit better. At least when you get a kid, you'll have had some practice.'

'Yeah,' I reply. 'I guess it's going to come in really handy some day.'

That's when I notice Miranda standing there, leaning against the doorway, watching her son. I know how she feels. What a beautiful thing to watch; what a painful thing to not be able to fix this for him.

CHAPTER THIRTY-TWO

Paige

'What will it take for you to change your mind? Because I was googling last night, and with the right monitoring, there's a chance I can make it through this pregnancy without complications,' I say to Nick the next night before bed.

'Google,' he says, deadpan, with a mouth full of toothpaste. He spits into the sink and starts rinsing his mouth out.

I knew there was a chance Nick might respond like this. He isn't intentionally making me feel stupid, but that's how I feel. 'Well, I didn't get to the academic research papers yet.'

'I've already read them,' he says, matter-of-factly, as he reaches for the mouthwash. 'All of them. *And* I spoke to a specialist doctor in the US.'

Of course he has.

'I also consulted three cardiac specialists and another obstetrician. Just to be sure.'

'Nick, you want us to terminate our baby. We *want* this baby. Like we wanted Max.'

He gargles and spits before replying.

'This is about your life,' he corrects. He pauses, reaching for the deodorant. 'It's not like we *want* to do this.'

'And we don't *have* to do it.'

Our life, like the life of any couple, is filled with choices and decisions. Give here, take there. Surely we can find a way to agree on this one.

'Paige,' he says, turning around to face me. I can tell he's sorry about what he's about to say by the way he blinks, the way his mouth curves a little at the edges. 'I don't feel confident about the outcome.'

And there it is. Nick's clinical justification of why we should abort our baby.

My thumb breaks through the hole I've been making in the cuff of my sleeve, a bad habit of mine. Nick moves closer and tries to hug me but I raise both hands to stop him.

Nick flinches. 'Paige, I devote my working life to saving people's lives.'

'That does not make you always right.' My voice wobbles. Maybe because part of me knows he is right. My life is at stake. I could *die*.

'No, it doesn't. But do you want to know what it feels like? To be operating on a patient for hours – a child – and experience that moment when you realise that you're losing them and there is absolutely nothing you can do to stop it? Knowing that after that child dies in front of your eyes, you're going to have to walk out the door and face the people who love them more than anything in the world and let them know their child is gone? I never, *ever* go in believing that loss is an option. Even when I know the stats aren't on our side, I try to maintain the belief that things will work out, so I can do the best job I can, but I still have to be realistic about things.'

I understand what he's saying, but surely there's a chance he can see that we can choose to be positive about this. 'Why can't you believe things will be okay? Why can't you bring your positive attitude to this – to us?'

Because he's scared, whispers a voice in my head.

'I think it's important to realise that we don't need to rule out the fact that we might become parents some day. Right now, we need to see how your recovery goes, and from there we can work out how to become parents. Okay?'

'I'm really not buying this right now,' I say flatly.

'I'm not trying to sell you anything. I'm trying to reassure you. Termination isn't going to be the end of the world.'

I shake my head, trying to block out the idea. If I do this, how will I manage to cope afterwards? 'That's not how it feels. And this isn't how it's meant to be. This is not how it was supposed to go, Nick. We were meant to be... happy about this.'

'I know,' he concedes. 'I want nothing more than for us to be happy about a pregnancy. But this one... it's not the right time. I'm sorry, but it's not.'

'Are you going to die, Aunty Paige?' asks Ella. She's using my face as a make-up canvas, caking it with finishing powder.

'Uh... what?'

'Keep still!' she says, brandishing my good red lipstick. We're in Caitlin's back garden. I'm lying down on an outdoor lounge chair, babysitting Ella while Caitlin is at Ethan's swimming lesson. 'Close your lips and do this,' she says, making a face so her lips are taut. She leans her body over me, steadying herself on me with her elbow.

'Okay. But what makes you think—'

Before I can finish my sentence, Ella is colouring my lips, my teeth and the area around my mouth with my sixty-dollar lipstick.

'Want to see?' she says, reaching for the mirror. She holds it up for me. My eyes widen as I take in my wild hairstyle, purple eyelids and fire-engine-red cheeks. 'What did you say you wanted to be when you got older?' I ask suspiciously.

'A gymnast,' she says matter-of-factly.

'Oh, great. That's good,' I say, thinking this child would have no hope as a make-up artist. I sit up. 'So, who told you—'

'Mummy was talking to Daddy and then Mummy was talking to Nanny on the phone and Nanny was crying and then Mummy was crying and Daddy said you weren't going to die because Uncle Nick would never let you die, and then Mummy said you were going to die.' Ella lifts herself off the side of the chair, does a series of cartwheels across the lawn, rolls her way back to me and says, 'So are you?'

'Am I?'

'Gonna die, silly!'

'We're all going to die some day, Ellabella,' I say, squinting into the sky. 'But hopefully I'll be really old when it's time for me to go to heaven.'

'Heaven must be full of old people.'

I fake a smile for Ella's sake. 'Mostly old people. But not always.'

Ella giggles.

'So, do Mummy and Daddy and Nanny always talk about grown-up stuff in front of you?'

'They thought I was *sleeping*.' She presses a finger to her lips. 'Mummy says you're having a baby. Will the baby go to heaven? Like Max?'

'I hope not.' I start threading a daisy chain to make a bracelet.

'Can it be a girl?'

'Maybe,' I say. 'Would you like it to be a girl?'

'Yes! I hope it's a girl. We could call her Susie.' She sits up and kneels down beside me, and I fasten the bracelet around her wrist. 'If you die, we'll all have to help take care of the baby because that's what families do. If it's a girl, she can have Wally giraffe. I don't play with him any more.'

'What makes you think… How do you know this, Ella?'

'Nanny,' she says. 'Nanny told Uncle Nick and then Nanny told Mummy and then Mummy told Daddy.'

'Oh. While you were *sleeping*?'

She giggles melodically and cups a hand over her mouth. 'Yeah. But don't tell Mummy.'

*

Two hours later, Caitlin and I are unpacking groceries in her kitchen while Ella and Ethan are happily seated at the outdoor table playing with Play-Doh. After our argument the last time I was here, things haven't been the same.

'So, how are you feeling?' I ask. With her last two pregnancies, she told me about every single itch, pain, cramp and craving, but this time I know nothing about how things are progressing. In a way I suppose that's been my fault. I've been the one keeping my distance.

'I'm fine,' she replies dismissively, which implies the exact opposite of course. Caitlin, like me, is a terrible liar.

'Was everything okay with your last scan? Did you find out the sex?'

'Yes, all okay. And no, not this time.'

'Mark didn't want to find out? I thought he said—'

'We didn't find out, Paige. Okay?' So much for the tiptoeing around. This is regular old Caitlin speaking.

'Woah,' I say, holding up my hands.

'Sorry, I'm very tired at the moment. Mark's been working long hours and spending a lot of time renovating the cottage. We're in the final stages now, thank goodness.'

'If you need a hand with things, all you need to do is ask. I'm here.'

Caitlin tips some peaches into the fruit bowl. 'I think you have enough going on right now. But thank you.' She straightens up as if to regain her composure and then empties the contents of another shopping bag onto the counter.

'If there's something wrong, you know you can tell me.'

She flips around to face me. 'I don't know where you got the idea something's wrong, because there's not, but I do wish you'd drop it. I'm fine.'

'I'm sorry about what I said to you – about the whole surrogacy thing.'

With that, she starts busying herself by emptying sugar into a Tupperware container. 'I know you didn't mean it.' She briefly looks up and her eyes lock with mine. 'I'm sorry for what I said, too.'

We leave the conversation at that, and I take the carton of milk from the pantry and put it in the fridge. If she notices, she doesn't let on. 'Fine,' I say. 'If you say you're fine, then I suppose I will have to believe you.' I hold up a bag of Brussels sprouts. 'Please don't tell me your kids actually eat these?'

'I pack Ella's lunch box with them.'

'Since when do kids love Brussels sprouts?'

'Since never,' she says.

I raise my eyebrows. 'Well, of course. They're…'

'Revolting.'

'Then why do you buy them?'

She shrugs. 'Mum used to. They're good for you. Varied diet and all that. They say if you expose children to a variety of different foods, it's good for them. So I do what I think is good for them.'

'You're an adult now. You get to choose to not feed your family Brussels sprouts. Even if the literature states you should. Just because research says something doesn't mean it's going to happen. The research can be wrong. The so-called experts can get it wrong.'

Caitlin's eyes widen. 'Hold on,' she says, raising a hand. 'Are we still talking about Brussels sprouts here?'

'I'm not going to die,' I say, helping myself to a peach. 'I know you're scared but I don't want you to be scared. I want you to… be here… for me.'

She blinks slowly, taking the news in. 'So you've decided, then?' she whispers.

'I'm in the process of deciding. I have an appointment booked with a counsellor at a clinic to talk about things.'

'An abortion clinic? Do you… want me to come with you?'

'Thanks, but this is something I need to do alone. And I really need you on my side, regardless of what I decide,' I say. I bite into my peach. 'Because I'm fairly sure I want to keep the baby.'

'And Nick?'

'Does not want what I want.' I gaze out the window. 'But not because we want different things. We both want *a* baby. The problem is *this* pregnancy.'

'My God, Paige.' Her hand rises to her mouth. 'How can you be disagreeing on something like this? How can you decide on something like this with him not being on board? Have you thought this through? I mean, properly thought this through? You still have a few weeks before you need to make a final decision. It's not too late…'

I swallow a mouthful of peach. 'Look at them, Caitlin.' I point out the window to Ella and Ethan. 'They're here because of you.'

I tear my gaze away and let it fall on her belly. Caitlin's hand slides over it. 'They're here because of me… but they also *need* me.'

Of course Caitlin is going to take Nick's side. She's not the one that's childless.

'I think it's better that we don't talk about this together,' I say sharply. Too sharply, perhaps.

'You're impossible,' she mutters.

'Don't treat me like I'm stupid, Caitlin.'

'I'll do it. I'll be a surrogate for you when the timing's right. I'll give you what you want, Paige. If you can't do this down the track, I'll help you.'

The problem is, I don't want her help. I don't want anyone's help. I want this baby.

I meet Mum and Caitlin at the local farmer's market around the corner from Mum and Dad's place on Sunday morning. The two of them are trying out home-made hand cream at one of the stalls when I show up.

'How's the rest of your week been?' asks Caitlin casually as we stop at another stall, this one for honey.

'You don't need to be weird about this. I don't want either of you to tiptoe around me. What I need from both of you is for you to act normal. Be normal, act normal.'

'Sure,' says Mum, a little too chirpily. 'So, what's new?' she says as she selects a container of honeycomb and hands over a ten-dollar bill to the vendor.

'Our baby is as big as a blueberry. Did you know that?'

'No,' says Mum, sounding interested. 'What about yours, Caitlin?'

Caitlin shoots her a look.

'Oh, Caitlin, yours is more like the size of a butternut pumpkin.'

'Paige…' says Caitlin quietly. 'We really need to sort this out. I thought we'd moved on.' She pauses. 'What did they say at the clinic?'

'Yum. Poffertjes,' I say, spotting the food trucks. 'Have you both eaten?'

'Uh, no, not yet. Should we get some?' suggests Mum.

'Definitely. Yes,' says Caitlin.

'About what you said before,' says Mum as we stand in queue waiting. 'So, have you? *Decided*?'

'I think I have.'

'Right, but are you still considering the other option at all?' asks Caitlin.

'Yes, but I'm pretty sure I know what I want.' After I say this, I realise I'm not totally sure about things. I *think* I know what I want but *committing* to that decision is a step I'm not yet ready to take.

'Where does Nick fit into all this?' asks Caitlin. 'I can't imagine he... Is he on board with this? I mean, he's a medical professional, so of course he's going to know what's best,' Caitlin deduces.

'I know you're both worried about me, but this isn't helping. And to be honest, I'd like to talk about what happens if—'

Caitlin stiffens. 'I'm sorry, Paige, but I can't do this. I can't talk to you about that right now. I think you're rushing into this decision. Too quick.'

'You can't "do this"?' I say, making air quotes. 'Really? Because *I* had an appointment the other day at a clinic to discuss an *abortion*. The woman there, she told me everything I needed to know and everything I could expect. And I listened. I *listened* to her. I considered it. I walked out of there thinking that maybe I could do it. Maybe I could do this thing and be okay with it. Maybe not right away, but maybe with time. But I got into the car and I put the key in the ignition, and all I could think of was how I felt about this baby.'

'But what if you leave us all behind? What are we supposed to do then? How are we going to live without you? And how are we going to live with ourselves knowing we didn't try to prevent it from happening?'

'Nobody is forcing me to take this risk.'

'Mum, say something! Tell her this is crazy!' says Caitlin.

Mum's face pales. 'Listen, honey, why don't you spend a bit more time talking to Nick about his concerns? Take it slow, listen to each other, think about the future and what it might be like for either of you.'

'Exactly,' says Caitlin. 'Ask him if he knows how often he should be changing a kitchen sponge or a set of bed sheets before you essentially ask him to become a single parent to your baby.'

'There are millions of amazing and happy single parents in the world, Caitlin. You're overstepping the line.'

'Just telling it how it is.'

'How dare you?' I spit. 'Do you have any idea how hard it was for me to show up at a clinic to discuss and seriously consider an abortion? After I gave birth to a baby that was not breathing and I nearly lost my life? He died inside of me! You held him in your arms! My life will *never* be the same after losing him, so you tell me how I am supposed to carry the guilt of willingly losing another baby.' I throw my hands in the air. 'Go on, tell me. Tell me how I am supposed to do that.'

'Sweetheart, calm down, pleads Mum. 'This isn't healthy for you.'

Caitlin is staring at me, tears streaming down her cheeks.

'Next, please!' calls the guy in the food truck.

Through gritted teeth I tell her, 'You're my sister. You're supposed to be here for me. You're supposed to tell me you'd be here for *Nick* too.'

'Next!' the vendor repeats.

Mum takes me and Caitlin by our wrists, the way she used to when she'd march us out of a shop for touching what we shouldn't have, and we step out of the queue.

'Weekly! You're supposed to change bed sheets weekly! But not everybody always does!' I shake my arm free from Mum, who's still holding onto me.

'You know what, Mrs Perfect? I am sick and tired of you rubbing it in with your perfect life and your way always being the right way. Not everyone has or aspires to have the kind of life you have. And you might have a perfect house and perfect kids and a perfect husband, but—'

'Actually, Paige, nobody has a perfect life, least of all me. You know nothing of my so-called perfect life.'

I cross my arms. 'Oh, please.'

'Well, you wouldn't be saying that if you…' She stops herself and her body suddenly stiffens.

'If I what?' I demand.

She presses her lips together. 'Nothing. It's nothing you need to concern yourself with.'

'Oh, so you know all about my business and you're allowed to interfere in it, but you can't even tell us what's going on with you?'

'What's going on with her?' asks Mum.

'This has something to do with the night Nick and I babysat for you, doesn't it?'

Caitlin crosses her arms. 'This isn't the right time or place. We have more pressing things to worry about in this family right now.'

'Oh, like what?'

'Like you,' she says.

'Wow,' I say. 'I'm done here. Sorry, Mum, but I need to leave.'

I reach the main road around the corner and start gasping for air. My bus comes to a stop across the street. On it is an advertisement for wristwatches currently on sale.

Time is running out, reads the advertisement.

I catch the third bus home. The one promoting seat belt safety. *Keep your kid safe*, it says.

CHAPTER THIRTY-THREE

Nick

I'm in between appointments when Sarah pokes her head round the door and tells me there's someone insisting on seeing me. 'Apparently it's urgent. Her name's Caitlin Callaway. Is that your sister-in-law?'

'Show her in,' I tell her.

Moments later, Caitlin practically storms in and whips the patient chair out, plonking herself in it.

'Nick, this is serious.'

'I know. I know it's serious.'

'No, I mean it's beyond. My dad is sleeping on the sofa. The sofa! In over thirty years of marriage, my dad has never by choice slept anywhere in the house but his bedroom. And do you want to know how many nights he's been taking up residence on the sofa?'

'How many?' I ask, going along with it.

'Seven. Mum's a mess. She doesn't even *want* him back in the bed!'

'I got the impression they weren't seeing eye to eye.'

'Nick, they've progressed to the silent treatment. My mother, who has advocated my entire life for "open communication", is not only ignoring my dad, she isn't even cooking for him since his risotto went cold or some stupid reason.'

I think to myself there's no danger of David starving to death but I get her point.

'Listen, Caitlin, I understand you're concerned, but I have another six patients to see today. Is there anything else you need?'

'This is an emergency. I've called Ryan.'

'Right, and you need me to pick him up from the airport? When does he arrive?'

Caitlin gives me a look that says, *Why would you get that impression?* 'No, he can get an Uber. A couple of weeks. He can't get here any sooner, which means I'm going to have to hold the fort in the meantime.' She groans.

I sit back. The only thing to do is wait for her to run out of steam.

'What I'm trying to say is you need to do *something*. Paige won't listen to Dad, she won't listen to me, and whatever approach you're taking, she's obviously not listening to you either. This is a hospital – you must know some husbands that have lost their wives that can talk to her. Make her see some sense?'

I let out a sigh. If this is the best suggestion Caitlin has got, we're all in trouble.

'This is a children's hospital. No dead mothers here.'

'Nick, I know my sister. There is every chance she is going to make a decision and stick to it. We can't let her, we just can't.' She pauses. 'I even offered to help. I'm serious. I'll be a surrogate for you both if that's what it comes to.'

'Thank you,' I say, trying not to sound blindsided, which is exactly how I feel. 'That's… uh… that's very generous.'

'So what's your plan?' Yep, this is Caitlin, straight to the point.

'I'm trying. She might need a bit more time to come around. We've got an appointment with the cardiologist – maybe that will help her reconsider things.'

'I know my sister. It won't. So you're going to have to find another way because this is the last resort.'

I nod, knowing that what Caitlin is telling me is right. And I feel sick at the thought of what it means.

*

I'm outside, hosing down the driveway, when Hope turns up. 'Hey, is Paige home from Windsor Lakes yet?' She stops in her tracks and takes in the sight of me. 'God, Nick, how are you doing? You look like you haven't slept in days.'

Never mind what I look like. I *feel* like I haven't slept in days. 'She should be home soon. Want a coffee?'

She follows me inside and deposits the foil-wrapped tray she's carrying on the bench. 'I brought over some food for you both.'

'You shouldn't have.'

'Oh, it's nothing special.' She winks. 'Just some lasagne I picked up from Romano's on the way. Don't tell Paul, he thinks I make it from scratch.'

'No, he doesn't,' I say, smirking.

'Yes, he does,' she insists.

I waggle my eyebrows. 'Why don't you go home and ask him?'

'I knew there was a reason I loved that man,' she says, chuckling. She claps her hands together. 'So, she's leaning towards keeping the baby. You don't think she should. Are you okay or is that the dumbest question I could ask you?'

Hope makes her way to the oven, turns it on and slides the tray of lasagne in. 'Yes? No? Getting there? Do I need to arrange a weekend away for you and Paul?'

I give her a half-hearted smile. 'Not at the moment. But thanks for the offer.'

'Okay, Bellbrae. Talk to me. Or Paul. We're here for you.'

I rub the stubble on my face. 'There's nothing much to talk about. I can't let her do it and I don't think she's going to change her mind.'

'Exactly. So we're all going to need to accept the decision she makes and support her. Aren't we?'

I clear my throat. 'Maybe not.'

Hope shuts the oven door and gives me a piercing look. 'What do you mean by that?'

'Actually, I was planning to call you. I wanted to talk to you about something – as a friend.' I steel myself, not quite knowing how she's going to react. 'A legal matter.'

Hope's brow wrinkles as Paige steps through the door and into the kitchen. Her timing couldn't have been better if she'd planned it.

'Hey! Is that lasagne I can smell?'

Victoria's waiting room smells like lemon essential oil and fresh paint. Two men are working in the far-right corner, laying paint-splattered cotton sheets on the floor, while another stirs the contents of a tin with a stick. All the artwork has been removed from the walls, aside from a small poster affixed to the reception counter that says: *Heart failure. Recognise the signs!* Paige switches seats so she doesn't have to look at it.

Paige and I sit next to each other, flicking through old magazines and calendar appointments on our phones until Victoria finally calls us in.

'Take a seat. Wherever you like,' she says, motioning to the grey fabric sofa. Her receptionist, Fiona, shuffles towards the small round table in front of us with a jug of water before leaving the room. I claim the seat closest to the window, next to Paige. She sits on her hands, something she always does when she's nervous.

'Hi, Paige. Nick, good to see you,' says Victoria, taking a seat opposite us.

'Likewise,' I reply.

'Work treating you well?'

I glance in Paige's direction. She seems terrified. 'Yeah, it's great.'

Victoria nods before turning her attention to Paige. She gives a tight but warm smile and says, 'Paige, how are you feeling about everything?'

'A little nauseated,' she replies quickly, and then she blushes, realising this isn't what Victoria means. She slips her hands out from underneath her and starts fiddling with them.

'Did you manage to have the date scan?'

I reach across and clasp my hand over Paige's.

'Yes. I'm seven weeks.' She hands Victoria the envelope with the ultrasound results and her expected due date.

Victoria accepts it and jots down some notes. 'Okay, so it's early. And how are you going with the new meds? Any Issues?'

'So far so good.'

'Any general changes with how you're feeling?'

She shakes her head.

'No symptoms?'

'Nope.'

'That's good. I'd like you to come in right away if you experience any symptoms at all from the checklist I gave you. Any sort of difficulty breathing while lying on your back, shortness of breath, especially on exertion, palpitations, swelling. If you feel out of sorts in any way, best to get checked out, okay?'

'Yes. Of course.'

'Good. So I took a look at the blood test results, where we checked your plasma BNP levels again. High levels of this hormone in your blood essentially tells us whether you're experiencing heart failure. If you do continue with this pregnancy, we would be looking to monitor you very closely with regular echoes as well. I'd be looking to repeat these tests in four weeks.'

This is where I want to jump in. I let out a discreet cough and try to speak but Paige jumps in with her question first.

'It's safe for me to keep the pregnancy and see you in four weeks then? With regular monitoring, things should be okay? Is that what you're saying?'

Victoria puts her pen down. 'Not exactly. We should talk about this now. I know that some of this would have been explained to you when you were in hospital last year, but I'm going to go through it again for you because I think it's important for you to be as informed as possible about the situation.' She pauses again. 'Because you… and Nick… *are* going to need to make a decision.'

Paige lets go of my hand and Victoria pretends not to notice. 'Oh. Yes. Sure.'

'I'd like to explain some of the implications of cardiomyopathy, to give you the chance to ask any questions.'

Paige nods, encouraging Victoria to continue.

'Do you remember what I told you about PPCM and eventual pregnancy?'

'Yes, you said that pregnancy was contraindicated until my ejection fraction was at least fifty-five per cent. That it would be too risky otherwise. That's the number we agreed on.'

'That's right. However, we still need to think about the likelihood of a recurrence given your history. We consider the safe zone for pregnancy to be fifty-five per cent because anything less than that is going to mean your heart isn't as strong as it needs to be to carry a pregnancy to term. During pregnancy, your heart works harder – your blood volume increases by thirty to fifty per cent. And when we're looking at cardiomyopathy – when we literally look at the size and function of the heart on the monitor – we're dealing with an already enlarged heart size.' She shows Paige a diagram she's been sketching.

'I understand,' she says quietly.

'So when we're looking at a case like this, where your EF levels aren't where we'd like them to be, we, as medical professionals, need to look at the risks involved – not only the maternal risk but also that of the foetus. The added strain that pregnancy puts on a woman's body is something that puts you in a precarious situation.' She folds her hands. 'Paige, what I'm trying to say here is that from what I've been able to determine, there's a high rate of relapse and about a fifty per cent chance of maternal fatality, and in cases like yours…'

Paige clenches her jaw, nails digging into her palms as we wait for Victoria to confirm our worst fears.

'There is a chance your heart, with time, will get back to where we need it to be. That means there is every possibility that in the future, you and Nick will have the chance to become parents.'

'I'm sorry, I still don't think I understand what you're trying to say. You're saying there's a fifty per cent chance I could survive pregnancy?'

'The risk is way too high, that's what she's saying,' I say, interjecting.

'Hold on a second. She didn't say that. And that's not what I asked. It's not a sure thing. That I'd die, I mean?' She pins Victoria with her gaze.

'Maybe you could explain that—'

Victoria raises a hand to stop me from saying anything more.

'From a professional standpoint, I need to emphasise that attempting to carry a baby to term in these circumstances is extremely high risk, especially when we look at your history and how close we came to losing you with your first pregnancy. We need to consider the way your body reacted and responded to the drugs we gave you. We doctors don't have crystal balls and we don't know how things will go this time. Your heart could go into failure sooner this time around. What I wanted to reassure you with today is that there is hope, and you don't need to rule out the possibility that you may become parents once you've recovered fully.'

I rub the stubble on my face. I need Victoria to be as clear as possible here. No skirting around the issue. 'What's your advice?

Given the circumstances?' I glance over at Paige briefly. She isn't going to be impressed with this question.

'I know this isn't what you want to hear and it's not easy for me to say this. I discussed your case with some colleagues, both here and overseas.' She pauses and I catch the brief expression of sorrow that flickers on her face, like a quick flash of a camera, and then I know. I *know* what is coming. 'As a woman, and as your doctor, there really is no easy way to say this to you.' She uncrosses her legs and then says, 'I recommend terminating the pregnancy.'

Paige lets out a noise – a sigh, or is it a small moan? I can't be sure, but then Victoria is sitting next to her and her hand is on her knee, which is more comfort than I can offer her right now. 'I wouldn't be recommending interrupting a pregnancy unless I thought it was going to be the safest option for you and your developing baby,' she tells Paige gently.

'I'm sorry, but she's right,' I say quietly when Paige looks up at me for confirmation.

At first I think she might burst into tears, but she takes a moment for the information to sink in and then she stands up and snatches her handbag from the floor. 'Thanks for your time, but you can tell your colleagues and specialist team that my baby and I don't want to be interrupted. We want to be left alone!'

Both Victoria and I jump out of our seats. Victoria moves closest to her, one hand on her hip, an expression of concern on her face, the other hand rubbing Paige's upper arm.

'I really am sorry, Paige, but I have to be honest with you.'

'Paige—' I say.

'You're all for *interrupting* things. You agree with Victoria.'

'We're dealing with the facts as best we can. We're on the same side here.'

'Well, it doesn't feel like it.'

And just like that, right in front of Victoria, Paige and I are arguing again.

CHAPTER THIRTY-FOUR

Paige

The flowers in Imogen's waiting room are wilting. They aren't completely shrivelled, but a few rogue rose petals have found their way onto the coffee table.

'Paige?' calls a female voice.

Jerking my head up, I notice Imogen standing there, a gentle smile resting on her face. She's wearing a floral tunic with a pair of ankle boots, and her wavy russet-brown hair is swept into a loose bun.

'Come on in.' She motions to the door and I follow the scent of pear into her office. Imogen always has soft music playing in the foyer and a scented candle burning in her room. She sits down on the sofa and crosses her legs, and I sink into my regular place opposite her.

'The flowers are wilting,' I say quietly as I reach for one of the cushions and run my finger over the piping.

'You mean the ones in the waiting room? They get replaced every Monday.'

'They're dying.'

'It's Friday. They'll be fine until...' She uncrosses her legs and observes me for a moment. I'm trying to hold myself together, but Imogen has seen me at my most vulnerable, and it's impossible to hide my feelings from her now.

'Paige?'

'I'm pregnant.'

Imogen blinks in surprise. 'Pregnant,' she echoes, as if trying the word on for size.

'Mmmhmm.'

'A surprise?'

'Mmmhmm,' I repeat. 'Seven weeks.'

'Still processing?'

'Mmmhmm.'

She scribbles a note onto her pad before setting it down. 'Okay, so tell me about it,' she says in the casual tone she always uses.

I sip my water, thinking about what I want to say, but all I can think of are the blooms. 'Nick rarely buys me flowers. He used to, when we were dating, and then for a while after we first got married. But now he usually buys them for special occasions. I always keep the cards. I store them in a shoebox in my wardrobe.' I smile to myself. 'I've kept every single card, letter and memo. Sometimes when he leaves for work he leaves a Post-it note on his side of the bed for me because he knows how hard it is to have to wake up without him beside me when he's on call. Sometimes I can barely make out his handwriting. Those notes – those tiny reminders of how much he loves me – they mean so much.' I feel the tears prick my eyes. 'I don't think he knows this, but I keep them. I keep them all. I'm on my fifth shoebox.'

'Why do you keep them?' she asks.

'I've never really given much thought to why I keep them. It's kind of like how my mum kept all the cards my sister and I gave her when we were growing up. But I think that… I think I hold onto Nick's notes so that one day we'll have a reminder – and our children will have a reminder of us and… how much we loved each other.'

Imogen waits for me to continue.

'I don't remember the flowers once I toss them out. Once they're gone, they're gone. But somehow I need to find a way to still be there, even if I'm not there…'

Imogen blinks at me, registering my words. 'I'm hearing you, Paige, and I know where you're going with this, but why don't we unpack this first.'

Imogen asks me what the doctors have told me and I explain the risks to her.

'Tell me, how did Nick react to the news? How's he feeling about things?'

'Nick, the doctors… well, actually, pretty much everyone I know except Mum and Hope are telling me to end the pregnancy.'

'And how are you feeling about things?'

I give a deep sigh. 'I understand why they're saying what they're saying. The thing is, if I terminate this pregnancy, I don't know how I'd go back to living life in the same way as before, knowing I did that.' I frown at her and shrug.

'Let me tell you something. The emotional distress you're experiencing right now is normal. Motherhood goes hand in hand with an innate and very strong sense to protect. These things don't always need to be logical. So your feelings are your feelings, and you can give yourself permission to own them.'

'I think I love this baby.'

Imogen nods. 'And I believe that you do. Women experience love for their babies at vastly different points: early pregnancy, late pregnancy, at birth or even much later once they've had a chance to get to know the infant. What you're feeling is real, and that's okay. You're allowed to feel it.'

'It would be easier if I didn't. I told Nick I'd at least consider the alternative. I had an appointment with a counsellor at an abortion clinic.'

'So you're considering the alternative? You've weighed up the risks to your own life?'

'I don't want to die, but when I think about how we lost Max the way we did, I don't think I can do it. I'd never judge a woman for terminating a pregnancy, but for me personally, I can't seem to separate the emotion here.'

I stare at the abstract painting on the wall for a long time.

'Is there a chance that continuing this pregnancy could risk *both* your lives?' she asks.

'Yes. The doctors are aware of the issue though, and I'll be given proper monitoring. I know what to look out for in terms of heart failure symptoms this time.'

'What if the worst happened to you? Where would that leave Nick? Have you thought about what that might look like?'

It is the unthinkable, and even briefly allowing myself to imagine what it would be like for Nick to care for our baby without me sends a crack through my heart. It would be unfair. For everyone.

I wring my hands together and twirl my wedding band around. 'It's not only my decision, is it?'

'If your baby makes it and you don't, your husband is going to be left to pick up the pieces.'

'He would be a great dad,' I offer.

Imogen presses her lips together and then pauses, as if she's thinking about what to say and how to say it. 'I don't doubt that for a second. The thing is, does he want to be a single dad – without you?'

I swallow uncomfortably, feeling the hopelessness of this situation tighten around me like an impending storm.

'It's not about what we want. None of us *wanted* this.'

'No, I know, of course not,' she says, shaking her head. 'It's something to consider. The fact is there are going to be implications beyond this one decision, and those implications might not involve you.' Imogen pours herself a glass of water. 'I know this conversation is uncomfortable so I think we should wrap things up for today. I want you to keep my number handy and call me – call me any time, day or night, if you need to. Okay?'

'Okay,' I reply. But a phone call with Imogen isn't what I need. What I need is a way to make a final decision. Because once I make it, that would be that, and there'll be no turning back.

'What are you doing?' asks Nick the next evening as he joins me in the living room following a fourteen-hour shift. I'm sitting on the floor, legs crossed, watching back-to-back episodes of *Gilmore Girls*. I've lost count of how many times I've watched this series, always slightly in awe of the kind of relationship Lorelai and Rory had together as mother and daughter.

It's an unusually cold day and it's been raining outside. Nick let a draft in when he opened the front door and I can still feel the cold air radiating from his body as he bends down to kiss me before plonking himself down on the sofa.

'I got these photos developed this afternoon. They've been on the memory cards since forever.' I sit down next to him and show him a photo of us together. It was taken on one of our very first dates to Max Brenner. We sat in that chocolate bar booth together sipping on hot chocolate until the owner turned off the lights and we had no choice but to leave. Nick walked me home in the rain – slowly, the whole trip taking us a little over an hour. And when our lips met when we said goodbye, our bodies shivering in the cold, I invited Nick in. We've been inseparable since.

Nick stares at the photo before his eyes travel to the ones spread out on the floor.

'Uh, so why now?' he asks. He pops the cap off a bottle of beer and takes a sip.

'I, uh, I just felt like it.' I flick to the next photo. 'Do you remember this night? When we drove all the way to Ocean Grove and then realised we'd made the accommodation booking for the wrong weekend? We ended up sleeping on the beach and then we drove back home the next day.' I laugh, recalling the memories.

'No, you didn't just feel like it,' says Nick, piercing me with his gaze.

I tilt my head, trying to gauge what he means. 'Yes, I did.'

'Uh-uh. I know what you're doing.' He fiddles with the beer cap.

'Well it's pretty obvious, isn't it?' I motion to the photos on the floor.

'You've decided, haven't you? So that's it?'

'What? No,' I say, shaking my head. 'It's complicated. I'm trying to find a way to…' What I want to say is that my session with Imogen has left me feeling more confused than ever. I can't properly explain why I've decided to drag out all our old photos but it seemed like the right thing for me to do. Yes, my first instinct is telling me that I want to keep this baby, but I can't fully decide until I make myself think about all the things at stake. My life. Nick's life. Our life together.

'I knew it. Once you get something in your head…' He picks at a piece of lint on the sofa.

'Hey, what I was going to say is that I went and saw Imogen.'

'Oh? And? Were the photos her suggestion then?' he asks, gesturing to the floor.

'You know she mostly sits there and listens.'

'I think you're doing this because you still feel guilty about Max and you're more scared about having an abortion than losing your life. It wasn't your fault.' His eyes land on one of the pictures in front of his left shoe, the one of us in a hot air balloon in the Yarra Valley. Silence lingers in the air until he eventually picks up where he left off. 'There is nothing you could have done to prevent what happened with Max, and I know you were making really great progress in getting past all of that, but I think this has brought up a lot of stuff for you.'

'Mothers do things to protect their children all the time. They make decisions based on what's best for their kids. Look at Emily! She's travelling to the other side of the world because in the sea of a billion guys out there, she's trying to find the father of her unborn child.'

'Are you serious? You're comparing our situation to Annoying Emily?'

'That's not what I'm doing. You're missing the entire point.' I push my thumb through the hole I've made in my sleeve to the satisfying sound of thread breaking away from the fabric.

'Well, you're the one who brought her up.'

'Oh my God, I can't believe we're arguing about Annoying Emily.' I get up from the sofa and pick up Piper's water bowl to refill it in the kitchen. Nick follows me.

'Our problems have nothing to do with Annoying Emily; they have everything to do with your life.'

I finish filling the bowl and flick off the tap.

'You know what?' continues Nick, his voice rising. 'Annoying Emily isn't annoying. You're the one who's annoying.'

'We're yelling and babies in the womb can hear!'

'Not until eighteen weeks they can't.'

'See? Annoying!' I tip the water from Piper's bowl down the sink, set it on the bench with a clang and storm to the bedroom.

'Paige, wait!' says Nick, trailing behind me.

I slam the door behind me and flop onto the bed. I wait for Nick to knock, to let himself in, to comfort me, make things better – easier. But there is no knock. Instead, I hear the tinkling of keys and the front door opening and closing, right before the car motor tells me my husband has driven away. Who'd have thought that becoming parents would potentially cost not only a life but what it means to be *us*.

CHAPTER THIRTY-FIVE

Nick

Paige and I are in the cereal aisle the following morning, doing our weekly grocery shop. She picks up a box of Weet-Bix and tosses it into the trolley. I take it out and replace it with a box of Crunchy Honey Weet-Bix Bites.

'Bites?' she asks, eyeing the box with suspicion. I don't blame her for questioning what is, in fairness, strange behaviour on my part. I'm a creature of habit when it comes to my breakfast choices. It's either Weet-Bix, cold toast or an apple, with no room for negotiation.

I shrug. 'I want the Bites.'

'But you don't like them. I bought them for you when they first came out. You said they're too sweet. You—'

'I want the Bites,' I reply curtly, avoiding eye contact. My mood is not helped by the fact I'm running on less sleep than usual.

'But you don't *like* the Bites,' she mutters under her breath.

'I think I can make my own decisions about my breakfast cereal choices, Paige.'

She inhales deeply, grips the trolley handles and moves forward, choosing to ignore me. We make our way to the toiletries aisle. She picks up a can of hairspray, two bulk packs of toilet paper and three tubes of toothpaste. I do not know why we need that many tubes of toothpaste. I also don't know why she's stockpiling toilet paper and hairspray. Not only do I not understand Paige's shopping habits, I don't know how to do a multitude of other things. For example, I have no idea who our cars are insured with. I don't know what products to use to clean an oven. I am hopeless at changing bed sheets and have never negotiated a better rate for our mortgage repayments.

'Do we need all of those?' I ask.

'Uh, yeah. We're almost out of toothpaste.'

'But you have three tubes.'

'And? Since when have you taken this kind of interest in my grocery shopping choices?'

'Do we really need them all? There are only two of us,' I counter.

Paige's body stiffens. 'What's the matter with you?'

'I don't understand why you need to buy three tubes of toothpaste when one will do. It's not like we live in a remote area 200 kilometres from the nearest supermarket.'

'That's not the point. I always stock up. So if we run out we have extras. We've been living together for years. You already know I do this. Why is this an issue all of a sudden?'

'In case of an emergency?'

'Well, yeah. Kind of. Why are we even standing in aisle six discussing this?'

'That's not how I'd do it,' I say, reaching for a stick of deodorant. I toss it from one hand to the other while I think about this. I am potentially going to be the one having to work all of this stuff out and more. On my own.

'Hold on. What do you mean by that?' Paige manoeuvres the trolley forward so a woman can pass by.

I reach for two more sticks of deodorant and throw them in the trolley. 'Actually, while we're at it, let's make it five or six,' I say, sweeping several cans into the trolley at once.

'Nick,' Paige whispers, reaching for my arm. 'What the hell is going on with you?'

I turn to face her. 'I'd run out of toothpaste and toilet paper and deodorant.'

'But how is that a problem?' she says, searching my eyes. I blink – once, twice, three times. I don't want to do it alone. 'It's not your problem and it won't be your problem,' I tell her, this time reaching for the shaving cream. 'It'll be *my* problem.'

With that, I forge ahead towards the checkout. We line up behind a woman trying to unpack her trolley with a baby in a carrier. She struggles to reach for a pack of baby wipes in the corner of her trolley.

'Here, let me help you,' I say, retrieving it for her.

'Thanks,' she says.

My eyes fall on the baby, who can't be older than a few weeks. Paige and I both take in the infant's tiny features, translucent eyelids, fuzzy facial hair, apricot-coloured cheeks and a hand-knitted beanie. Eventually, the mother catches us looking and smiles at us as if to say, *Yes, I know, isn't she perfect?*

Paige and I exchange a glance, our eyes locking, saying everything our words can't. We miss our son. We wish things didn't have to be this way. Here we are, meeting in the middle, for one brief moment over this beautiful, healthy baby. And then, as quickly as it's here, it's gone. I rake a hand through my hair. 'I need a coffee. I'll meet you at the car,' I say, excusing myself.

After I pose my question to Hope, there will be no taking the words back. And no matter how I try to justify it, it isn't going to make me popular.

'What are you really doing here, Nick?' she asks as she opens the fridge. Hope's tone is friendly but direct. I've been here for around ten minutes and the conversation hasn't progressed from the weather, the news, Ollie's sleeping habits and how well Melbourne City is doing. She takes two bottles of Coke out of the fridge and nudges the door closed with her leg before handing me one.

I twist the cap off the bottle. 'There's no easy way to ask you this. I want to know if...' Hope keep her eyes trained on mine as I search for the words. 'I want to know if there's a way I can stop this from happening.'

'Mmm.' She nods for me to elaborate.

'I need to know what legal avenues might be available to me.' There it is. I've said it. It's out in the open and there's every chance Hope is going to tell me to leave.

'Oh God. Nick, you can't be serious.' Hope twists the cap off her bottle and spins it around in her fingers before looking up at me again. 'You really are serious, aren't you?'

My jaw tightens. 'I wish I wasn't.'

'Sit down, Nick,' she says, moving a soft toy off the kitchen stool. 'I'm a little rusty on things but here's what I can tell you. According to the Family Law Act, a baby does not exist until it's born.'

'Right.' I know this already, of course, but I let Hope continue.

'So if you're asking what I think you're asking, you need to be totally aware that this could completely destroy everything you have with Paige. I mean, is that what you want? Is that what you're willing to risk? Because when she finds out, and she *will* find out, there's no turning back. This would be the ultimate betrayal.'

I know what's at stake. Of course I know. I don't *want* to do this. But I feel like I have no other choice. I rub my throbbing temples; the headache that started between my eyes this morning is making it hard to focus. 'I've been turning it over and over in my mind, and at this point I need to know whether it's possible. Is there anything I can do?'

'This isn't the kind of law I practise, Nick, you know that.'

'Yes, but there's a reason I came to you and didn't go straight to a family lawyer.'

She nods. 'I know. And I'm glad you came to me because someone else might take your money and not tell you that that he or she really loves Paige and does not want to see her suffer any more than she already has.'

She lets the words sit there, and they do exactly what she wants them to. They seep in, weighing on me. I am officially the world's worst husband.

'Technically, you have standing to make a claim. That would involve making an application to the Family Court to make a decision about the fate of the foetus,' she continues.

'So, what you're saying is, it can be done?'

'Well, it can, but you can't take a step like that without giving it more serious consideration. This is your wife we're talking about. And let's not overlook the fact that she's my best friend. Like I said, she will never forgive you if you go down this path.'

'I know that.' I've asked myself countless times whether I'm prepared to take this step. Whether losing Paige because of this is better than losing her all together. Will I hate myself for it? Probably. Will I hate myself if I do nothing and things go wrong? Definitely.

'You also need to be realistic about this because your prospects would be uncertain in the legal environment. Not to mention costly.'

'Money isn't an issue.'

'No, but your health and happiness are,' she says. 'At some point you need to let go and see how things land. And I know you, Nick. I know you don't want to lose your wife like this.'

She's right. I don't. But the alternative is unfathomable. I spin my bottle round in circles. 'Noted. But please tell me what I'd need to do if hypothetically I were to give this a try.' Facts. I need facts.

She sits there chewing her lip in contemplation, and when I think she isn't going to tell me, she gives a little shake of her head and starts talking. 'For a start, you'd need independent evidence – medical evidence – to prove the risk to the mother's life. Remember, the law doesn't support your desire for your wife to have an abortion for medical reasons. It's untested and, as far as I know, there are no precedents. You'd likely need to seek the advice of a family barrister before a lawyer would agree to act for you on something like this.'

'Okay, anything else?' I know I'm prodding now, but I need to know.

Hope lifts her hands up. 'Conversation ends here. I'm sorry, but I can't help you.'

I nod, understanding. 'Yes, of course.'

Hope looks me squarely in the eyes. 'You put me in the middle here, and I don't want to be in the middle. So I'll give you a week to consider things. If you don't tell her about this conversation or whatever intentions you might be having beyond this discussion by then, I will. And if she asks me anything, I won't lie for you.'

'Yes. Of course. That's a fair call. Thank you.'

She reaches for my hand and gives it a squeeze. 'You are a good man. A really good man. And I understand where you're coming from with this. But please, don't prove yourself to be the kind of man we thought we knew but didn't.'

I leave Hope's place, walk down two blocks and into the first bar I can find. After my second Scotch, I look up the number for the closest family law firm to the hospital I can find: Jim Lawrence & Associates.

I drain my glass, motion to the barman for another, dial Jim's office number and effectively wave my marriage goodbye.

Just checking in. Did you forget we were meeting up? Should I wait?

The following morning, I'm three kilometres away from home, jogging along the beach, when this text message pings on my phone. Miranda. If I don't go home to shower and change out of my gym clothes, I can meet her in twenty minutes.

Sorry, running late. I can be there in 20.

A second later, her reply comes:

Okay! I'll make sure your coffee's ready.

I spot Miranda at a table at the back of the The Split Bean café. Unlike me, she's put together and ready for a day's work.

'Jesus, Nick, you look like you pulled an all-nighter,' she says as I slide into the seat opposite her.

She's not wrong about that. I haven't slept a wink. My phone pings then with a message from Paige, wanting to know if I can meet her at The Butter Dish. She wants to discuss something important. Hope, I think to myself. What did I expect? Loyalty from Paige's best friend? An uneasy feeling swirls in the pit of my stomach.

'Nick?'

'Uh, I'll have a flat white, no sugar.'

Miranda smiles. 'I know. And it's right there in front of you, actually.'

She's right. There it is. A steaming-hot flat white with my name scribbled on the paper cup. 'Sorry.'

'Want to talk about it?'

Of course I want to talk about it. I am the world's worst husband. I'm a shitty person doing something unforgivable. If my wife doesn't die, I'm going to lose her anyway. Me, the guy who has lived his life trying not to screw up, has done just that.

My phone beeps with another message from Paige.

So? Is that a yes?

I type back:

Yes. See you there.

I am literally breaking out in a post-run sweat as my thumb hovers over the send button.

Miranda, sensing something is off, leans forward. 'Nick, can I ask you something? Does Paige know we've been seeing each other?'

I put my phone away. 'Ah, no, I haven't told her yet.' Another compelling argument for the shitty husband category, I think to myself.

'It might be a good time to tell her,' she suggests. 'Nobody likes being lied to, and Paige is feeling extremely fragile at the moment.'

This isn't so much a lie as it is an omission of information, I reason. But I know exactly what she means. 'I will. I plan to. I've needed some space... to wrap my head around it all.'

'Don't leave it too long, that's my advice,' she says, sipping on her coffee. 'So, what was it you wanted to talk to me about?'

'I'm thinking of meeting with a barrister.'

Miranda runs a finger along the rim of her cappuccino mug, and I get the impression she already knows what I'm going to say. 'Isn't that a little... I don't know? Extreme?'

'It's...' I need to land on the right word here. 'Necessary.'

'But is it?'

'I can't sit back and let her die, can I?'

'But you're not *letting* anyone die, Nick. This is a huge decision. And I can't begin to imagine how torn you both must be. But ultimately this rests with Paige. You can't be responsible for her like this – she's her own person and has every right to make a decision according to what feels true and right for her, no matter the consequences.'

'Her sister, my father-in-law… they expect me to resolve this, to make sure she changes her mind. Maybe this will help her see that the risks are real.'

'The way I see it, your job here is to support her. She knows the risks. I think she also knows there's a chance she may lose this baby too.'

'It'll be my fault.'

'It won't be,' she counters.

But that's the problem. It's on me. It always is. Ever since Zac, it always has been.

CHAPTER THIRTY-SIX

Paige

Half an hour passes, then an hour, and Nick still hasn't shown up. I keep my eyes trained on the family of three on the other side of the park: a mother, father and an infant, who keeps insisting they continue pushing him on the swing. And then I imagine Nick playing the role of a single father – of him bringing Piper and our child to the park without me. Will he remember to pack snacks for car rides? Will he enrol our baby in swimming classes at three months of age like I plan to? Will he spend time making sandcastles and say no to ice cream before dinner? And will he be able to give our son or daughter the kind of life that I dreamed of, one that will ensure that he or she grows up knowing that the life I had was one that I was willing to give up? And will that make a difference to making the pain of growing up without a mother less apparent?

I wait for Nick for over an hour. Finally, when I haven't heard from him, I send him another message.

> *How far off are you? It's getting a little cold. Should we meet somewhere else?*

Ten minutes later my phone buzzes.

> *I'm sorry. Walking out the door now. Give me half an hour.*

I find a spot for us in the back corner of The Butter Dish, the local eatery that Nick and I have been coming to since his university days. We always order the same thing here: two milkshakes – one chocolate, one vanilla – and a bowl of nachos to share. I place the order while I wait. When our food shows up, Nick still hasn't, and I dial his number. It rings out. I try again, and this time he denies the call. It goes straight to voicemail. I don't bother leaving a message. Instead, I wait five minutes, hide my number and then try again. He answers on the second ring.

'Hi, this is Nick.'

'Hey. It's me.'

'Who? Uh, Paige?'

'Ah, yep. Your wife.'

'I'm on my way.'

I can hear the clatter of plates and the buzz of voices in the background.

'Where *are* you?'

'I stopped by a café and I'm literally leaving now.'

'A café? For what? Why would you—'

'Coffee.'

'It couldn't wait until you came here?'

'I needed to talk to someone about something.' The background noise gets louder and then recedes. 'Give me twenty minutes. I'm sorry. Time slipped away.'

'I've been waiting for you for hours. Our order's on the table.'

'I know. I'm sorry. I'll be there as soon as I can,' he says, cutting me off. 'Promise.'

'Hey, sorry,' he says, twenty minutes later, giving me a quick peck on the lips before he pulls out a chair.

'You already apologised,' I say tersely. I bite down on my straw to stop myself making another smart comment. 'So, uh… how was your morning?' I say, neutrally. 'You went for a jog, obviously. And detoured past a café and now you're here.'

'Yes, I know.' He rubs his cheeks. 'Should we cut to the chase?' His brow is creased, and even as he sips on his milkshake, it doesn't smooth out.

I reach for a nacho. 'Okay, fine. Well, I've thought about it. About both sides. And I know you're concerned about the worst-case scenario, and I agree that if it comes to that, your world is going to change. *Our* world is going to change if I can't carry this pregnancy as long as I hope I'll be able to. I don't want you to be hurt. But I don't know how to get us out of this.'

'Well, it's pretty straightforward, isn't it?'

'Hear me out,' I say, pushing my plate aside. 'Losing Max was the hardest thing we've ever had to deal with. It derailed me. I mean, how can the way you see life not change after something like that, right? And every time I think about the possibility of putting myself through another loss by choice, I fall to pieces. How do I do that and come out the other side unscathed?' I glance over at the waiter serving the couple behind Nick and wait for him to step away before continuing. 'I know this decision is potentially going to put you in a situation that you don't want to be in. One you never dreamed of and never asked for. And I know it won't be easy if things don't work out for us the way we hoped they would. I know what it means to give this a shot. I know what this could lead to. And I also know you're stronger than me – you'll be able to deal with it. You'll be the best dad...' I feel my eyes going misty. 'I know this is a sharp turn in our lives. And I know what I'm asking of you.'

'God,' he says, blowing out a breath. 'What if I told you that, with time, the pain of going through something like a termination would fade? What if I promised to be there for you to help get you through it? I could take time off, change careers even... anything you want.'

'I still can't do it. I'm sorry, but I… can't… do it. I've decided.'

I want Nick to reach across the table for my hand, take it in his and tell me that he's on board.

Instead, he gives me a steely look.

'What? What is it?'

'I never thought I'd be saying this, but…' He draws a deep breath, his eyes trained on the salt and pepper shakers in the centre of the table. 'I don't know if I can be with you if you make this decision alone and make it through.'

It's like someone has robbed me of my breath. 'Huh? What did you say?'

'We're a couple, a married couple. A couple that's supposed to make decisions together. And if we can't see eye to eye on life's major curve balls, and you'd be prepared to disregard me and everyone else around you in a decision as big as this that affects both me and our future child, then I don't know how I'm going to get past that.'

'What? I can't believe I'm hearing this. What about me? Maybe I should be the one reconsidering our relationship based on the fact you want me to have an abortion!'

A pair of eyes from the table across the room follows us. I fire a scathing look in their direction.

'Because I don't want you to die! How am I going to explain it to our child *if* he or she survives? Have you thought about that? When he or she asks about you and you're not here – what am I supposed to say? I never signed up to be a single father, Paige! How do you expect me to take your place?'

'You tell the truth. You be you. You are enough.'

'Oh, come *on*, Paige! You and I both know that's bullshit. This is a selfish decision.'

'Not all kids have two loving parents and they turn out fine. I'm choosing to believe that he or she would be fine. Our family is tight, Nick. Everyone is going to be there for him or her.' I hesitate. 'And for you.'

'Really? Is that what you're telling yourself?' He crosses his arms and leans back in his chair.

'I don't really have any other choice.'

'So you admit that it's not the best outcome for this child, to be motherless.'

'Jesus, Nick, what do you think I am? Of course it's not the best outcome!'

'Then why set him or her up for a life without you in it? Why leave our child wondering about what it might have been like to be loved by you? This baby might never get to hear you say, "I love you." They might never know what your hopes and dreams are for them. Or how much you love being their mother.'

I'll find a way, I want to tell him. *I'll find a way to make this better*. Only I don't say that. Because I know it's going to be impossible to be there, to fill the void, to kiss it better, to laugh or cry or cuddle or watch with pride from the sidelines if things go wrong.

'Could we order a bottle of water?' asks Nick as a waiter passes by our table.

'Sure. Still or sparkling?'

Nick looks at me and shrugs, inviting me to answer for him.

'I don't know,' I reply, staring at the waiter dumbfounded.

Forty-five minutes later, when the waiter clears our barely touched meals from the table, I reach for a headache tablet. Nick motions for me to pass him the packet.

'So, this is it?' he says as he pops two pills from the packet. 'It's your body, so obviously you're the one who gets the final say here?'

The tablets that do not want to go down are dissolving at the back of my throat, leaving a bitter taste in my mouth. I pour more water and try again, swallowing hard.

'We've officially graduated from embryo to foetus, and yes, this is it.' I drain what's left in my glass, unable to meet Nick's gaze. And as I do this, I swear I hear him utter a string of muffled words under his breath that sound something along the lines of, *'This can't be it.'*

CHAPTER THIRTY-SEVEN

Nick

I spend the better part of the next morning doing two things in between patient consults: picking up the phone and putting it back down again. In theory, I know Miranda and Hope are right. But there is something bigger at play here, something I can't seem to get past – the fact that if I don't do this, if I don't take this step, I might live to regret it. And with that thought, I dial the number to Jim Lawrence & Associates and make the damn appointment with one of Jim's associates.

'Barry will be glad to see you at one o'clock next Friday,' says Bev, Barry's receptionist, who sounds like she's smoked three packs of cigarettes in a row. With what he charges, I'm sure he will be.

It's settled then. I have officially made an appointment to see a barrister. A family barrister. It's ironic, really, how all we ultimately want is to have a family, and here I am, potentially destroying the chance to have one.

Piper starts barking when she hears me enter the otherwise empty house. I take her outside, toss a ball around for a bit with her, and retreat back inside where I find a note stuck to the fridge with Paige's scribble on it.

Back soon! Just grabbing some bread and milk from the supermarket.

I lean against the kitchen bench, where Paige's collection of cookbooks is stacked in one corner. She's been collecting recipe books for years. Last night she spent an hour searching for a vintage cocoa chiffon cake recipe that she never managed to find. I think she mostly did it for the distraction. She ended up trying to make a croquembouche and never got far enough to even attempt the spun sugar. The squishy, eclair-like balls have collapsed onto themselves on the white porcelain plate next to the hob, and the mere sight of it causes my throat to tighten.

The house is quiet – too quiet – without her. But she's every-where. Reminders of her are everywhere: the pictures on the walls mounted in frames that took her eight months to find, the shoe closet she will never ever cull from, the books of recipes she will never master the art of following. The bottom line is that the world – my world – will not be the same without her. Nobody's will.

An hour later, Paige dumps the bag of groceries she's carrying next to the bench. So much for a quick dash to the supermarket for milk and bread. This is typical of Paige and it's something we normally laugh about. She can never come out of a store with less than an armload of shopping. 'There's still a pumpkin in the boot,' she says.

She goes to smile but pulls back like she's not sure if she should go through with it or not. It most likely has to do with the fact I'm having trouble looking her in the eyes. 'I'll go get the pumpkin,' I say, giving her a quick peck on the cheek.

'Nick,' she calls out softly as I start walking away. 'About last night, the whole decision thing. I know it's going to take you some time to get your head around things.'

I swallow back the lump forming in my throat and nod stiffly. 'Yes, I know. Can we park all the talk about it for tonight?'

She nods. 'Yeah, sure.'

'So, what's this?' she asks when I get back. She points to the line-up of ingredients on the bench and the recipe book flipped open to the page for the croquembouche recipe.

I shrug, 'I don't know. I thought, maybe if you're not too tired, I could help you figure out how to make it without that happening?' I point to the failure next to the hob.

She tilts her head, her eyes filled with intrigue. 'Really? You want to bake?'

'Yeah, I thought we could figure it out together.'

'Okay,' she says enthusiastically. She opens a drawer, tosses me an apron and it's almost like old times. Everything about this moment reminds me of what things were like for us before everything changed.

I pull the too-small apron over my head and pick up the measuring cup. 'Are you measuring or whisking?' I ask her.

'Thanks for believing in me, but I don't think I can be trusted to do the measuring. I'll read the instructions.'

I'm warming some milk in a pan when a phone rings.

'Oh, that's you,' says Paige, leaning over the bench to peer at my phone. 'Miranda Summers.'

The milk starts steaming. 'Oh, it's nothing urgent.'

Paige flips around, the phone in her hand. 'You sure you don't want to answer it?'

'No, no need. I can call her back.'

'Okay,' she says with a shrug. She puts the phone down and reads out the next steps for the recipe. 'Now we need to whisk the egg yolks, sugar, flour and cornflour.' She pauses. 'Last night I used whole eggs.' She presses her palm against her forehead. 'And no cornflour.'

'That'll mess up a recipe.'

She laughs and I can't help wondering if this might be the last time Paige and I will be spending time together messing around in the kitchen, trying to master a croquembouche.

'When you add the milk to the egg mixture, do not stop whisking,' she warns. 'Trust me. It took me two attempts last night because Piper rang the bell to go outside.'

'Got it,' I say, transferring half the milk to the bowl.

'So, who's Miranda? I feel like I know her name,' she says casually after a beat.

I pause.

'Keep whisking,' Paige says, motioning to the bowl. 'You can't stop at this critical moment.'

I put the whisk down and Paige looks at me quizzically. 'What's wrong?'

'You do know her name. We were meant to go to her son's birthday party together.'

'Miranda Summers,' she says. 'Yes, I remember something about that party.' She pauses. 'You went on your own,' she says sheepishly.

'Yes. I did.'

'I never even asked you who she was.'

'I guess we had other stuff going on.'

Paige looks momentarily perplexed. We have always valued our independence, but for the most part I know all her friends and she knows all mine.

'Yeah, I guess we did,' she replies sadly.

CHAPTER THIRTY-EIGHT

Paige

Days later, I'm knee-deep sorting out a pile of old bills and papers in the study when Nick's phone rings. It's an unknown number.

'Hello, this is Paige.'

'Hello, may I speak with Nick Bellbrae please?'

'Nick isn't home. He's taking the dog for a walk. This is his wife, Paige. Can I help you with anything?'

'That won't be necessary. A message will be fine.'

'Sure. Um, where did you say you were calling from again?' I search the desk drawer for a pen.

'It's Barry from Jim Lawrence & Associates. He has our number.'

'Sure, I'll let him know you called.' I hang up the phone, scribble *Call Barry – Jim Lawrence & Associates* on the back of an old water bill and stick it on the fridge.

And suddenly, I'm overcome with a sense of dread. I've seen the ads on TV. Jim Lawrence & Associates is a law firm, I'm sure of it.

A quick search on my phone reveals the number. I hold my breath as I dial it. A receptionist answers.

'Um, yes, hi, I was given your number by a friend. I'm wondering if your firm deals with medical negligence cases at all?' Naturally, I think of the worst-case scenario. After all, this is a law firm Nick's been in touch with, and for some reason he hasn't told me about it. Why else would he keep it a secret except to not worry me?

'No, I'm afraid we don't, sorry.'

'Oh, okay. And what sort of cases do you deal with there?' My mind is racing, building potential scenarios in my mind. Maybe it has something to do with a parking infringement, or maybe Nick wants to update his will. Maybe Nick has finally had enough of our neighbours, who refuse to trim their wisteria that encroaches on our side of the fence.

'Our lawyers work in family law exclusively.'

This can't be right. 'Even Barry?' I press.

'That's right. He's one of our barristers.'

I need a second to catch my breath.

'Exclusively family law,' I repeat. 'Are you absolutely sure?'

'Yes. Is there anything else I can help you with?' she says in a clipped tone.

I hang up the phone, my heart hammering in my chest so hard I can barely breathe. What on earth would cause Nick to be in touch with a family lawyer?

My breath is shaky as I dial Hope's number. Her phone goes to voicemail.

'Hope, it's me. Call me back as soon as you get this message. I think it's urgent. I think Nick wants a divorce.'

I don't see Nick until the following day when he walks in the door after an emergency at the hospital. Instantly, I know it must have been a bad one. It's funny how years of marriage give you the kind of superpowers to know when your other half has had a bad day, or a good day, or even an average day, yet you can completely underestimate how quickly a relationship can unravel.

'Morning,' he says. He leans forward to peck me on the lips but I awkwardly step aside, bumping into the kitchen bench.

'What's wrong?'

'What do you think is wrong?' My voice is even, measured, despite the fact my insides are churning. I've been waiting all day to confront him about his not-so-secret appointment.

'Caitlin giving you a hard time?'

I shake my head slowly. 'No, actually, this is not about my sister not knowing when to stop interfering.' I emphasise the word interfering. 'But even she knows where to draw the line.'

He flinches. He knows I know. Nick turns around to face the window.

I stand there, taking in the broad curves of his shoulders, the dip of his head, the way he lifts one arm and runs a hand through his hair – something he only ever does when he's stressed. I wait for him to talk. To say *something*. When he doesn't, I can't help myself. 'I left you a note on the fridge yesterday. You might not have seen it. It was still there this morning. Someone from…'

He's nodding slowly. 'Jim Lawrence. Barry.' He still doesn't turn around to face me.

I click my fingers. 'Yep, that's right. He said you'd have their number.' My tone is bordering on condescending now, but I can't help it. I can't believe Nick has betrayed my trust like this.

'I'm sorry.' He flips around to face me and it takes everything to not burst into tears. I *trusted* him.

'I'm not ready for you to apologise yet.'

He gives a small nod.

'At first I thought it might have been a medical negligence issue, because why else would you be calling a law firm? But then, they tell me it's a *family* law firm. And I'm left wondering how on earth you could go behind my back like this. *How* Nick? How do you go and break my trust like this?'

He's staring at my midsection as if he's noticing it for the first time. The bulge that could easily be mistaken for an extra serving of Mum's bucatini – not quite yet an unmistakable baby bump, but nevertheless the first glimpse of a baby bulge, accentuated thanks to my tight-fitting yoga leggings and cotton tee.

An unbearably long silence envelops us. 'I made an appointment with him,' Nick starts. 'With Barry. You're right. He's a barrister. A family law barrister.' His voice is measured, even, a bit too formal for my liking.

'An appointment for what, exactly?'

'I went to see Hope last week. I went to ask her if… if there was anything I could do to stop you going ahead with this decision. She gave me some general information and told me I'd need to see a barrister in order to look into taking things further.'

Of course Hope has told me everything, but hearing it from him makes me feel sick, like there's an undigested meal sitting in the pit of my stomach.

'Taking things further,' I repeat. 'Maybe now it's all out in the open, you could enlighten me by telling me exactly what you mean by that.'

'I'm guessing Hope already told you.'

'She did, but I want to hear it from you so you can listen to yourself, Nick! How are you planning on taking things further?'

Nick bites his lip. 'This hasn't been an easy decision.'

I furrow my brow. 'You met with a barrister to see if you can legally force me to have an abortion. You do realise the law is not on your side here?'

'I don't think I have any other choice.'

'Actually, you do. And it also means your apology is redundant. You're not sorry. If you were sorry, you'd back off. If you were sorry, you'd have told me before I had the chance to find out on my own.'

'Paige, please.' He moves forward, closing the distance between us.

'Stay there. Do not come any closer,' I say, holding up a hand. 'You have no leg to stand on. I know this because I had an appointment at a family law firm today. The same law firm *you* went to. Only *I* spoke to Cecelia, and Cecelia is much more confident than Barry.'

'I—'

'You need to calm down about all of this. You, Caitlin, my dad – you all need to stop this craziness!' I cross my arms, and my knees wobble. It takes everything to stand upright. 'I think it's better that we have some space.'

I call out for Piper so I can say goodbye to her. She comes hurtling down the hallway into the kitchen.

'I'll sleep on the sofa tonight,' offers Nick.

'Actually, my overnighter is already in my car. I'm staying at Mum and Dad's, and you're not going to fight me on this. I think you've overstepped the line already this week, and you need some time to put it into perspective.' If I can just keep it together until I walk away…

Nick balls his hand into a fist, closes his eyes and shakes his head. 'For how long?'

My eyes fill with tears at the way he asks this question – he sounds so… *defeated*. 'I don't know.'

Nick runs his hands through his hair. 'Jesus Christ, I knew it would come to this.'

I turn back to face him and shake my head in bemusement. 'Then why would you go and involve Barry?'

'You don't have to do this.'

'You asked for it,' I say.

And as soon as my eyes lock with his, I know it's not true. Neither of us asked for any of this.

CHAPTER THIRTY-NINE

Paige

'You all knew?'

Within half an hour of my arrival at Mum and Dad's, we are in the midst of a family meeting, though it's more like an argument, Hutton style, which means we are having several arguments at once. Mum is brewing tea – chamomile, of course – while Dad sits on the sofa, mostly watching and waiting for his chance to intervene. The only person missing is Ryan.

'I didn't know this was what he was going to do,' says Caitlin, who is perched on the kitchen bench, helping herself to a tub of chocolate ice cream.

'What does that even mean?'

'She went and had a word with Nick,' pipes up Dad. The three of us – me, Mum and Caitlin – flip around to face him. Mum keeps her fingers on the teabag.

'I'm sorry, what—?'

'Paige—' interrupts Caitlin.

I hold a hand up to quieten Caitlin. 'Dad, what does that mean? She was in on this? Were you in on this, too?'

'It's my fault,' says Dad. 'I didn't think Nick would go this far.'

'What did you expect?' says Mum, chiming in. 'Though, to be honest, I don't think he'll go through with it. It's probably just a step he needs to take to sort himself out, know what I mean? No point getting yourself tied up in knots over it.'

'It's not your fault, Dad,' says Caitlin. 'You didn't make me go talk to him.'

'Talk to him about what?' I say, raising my voice. 'Would you please tell me what's going on?'

'Dad and I discussed things. We both thought Nick should be doing more to convince you to put your life ahead of...' Her voice fades, like it's trickling away. I know it's because she can't bring herself to say it. *Your baby's.*

'That's rich, coming from you at twenty-four weeks.'

'Oh, Paige,' says Mum, relinquishing the teabag. 'This is a nightmare. Just a nightmare.'

'Evelyn, don't make her more upset than she already is,' says Dad with a hint of impatience.

'I think you and Caitlin have done enough in that department. What were you both thinking, interfering like that? Don't you think Nick has enough to deal with? I knew you were putting undue pressure on him! You should both be ashamed of yourselves,' Mum retorts.

'Whose idea was it?' I ask.

'I promise you, Paige, this was not my idea or Dad's. I thought by going to talk to him, he'd find another way for you to reconsider things,' says Caitlin.

'What's happened has happened. You can't stay here, Paige,' says Mum.

'Course she can stay here,' says Dad.

Mum fires him a look. 'She needs to go home and sort this out, pronto, and she can't do it from our living room.'

'He went behind my back, Mum!'

'Because he's scared of losing you! Can't you see that?'

'It was wrong!'

'Of course it was wrong, but he's acting out of desperation. Surely that's obvious to you?'

'And do you really want to lose your marriage as well?' says Caitlin.

'I suppose we can't all have perfect marriages like you,' I spout. 'It's easy for you to say since you have a family, another baby on the way, a country house and all the pieces of your life that fit perfectly together. It's always easy for people like you to point a finger.'

Caitlin flinches, like I've hit a sore spot. 'I'm concerned about you,' she says.

'Your concern is why I'm here tonight.' I know this isn't totally fair – it's not Caitlin and Dad's fault that Nick did what he did.

'One night, Evelyn. Let her stay the night, and she can sort things out in the morning,' says Dad.

I have to give it to Dad for his optimism; I don't plan on leaving any time soon.

'Since your father's sleeping on the sofa, you'll have to sleep with me until I make up the guest bedroom.'

'Hold on. Why is Dad sleeping on the sofa?'

'They've been arguing non-stop over you,' says Caitlin, matter-of-factly.

'This is ridiculous. Dad, I've made my decision.'

'Did you hear that, David? She's made her decision.'

'Dad, this is serious. You can't be arguing with Mum over this. It won't change anything.'

Dad stares into his lap, silence filling the room. He gets up and turns his body towards me. 'It'll break her, Paige. Losing you will break her. And me.'

We all look across to Mum, who is now staring at us all, misty-eyed. She relinquishes her grip on the teabag. Then she turns around and leaves the room. We stand there, the three of us, watching her go.

And I am left wondering whether I've made the right decision after all.

CHAPTER FORTY

Nick

Midway through my rounds, I bump into Ben in the corridor of the hospital. As in, I literally bump into him. My folder falls to the ground, spilling papers everywhere.

'Sorry, mate, I didn't see you there.'

He starts to laugh as he scoops together my folder, but when his eyes meet mine he studies my face for an unusually long time. So long in fact that I instinctively wipe my mouth in case I've got crumbs from this morning's toast on it.

Ben quietly observes me, pressing his lips together, like he's thinking. I've known Ben long enough to know he is always careful with his words. It's one of the reasons we get along so well. That and the fact I can trust him with almost anything. Ben will always tell me what I need to hear even if he is careful about the way he tells me.

'Pamela said she spoke to Paige the other day. You look terrible, Nick. How many hours of sleep did you get last night?'

'Since when do we have trouble running on little sleep?' I'm avoiding his question completely, of course. The one where he really wants to ask me how bad things are.

'If you really want to know how I'm sleeping, the answer is on my own.'

Ben shakes his head. 'Wait. What? Where's Paige? She's not in hospital, is she?'

'No, she's at her parents. I guess she didn't tell Pamela that.'

'No. She didn't.' He nods towards one of the empty wards. 'Why?' he asks, once he shuts the door behind him. 'Are things really that bad between the two of you?'

'I messed up.' There's no point in framing this any other way. I knew what I was doing, and I knew it might put me in the position I'm in now.

'She's blaming you for getting pregnant?'

I let out a sigh. 'I went to see a barrister.'

Ben frowns at me as if I've completely lost him. 'A barrister? Why would you need to see a barrister?'

'To see if there was anything I could do legally to prevent Paige from…' My God. I can't say it out loud. My skin burns red-hot from the shame. What *was* I thinking?

Ben's still standing there, his mouth practically agape. This is not the Nick he has known since his university days. This is not his best friend talking. It's someone else.

'I'm an idiot, okay. I don't need you to tell me that.'

'You should have come to me. I told you I was here for you. I would have set you straight, man. That is not cool.' That's when I realise why I never went to Ben with this. I know he would have shaken sense into me in a way that nobody else could. I know I would have listened to him. 'Why would you do that? You know you can't dictate whether your wife continues a pregnancy, and neither can the law.' He shakes his head like he's overwhelmed with a problem that has now become his.

'Yeah, well, I don't need the lecture right now, do I?'

'Why didn't you talk to anyone about this first? Why didn't you talk to *me*?'

'I talked to someone else.'

Ben's phone rings. He turns it on silent and flicks his attention back to me, looking at me knowingly. 'You've been taking advice from the woman downstairs, haven't you? The one you "bump into" for coffee every second day?'

'Her name's Miranda. And I don't need this, Ben. Not now. And not from you.'

'From me? The guy who's known you for years versus someone you just met in the hospital cafeteria?'

'Leave it alone,' I say gruffly. 'You have no idea what's going on.'

'What's going on? So there's something going on?' Ben flicks his eyes to the door to make sure it's still closed. 'Does Paige know?'

'There's nothing for her to know,' I say firmly.

'Man, you are really treading on some thin ice here. Paige is everything to you, Nick. Everything. Don't mess it up any more than you have. You don't want to lose her either way.'

There's nothing more I want to hear. Ben's phone lights up again and I take the cue to storm out of the room and to the bathroom. No amount of cold water helps take away the heavy feeling in the pit of my stomach. Maybe it's too late.

CHAPTER FORTY-ONE

Nick

First, the coffee machine breaks. Then, I realise we're out of dog food. Paige has been staying at her parents' for a week and is completely ignoring my calls. I know this won't go on forever – she has surely got to talk to me again some day, but there's no denying the fact I'm a lost man without her, and it has nothing to do with the fact the only things in the fridge are sour milk, some limp lettuce and a yellowing head of broccoli.

I miss my wife.

And I wish I could go back to a time before I made that stupid phone call. I knew, even before I made the appointment, that I wouldn't go through with it. I just had to try. It was like ticking a box, appeasing my ego, giving myself an insurance policy to fall back on if ever in the future I started to question whether I'd done enough.

Outside, it's warm, the sky a golden pink.

'Come on, Piper, rise and shine.' I dangle the lead in front of her and she races towards me. 'Looks like it's your lucky day. We're doing breakfast at a café this morning.' She wags her tail and pants at me.

We reach the foreshore and I let her off the lead and she runs alongside me. At this hour of the morning, there's nobody here but a few other joggers and a couple sipping their takeaway cappuccinos from the café across the road. I reach the pier and am ready to turn back when I notice the body in the water. I stop, bend over, hands on my knees as I try to catch my breath. The sun is shining directly onto the glistening water, making it hard to tell whether this kid is swimming or waving. I squint, trying to get a better view.

For twelve years I was a member of my local Surf Life-Saving Club. I learnt enough to know that an arm in the air isn't a wave. It's a cry for help. I have no board and there's nobody to call out to since it's too early for anyone to be patrolling the beach. Before I can think, I'm swimming towards her, Piper barking at me from the water's edge. The glaring sun in my eyes makes it almost impossible to find her. I stop in the area I thought I last saw her but there's nobody to be seen. But then I catch a glimpse of blonde hair and my body lurches towards it. My arms grip a body part. An arm? A leg? I drag her up to the surface. She can't be older than twelve or thirteen. She's unconscious and not responding.

I tow her behind me to the shore, where Piper is waiting for me. Now the couple who were sipping their coffees are standing there with her.

'Call an ambulance!' I yell as I carry the girl in my arms to the dry sand.

'Hey, darling, can you hear me? Open your eyes.'

Nothing.

'What's your name?'

After no response, I check her airways, positioning her chin in preparation for CPR.

Someone is kneeling beside me, asking what they can do to help. 'I need you to get to the Club. Check if anyone's opening up and see if you can get a defibrillator here. If nobody's there, try the supermarket.'

Suddenly, there's a flurry of activity around me – fumbling and panic as the child's mother starts yelling. Someone holds her back. 'I left her on the pier. She was feeling faint. I went to grab something to eat. She must have fallen! Cleo, baby! Wake up!'

My training kicks in, and I'm suddenly on autopilot, but this time I don't have the team I normally rely on to help me. It's like how it was with Zac, only now I have the training – the know-how – to save this girl's life.

I start delivering compressions.

Thirty compressions at a rate of one hundred per minute.

One, two, three four…

All I can think of is how this young girl doesn't deserve to die today. Her parents don't deserve to lose her.

Two rescue breaths…

Five minutes pass, then another three. There's still no ambulance.

'Come on!' I yell.

One, two, three, four…

The paramedics arrive and they want to take over, but I don't know if I can take my hands off her.

'We'll take it from here, sir.'

Before leaving, I brief one of the other paramedics and pass on my details. I take one last glance at Cleo. And then I turn around and start to walk away, realising that maybe it really is time to let go. Because I did my best, and maybe that was enough.

Throughout the course of the day I leave three voicemails for Paige. She finally calls me back before seven, right as I'm opening the door to the pizza delivery guy.

'How's Piper?' she says.

'She's fine, but I think she misses you.'

'I miss her too.'

'Listen, I know you need your space. There's something I have to tell you.'

'If this has anything to do with—'

'No, not at all. There's someone I need to tell you about. Someone I knew vaguely from uni. She works at the hospital in the psychology clinic. She's a friend.'

'Does she have a name?'

'Miranda Summers.'

'The woman who called the night we were making the croquembouche?'

'Yes. She's the one who asked us to her son's birthday.'

'What kind of friend is she, Nick?'

'She's a psychologist.'

There's a pause.

'You went to the birthday party alone. At her house…'

'Yes. I ended up getting there late, actually. I wanted to drop Will's present off. He… he reminds me of Zac in a lot of ways.'

'Nick, the way you're talking, you're making me wonder if there's more to this.'

'There's not. There's absolutely not. But I've been meeting with her. Talking to her. Just talking to her… about how I've been feeling about things.'

'Because you can't talk to *me*?'

'It's not like that. I've needed to talk to someone who isn't… close to all of this.'

'And you kept it a secret because…?'

'Because I… because maybe I haven't been handling this all very well,' I admit.

'Wow.'

'For what it's worth, it's been helping.'

'Well, I'm glad Miranda has been so helpful.'

'I met with her a few times, Paige. Inside and outside the hospital. I don't know why I didn't mention it earlier. It's stupid, really, but I think I was embarrassed.'

'Why would you feel embarrassed? Look at what we've been through. I still talk to Imogen.' Paige pauses. 'But you're only talking?'

'Yes. Just talking,' I say quietly, and I'm pleasantly surprised at how calm we're both being. The way things have been, it's not how I envisaged this conversation would go.

'So, is that all you wanted to talk to me about?' she says eventually.

'Well, I really want to ask you if you're ready to come home but I think I should give you some time.'

'Okay,' comes her response. I don't know what I was expecting but it isn't this.

'Paige?'

'Yes.'

'I love you.'

'Goodnight, Nick,' is her only reply.

CHAPTER FORTY-TWO

Paige

I'm driving home to pick up some clothes, thinking about Nick and the fact he's been talking to Miranda about our problems. Naturally, I've googled her, read her online bio and also checked her LinkedIn, Facebook and Instagram accounts. She's a single mother of a really cute kid, worked as a counsellor for bereaved parents, loves snow skiing and winery hopping. She runs the Mother's Day Classic every year, and ever since her husband died, she takes her kid go-karting once a month because apparently that was what her husband and son used to do. According to Facebook, she's the perfect kind of person to listen to the guy – my husband – who has quietly been falling apart without his wife noticing. As I turn onto the main road towards home, I realise I don't blame Nick for reaching out to someone to talk to – someone to listen. In fact, I'm glad he's been talking to Miranda. Nick is trying to deal with all of this in the best way he can.

My phone buzzes, and I answer, even though I'm not in the mood to talk.

'Nick, hi.'

'Hey, I… I wanted to call and make sure you were okay after what I told you last night. You were pretty quiet on the phone.'

'I'm fine with you talking to her, Nick.'

'About that, actually – she told me not to do it. I didn't listen.' He pauses. 'Anyway, we can talk about that when you're ready. The other reason I'm calling is that I wanted to ask you a favour.'

'Sure,' I say, unsure of what he means by this. Nick asking me for a 'favour' is a totally foreign concept to me. We don't ask each other for favours. We help each other out. I don't like the way it sounds – like the distance between us is real.

'Would you come with me to visit Zac?'

In all the years I've known him, Nick has never visited Zac's resting place. Ever. He told me he didn't need to, that Zac was with him without him needing to see his memorial.

'Um, yes, of course I'll come with you. Tell me when, and I'll be there.'

Shortly after I hang up, my phone rings again, this time from a private number I don't recognise. I turn the radio down and accept the call.

'Hey, sis.'

'Oh, Ryan. I didn't recognise your number. It's late over there. What's up?'

'Nothing. Just wanted to hear your voice. Where are you?'

'On my way home from the hairdresser. Nineties perm, purple highlights.'

It doesn't take much for Ryan to laugh, and soon I find myself laughing at his bad jokes too.

'You going to be much longer?' he asks once I finish telling him about my latest kitchen fail. Cupcakes where I accidentally substituted turmeric for the cinnamon. Hope thought it was a hoot.

'That's it. That's the end of the story. It's all I have for you.' I flick the indicator on and turn into the driveway. And that's when I see him. Ryan, my big brother, sitting on top of his red suitcase on my front porch with a goofy smile on his face. He waves and approaches the car, opening the door for me.

'Oh my God! What are you doing here?' I punch him play-fully in the arm and he envelops me in one of his signature hugs. 'Have you been going to the gym?' I say, squeezing his biceps. 'You look great.'

He grins. 'You look good too, sis.'

He ruffles my freshly blow-waved hair and I don't even care.

'I know. Just got my hair done.' I flick my hair over my shoulder to show it off.

Ryan looks at my midsection. 'If you look closely, you can sort of see a bump.'

I lift up my T-shirt to show him. 'No, you can't. That's the risotto I had for lunch.' I grin at him. It's impossible not to feel like smiling when Ryan is around.

'So, how's Susannah going?'

'She's great, but the IVF is kicking our butts at the moment. We did another round a couple of weeks before I left and nothing. Didn't take. We're gutted. We didn't think it would take this long. You wait, get your hopes up and then *whoosh*, it's over and you have to find a way to find more hope for next time.'

'That really sucks.'

He shrugs it off. 'Yeah.'

'Mum and Dad didn't tell me you were coming.'

'That's because I didn't tell them I was coming.'

'They don't know you're here?'

He shakes his head.

'Does Caitlin know you're here?'

He nods. 'Yeah, she does.'

'Well, just so you know, things have kind of been a bit tense lately in our family. I've been causing a bit of trouble, so try to ignore us all if things get heated.'

'She said things are getting out of control. She wanted me to come home.'

'That's a bit of an exaggeration, isn't it?'

'She said you're living with Mum and Dad.'

'I'm not living with Mum and Dad. I've been staying with them for a while, that's all.'

I push the door open and notice the scent of lemongrass. Nick's been burning the candles. I like to light them every morning.

'Come inside and take a shower and then I'll take you to Mum and Dad's.'

'I already organised dinner and a movie with Caitlin. You're coming too.'

'Nope.'

'It's non-negotiable.'

'I can't, Ryan. Things between me and Caitlin are strained right now. Trust me, you don't want to be around us both. Can't the two of you go and I'll sit this one out?'

'I flew halfway across the globe to be here with you all. Think you could make an effort? Just for one night? I'll let you choose the movie...' he teases.

I blow out a breath. Ryan's half-joking but deep down I know he's not. He's always been the peacekeeper of our family and I don't want to disappoint him.

'Mmm, well in that case... rom-com it is,' I concede. 'But you're paying.'

He winks in response and goes to shower. I head to my bedroom to pack some more clothes. There's a Post-it note on my side of the bed. It's the first one Nick ever left for me.

Can't wait to see you again. Miss you more than words can say. N x

'Paige? Are you okay?' asks Ryan, when he walks in to find me standing on the tufted bench in my wardrobe, trying to reach the shoebox.

He rubs his wet hair with his towel and tosses it aside. 'Get down from there before you fall.' He helps me down, jumps up and brings one of the five boxes down.

'Yes, this is the one.'

I lift the lid, and the Post-it notes spill out.

'Post-it notes?'

'I keep them. I kept them all.'

Ryan fires me a look that says, *Really? You're getting worked up over a bunch of Post-it notes?*

'I thought I knew him. The Nick I know wouldn't go to a lawyer about this, Ryan. How do we go back to normal after this?'

'Well, you know, the past year has been pretty stressful for the both of you.'

'Are you justifying it for him?'

'No, but I kind of feel for the guy. He's clutching at straws and I think he knows it. But something's driving him to take this drastic step. Maybe he won't be able to forgive himself if things go arse up and he didn't try harder.'

I show Ryan the note.

> *I can't imagine waking up without you by my side. Move in with me?*

He reads it and lifts his eyebrows. 'You need to work out what it is you want, Paige.' And then he walks away, leaving the conversation there.

Ryan is staying at Caitlin's tonight. I don't know where he finds the energy, considering he's just come in off a long-haul flight. He has the energy of a bouncy toddler. If he's less than impressed at our choice of film, he doesn't show it. We finish watching the movie, and as we stroll back to the car, he swerves towards the door of a pub.

'Uh-uh,' says Caitlin, shaking her head. She motions to her belly. 'Me and pubs, we don't go together.'

Ryan and I roll our eyes. 'I might not see you again for another three years. You're coming into the pub,' he says. He leads us to a table in the corner, which is as far away from the live band that is playing as you could get.

Caitlin fumbles with her necklace while I rummage through my bag for some lip gloss.

Deciding I'll be the one to break the silence, I ask her if she liked the movie.

'Hated it.'

'Oh, come on. You laughed the whole way through,' comes Ryan's voice.

'I thought it was pretty great, actually,' I say.

She rolls her eyes.

'Hey, enough of that,' says Ryan.

We both ignore him.

'I'm serious. Enough. I didn't come home to watch you two act like children. In case you haven't noticed, I'm trying pretty hard here. I'm going to go get us some drinks. Do me a favour and sort it out.' He flips around and makes his way to the bar.

'He's right,' I say.

'He doesn't deserve to come home to this.'

'Nope. Maybe we should try to get along for now – for him.'

Caitlin raises a brow. 'So, truce?'

'Truce.'

She nods, picks up her phone and starts texting someone. As she reads her messages, her expression hardens.

'Let me guess. The kids are giving Mark trouble?'

She stares at the bar, a steely look on her face. 'No, actually. The kids are apparently with my in-laws because Mark decided *he* needed a night off.'

'Well, he's been working pretty hard, what with work and the cottage in Castlemaine. Maybe he's tired,' I offer. Mark isn't my husband, of course, but if he's anything like Nick, it would take the earth to stop spinning before he admitted to me outright he was tired.

'Of course he's tired,' she says.

'So what's the problem then?'

Caitlin looks at me as if I've asked her to come up with the winning lotto numbers. 'Nothing,' she says, pressing her lips together. 'It's not a problem.'

The way she spits it out makes it obvious that it's an issue – at least to her.

'How long until he finishes the renovations on the house?' I press. It seems like he's been working on them for far longer than they'd anticipated, and I can't help wondering if this has something to do with Caitlin's secrecy.

'No, the country house is all finished now.' She tosses her phone back into her bag and starts fiddling with the buttons on her cardigan. 'It's been finished for two and a half weeks.'

'What's wrong?' I say, frowning. Over the past year or so, Caitlin has shared her Pinterest board and all of her 200 or so images with me. She dragged me round to interior design shows and furniture showrooms, and now that her beloved luxury house in the country for weekend getaways is ready, she sounds as if she couldn't care less. Now that I think of it, Caitlin has seemed a little snappy around Mark.

Caitlin pretends to be looking for Ryan in the sea of people waiting around the bar.

I raise my voice, in case she hasn't heard me over the music. 'I know something's wrong. What is it? Is it Mark? Because if it is, you can tell me. It's not like I'm going to judge you if your husband's being a bit of an ass.'

Caitlin doesn't laugh. She sits there looking as if she's going to burst into tears if I say another word.

'Hey,' I say, reaching for her shoulder, which I shake a little so she'll look at me.

Ryan is approaching the table, holding three glasses. As he sets them down in front of us, Caitlin blurts out, 'I think he might be having an affair.'

'Who's having an affair?' says Ryan, pulling up a low stool. 'I turn my back for a second and miss out on all the goss.'

I make a sign for him to stop. He questions me with a look. *No*, I mouth.

'Shit, is it Dad? Is Dad having an affair?'

'What? No!' I say, shaking my head at the absurdity of it.

'Jesus, then don't tell me it's Mum,' he says with a horrified look.

Caitlin's head is in her hands at this point.

'Oh my God, Ryan, be quiet, okay. Let her talk.'

'He's late home *all* the time. It doesn't feel like we're a family. It's like we're so focused on keeping everything ticking along and running smoothly that we've forgotten who we were, and we don't know who we are any more. We don't talk unless it's about the kids, and it's not the same as how it used to be with us.'

'Right… but an *affair*?'

'Are we talking about *Mark*, here?' says Ryan, clearly confused and equally frustrated.

She lets out a deep sigh. 'I saw a text message.'

'Mmm… and…?'

'From one of his colleagues, Natasha. No kids, go-getter, amazing legs, amazing boobs, amazing everything.'

'Oh, come on! You're beautiful, and pregnant, and… your hair's not out of place, your skin is flawless, your legs are way less hairy than mine right now, and let me look at those hands…' I take one in mine. 'Where do you even find the time to get a manicure when you're raising those gorgeous little people you have at home? Caitlin, you are beautiful. Isn't she, Ryan?'

Ryan nods and produces a delayed, 'Yes. Of course you are.' He still seems disconcerted.

I continue. 'You're also loving, and committed, and smart, and you can bake a mean cake, and you run rings around Betty Baker any day of the week. And Mark loves you. I know he does.'

Caitlin's lower lip turns downwards. 'Then why don't I feel it?'

I blink at her, trying to think. 'Maybe you're feeling a bit overwhelmed with your life. You have every detail under control. Could it be that maybe you're exhausted? I mean, you are carrying a little person inside of you.'

Tears start streaming down her cheeks. I grab my bag and haul it towards Ryan. 'Tissues,' I order.

Ryan reaches into the depths of my bag, but before he can rummage through it, I snatch it away from him and swap it with Caitlin's. 'Forget it, you won't find any in there, I'm disorganised.'

Caitlin starts crying harder.

'What? What did I say wrong?'

I look at Ryan. 'Go see if you can find some napkins or something.'

Ryan holds up three small tissue packets. 'Uh, no need. We're good.' He peers into the bag. 'And we've got a Lego figurine, gum, lipstick, deodorant, a princess tiara, wipes, pads, tampons…'

'Thank you, Ryan,' I say, taking a packet from him.

'I *don't* have everything under control. Do you know how exhausting it is to be at home full-time with Ethan? He hardly naps, and he's so active. And he's been throwing these tantrums because he's not speaking the way he should be, so we started seeing a speech therapist and I keep losing sleep over it. I mean, what if there's some underlying problem with him and I missed it? They want to do further testing – whatever that means! And since Ella started school this year, I've been going to bed later and later every night to get all the stuff done for the PFA because I want it to go smoothly.'

'I thought you loved all that,' I say. 'Don't you?'

'I do.'

'And it's normal to worry about your children.'

'Yeah.'

'So you're allowed to talk about being worried about your kid. You don't need to pretend like it's all perfect at the Callaways', especially around us.'

Ryan nods. 'Even if you were half as perfect as what you are, you'd still be doing an excellent job raising those kids. Cut yourself some slack.'

'So what about Mark and the text message? Do you really think there's something going on?' The logical part of my brain tells me there is no way Mark would risk his marriage. He and Caitlin are solid, I'm sure of it. And Mark is a good guy. A family man. And he still looks at Caitlin with the same admiring stare he had as a teenager when he lived across the road from us. They know each other inside out though, and if Caitlin is suspicious, then maybe she has every reason to be.

'I don't know for sure. I thought she might have been meeting him at the cottage. You remember that night I asked you to babysit?'

'I remember,' I say. I knew something wasn't right. 'You drove all the way down there to see if he was with her? Was he?'

'I don't know because I stupidly parked the car down the street, climbed over the front fence, peeked through a window, and then a neighbour called me out.'

My eyes widen. 'What?'

Ryan is staring at her in disbelief. 'Couldn't you have just opened the gate and walked right in?' he asks.

She lets out a loud sigh. 'I think I was too scared to.'

'But that was months ago. Since then you haven't noticed anything that's made you suspicious, right?'

Ryan's quick to get a word in. 'Hold on a second. This Is a no brainer. None of this beating yourself up for months on end *wondering* about it. I think you need to resort to plan B. Come right out and ask the guy.'

CHAPTER FORTY-THREE

Nick

I wake up to loud knocking on my front door, and for a moment I'm hopeful that it might be Paige and she's forgotten her keys. But no, it's her brother, Ryan, standing there with two steaming-hot cappuccinos and a smile on his face. It's six o'clock in the morning, way too early for anyone to be smiling this widely.

'Morning,' he says chirpily, stepping past me and down the hallway. It's like he's never been away.

'Hey, when did you arrive? Did Susannah come too?' I accept the coffee from him and take a sip. I squeeze his shoulders, broad and firm from all the exercise he does – Ryan is a fan of all sports, especially adventurous ones. 'It's good to see you.'

'Yesterday. And it was mostly a surprise. And no, she couldn't make it.'

'But Paige knew?'

'Nope.'

'Uh, in case you're wondering, she's not here, she's actually… Wait, didn't you see her at your parents' place?'

Ryan waves a hand in the air to stop me. 'I stayed at Caitlin's and I already know.'

I let out a huff of breath. 'It's a mess.'

'She'll come around.'

I shake my head. 'Mmm, I'm not so sure about that.'

'We came by yesterday. She picked up some clothes. I saw the way she looked at your notes.'

'The Post-its?'

Ryan lets out a little laugh. 'They're kind of cute. I would never have picked you for a romantic like that.' He gives my arm a little punch.

I grab a few slices of bread and drop them into the toaster.

'Got any Vegemite?' Ryan opens the pantry and looks for it. I try my hardest not to appear embarrassed at the boxes of last night's takeaway stacked beside the rubbish bin.

'She keeps it in the fridge.'

'Who in their right mind keeps Vegemite in the fridge?'

'Paige does. She also keeps her car keys in there.'

Ryan frowns. 'Huh. Now that's just weird.'

I start buttering a piece of toast. 'So she never forgets where they are.'

'And she can't use a fruit bowl? Or a hook on the wall?'

What can I say? 'That's Paige for you.'

Ryan pinches the slice of toast I've buttered. 'You need to hurry up and shower. I booked us in at the driving range.'

'How'd you know I wasn't working?'

'I asked Ben.' That smile again.

'So how long are you staying for?'

'A couple of weeks. I wanted to come spend some time with Paige.'

I flick my eyes up and notice the way the smile is gone, his expression darkening.

'You know – just in case.' He sighs. 'I'm sorry. That was a stupid thing to say to you.'

'Don't apologise.'

'Susannah and I… We'll both come back, if you need us.'

'I don't want to see you for at least another three years.'

Ryan laughs half-heartedly. 'I know why you did what you did. I think Paige realises, or will realise eventually.'

'We'll see,' I say, scraping my toast crusts into the bin.

Ryan finishes his toast and starts packing the dishwasher. He searches the bottom cupboard for dishwashing powder. 'Why do you have so many boxes of this stuff?'

'In case I run out.'

'You live a block away from the supermarket.'

'Yeah. I know. It's complicated.'

I haven't visited Zac in over twenty-five years, but somehow part of me knows exactly which path to follow, and I find it easily; the white roses are still blooming prolifically after all these years. Sometimes my grandmother Elsie comes here with Mum, but they stopped asking me to join them years ago after I kept making excuses about why I couldn't make it.

It's silent here, except for the crunch of gravel under our feet. It's drizzling, and Paige is holding an umbrella.

'Do you want me to stay here?' asks Paige when we get closer to Zac's spot.

'I won't be long.'

'Okay, I'll wait here for you,' she says softly.

I stop in front of his memorial and read the plaque. He's been gone so many years now, I even forgot what it says. I lay the bunch of flowers I've brought with me next to it.

'Hey, little brother. I don't really know where to start. I'm not really good at this stuff. And it feels stupid talking to you, because who knows if you can hear me. Mum thinks you can. Grandma thinks you can. But me? I'm not convinced. But anyway, here goes… I miss you. Even after all these years, I think about you all the time. I wonder if somehow you're looking after Max.'

I reach into my pocket, take out a hard plastic figurine and place it on the ground. 'I promised you my Star Wars collection, but this is the only piece I kept. I've been waiting all these years to give it to you.'

I clear my throat and continue.

'I became a doctor, Zac – a paediatric surgeon. I've saved hundreds of lives, I've made a countless number of kids better. I love what I do. But it never feels like what I do is good enough. And I realise now, it's because nothing I do can ever bring you back.'

My eyes burn, and there's a lump in my throat I struggle to swallow past. 'I'm sorry, Zac. I'm sorry I couldn't save your life.'

I start walking back towards Paige, who is still standing there, waiting for me. Something causes me to glance back, and as I do, I feel the warmth of the sun on my face as the clouds part in the sky.

It's finally time for me to say goodbye. It's finally time for me to forgive myself.

CHAPTER FORTY-FOUR

Paige

Later that evening, the doorbell rings at Mum and Dad's. Of course I know who it is, but Mum and Dad have no idea. Much to Mum's delight, I've declared Sunday night dinners reinstated, on the condition she and Dad are civil with one another. So far it's working – things feel almost back to normal, minus Nick not being there.

Dad lets out a deep belly laugh when he sees Ryan standing at the door. 'Evelyn! Could you come down here to sign for a delivery please?'

Mum comes padding down the hallway and practically tackles Ryan to the ground when she sees him.

'Oh my God! What are you doing to us?' She presses her hands against his cheeks and then over the rest of his torso as if she's frisking him, or making sure it's actually him. 'Look at you!' She steps back to admire him from afar, her face looking like a kid who has set eyes upon Santa.

If Mum and Dad have any suspicions about Caitlin's issues, they don't let on during dinner. Ryan, on the other hand, pulls me aside in the theatre room after dinner to demand answers. Apparently I chewed my food too slowly and laughed at one too many of his bad jokes without making a sarcastic comment.

'Come on, the joke about the truck driver and the red bucket?' He reaches for the remote and turns the TV on.

'Okay, fine,' I say, crossing my arms. I take the remote and change channels. 'I miss Nick and I want to go home, but if he hasn't changed his mind about things, I don't know where that will leave us.'

'Leave it on that channel,' says Ryan, referring to *Top Gear*. 'Hold on.' He gets up from his seat and comes back a minute later with a bowl of microwaved popcorn. He drops onto the sofa, something that drives Mum crazy, and raises his feet onto the ottoman. 'We have about a minute before Mum and Dad join us,' he says, throwing a piece of popcorn into the air and catching it in his mouth. 'Mum wants to watch one of her movies. Dad tried to make a beeline for the garage but I stopped him.'

'Ugh, I am so not in the mood for *Grease*.'

Ryan makes a face and heaps a handful of popcorn into his mouth. He swallows and then turns to me. 'Anyway, I think you need to go home, Paige. Since I'm the international guest, I'm reclaiming the guest bedroom, so you're out.'

I roll my eyes.

'Seriously, you're never going to resolve things by being here. You need to talk to him. He's in knots about it, the poor guy.'

'You spoke to him?'

'Don't look so surprised. You've known about my bromance with Nick for years.'

'Oh, please.'

Ryan shrugs.

'So, what did he say?'

'He didn't need to say anything. He looks like he got hit by a garbage truck.' He punches me lightly on the arm. 'Seriously, Paige. Go home. He did something shitty but he's not a shitty person.'

'I'll go see him. After *Grease*.'

Ryan fist-bumps me. 'Yeah! She's doing it!'

I snatch the bowl of popcorn from him,

'Who's doing what?' asks Caitlin, stepping into the dark theatre room with a beanbag in hand, Mum and Dad trailing in behind her in their pyjamas. I have to give it to Ryan: he's got a knack for getting people to do things.

'Paige is vacating the Hutton family home tonight and will be resuming talks with her husband.'

Mum goes to sit on the far end of the sofa, but Ryan's quick to move. She gives a small shake of her head.

'Better view of the TV from this spot, Mum. That way you can also sit next to Dad.' He waggles his eyebrows and claims the beanbag once Caitlin decides that getting out of it is near impossible.

'And Dad, I was wondering if you could sleep in your old bed because I've asked Tim and Liam over for a movie marathon.'

He's good, Caitlin mouths.

I know, I mouth back. Lucky I have popcorn. Seeing Ryan in action is riveting. Especially since Mum's hand creeps forward on her lap and then Dad follows it with his. It's like they're hypnotised.

'Would that be okay, Mum?' Ryan asks innocently.

'Yes, I don't see why not. I've always liked Tim and Lachlan.'

Caitlin and I correct her. 'Liam.'

Dad's fingers curl themselves around her hand.

'Caitlin and I also hereby declare our support of Paige. And I want to say that no matter the outcome, no matter how bad things get, we are all going to manage. Even Mum.'

Mum nods.

All eyeballs are now on Dad, who lets out a heavy sigh and releases his grip on Mum's hand. Just when I think he's going to stand up and leave the room, he nods.

Ryan breaks out into a smile, pops the top off a beer, hands it to Dad and then clinks his against it.

'Mum, you're welcome. Dad, whenever you're ready, you can give your wife a kiss.'

'Oh, stop it! Enough now, Ryan, honestly,' says Mum, though we all know she doesn't really mean it. Without warning, Dad leans across, pulls her into his arms and kisses her.

Ryan chuckles and pushes play, and the intro music to *Grease* filters into the room.

'Meanwhile, I need to update you two on what fell out of my husband's mouth last night,' whispers Caitlin, directing this to me and Ryan, who is quick to turn the volume up on the TV.

'What did you say, sweetheart?' says Mum, straining to hear. 'What fell out of Mark's mouth?'

Dad points to the TV. 'What happened to *Top Gear?*'

'Turn the volume down, we're having a conversation here,' Mum says, firing Ryan a look of annoyance. 'And we're watching *Grease.*'

Ryan rolls his eyes and Dad shrugs in defeat.

'Nothing, Mum,' says Caitlin. 'I wasn't talking about Mark.'

'Then which husband were you talking about?'

I bite my bottom lip. Ryan grimaces. 'Here we go,' he mutters under his breath.

'Why am I always the last to know things when it comes to the three of you?'

'It's nothing to worry about, Mum. Caitlin and Mark have been a bit tired and snappy with each other lately, that's all. His long hours, her hormones...'

'There's no use, Paige. They're going to find out sooner or later,' says Caitlin.

Mum's eyes swing back to Caitlin. Even Dad perks to attention. I'd be almost relieved the spotlight isn't on me for once if it weren't so troubling.

'Mark did not have an affair with Natasha,' she declares.

'Oh, thank God for that,' I say.

'Who's Natasha?' ask Mum and Dad in unison.

Caitlin gives them an abridged rundown of things so they're up to speed. 'You probably think I should be thankful that he didn't have an affair, right?'

We all nod.

'Well, it's a cruel blessing, actually. Because while she sent him four flirty text messages, which he didn't act on, he contemplated things. As in, seriously contemplated. And I don't know how I feel about that yet. He said he was starting to have feelings for her.' Caitlin's voice catches in her throat. 'While I've been busy raising kids and keeping our life ticking along, it seems Mark has been travelling on a different train. And I don't know how we're going to fix this. I don't even know if, once a marriage is broken, it can actually get back on track.'

'When you figure it out, let me know,' I say, dryly.

Dad chimes in then, surprising us all. 'Oh, come on, course it can.'

'David,' says Mum, softly.

Caitlin, Ryan and I look at each other, and then back at Mum and Dad.

'Go on, tell them. They're old enough and there's no use pretending everything was always rosy.'

Mum sighs. 'Your father's right. Marriage, like anything else, takes hard work. Sometimes…' Mum pauses, choosing her words carefully. 'Sometimes couples drift so far apart, it's hard to remember why they chose to be with each other in the first place. And that's what happened with Dad and me.' She moves a strand of hair behind her ear. 'But it was a very long time ago and Dad was away a lot and I was very lonely. I was happy, staying home and raising the three of you, but there were times when I felt like things were missing from my life – as if the life I was living wasn't exactly what I'd signed up for. I lost sight of who I was for a little while.'

'Oh my God, Mum, you had an affair?' whispers Caitlin, her eyes wide.

'No. But I did meet a man and started to have… well, feelings for him. It was wrong. I knew it was wrong. And I told your Dad as soon as I admitted it to myself, because it scared me. It took us a while to sort ourselves out, but we eventually did.'

'That's right,' says Dad. 'That's when I stopped doing the international flights and I started spending more time with her and the three of you.'

I nod, the vague memory surfacing of Dad declaring a change in his roster over a roast chicken dinner. Mum had burst into tears and excused herself to the bathroom.

'Anyway, what Dad's trying to say is that if Mark loves you and you love him, it might not be easy, but you can work towards making some changes to address the things that haven't been working. The main thing is that both halves of a couple are willing to see eye to eye. Because a man can't spend his life sleeping on a sofa, can he?'

Before I leave, I pull Caitlin aside.

'Hey, I need to talk to you.'

'What is it?'

'You're going to be okay, Caitlin. I know you are. No matter what happens with Mark, this isn't going to be the end of the world, even if it feels like it.'

She presses her lips together. 'Everything I ever wanted was a happy family.'

'Yeah, me too.'

'God, I can be so insensitive. Sorry. I'm just so scared. I'm not like you, Paige. I'm not as strong as you.'

'Well, you don't need to be. Because you have me. And I'm here for you.'

Caitlin bursts into tears. 'Oh, Jesus, Paige.' She lifts her hands to her face and cries into them.

'Hormones?'

'No, not hormones. You. It's all you.'

'All me what?' I whisper.

'I've been awful to you. Causing you so much added stress when maybe I should have been doing what you said. I should have been supporting you. You're going through the worst time in your life and I've been thinking of myself.'

'It's only because you love me,' I tell her.

'Yes,' she says, sniffling. 'Even if I don't always show it, I really, really do. We all do. And from now on, I'm going to be the kind of sister you deserve.'

'Caitlin,' I tell her, 'you already are the sister I deserve.'

CHAPTER FORTY-FIVE

Nick

Every night since Paige left, I've been coming outside to look at the stars. It's become sort of a ritual – one that beats tossing and turning in bed, anyway. At the same time, it reminds me of how lonely the house feels without her.

Piper starts barking, and a few seconds later, Paige steps through the back door into the moonlight. 'Hey there. Couldn't sleep?'

'Paige… I, uh… it's late… What are you doing here?' I give a small shake of my head, and at the same time, I feel myself come alive. There she is, my beautiful wife – the wife I've lost – standing right in front of me. 'I mean, it's good to see you. I'm glad you're here. Is everything okay? Are you feeling all right?'

'I know it's late,' she says, positioning herself beside me so our shoulders are touching. 'I'm fine. Well, not fine, but healthy-as-can-be-expected fine. I've been thinking about you all day.'

I've been doing the same.

'I miss you, Nick.'

'I miss you too. A lot. More than you can imagine.' I hesitate. 'But I understand. I know I did the wrong thing by you.'

She presses a hand to my lips.

'There's something I want to ask you. What made you want to go see Zac, after all this time?'

The question stuns me a little – it's not what I expected her to come here for. 'I suppose I've been feeling guilty. Ever since Max, mostly, but even before then.'

'Oh, Nick.'

'I've been finding it hard to deal with not being able to make sure the people around me are okay. That's partly what I've been talking to Miranda about.'

'And it's partly why you called Jim Lawrence & Associates.'

'I tried calling you to explain. I wanted to let you know I never went back to Barry, and not because you found out about things. I couldn't have gone through with it. I think I knew that all along. It was stupid. I was stupid.'

'You made a stupid mistake,' she says.

'I hurt you, and I'm so, so sorry.' I feel my shoulders slump, and Paige reaches across and rubs my back. This small gesture almost makes me choke up.

'It's okay. I understand why you did it,' she says softly.

I take a deep breath and look up at the sky. There are an unusual number of stars tonight, and for a minute or so we simply stand there, gazing up at them, each of us lost in our own thoughts.

'You know, my dad bought Ryan a telescope for his eighth birthday. Ryan never let me touch it, and I was so envious that I saved up three months' worth of pocket money – all of thirty-six dollars – and finally asked Dad to buy me one too. He did, and together we'd spend hours looking up at the sky on nights Dad was home with us. I haven't thought about it in years,' says Paige.

'I never knew any of that.'

'Back then, I thought I had my whole life mapped out in front of me like the night sky and its stars. But I think I've realised that the sky can present a completely different view of itself depending on the time you look at it and from where you look at it.'

'I never took much of an interest in space as a kid. Zac was obsessed though. The entire ceiling in his bedroom was covered in stars. He was supposed to be the astronaut and I was meant to be the racing car driver. Funny how life turns out.'

'Sometimes not so funny,' she offers.

'I told him to go lie down and wait for Mum to get home from the pharmacy. I should have called an ambulance then, not when he was passing out on the bedroom floor. I could have saved his life. But I didn't.'

'Nick,' Paige says, 'you were twelve years old. How were you supposed to know?'

'Maybe that's true, but regardless, I always felt like I didn't do enough. The CPR – it didn't work, I got it all wrong.'

'You did what any child your age could have done. Twelve-year-old kids aren't trained in CPR. You did the best you could. Your mum took him to see a doctor twice before that day. It wasn't your fault. It's time you look at this differently.'

I scrunch my eyes closed as if I don't want to hear it. 'I was in *Singapore*, Paige. I could have saved Max. I was 6,000 kilometres away, and if I was here instead, with you, then maybe I could have seen it coming. Just like—' I stop myself.

'Right, like you can see what's coming now?'

I don't respond but Paige is quick to frame my face with her hands. 'Nick, listen to me. You are not responsible for what happened with Max. We *have* to move forward. You can't continue blaming yourself for your brother's death. And you can't keep losing sleep over me and what's going to happen if I get sick… if I—'

'Stop, Paige.'

'No,' she says adamantly. 'I won't let you carry this, Nick. I will not let you take responsibility for losing me too. Please, promise me.'

'Yes, okay,' I whisper. 'I want this baby too. More than you can imagine. But I don't want you to die. I don't know if I can *do* it without you. I *need* you, Paige.' My voice wobbles. 'I love you and I need you in my life.'

She slides her arms around me and squeezes. As we both stare up at the midnight-blue sky, I realise, finally, what it feels like to stand firm in a potentially life-changing decision with no more turning back. Paige's survival and that of our baby depends on how the next several months pan out. I've known this all along, of course, but now the reality of it all is pressing against us both.

And while I know she'll never admit it, at least not to me, I know that deep down she's scared too.

PART THREE

CHAPTER FORTY-SIX

Nick

Life in the aftermath of making the big decision carries on without a major hiccup for all of three days.

'What are you doing?' asks Paige, looking at the computer over my shoulder. She breaks a muesli bar in half and offers me a piece.

I slam the laptop shut. 'Nothing.' I have every intention of talking about this with Paige, but it's only a sliver of an idea and I haven't even had the chance to think about it properly.

'Doesn't look like nothing.'

'I was looking into something, that's all. Work-related stuff.'

Paige looks at me expectantly. I should know better than to not come out with it – and it's not like we've never spoken about this before. It's just that the timing makes it… awkward.

'I'm working out what's involved in case I want to move away from surgery and into teaching,' I tell her.

'What?' She raises her eyebrows. 'Wow, I wasn't expecting you to say that. Last time we talked about it was before Max. I didn't think this was something you really wanted to do.'

'I'm warming to the idea.'

'What does that mean?'

'We need to be prepared, Paige.'

'Isn't this a little… I don't know… pessimistic of you?'

'I don't really want to wait until it's too late. Think about it. What if things go wrong and I'm left to care for a baby alone?

Surely, in making the decision you've made, you've thought about that?'

She puts her hands over her mouth and huffs out a breath. I know this isn't exactly an easy conversation, but it's a necessary one.

'Well, have you?' I press. 'Let me ask you something. Do you want me to put our child into day care at six weeks? Or would you prefer I hire a live-in au pair?'

'Nick!'

'These are the things we need to think about. These are the things we need to talk about. I'll have absolutely no way of knowing what you want.' Heck, I don't even know what I would want. How can a parent be expected to plan for this kind of thing so early on in the game?

'Not now,' she says, like we have all the time in the world.

'You made a decision. This is the planning that comes as part of that decision. I know you don't want to hear it, but it's just the way it is.'

'I knew this wasn't going to be easy,' she huffs.

'No, it's not easy. Because all we ever seem to do is argue. It's one stupid argument after another.' I can't help feeling annoyed now.

'We're not arguing, we're discussing something. And I'd appreciate if you'd start to include me in your plans instead of going away behind my back to "sort things out",' she says, making air quotes.

'Oh, come on, I thought we were past the whole Barry thing.'

She crosses her arms. 'I've forgiven you, Nick, but I can't forget.' She starts to walk away.

'Hey! What does that mean? You don't trust me any more?'

She clenches her jaw, and I think to myself, *What did I expect?* Paige is home, but our problems aren't over yet. Not by a mile. Even if Paige does survive, I'm starting to wonder whether our marriage will.

*

The following week, I confess to Ben that I'm thinking of moving away from surgery and into teaching. We're at the local basketball courts, shooting hoops, something we haven't done in months.

'That'll be the day,' he says, laughing as he dribbles the ball past me.

This disarms me. Moments ago I was very open to this, and Ben's reaction makes me wonder if he has a point. I might be a hopeless educator. 'I'm serious.'

Ben wipes the sweat from his brow and tosses me the ball. 'Why would you want to do that, Nick? You are one of the best paediatric surgeons in Melbourne. You'd be crazy to throw all that away.'

'I wouldn't be throwing anything away.'

'Yes, you would be. You're a surgeon. Not a teacher.'

'I want to do this.' I bounce the ball in his direction.

'Really? Then why do you sound so miserable about it?'

I don't reply.

'Is that your answer?'

Ben throws the ball back to me. 'I might not have a choice, Ben, okay?' I shoot and miss. 'Someone is going to have to be around to raise the baby, assuming…' *Assuming he or she survives.*

Ben rests his hands on his knees and catches his breath. 'You want my advice, Nick?' Ben poses this as a question but of course it's not a question at all. 'Instead of spending time focusing on the worst that could happen, maybe you should spend your time making the most of the time you have left. I'm pretty sure that no pregnant woman out there ever wants to have to see her husband getting ready to live a life without her. Let her enjoy the months ahead. Deal with the rest later.'

I hurl the ball in Ben's direction. He catches it and tosses it back. 'Easy for you to say.'

'She just moved back in. Let the dust settle, work on finding some normality in your lives again so your life doesn't fall apart if she survives.'

Ben walks off the court and holds out a towel and a drink bottle for me. 'Remember, that's what we're all praying for here.'

CHAPTER FORTY-SEVEN

Paige

Windsor Lakes isn't quite the same when Elsie and Frank aren't sitting together in the common room. Elsie has come down with a chest infection, which means she's confined to bed. Frank is positioned on an armchair in one corner of her room, snoring, with an unfinished crossword on his lap. Elsie's room is small but comfortable. Her walls reflect her love of art. From them hang bright abstracts and verdant landscapes with blue skies and richly coloured autumn leaves. She keeps only three things on her dresser: her reading glasses, a butterfly brooch her mother gave her and a copy of the Bible. Elsie has been a resident at Windsor Lakes for over ten years. Glancing around her room, I marvel at how such a long life can fit itself into the confines of a compact room like this with so few belongings. You could count on one hand the things that matter to Elsie.

I perch on the edge of the bed. 'Looks like you're keeping the doctors and nurses on their toes,' I say, adjusting her blanket.

'We're all old here, Paige, it's our job to keep them on their toes.' She coughs into her elbow before sinking back into the pillows.

'Can I get you anything? Those ginger snap biscuits you love? I know where Viv keeps them hidden.'

'My wool and needles.' She points to her basket on the floor. 'And tell that husband of yours to come and visit his grandmother every once in a while.'

'I'll tell him,' I say. 'He's going to be home this Saturday. I'll make sure he visits then. Is Bette still planning on visiting next week?' I pick the basket up and lift several balls of yarn in varying colours from it.

'That one,' says Elsie, pointing to the mint green. 'And yes, she is, but she can only manage a couple of days. She's run off her feet with the B & B.'

I hand Elsie the yarn and a crochet hook and watch as her long, knobbly fingers start to move, hooking the wool and weaving it in and out. While she sets to work, I examine the burgundy pouch in the basket, which holds an assortment of knitting needles and crochet hooks in various colours and sizes. 'You don't even need a pattern?' I ask, noticing there aren't any patterns or booklets in the basket. An idea is taking shape in my mind.

She taps the frame of her glasses. 'I've got these. And my memory.'

'My grandmother used to crochet. Apparently, she used to make sweaters for her chickens.'

Elsie laughs. 'Well, if a teapot can have a jumper, then why not a chook?'

'What is it you're making?'

'A matinee jacket. For your little one.' She continues working her hook around the wool. Elsie coughs again, letting the crochet hook fall into her lap. She takes a laboured breath and sinks back into her pillows.

'Why don't you rest now? Finish it later. When you have more energy,' I suggest. I squeeze her hand. It feels cold, the skin loose and papery thin.

'How many times do I have to tell you that my clock's ticking? Knowing my luck, the doctors will be in here later tonight demanding to have me transported to the hospital. And then?'

'And then you go. You go to the hospital and you get better and then you come back here and finish it then,'

Elsie lets out a small laugh as she pats my leg. 'Innocent,' she murmurs. 'That's the thing about being young like you. You think you have all the time in the world to finish all the things you started and all the things you didn't.'

By the time I'm halfway through my second trimester, I've crocheted four amigurumi toys under Elsie's careful tutelage. A hedgehog (Alfie), a turtle (Mrs Go Slow), a bunny (Ginger) and a monkey I named Frank after one too many hints from a certain crossword-loving fellow at Windsor Lakes. Crochet doesn't come easily to me, and I struggle to finish one toy a week. Stitched into each one is a pocket just big enough for a letter.

Elsie's chest infection has escalated into pneumonia, and she's been transferred to hospital. She spends long stretches of the day sleeping, so I make an effort to visit her in the mornings when she seems to have a bit more energy. Nick and my doctors have warned me to be careful – in my condition, I need to stay as healthy as possible – but I can't stay away. This is Elsie, after all.

I show her my latest creation, a salmon-coloured starfish in the making. 'What do you think?' I ask, holding it up for her to see.

She nods approvingly. She draws in a laboured breath and winces, her eyes fluttering closed. I wait for her to open them again.

'I think it's perfect.' Her eyes drift shut again, her chest continuing to rattle with every precious breath she takes.

After a minute or so she opens her eyes. In a moment of pure lucidity, her face almost glowing, she tells me, 'In the end, what matters most of all is how much you loved. You made a difference to my life, Paige. Not because you're family, but because of who you are. Understand?'

'Yes,' I whisper. 'I understand exactly what you mean.'

'You rest up,' I say. 'Bette's flight is at six o'clock tonight, and she'll pop in with Nick later. She says she can't wait to see you. I'll be back in the morning with Frank.'

Elsie keeps her eyes closed, giving the tiniest nod to show she understands.

CHAPTER FORTY-EIGHT

Nick

Usually, whenever Paige and I are invited to a barbecue or a dinner with friends, we stop by Mrs Betty Baker's, and Paige skilfully manoeuvres whatever cake or tart she's bought into her trusty old Tupperware container. Of course all our friends and family members know she does this but are too polite to say so. It's not like Paige doesn't know they know – she does, but it's something we all go along with. Tonight is different. Tonight, Paige is in the kitchen, attempting the same old croquembouche we attempted weeks ago. She's been in the kitchen for hours.

'It's looking good.' In all fairness, it's coming together nicely, even if it is a little out of proportion.

I check my watch. 'We said we'd be there at seven.' Ben and Pamela have invited us around for a barbecue, which puts the croquembouche into misfit territory.

'Being late is a small price to pay here, Nick,' she says, working on the spun sugar. She concentrates, her tongue poking out the side of her mouth.

'You couldn't have chosen a different day?' I say as we finally carry it to the car.

'I don't want to die without mastering a croquembouche without your help.' Her lips form a smile, one that reaches her eyes. 'It's fine, Nick. You can laugh. It's a joke.'

I want to tell her it's not a joke, or at least not a funny one, when I realise this is exactly the kind of joke she and I would make before. Before everything changed us.

'Please do not tell me you've got a bucket list.'

She chuckles. 'You'll be pleased to know I do not have a bucket list,' she confirms.

We get back from Pamela and Ben's before eleven, but no matter how hard I try, I can't seem to fall asleep, so I go outside and light the outdoor fire. Evelyn keeps a gardening notebook on one of the shelves near the potted flowers. I take it down, and as I sit there under the moonlight on the lawn in one of the old white wicker chairs, watching the crackle of the fire, I start to do something I haven't done in years.

I start to pray.

Please God, if you can hear me, let this all be okay.

Please God, don't take her away.

Please God, let them both make it.

I don't know how long I've spent out here by the time Paige joins me, carrying a couple of blankets with her. She pulls out a chair and sits next to me.

She tilts her head up to the sky. 'I couldn't sleep either. I kept thinking of Pamela's face when the croquembouche collapsed.'

I laugh. 'She didn't know whether to laugh or cry.'

'I did it though. I made it. It was in tip-top condition when it left this house, Nick. So, whatcha doing out here?'

'I keep thinking about us. Whether we're actually going to be okay.'

Paige pulls the blanket around herself. 'Yes, I think we will be fine. People do and say things they don't mean when they're faced with life-altering decisions. We both know that.'

'I lost your trust.'

'And I lost yours.'

'No, you didn't.'

'I made a decision and put our baby ahead of you. I put what I wanted ahead of what you wanted.'

'We're here now. Dealing with it.'

'Losing sleep over it,' she says, smiling. 'What are you writing, anyway? Don't tell me you've turned to poetry.'

Paige and I barely talk about God, or religion, even if we were baptised and married in church. So when I tell her I'm praying, she looks at me as if I've totally lost it.

'Praying,' she repeats, her eyes moving from my notepad to the basket I'm filling with notes. She nods slowly, understanding.

'It's silly, isn't it? Given I never go to church. I probably should have lit a candle or be on my knees or something. I'm doing it all wrong, huh?'

Paige smiles. 'I don't think it matters. What are you praying for?'

I lean back in my chair and look up at the sky, filled with tiny white stars, and let out a deep sigh. 'I'm praying that our baby will be okay, that you'll be okay, that… everything will be okay.'

Paige's hand reaches out and clasps mine. 'Can I pray with you?'

I hand over the notebook and she tears a few pages off and hands it back to me.

She scribbles on a few and tosses them into the basket. Within minutes we are immersed in this activity, silently sharing our prayers and wishes on paper, hoping they'll be answered.

When we finally run out of paper, Paige shows me her last note.

Thank you, God, for everything in my life, especially my husband. You brought us together, so I'm hoping, somehow, you'll find a way to keep us together. Over to you now, big guy.

She stands up and manoeuvres herself onto my lap. She kisses me, so deeply and passionately, and all I can think of is that I wish it will never, ever, ever come to an end.

In the morning, when I go to the garden to collect the notes, they're gone, the wicker basket empty. They've been swept away by the wind and are no longer in our hands.

'I know how hard this is for you,' Paige says to me.

'I need you to know that I might run out of toothpaste, and toilet paper, and if it's a girl, I have no idea how to style hair, and if he or she ever needs a tonsillectomy, I'll probably rock up at the drop-off zone, go play a round of golf and come back later.'

'I'd pace the hall for tonsillectomy,' she says. She frames my face with her hands and smiles.

'Of course you would. And it would be perfect.'

CHAPTER FORTY-NINE

Paige

On Tuesday evening, Hope turns up at my doorstep in her gym gear demanding I join her at her evening Pilates class. A heart condition is not going to be an excuse for me to let my pelvic floor or my abdominals suffer.

Eloise, the spritely instructor with a shock of pastel-coloured hair that is lavender at the roots morphing into shades of mint green and aqua by the ends, thrusts a sign-up form my way. I've ticked my way through boxes that six months ago would have made me turn around and flee.

Are you pregnant? *Yes.*

Are you suffering from any of the following conditions? *Yes. Heart condition – PPCM. It's rare and a huge pain in the butt!*

Are you on medication? *Yes. Lots. See following page for a list.*

And then… Have you any children? *Yes, one.*

What are their ages? *Max would have been one.*

Eloise gives me a shaky look as she scans the form and flips over the page.

'I'm not going to die in the middle of your class, I promise,' I tell her.

'I can vouch for that. The new season of *The Crown* comes out tonight and there's no way she's missing it,' Hope says, taking hold of my wrist and leading me to the mats.

The workout is hard, and Eloise keeps pointing out all the things I'm doing wrong. 'Watch your posture, Paige. Strong through the centre. Draw those shoulder blades down your back. No slouching.'

Once we're done, Eloise strides over and congratulates me on my effort. 'Did Hope tell you about our current promotion? If you sign up for twelve months, you get three months free.'

Under normal circumstances this would be a fantastic deal. Under normal circumstances I'd pull out my credit card and sign on the dotted line. But not today. This information makes my stomach lurch. It's possibly the first time I'm registering the fact that my decision equates to disruption when it comes to planning my life.

'Um,' I say, 'let me give it some thought.'

'Sure. Promo ends next week.' Eloise goes to push a flyer into my hand, which Hope is quick to grab. She folds it in half and tosses it into her bag. 'Thanks, Eloise.' She grabs me by the hand.

'Come on, let's go.'

'Hope—'

'Don't think about it,' she says firmly.

'But—'

'Don't think about it,' she repeats.

We have tickets to see Ed Sheeran in late February. Grandstand tickets for the Grand Prix in March. I'm supposed to take Ella and Ethan to see Disney on Ice in early July. And Mum is turning sixty in the spring. We're buying her and Dad tickets to the United States since she's always dreamed of going cruising in Alaska. Caitlin has already booked the venue for her surprise party. I'm in charge of the table centrepieces. What if I'm not there for it? What if I can't be there for any of it?

If I don't make it, what will our baby have to hold onto? How will people, generations from now, remember Paige Hutton, wife of Nick Bellbrae? I've quietly sailed through my thirty-four years without ambition or footprint. And it suddenly bothers me. Much more than I ever thought it would. How will my son or daughter remember me if he or she doesn't have the chance to know me?

I think about the storage boxes in my garage, which is pretty much empty aside from a camping tent we used circa 2010, a set of Nick's dusty golf clubs, a pair of old roller skates (no idea how they got there) and my old violin (I played for six years). Most of our photographs are digital. It dawns on me that Paige Hutton, wife of Nick, daughter of David and Evelyn, sister of Ryan and Caitlin, aunty of Ella and Ethan, has no heirlooms or significant *things* to pass on to a child apart from some lumpy, misshapen toys. You can hardly count my recipe books, of which I have many – but of course they mean very little. I can't blind bake pastry properly or pull off a pavlova and probably never will. Maybe that's what they'll remember about me. Terrible cook. Loved recipe books. Worked at an oldies' home. Excellent Snap player.

What else?

'Hey, are you okay?' says Hope in the locker room, startling me from my thoughts. I've showered and dressed, and am now just sitting, staring into space.

'What if I actually don't make it?'

Hope tries to laugh it off, like it's an overreaction, some ridiculous notion for her to entertain. 'Look at you. You just did an hour of Pilates.'

More like forty-five minutes, and what she doesn't know is that I feel like I could sleep for three days.

'It's not a guarantee that you won't make it, Paige, so stop acting like it is.'

'I'll wait for you outside,' I say, scooping up my gym bag and mat.

She follows me out the door, 'Get back in there,' I tell her, 'You're practically naked.' That doesn't stop her. She waltzes out in her underwear like she's walking around in her bedroom.

'Well, I'm not going to let you walk away like that. Did you hear me?'

'My ears are working fine.'

'I mean, did you really hear me, Paige, because this is important.'

'Yes. I heard you.'

'Good. Now maybe you need to work on Nick.'

CHAPTER FIFTY

Nick

A couple of weeks later, my phone rings while I'm in the middle of surgery.

'My right pocket,' I say.

Allison, one of the nurses, slips her hand into my pocket.

'It's your wife,' she says.

'Go ahead and answer,' I tell her.

Allison puts the call on speaker while I prepare to suture up a patient – Hannah, who is going to be fine after her hernia operation. 'Hi, Paige, it's Allison, answering on behalf of Nick.'

'Oh, hi, how are you? Is he around by any chance?'

'He's got his hands in a patient but let me see if he can talk.'

'I'm fine to talk, thanks, Allison.' Allison moves the phone closer to me, holding it up so I can continue working.

'Paige, hi.'

'Oh, hey, sorry to interrupt. I'm in possession of doughnuts from Mrs Betty Baker's. Do you have time for a break at all today?'

'If he doesn't, I do,' pipes in Allison with a melodic chuckle. 'God, how I love those doughnuts.'

'So good. You know they're opening a new shop downstairs next month,' comes another voice, this one from Christian.

I almost forget Paige is still on the phone. 'Did you hear me, Nick?'

'Yeah, sure. Can you swing by at around twelve? I'll meet you outside. The usual spot.'

We sit together on the grassed area outside the hospital. Most of the lunch crowd has thinned out but there are still groups of people spotted over the lawn and under some of the trees.

'Bet you're wondering why I'm here,' she says, wrestling our drinks from a cardboard tray. Flat white (for me) and a berry smoothie (for her).

'Does it have anything to do with the dozen lemon curd doughnuts that are in there?' I say, pointing to one of two boxes beside me. Being out here, on the lawn on a lunch break, reminds me of the early days of our relationship. Paige used to visit all the time. All the cafeteria staff knew her name.

'Maybe,' she says. 'Or maybe it has to do with the fact that you have been calling me twice a day for the past five days and I figured we need to get to the bottom of it.'

This is something I hoped she wouldn't notice. I'll admit, it is unusual for me to call her more than once a day.

'Don't worry,' she says, lifting her hands up. 'I know it's your way of dealing with this. And it's fine, really it is. I love talking to you. But if Paige Hutton is going to have an expiry date that comes sooner in life than later, then I am hereby making it my mission to make sure that I come visit more regularly.'

'Please don't talk like that.'

'It's fine.'

'It's not fine. You can't joke about it like that.'

'What else can I do? This is it, Nick. My life, our baby's life – it all depends on the way the months ahead pan out. Living with this huge question mark over our heads like some nasty grey cloud is exhausting. And, honestly, we both need some good-quality sleep. Do you know how bad sleep deprivation is for your skin? People who do not have a baby yet should not be waking at all hours of the night like us.' She gives me a knowing look.

'I'm sorry.'

'I know you can't turn the worrying off like a switch, and neither can I, but please, Nick – let's try to enjoy things day by day? Please try not to worry about me or what lies ahead.'

Her fingers trace one of my eyebrows – the one missing a tiny patch of hair. She slowly opens one of the boxes to reveal a single white envelope.

'No doughnuts? I don't know how I'm going to walk back in there and tell my team that there are no doughnuts. You can't mess with my team, Paige.'

She holds the envelope up, teasing me.

'If this is a bill, I'm afraid I don't want it.'

'I've been holding onto this since I had my last ultrasound… I've been waiting for the right moment to open it. That's if you want to know…'

I jerk my head up. 'You know what we're having?'

'Not yet,' she says. 'It all depends on whether you open the envelope. For all I know there could be a rates notice in there.'

I tear the envelope open and she pulls the card out. In our doctor's scrawly handwriting are the words:

> *Congratulations to the most wonderful couple I know! You're having a GIRL!*

I blink, staring at the most amazing words I've ever seen written on paper, while Paige laughs, the goofiest of smiles appearing on her face. 'It's a girl. We're having a girl.'

'Yes,' I say, nodding as I turn my face towards hers. There they are: Paige's eyes, sparkling with happiness. 'We are having a baby. We're having a girl.' A surge of elation simmers away and I marvel at the way it feels. Paige is keeping the baby. Our baby. Here we are, Paige and me, in this magical moment that, no matter what happens, nobody can take from us

Now that we know we are having a girl, I find myself imagining her life. In my mind's eye, Paige is there, *with* us – pushing her on a swing, teaching her how to read, feeding her in her high chair, reading to her in the cubby house.

'Earth to Nick,' comes Paige's voice as I finish shaving. She's standing in the doorway of the bathroom in her robe with a piece of toast in her hand.

'Hey, I meant to ask you. How's Grandma doing?'

'Not so great. Apparently, you told her you were bringing her a new pair of slippers.'

'I might have. Wait till she sees them. They're leopard print.' She laughs. 'Bet she'll love them.'

'If we leave soon, maybe we can pop past to see her on our way to the Yarra Valley.' We've organised a day out at a winery, not that Paige can drink wine, but she loves the scenic drive anyway.

'Yeah, sure.' She finishes her toast and towel-dries her hair. 'I've been thinking that, when you're ready, we could talk about the nursery. I'd like to make a start on it even if it's early, and maybe we should book some painters in this time?'

'Course, yeah, I'll get onto it straight away. Leave it with me.'

Paige starts tearing through her dresser, trying to find a pair of clean pants.

'I think we should try to take this day by day but also treat it like any other pregnancy. I want things to feel normal, and I want our friends and family to feel happy for us. I want them to be involved and not feel awkward in any way.'

'Got it,' I say. 'You don't want anyone worrying about you.'

'Right. That's exactly what I don't want,' she says, pulling up her pants. 'Ugh, they're on backwards.' She wriggles out of them, tries again and then heads to the bathroom to brush her teeth.

'I've been making a list of baby names,' I call out. 'And Harper is definitely looking good but I found another name I think you might like.'

'Mmm?' she says, her mouth full of toothpaste.

'Aveline,' I say, stepping back into the bathroom. 'French for Evelyn. Ava for short.'

Her eyes widen. 'Yes,' she whispers as she turns to face me. 'I love it.'

CHAPTER FIFTY-ONE

Paige

I reach my third trimester. My heart seems to be doing fine, and for the most part, life's been passing by as normal. Sunday night dinner at Mum and Dad's is back on. Ryan called three days ago to let us know Susannah is pregnant. It's early, but they're hopeful, as are we. Elsie passed away a few weeks ago, with Frank by her side. She'd finished not only the matinee jacket but a pair of matching booties and a beanie for Aveline. Windsor Lakes isn't the same without her. Immediately following the news, for the first time ever, Viv did not bake any sort of comfort food. Instead she learnt to play bridge with Frank.

Caitlin gave birth to a baby. Another boy. They named him Jordan. Her contractions started at eight in the evening and she delivered him close to midnight. He's perfect, from his soft peach skin to his mop of light brown hair and tiny button nose. We can't decide whether he looks more like Mark or Caitlin, though Dad is convinced he can see something of himself in him. Nick's face lit up when he laid eyes on Jordan for the first time, bundled up in a white blanket with a blue beanie on his head. Caitlin asked him to pass him to her as he was due for a feed. Effortlessly, his strong hands dipped into the crib, lifting up baby Jordan as he brought him to his chest.

'Hey, little guy. Looking pretty perfect to me,' he said softly before handing him over to Caitlin. He looked over at me then and winked reassuringly. I haven't been able to get the picture of him doing that out of my mind since.

I finished the eighteenth amigurumi last week. I'm writing Aveline the last letter to slide into its pocket when Nick snuggles up beside me on the sofa.

'What are you up to?' He flips a banana in the air, catches it and starts peeling it.

I shake my head in amusement. Nick has a strange habit of playing with fruit before he eats it. Rolling it, tossing it, spinning it. 'Child,' I mutter.

Nick picks up a stuffed donkey. 'Is this what she gets for her sixteenth? Pedro the donkey?'

'Whatever happened with Annoying Emily? Did she ever end up finding her Pedro?'

'I didn't tell you? Oh my God, Paige. She found him. In Valencia.' He frowns. 'Or was it Madrid? Either way, it was in Spain. She actually found the guy.'

'And he's on board? Like, they're sticking together now?'

'She hasn't come back yet.' He shrugs. 'So I guess so.'

'Good for her,' I say, smiling.

I look at Nick, biting into the rest of his banana, and the enormity of what I've asked him to do for me, for our baby, hits me like a ton of bricks. Nick will potentially be the witness to our child's first everything. He is the one she will come to for... *everything*. Nick and I are bound by love, and he is going to be the glue that will keep our family, and the memory of me, together. He will be the one to explain to our daughter that the love that binds us is not always straightforward, but it is strong.

I point at the donkey Nick is still holding. 'These toys, Nick. They're not just toys.'

'Oh, really? Do they come alive at night?'

'Better.' I pick up another one of the toys – an owl. 'On the bottom of each of these toys I attached a little pocket – like an envelope, which you unbutton like this.' I show him. 'And inside are letters. To Aveline. From me.'

'Eighteen of them?'

I nod. 'Yes, one for every birthday until she's eighteen.'

Nick blinks, showing me he understands.

'They're not perfect, but I tried my best. I think this is the best I can do.'

'I love that they're not perfect,' says Nick, picking up another toy. 'There's something human about them being a little wonky, and the stuffing not being even, and... look, these eyes are a little lopsided, too.' He laughs as he gives a little pig a squeeze. 'Imperfectly made with love by your perfect mum. That's what I'll tell her.'

A month later, once Jordan has settled into a routine – albeit a loose one – Caitlin and Mark decide to venture to the country house with him for a quiet weekend away. Now that Jordan has arrived, she seems less uptight than usual, something I suspect has to do with the counselling she and Mark have been having since his birth. In true Caitlin fashion, she's stocked up on self-help books so she can collate her own theories on how to make a marriage last a distance. Even Mark seems happier, more talkative and attentive than usual.

It's Nick's weekend off so we've made plans to take Ella and Ethan to the zoo.

'Are you sure you'll be all right with them? They can be such handfuls. I don't want you over-exerting yourself,' says Caitlin, momentarily resting her bag on the floor.

'Nick's home all weekend. Plus, Mum's only a phone call away. I promise you, it'll be fine,' I reassure her. 'Repeat after me: the children will be fine.'

Caitlin nods and repeats. 'Fine.'

'Yes. Absolutely fine. We even have a surgeon on standby should any emergencies arise.'

Caitlin groans. 'You are playing into my biggest fears.'

'Don't worry. He's a fantastic doctor.'

As Caitlin picks up her overnight bag, I reach out for her arm. 'Caitlin, there's something I need to say.'

She gives me a questioning look.

'You're enough. More than enough. Even if you weren't on the PFA and were late for meetings and didn't manage to get your nails done or your face made up before you left the house, you would still be *Caitlin*, my big sister – the one who has the biggest heart and the smartest comebacks, and the most reliable shoulder to rest a head on when things go wrong.'

'Paige…'

'What I'm trying to say is that you don't need to try to be perfect all the time. You don't need to hide from me or anyone else who matters in your life. You hold yourself up to these impossibly high standards but we all love you even if you don't meet them. Understand?'

'Yes,' she whispers. 'I don't want things to fall apart.'

'They won't. But if they do, you'll deal with it. The world won't stop turning if you take a step back and relinquish a bit of control over things.'

Caitlin rubs her forehead. 'You're right. And maybe that's also something Mark and I need to discuss.'

'There's one thing you're wrong about though.'

'What's that?'

'It's you who has the smartest comebacks.'

I laugh. 'Practice. Go on, get out of here,' I say, hands on her shoulders as I steer her towards the door. Mark is already waiting in the car. 'My husband and I would like to commence spoiling your kids in peace. We plan on breaking lots of rules.' I smile at her cheekily.

'Okay, well, good luck with it and let me know how it goes.' She pauses. 'Or not.'

CHAPTER FIFTY-TWO

Nick

We are three hours into our long day at the zoo, and both kids are reaching the point of exhaustion.

The queue for ice cream is a mile long, but a promise is a promise, and after thirty minutes, I present Ella and Ethan with two half-melted bubblegum ice-cream cones.

'This should hopefully make them forget about the long walk back to the car.'

Paige smears a squirt of sunscreen onto Ethan's arm, which he tries to pull away, and then hands the tube back to me. 'Hey, do we have any more water?'

'Yeah, check the backpack,' I tell her. Ethan's about to lose his ice cream. I reach out and steady his hand so he doesn't drop it.

Paige tips the bag upside down, but no bottles fall out. 'Looks like we're out. Let me go grab some more.'

'I can go,' I offer.

'No, it's fine. Also need to pee.'

'Again?'

'Again,' she says, rolling her eyes.

'Okay, well, sure, I'll wait with the kids.'

By the time Paige finally returns half an hour later, the kids are well and truly ready to go home. About five minutes before Paige got back, Ella decided to climb a tree, tripped on a stump and cut her knee. She's now crying uncontrollably.

'Hi, Nurse Paige, this is Ella – 101 years old, funny little laugh, freckles, pet giraffe called Harvey. She's had a fall and grazed her knee but it looks like she should be able to keep her leg if everything goes smoothly.'

'Got it,' says Paige, rummaging through her handbag for a wipe.

I fake-cough into my fist. 'We are also going to need Harvey.'

'Yes, course,' she says, breathlessly, turning to the backpack.

'Afternoon, Harvey!' I say, holding up the worn-out giraffe that Paige and I gave to Ella when she was born. She still takes it everywhere.

Ella giggles.

'How's your friend Ella feeling today?'

'Good,' replies Ella, sitting up straighter.

'Mind if I check her knee out?'

Ella shakes her head.

'Okay, this won't take a second.' I clean up Ella's knee and then say, 'Harvey, I hereby declare Ella ready to get up.' I turn to Paige. 'Crisis averted.'

She returns a half-hearted smile.

'What is it? What's wrong?'

'Hey, Ethan, let's go see those real giraffes on the way back to the car,' says Paige suddenly. Ethan extends a pudgy hand, which she takes hold of.

'But we still need to see the—'

Paige shakes her head. 'Car,' she replies. 'It's not an emergency... I just... I'm feeling a little off. Light-headed. I think I've overdone it. I had a little... flutter.'

'What? Like an arrhythmia? Shortness of breath?' I feel the adrenaline kick in. This cannot be the start of the end. She's only twenty-nine weeks.

'Yeah, just subtle. And no, my breathing's fine. But I'm also feeling a little tired. I don't know… Do we need to get it checked out?'

I lift Ethan into my arms and onto my shoulders. 'Okay, little guy, let's go see these giraffes.' I pull my phone from my pocket and make a call.

'Hi, James, it's Nick. Are you in clinic today?'

Paige takes Ella by the hand. 'Let's go, sweetheart. Did I tell you you're going to Nanny Evelyn's today?'

Dr Sanders is wearing a light pink polo and a pair of beige trousers, looking like he's come straight from the golf course.

'How's my favourite patient?' he asks, flashing Paige the kind of smile that would make any patient relax.

'I don't think I've had enough to drink today,' she says, her voice quiet as she sits back on the crisp cotton sheets.

'Nick wouldn't have called me on a Saturday if he didn't think it was important.'

'I know. I'm only twenty-nine weeks, though, and I can't let this happen. Not now. It's too soon.'

'Right. So tell me about things.'

Paige tells him about the symptoms she's been experiencing.

'All right, so let's see – any difficulty breathing when lying down?'

'No, not really.'

'We'll see what's going on today, and if we need to adjust your meds, we'll look at doing that first before we suggest any other kind of intervention. Sound okay?'

'Yes,' she tells him.

'When was the last time you had an echo?'

'Three weeks ago.'

Dr Sanders keeps his focus on the monitor. 'And there was nothing significant to report?'

'Nope.'

'A slight enlargement,' I tell him. I reel off all the figures for him. And then I show him the report on my phone.

'Ah yes, I remember seeing that one. Okay, so Paige, you're not going to like me for asking this one, but what's your weight gain been like?'

She groans. 'Um... well... I've been giving into my cravings lately. I figured I should fully step into the role of impending motherhood and take advantage of poppy seed bread.'

'I see. And this equates to how many grams exactly?' asks Dr Sanders.

She gives him a sheepish look. 'Well, I'd say more like two kilos. Or... well, actually, two and a half kilos and a new pair of jeans.'

'In what? A month?'

'Um, more like the past two and a half weeks.'

Dr Sanders clicks his tongue.

'Are you worried?'

Dr Sanders rests a light hand on my shoulder. 'Just cautious.' He arranges for an echo and runs some blood tests.

After a four-hour wait, the results confirm Paige has probably overdone it. He sends us home with a warning to continue watching Paige's salt intake. 'Oh, and Paige?' he says as we're walking out the door.

'Yeah?'

'Poppy seed loaf is my favourite too. I don't blame you.'

She lets out a small laugh.

'See you next month.'

'Can I have a word please?' I say to James before I leave the room.

'I'm going to grab some water,' says Paige, taking this as her cue to leave us to it.

'Do you think she'll be back before the month's out? What exactly did today's echo show?'

James puts a hand on my back and leads me out of the room. 'It showed another slight enlargement, Nick. This is where I tell you to go home and enjoy the next few weeks with your wife. At this point we need to wait and see.'

CHAPTER FIFTY-THREE

Paige

'Nick and I decided on a name a while ago,' I say to Mum after work a few weeks later.

She presses a hand to her mouth. 'And?'

'Aveline. It's French for Evelyn.'

'Oh, Paige.' Mum looks like she might cry. 'I'm honoured.'

'It was Nick's idea.'

'Come upstairs, I want to show you something,' she says.

I follow her to her bedroom and she hands me a box. 'This is for you.'

Inside, there's the outfit I came home from hospital in. I move some of the tissue paper and discover a few loose photographs: my first birthday, my first day of school, my graduation. There are photos of Caitlin, me and Ryan in the back garden, bare legs, faces smeared with fluorescent zinc cream, arms wide open feeling the spray of water from the sprinkler on our bodies. The mud cakes I'd forgotten about. The fairy garden under the pomegranate tree. Dad dressed as a superhero, sitting on an upturned crate reading the newspaper.

Looking across to Mum, standing there, a serene expression on her face, her eyes blinking at me thoughtfully, I swear she's almost seeing the memories playing themselves back in her mind. I set the photos down and take one of the last two items from the box: Ruby, the doll that saw the best of days and the worst of days, and was with me through it all. Her left eye is hanging on by a loose thread, and her cheek is grubby with dirt, and she has one shoe missing, but I feel a surge of emotion ripple through me as I turn her body over in my hands, which are so much bigger than the last time I handled her. 'You left her on the bed for me at Grandma Beth's when we came home from the airport after saying goodbye to you and Dad when you went to Malaysia.'

'Yep,' says Mum. 'And she didn't leave your side for years.' Mum rolls her eyes. 'I set a place at breakfast for Ruby every morning for six months after that trip.' She laughs, taking her from me. 'Snickers was very jealous.' Snickers was the toy elf I won at a beach carnival when I was seven. She adjusts Ruby's coat and hair as I lift out an envelope with my name on it. As I open it, Mum walks towards the window, suddenly appearing smaller to me than she ever has before. She keeps her body turned away from me as I read the note she's written for me, in her beautiful cursive handwriting I spent hours trying to emulate as a child.

My dearest Paige,

I've always felt blessed to be your mother, and I've lived my life cherishing all the times you enriched my life, simply by being in it. When you're potentially faced with losing your daughter, those cherished moments have a way of becoming even more precious. Each of these items are tied to moments of joy, moments I so wish I could go back and relive, just to feel your tiny body close to mine, or your face light up when Dad told a joke. Those were times when I had the power to make things better. And oh, how I wish I could make things better now.

You know, when I close my eyes, I can still hear your voice as a toddler. When you smiled, I couldn't help but smile, when you laughed, I couldn't help but laugh, when you cried, I'd wipe away a tear, and now that you're all grown up, it warms my heart that nothing has changed. The only thing that really changes is time. And none of us get enough of it.

I am praying every moment of every day that you'll know the joy of having a daughter to pass these items onto. I am praying that she might know first-hand what it is like to be loved by you. But if things don't go the way we want them to for our family, I want you to know that I will make it my job to ensure she knows how much you loved her and how brave you were to sacrifice everything, including your own life, for her.

I am so proud of you, Paige. You make my heart burst with love every time you walk into the room. You always have, and you always will.

Your loving mother,
Evelyn

I fold the note. 'Mum…'

Mum simply nods and holds her arms open for me to fall into them. We stay there like this, swaying ever so gently, Mum pressing her lips against my head and patting my back.

'I love you, Mum. So much,' I muster.

'I know… I know… I know you do,' she whispers back. 'You don't even need to say it.'

I close my eyes and press my ear against her chest, listening to her beating heart. I don't want to leave the comfort of her embrace. I could listen to her heart beating like this forever.

CHAPTER FIFTY-FOUR

Nick

The phone rings at 4 a.m., with a call letting me know I'm needed at the hospital for an emergency. Paige is sprawled across the bed, fast asleep. I roll onto my side and stroke her face, thinking about how lucky I am to have her in my life, and I know this is something I will never, ever take for granted for as long as I live. The feeling of wanting to stay here – with her – to miss a day of work, is foreign to me, but I have to go; someone's child needs me.

Before I go, I search the study drawer for the Post-it notes I haven't written on in a long time.

Didn't want to wake you. You're beautiful when you're sleeping. Call me when you get up. Nick x

It's almost lunchtime by the time I realise that Paige hasn't called me. I try calling her during a short break, but she doesn't answer. An hour later, I try again to no avail. It's then that I remember that Piper has an appointment with the vet today, but I can't recall whether Paige said it was before or after lunch. Either way, I can't help thinking something is off. I call Evelyn and leave a voicemail for her to check on Paige as soon as she can.

I'm prepping for surgery when I'm interrupted for an urgent call late that afternoon.

'Paige, it's me. They said it's urgent.'

'There's a hammering in my chest that isn't stopping.'

'Did you just climb the stairs? Or have you been resting?'

'Resting. I slept in until midday. I'm tired, so tired. And when I lie on my back, it's hard to breathe.'

The blood drains from my face.

I turn to Kerry, one of the nurses, and let her know I won't be able to perform the surgery. I keep talking to Paige while I go back for my keys, taking her through the checklist Victoria gave her. This doesn't sound good.

'I don't know if it's anxiety or something else, but it feels like there isn't enough air, Nick. How far off are you?'

'Too far. I want you to get off the phone and call an ambulance. Get yourself ready, call your parents, and tell them to come straight to the hospital. I'll meet you there.'

The lift doors seem to be taking forever to open.

'Tell me on a scale of one to ten,' she presses. 'The likelihood that they'll be wanting to deliver the baby today.'

She's almost thirty-two weeks, which means Aveline will be born moderately pre-term. And there is every chance she will be delivering her today.

'Paige, I need you to get off the phone now. We'll talk about it when I get there.'

'I need to know, Nick. If they don't send me home today, I need some time to let people know… I haven't said goodbye yet…'

'I'll see what I can do. I'll call them for you.'

The lift doors finally open and I step inside. Which level did I park on this morning?

'This is it? Is this it?' She sounds panicked now. 'My hospital bag isn't packed yet. I'm not ready, Nick.'

The lift doors close, and my call is going to cut out any moment. 'Just stay calm and forget about the hospital bag. I'll be there as soon as I can.' And then… 'Paige?'

'Yes?'

'I love you. I love you more than anything in the world.'

CHAPTER FIFTY-FIVE

Paige

The paramedics arrive before I get the chance to call everyone. They have just closed the doors to the ambulance when we hear a frantic knocking on the side of the vehicle.

'Wait!'

The female paramedic opens the door and looks at me for an answer.

'Dad,' I say. 'It's my dad.'

He's puffed out, perspiration running down his face.

'I came as soon as I could. Mum called me and I was only a street away helping Ted with his front landscaping.' He shakes his head. 'Never mind. I just wanted to see you before...'

'Would you like to ride with her?' she asks.

Dad looks at me for an answer.

I manage a thumbs up, and Dad clambers in. He leans in for an awkward hug.

Just as the paramedic closes the doors again, Mum turns up in her car and toots. She rushes out of the car and runs towards the ambulance.

'We really need to get you to hospital,' says Holley.

'Evelyn, swap places with me, darling,' says Dad.

'No, it's fine. I'll meet you both there. I wanted to see her...' She mouths a quick, *I love you.*

I lift a hand to wave goodbye as the doors finally close. As we pull away I picture Mum waving back until we turn onto the road. It reminds me of how she would sometimes let us say goodbye to Dad at the airport. The four of us would wave at the sky, watching his plane disappear behind the clouds. And every single day he was away, we would ask Mum how long it would be until we would see him again. This cannot be it. It simply cannot be the last time I see my mother.

Nick is there, waiting in emergency with Dr Sanders and Victoria when I arrive. But there's also Caitlin and Mark, and Hope and Paul. Someone's also called Viv because she's there with Frank in a wheelchair. They're all there, huddled together watching, and the only thing I can do is wave. I don't know if I will ever see them again.

Mum arrives as I'm being rushed into a cubicle. 'Darling, Paige. I'm here. I'll be out here waiting for you, okay?' She leans in and kisses me, the moisture from her tears brushing my cheeks. She lets go of my hand and walks away, and then the doctors, nurses, they're suddenly all around me. Memories of Max swoop into my mind, but this is different. It is calmer. Quieter. I feel Aveline moving. I keep my hands on my belly and tell her to hold on. To be strong. To be brave. To be okay without me. There are medical professionals buzzing around, but it's like everything is in slow motion. They're helping me into a gown, giving me an echo, hooking me up to monitors, drawing blood, and yet it feels like I'm not inhabiting my own body. Nick is beside me, holding my hand the entire time, watching intently as my dilated heart determines what will happen next.

Then, Dr Sanders says in a sandpapery but kind voice, 'Paige, you won't be able to give birth naturally – the stress on your heart would be too great. A vaginal birth could potentially take more than twenty-four hours, and the baby isn't turned the right way. We're going to need to perform a C-section. It's the safest option to deliver the baby in this controlled situation where we can monitor everything.'

I close my eyes, letting the confirmation of what I know is coming wash over me.

Nick squeezes my hand.

'Once again, you're experiencing heart failure. The C-section is still going to be a risky operation.'

I turn my head to face Nick. 'I love you. So much.'

'You're my everything, Paige. She's my everything,' he says, pressing his hand against my belly while he rests another on my cheek. 'I love you both more than you could know.'

The only thing I can find to write with is a stubby pencil from IKEA. I chew on the end of it while we wait for Dr Sanders to return. Nick leaves the room for what he promises will be less than three minutes so he can talk to Victoria.

As nurses and midwives continue busying themselves around me, I think of Mum and Dad, Ryan and Susannah, and Caitlin and Mark. I think of Ella and Ethan and the way their giggles are like sunshine, of Jordan and the tiny gumnut hat he was wearing the last time I saw him. And I think of Bette and the rhythm of the ocean and our walks along the beach. I think of Hope and Paul and Ollie. And I think of Nick. My pencil is almost blunt, I only have one sheet of paper and I need to make the words count. But how to pen a lifetime of thoughts onto a single page? There are so many things I want Nick to know – things he might need to know about continuing life without me. Does he have any idea that mattresses should be changed every seven years instead of ten or fifteen? We have three years left in ours at the most.

The heating ducts should be cleared out yearly. Every autumn I always call the same guy, Brett. He takes his coffee white with three sugars.

Does any of this even matter? I need more time to work this out. I ponder as my pencil hovers over the sheet of paper.

Dear Nick,

If you're reading this letter, I'm sorry. I'm sorry that you're going to have to do this without me. I know it's going to be hard without me. I know there will be times you will look into Aveline's eyes and see me. When that happens, I want you to find a way to smile, Nick. Everything I ever wanted was to become a mother and live a happy life with you. I was so very lucky to get everything I ever wanted.

When she's old enough, tell her, Nick. Tell our baby girl that Mummy said, 'The sweetest part of loving you was when I was waiting for you.' I hope she likes the toys I made for her.

I love you. I will always love you.
Your loving wife,
Paige

P.S. Don't ever worry about running out of toilet paper. All that matters is how much we loved.

EPILOGUE

Eighteen Years Later

'The winner of the Victorian Young Australian of the Year is Aveline Bellbrae.'

Nick takes a deep breath and squeezes Ava's shoulder. 'Well done, cricket. Knew you could do it,' he whispers as she squeezes past him.

Nick, Evelyn and David watch as Ava makes her way towards the stage, one hand in her pocket, holding on tightly to the good-luck charm her mother left her – a silver four-leaf clover. She carries it with her whenever she needs a little more confidence.

Ava steps towards the microphone, taking her time and clearing her throat as she scans the room.

'Look for the three of us and you'll be fine,' Nick said to her earlier when she'd told him she was feeling nervous.

She reaches for the microphone, lowering it slightly. She's wearing the navy-blue dress that Hope bought for her this morning after she'd decided that the floral one Ella had loaned her was too short and wouldn't do. Nick doesn't understand anything about dresses or fabrics, but all he knows is that in this moment, his daughter is beautiful, and every bit as special, kind and caring as he and Paige had hoped she would be. She has the same facial features as Paige: large blueish-green eyes, full lips and the hint of a dimple in her right cheek, which, for some reason, is always more prominent when she's tired. Her hair is darker than

Paige's but lighter than Nick's, and she often wears it tied back in a ponytail. Tonight, she had it professionally blow-waved. She looks older than her eighteen years, standing there all dressed up, accepting such an exceptional award, and Nick feels his eyes beginning to water as he compares the memories of her as a baby to the moment he's witnessing now. A moment he never thought he would see.

Ava grips the microphone. 'Good evening, everyone. It's an honour to receive this award for the work I've been involved in, raising awareness for a rare condition affecting women in late pregnancy or post-partum, called peripartum cardiomyopathy. I'd like to thank my dad, who is here tonight, along with my grandparents. Dad, thanks for always encouraging me and making me feel like I can achieve all the things in life I want to achieve.'

Nick clears his throat, feeling a mix of emotions swell inside him. Pride, happiness, a sense of longing for Paige to be here to share this moment with them.

Ava continues, her voice steadier now, more determined and even. 'I'd like to dedicate this award to my mother. Through the very act of becoming my mother, she demonstrated courage and determination, but also the kind of dedication and sacrifices we sometimes need to make in order to save a life. Even though you're not here, Mum, I love you and thank you. I wouldn't be here if it wasn't for you.'

It's almost eight thirty by the time Nick and Ava arrive back home. Evelyn and David have been following behind them in their car. 'Hey, sport, you're a little quiet,' says Nick as they take their coats off in the entrance. 'Everything okay?'

'Yeah, everything's fine. I wish Mum could have been here, that's all. If it wasn't for her, I wouldn't have gotten involved in the advocacy work in the first place.'

Nick keeps a straight face, trying not to reveal any emotion. 'Me too, cricket.' He hangs her coat on the rack beside his and follows the scent of party foods.

'I just pulled the sausage rolls out of the oven,' says Caitlin as Nick and Ava enter the busy kitchen. The bench is covered with platters of canapés and dips. 'Congratulations, sweetheart,' she says as she envelops Ava into a warm hug. 'I'm so proud of you.'

'Happy Birthday!' says Hope, handing Ava a gift. 'I can't believe you're already eighteen. So… I take it you won?' She holds Ava at arm's length. She's like the daughter Hope never had. '*Love* this dress on you.'

Ava holds up the award and grins sheepishly.

Hope puts her hand over her heart. 'Oh, sweetie! Congratulations!'

'Well done,' says Paul, grinning.

'Ollie! Will! Come in here! Ava's back and she has some news!' calls Miranda. 'God, I am so proud of this girl. Nick, you really hit the jackpot with this one.'

Nick laughs. 'On a good day I guess she's not too bad.' He winks at Ava, who gives a dramatic roll of her eyes in response.

Ollie and Will filter into the kitchen, alongside Ella, Ethan and Jordan. 'Happy Birthday!' they all shout.

Once their greetings are out of the way, Ava slips into her room to get changed. 'Knock knock, are you decent?' calls Nick from behind the door. They are long past the days where he can fling open the door to his daughter's room. He can still remember clearly the day they decided on her name. Paige had been brushing her teeth in the bathroom, her pants on backwards. It was the day she'd told him about the toys she was making for Ava. He is holding the last one – the *eighteenth* one – in his very hands now.

'Yep! Come in,' calls Ava, rolling a T-shirt over her head. 'Oops, put this on backwards,' she says, wriggling out of it. She turns her body away and tries again.

'You did great,' says Nick, turning to face the other side of the room to give her some privacy. 'Of course we always knew you had a good chance of winning. You're amazing. Just like your mum. Speaking of which…' He holds up the package, high above his head.

Ava jumps up to grab it from him.

He turns around as she gazes down at the package pensively.

'It's the last one. She asked me to give it to you. She wishes she could have been here.'

'Another one? Aren't I getting too old for these knitted toys now?'

'They're crocheted,' Nick corrects. 'Not knitted. Knitting's what you do with the two metal sticks.'

'Needles,' she corrects. 'Anyway, close enough.' Ava's fingers are already tearing the package open. Despite her age, she looks forward to these packages and her letters. She keeps the toys lined up on a shelf above her bed, and nobody except her is ever allowed to touch them. They are, of course, the most precious things she owns. She'd been particularly attached to Tabitha the whale when she was six, and Mrs Go Slow the turtle from the age of seven to twelve.

'A squirrel,' she says, letting the brown paper drop to the floor. 'I love it.'

Nick casts his mind back to the day Paige had finished making it. She was sitting on the sofa, her tongue poking out the side of her mouth while she tried to sew the eyes on straight.

Ava is now concentrating on opening the little pouch that contains a handwritten note from Paige.

'Should I leave you to it?' asks Nick, turning towards the door. He still finds it emotional, watching Ava read these letters.

'No,' she says, shaking her head. 'Stay.' She pats the bed.

Nick sits down beside her. 'Will you read it for me, Dad? Please? Since it's the last one?'

He clears his throat. 'Uh, yeah, sure.' He unfolds the letter, unsure of what it might contain.

Dear Aveline,

By now you're no doubt used to how these letters go, right? This is where I'm supposed to tell you all about my hopes and dreams for you and what to look out for in the year to come. Well, this letter is different. Writing these letters to you has been one of the sweetest parts of loving you. Through them, I've been able to dream for you – the Peter Rabbit cake for your first birthday, the pony party for your fifth, the sleepover for your sixteenth. Did you manage to read all the wonderful books I've told you about over the years? And in those times you were feeling a bit down, did my list of tips and tricks work? If they didn't, you can always go to Hope. Or Aunty Caitlin, or Uncle Ryan (depending on the problem). Anyway, now that you're an adult, you get to dream for yourself.

I want you to remember always that you are a gift. Your life is a gift, Aveline. Make the most of every minute. Enjoy all the wonderful things life has to offer.

Happy eighteenth birthday. I love you.
With all my heart,
Mum xo

P.S. Go give Dad a big kiss from me and remind him how much I love him. You got a good one, didn't you?

Nick swallows past the lump that has caught in his throat. 'You okay?' he asks, slipping his arm around Ava's shoulders as he plants a kiss on her head.

'Yep,' she says. 'Are *you*?' She screws up her freckled nose at him and reaches a finger over the moisture around the corner of his eye. 'You're such a softie, Dad.' She tilts her head. 'Hey, is that the doorbell?'

Nick shrugs and his eyes dart to and fro as if he's trying to listen. 'Are we expecting anyone else?'

'Don't think so.'

By now someone has opened the front door, and he can make out the exchange of greetings. Seconds later, someone knocks on Ava's door.

'Can I come in?' calls a female voice. The door flings open.

'Mum! You made it? I thought your flight was delayed!' Ava stands up and throws herself into her mother's arms.

'Ugh, it was. I had to get on a different flight. I can't believe I missed the presentation. Nick, we are going to have a heck of a Visa bill next month. But I'm home now, and here with you both.'

Paige has been away on a trip to Africa as part of Hope's charity organisation. She travels over once a year, sometimes together with Nick, who provides medical assistance to children in need, but this year their schedules meant they'd needed to travel separately. Over the years, Paige, alongside Hope, has been instrumental in coordinating fundraising efforts from the sale of ethically produced crocheted dolls. Together, they've managed to raise enough funds to give millions of meals to children and families in need.

Paige guides Ava into another embrace. 'Happy birthday, cricket. I'm so sorry I wasn't there.' She pauses. 'Did you…?'

Ava nods excitedly. 'Yes! Yes, I won!'

Paige turns to face Nick and beams a smile his way. 'Oh my God, Nick. She won!' She throws her arms around Nick. He can smell her perfume and the mint on her breath. 'I am so proud of her!'

'So, you opened your gift?'

Ava nods. 'Thanks, Mum.'

'No, my darling. Thank *you*.' She envelops Ava in a hug and then tugs Nick's shirt. Their arms lock around Ava, and in that moment, Nick feels like the luckiest man in the world.

'Mum?' Ava says as they're about to step through the door.

'Yes, honey?'

'You're the most brilliant, beautiful, loving woman in the world. One day I want to be just like you.'

Paige laughs and runs her fingers across her daughter's cheek. 'Oh, sweet pea. You already are.'

A LETTER FROM VANESSA

Dear Reader,

I hope you enjoyed reading *My Life for Yours* and spending time with Paige and Nick! If you are interested in learning about my upcoming releases, you can sign up for my newsletter here. Your email address will never be shared and you can unsubscribe at any time.

www.bookouture.com/vanessa-carnevale

When I sat down to write this book, I knew I wanted to write about motherhood and the instinct we have to protect those we love. In this story, Paige and Nick are faced with an impossible dilemma, exacerbated by the events that precede Paige's second pregnancy. I found myself torn whenever I looked at the situation from one perspective or another.

In writing this novel, I was also faced with the challenge of writing about one of the most sensitive topics that exist: the loss of a late-term pregnancy. While I was working on the first draft, a friend of mine, who I'd known for many years, shared with me details of her own pregnancy loss, mentioning to me that in her experience, 'Nobody likes to talk about it.' Keeping this in mind is what kept me going over the many months it took to churn out page after page of Paige and Nick's story. My hope is that any parents who've experienced this kind of loss feel seen, acknowledged and hopefully understood after reading this book.

I love hearing from readers, and if you've enjoyed this book, please consider leaving a review or saying hello! You can reach me via Facebook, Instagram or my website, where you can also sign up for my newsletter updates.

With love and best wishes,
Vanessa

www.vanessacarnevale.com

vanessacarnevalewriter

vanessacarnevale

ACKNOWLEDGEMENTS

They say it takes a village to raise a child, but I tend to think this also applies to books. First and foremost, thank you to my editor, Lucy Dauman, for your tireless input and wonderful guidance in helping me shape this book into what it is today. Thanks also to the enthusiastic and hardworking Bookouture team. Your passion and enthusiasm for all of your authors is nothing short of amazing, and I am thrilled to be working with you all.

This book would not have been possible without the assistance of the medical professionals who so kindly answered my many research questions around peripartum cardiomyopathy (PPCM) and days in the life of a medical professional. In particular I'd like to acknowledge Associate Professor Alicia Dennis, Director of Anaesthesia Research at The Royal Women's Hospital, Melbourne, who generously afforded me time over the phone and email to answer questions, offer suggestions and read over my early drafts. Thanks also to Dr Joe Crameri and Dr James Fett. Any errors are, of course, my own.

To Janelle Moran at Sands Australia, a wonderful, volunteer-based organisation that provides support to bereaved parents dealing with miscarriage, stillbirth and the loss of newborns, thank you for your time in helping me understand this delicate topic and the extraordinary work your organisation does. Karen Gawne, I appreciate you sharing your knowledge and experience as a midwife with me.

I also owe thanks to Sarah Cypher for offering such brilliant feedback on my writing and the story in its infancy, and to Anna Collins for reading an early iteration of the manuscript and providing feedback.

To my dear friend, Alli Sinclair, I am so grateful for all your support, the laughs, the positive vibes and your general brilliance, especially when it comes to brainstorming!

I'd also like to send a hearty thanks to the 'Bellota Girls', who know who they are. May we never run out of wine or stories about living our best lives as authors.

Finally, thank you to Fabio and the darlings of my life, Christian and Alessia. Loving you and seeing you grow and mature into the wonderful human beings you both are is hands down the greatest honour of my life, and words will never be able to express how much I adore you both.

Finally, my dear readers, where would I be without you? I'm so blessed to be able to continue telling my stories – thank you for making that possible.